3152

W9-CKH-784

Lizzie and Caroline

BY THE SAME AUTHOR

Fiction
The Gold and Silver Hooks
The Sea Flower
Second Growth
The Walk Down Main Street
Speak to the Winds
A Fair Wind Home
Jeb Ellis of Candlemas Bay
Candlemas Bay
The Fire Balloon
Spoonhandle
The Weir

Verse
Time's Web
Cold as a Dog and the Wind Northeast

LIZZIE

AND

Caroline

A NOVEL BY

Ruth Moore

William Morrow & Company, Inc., New York   1972

Copyright © 1972 by Ruth Moore

All rights reserved. No part of this book may be reproduced or utilized in any form or by any means, electronic or mechanical, including photocopying, recording or by any information storage and retrieval system, without permission in writing from the Publisher. Inquiries should be addressed to William Morrow and Company, Inc., 105 Madison Ave., New York, N.Y. 10016.

Printed in the United States of America.
Library of Congress Catalog Card Number 77–182952

Lizzie and Caroline

PART ONE

Lizzie

THE LIZZIE MACOMBER *WAS* a schooner, an aged two-sticker, raised like a ghost from her grave in a Chesapeake Bay backwater and brought back into time by her present owner, Jasper Brown, who had had her old hulk rebuilt and fitted out as a dude boat. Her filthy and rotted insides had been torn out, her cargo hold replaced with slick and varnished cabins as lavishly equipped as modern motel rooms. The lockers were waterproof, the bunk beds had innerspring mattresses; each bunk had its built-in bedside dresser and lamp set in gimbals. No dude would have to rough it aboard the *Lizzie Macomber*. She had comforts for all and she looked nice, her decks scrubbed white as a tombstone, her rigging spick-and-span with new yellow cordage.

She had not been, in her heyday, either clumsy or crank. Her original builder, Neddie Macomber, of Lunenberg, Nova Scotia, had also designed her, and she had been the last of a famous line of coasting vessels turned out by him in the last half of the 1800's. In her overhaul and rebuilding, however, some liberties had been taken with Neddie's design. The inward and upward slope of her tumble home was now slightly different; she was stouter, overall. Her keel had been warped when she had come off her mudbank, and while efforts had been made to remedy this, she was still somewhat hogged, her bow and stern lower than her midships. Jasper Brown, who had sailed skipjacks for most of his life, grumbled about the *Macomber*'s tendency to spank all the water out of the bay and her distaste for beating against the wind. Jasper was sixty, retired from his oyster business but not wanting to go on the shelf. He was called some forthright names—"plain damnfool," was one around the shipyard— had auxiliary power installed, so that no matter what happened he'd be able to get the dudes home all right, and then applied himself to learning the *Macomber*'s whims and quirks. In the course of time, he got so he could handle them very well. She became a familiar sight, occasionally a nuisance, in the bay ship channels, fat-old-ladying it along, usually winged-out, taking enough seaway for two of her size and loaded rail to rail with women in bright dresses.

To Lewis Wyman, brought up on steam before he shifted to motorships of one type or another, the *Macomber* and all her tribe were dangers to navigation and ought to be against the law, which was strange considering that Lewis was Neddie Macomber's great-great-grandson. He had no quarrel with functional sailing craft. He had seen feluccas in the Mediterranean, junks in China, caïques in the Levantine, dhows in the Indian Ocean, sampans, praus—all useful, built for sensible purposes and handled by sailors whose skill could be understood and admired by a man trained in another brand of seamanship.

"All those old sailing vessels do," he told his young son, Adam, "is to clutter up the seaways. They ought to be forbidden the ocean."

But in Adam, on this subject, Lewis banged head-on into a stubborn stone wall. Adam was crazy over anything that carried sail; his dear love was for Neddie Macomber's schooners.

"He was *in the family*, Dad," Adam said. "Don't you care if somebody in the family was really great?"

[2]

"Sure, I do. I don't doubt old Neddie was the Shakespeare of shipbuilding, in his time. But that's over and gone. What do you think would happen if you went out on the ball field and started talking the way people do in a Shakespeare play?"

Lucile, Adam's mother, said, "Now, Lew, are you saying Shakespeare was great only in his own time? Pooh!"

"That's not the point. Suppose old Ad, here, laces into one and knocks it over the fence. Who says, 'The sphere is sock-ed to the setting sun. Haste, haste thy feet, O great and glorious one, maketh thy score, it is a homing run?' Shoot, everybody jumps up and down and hollers, and that's the difference. That's what I meant."

"A great many very intelligent and intellectual people *adore* Shakespeare." This was Amanda, Lewis' twelve-year-old daughter. Her troubles with first-year high school English had resounded through the house, and Lewis cocked an eyebrow at her.

"Ho, ho, another speaketh," he said. "Do you?"

"I was quoting Old Schnickelpenutz," she said, and added hastily, "Excuse me, Ma, I meant Miss Smith."

"You'd better," Lucile said. "You know what I told you would happen if you didn't stop battling with your English teacher."

"Well, it's a running battle," Amanda said. "*I* run."

Adam stopped the discussion by stalking away to his room before Lewis could get back on sailing vessels. It was no use having it over, his father would only make fun. "Why be a throwback?" he would ask, and Adam didn't really know.

He had never seen one of Neddie Macomber's schooners under sail and never expected to for the simple reason that there were none of them left to see. According to Lunenberg records, the last one had been the *Lizzie Macomber,* vanished at sea without a trace. Adam had copies of all available Lunenberg records; he had pestered librarians all over Nova Scotia with letters, until one of them, being a good soul and interested herself, had hunted up everything on the subject she could find and had sent him copies, along with some old illustrated books. Of late years, too, Lewis had moved his family around a good deal, establishing homes, which for one reason or another had always turned out to be temporary, in Boston, New York, Wilmington, and Baltimore. From the time Adam had been old enough to realize who Neddie Macomber had been and who Adam Wyman was, he had haunted libraries and marine museums in these coastal cities. Now, at fourteen, he was an authority. He knew the names of the schooners and of harbors where hulks lay drowned in mud; the names of rocky shores and breaker-buried ledges from Nova Scotia to Cape Horn, where, sunk deep or smashed to bits of sea-worm-eaten wood, Macomber schooners had died. From pictures, he knew, or thought he knew, Neddie's famous design. Nevertheless, he did not recognize his love when he first saw it from the deck of the cargo ship in the Chesapeake Bay channel.

She was heading down and the cargo ship was heading up the channel. She was winged-out, taking up lots of room, and if she held her present course, she would pass the cargo ship on the wrong side. This was already creating a flurry in the pilothouse—Adam could hear Charley Anderson, the first officer, swearing, while he tried to figure out which way to turn. Whatever she did, to Adam she was an old two-masted schooner under sail, and who ever saw one of them nowadays? Racing for the bridge ladder, yelling back to Amanda to come and look, he came within an inch of falling over his father's feet, sprawled in front of his chair. Adam running-broad-jumped just in time and landed six feet away with a thud that shook the deck.

Lewis Wyman had a thunderous hangover today and the headache that went with it. Earlier on, he had taken aspirin and had brought a chair out into fresh air, hoping to doze a little. He was just beginning to, when Adam's shrill shriek went through his eardrums like a needle.

Hearing the thud, he jerked awake, thinking for a moment that his head had dropped off and bounced on the deck. While it kept on bouncing, he couldn't get out a word. Then he let go with an outraged bawl.

"For chrissake, Ad! You clumsy damn gowk!"

Adam hadn't stopped. He'd run on to the end of the bridge's port wing. Lewis was just getting settled again when Amanda flashed by. Her sneakers made no sound and she sidestepped his feet neatly, but she made him mad, too. Anything fast-moving hurt his eyes. He glowered at her and said, "You kids beat it. Go somewhere else."

He hadn't wanted to holler again. His first yell had set his head to thumping worse than ever. This time, it seemed, nobody heard him. Amanda joined Adam and the two stood jabbering with excitement, watching something overside. Lewis couldn't have cared less what it was, but he did open his eyes long enough to see the vessel's masts. His mind was fuzzily registering, "That damned thing again," when Adam let out another screech.

"Look! It says *Lizzie Macomber.*"

Lewis leaped in his chair. "AD! WILL YOU SHUT UP AND CLEAR OUT OF THERE?"

An immediate dead silence followed; then Amanda said, "Come on, Ad. Let's go aft. We can watch her out of sight from there."

They walked soberly back along the bridge, giving Lewis a wide berth. As they came abreast, he said, "That caterwaul of yours is enough to kill the devil. You like to blasted my head off."

Adam said, "I'm sorry," but he was too excited to stop talking, telling Amanda, "I don't see how she can be, she doesn't look right. Maybe she's been rebuilt, she's got new masts and canvas. But no, it's impossible. That one was lost—"

"All right, take it aft with you," Lewis said. "And take it *now.*"

The kids said nothing more, but some words blew back

[5]

to Lewis on the breeze up the bridge ladder. Someone—one of the hands?—said, "Your old man's pretty poison, huh? It's his girdle. It's killing him."

Adam said furiously, "You lay off the cheap wisecracks, bigmouth!"

"Don't pay him any mind," Amanda said. "He's only half there, anyway. And look at his nasty complexion, all covered with spots."

The quick comeback, the sound of Amanda's voice so like Lucile's, made Lewis grit his teeth against pain that came neither from his head nor his hangover. Lucile, struck down by a hit-and-run driver on a Baltimore street, had died two months ago. Amanda was her mother's daughter; she took after Lucile in looks and in a good many other ways. At twelve, she was a perfect little Frenchwoman, practical, with a flashing wit and a quick, sometimes double-edged tongue.

She sure stopped that joker cold, Lewis thought. Spots, eh? That would be Joe Bellows, the cook's helper, known to his shipmates as Joe Blow. So what was he doing hanging around the bridge ladder? Well, ship's discipline was up to Charley Anderson now. I'm not the skipper of this tub any longer, or I sure as hell won't be when we dock.

So, who cared? What mattered now was the kids and how they felt. As soon as his headache let up a little, he'd go aft and hunt them up. See if he couldn't be decent for a change. One thing Joe Blow was right about and that was that crack about poison.

Lewis sat motionless, waiting for his head to let up. It felt as if it were going to crack open, and would, if he moved it. Seemed as if that thumping and banging must be something more than a hangover.

Hell, he'd been drinking liquor moderately, and handling it all right, too, ever since he'd been old enough to hold up a mug. He'd been handling it all right that day in Buenos Aires when the representative of the shipping company had refused him a cargo.

God only knew what kind of a hatchet job had gone on, but Lewis was sure something had. Charley Anderson, his first officer, had been thick as thieves with that fellow. And Charley had been oily as the devil when he'd said the company had wired the owners.

Brother! Lewis told himself. That was when I should've cottoned to it, kept my hand on my number.

He hadn't, though. He'd lost his temper and slapped the company representative on the jaw. Hadn't even bothered to double up his fist. It had been a good solid slap, but the fellow was a heavyweight, quite a lot taller and huskier than Lewis; Lewis had expected a fight and was ready for it. To his astonishment, the guy had folded down to the floor and had lain there, out cold. Later on, Charley had brought word to the ship that he had a busted jaw.

Good old Charley. In there, plugging. Thanks to him, first officer, now acting-captain, they'd come back with a cargo; but Lewis hadn't any doubt as to what would happen when the ship docked.

Out on my ass and blacklisted. With two kids and darned few savings, unless by this time the real estate agent has sold the Baltimore house. There's the car, too, a good one. Could surely get a few thousand for a practically new Mercedes.

Lewis was forty. He'd never done anything but go to sea. His master's license had been earned from the ground up. Now he'd lost it because Charley Anderson, in his fifties, had had his own certificate for years, and no ship. With reason. Charley was a slow thinker, no good unless somebody was around to tell him what to do.

Well, he's got a ship now. This one. Let's see how long he keeps it. With, already, a pantry steward hanging around the bridge, shooting his mouth off? So, who cares? Dammit, I care.

This thing he had now, with booze, was a puzzler. It had begun on the previous voyage when he'd got the

radiogram about Lucile. He'd been heading home, looking forward, presents for her and the kids in his bag. One
minute, a man with a job to do, the next, not a man but a
lunatic with a fiery sheaf of words spinning behind his
eyes.

Your wife . . . dead . . . hit-and-run driver.

Not able to realize at first, standing there with the paper
in his hand, mumbling idiot-wise to no one in particular,
"Oh, God, why did we ever move from Wilmington?"
And, "After the way I've kept after her about crossing
streets?" And, "Who ever could tell a Frenchwoman anything?"

Then it had hit him like a thrown brick in the face.
He'd grabbed the bottle out of the drawer. Anything to
stop the knowing. It hadn't mattered then that Charley
had had to take over. Everybody had been sorry, had
covered up when Lewis had to be carried off the ship.

From that time on, he had had to fight liquor. It was
almost as if the years of social drinking, the hundreds of
occasions when he'd been a little high but able to handle
it, had piled up into a vast craving, thrust at him from all
angles and at any time of day. He'd supposed, at first, that
shock had turned him upside-down, that he'd get over it.
He hadn't. Even when he'd found out from Charley that
Adam and Amanda had come down to the docks to meet
him on that day, and had seen the state he was in—"Some
lunk," Charley'd said, "told them what ailed you"—even
knowing that, you'd think would cure a man cold. They'd
had Lucile's death to face, too, and alone. And where had
he been? Dead drunk.

He'd done his best to explain what had happened, and
he'd thought they'd understood. But when it came to
going on the ship with him, neither of them wanted to.
Amanda had seen his point of view almost at once, but
Adam had fought. He was old enough now to have his
own interests and a life by himself at home. They hadn't

[*8*]

been in the new house in Baltimore a week before he had begun putting down roots.

What about his swimming lessons? His course in navigation and small-boat handling? What about school—how could he keep up and go on with his class in June? What about the house here? Who was going to take care of it, look after the things?

Adam argued, almost hysterically, going from one point to another.

Lewis had been in no shape to argue with anyone; he was still in a bad way from his collapse aboard the ship, his nerves raw with shock and grief. If he had been himself, he would have said that the idea of coming back, ever, to this house without Lucile in it made him sick at heart; that his kids were all he had left now and he couldn't bear to be separated from them. He found he couldn't say anything of the kind without losing control. At last he put his foot down, hard.

"Who's going to look after you while I'm away? I don't know a soul I could ask. We don't know anyone here well enough. You can both take books along and study aboard ship. I'll get you what you need from the school. I've got to take you with me, there's no other way."

If this sounded to his children as if they were nuisances who had to be looked after somehow, Lewis was not aware of it. What he had said was merely true. Neither he nor Lucile had any close relatives; if she had any at all they were in France, and his own people in Lunenberg had died out half a generation ago. He supposed he could have taken the trouble to find some decent woman to take over the kids while he was away, live in the house with them, perhaps; but who could he be sure of, on such short notice? It would mean leaving the children with a stranger. Anyway, he hated the house. It was in a development in a suburb—an hour's ride by bus or car from the docks. He had bought it outright, with savings, and had got merrily cheated. Developers, building in a hurry, had paid for the cheapest kinds of materials and equipment. By the time Lewis had had his family moved in, the place already needed repairs, the plumbing out of order, something always needing to be replaced. And, without Lucile, the house was nothing.

Unable to do anything he didn't have to do, or to explain what he did, he'd arranged at once to have everything taken to storage and the house put on the market. He hadn't told the children he'd done this, only to pack any treasures they wanted to take with them and get ready to go. Then, knowing his owners wouldn't like it, he'd smuggled them aboard the ship at night and bedded them down in his cabin.

This had been the beginning of ruptured relations with Charley Anderson. Charley, a bachelor, didn't like kids; he agreed with the owners that they had no business aboard a cargo boat. In the morning, when he first saw them on deck, the ship was well down the bay, too far to turn back. When he came on two seamen putting up a temporary plywood screen in his own stateroom, Charley went raging to Lewis. He got little satisfaction.

"What's wrong with you moving in with Pete?" Lewis asked. Pete was the second officer. "I want the kids next to me, and your quarters are big enough to take a screen. They're a little old to bunk in together."

"All right," Charley said between his teeth. "But, hell, you could have asked me."

"Didn't see you," Lewis said. He was tired out, and Charley was one more thing.

"No, and I guess you don't now," Charley said. "I don't like being shoved around, incommodated like this, let me tell you."

"Well, go spit fire somewhere else," Lewis said. At once, he was sorry at being on such a short string and turned around to say so, but Charley had stomped off, smoldering.

He told Pete Parrott, the second officer, that he guessed the skipper was lushing it up again, on the sly.

From the first, it seemed to Lewis, his children had moved into a world of their own. He had tried to shake them out of it, but after a while it had got to be like everything else, not worth bothering with.

Adam had started out by being sulky and sloppy, hadn't even tried to keep himself clean. For the first few days out, he'd been seasick, a terrible blow to him because he prided himself on being one of a long line of seafaring men. Then he'd got over it; but he'd appeared on deck looking shaggy, with vomit stains on his shirt. Amanda had snapped him out of that. She'd settled down aboard ship much more easily than he had. Somehow, she managed to keep herself looking fresh as a butterfly; she'd taken over Adam, cut his hair, seen to it that clean jeans and shirts were available, lambasted him into cutting his nails and taking baths. Lewis suspected that Jilson, the ship's cook, helped out with the laundry when necessary.

Jilson was a part of Lewis' past, a habit and, it could be said, a longtime friend. When Lewis had had his first ship, Jilson had been ship's cook. He had been, and still was, the best cook, bar none, that Lewis had ever seen. Two years later, Lewis had changed ships; he had gone to considerable trouble to wangle a job for Jilson along with him. On Lewis' third ship, no cook's job was available. Thereafter, he had been in and out of Lewis' life—traveling, he always said, and occasionally Lewis would get a postcard from some far-off place, like Madagascar or Taiwan or Tahiti. The postcard would generally have been a long time on the way, having followed Lewis from a previous address; as like as not, his answer to it would be returned, "Address Unknown." Jilson's postcards always said the same thing, "When you're ready, Cap'n, I am," which meant that Jilson would come aboard, from wherever he was, and cook for Lewis again if Lewis could open up a job for him. This last time, the postcard had come from Boston, and Lewis' answer had caught Jilson there.

He was a temperamental man, unpredictable and touchy; no person to fool with. Due to his unusual skinniness and height, he was known in some circles up and down the coasts where he traveled as "Old Walking Cane," though no man had ever called him that to his face without reprisals. His head was as bald as an egg and shaped somewhat like one, narrow at the top and widening downward to accommodate a droopy, handlebar moustache. He might have been any age; his brown, leathery, noncommittal face gave nothing away, and Jilson himself did not say. Lewis knew he had been in the Navy throughout World War II and that he hailed from Belfast, Maine. One other thing Lewis knew, and that was all. Jilson could be depended upon in an emergency; but he was incurious about other people's affairs. He would never volunteer. You had to ask him.

From the beginning on the cargo ship, the kids had made good friends with Jilson. Lewis had warned them. "Don't plague him. Don't bother him. Wait till he invites you." But at sea they spent most of their time in Jilson's galley. Sometimes, wondering where they were, Lewis had found them in there, jabbering away. Jilson had always been glad to see him. The kids' talk stopped, though, the moment he hove in sight.

Feeds them pie and cake, I guess. Well, I haven't got much in the way of pie and cake to offer them now.

That aspirin he'd taken wasn't doing any good. Didn't dare to take any more. Must have half a bottle inside him already. Perhaps if he got up and walked around, he could help this thumping in his head. Wouldn't hurt him to go aft and be decent to the kids. After all, they'd just stuck up for him. Handed quite a mouthful to Joe Blow. This defense, suddenly, made Lewis feel better. After all, he'd been—yes, that *was* the word—"poison," to them.

He eased himself out of his chair and went, stepping carefully, down the bridge ladder. The kids were out on the stern, as close as they could get to the rail. Adam was talking a blue streak to Amanda, waving his hands around, explaining something. The *Lizzie Macomber,* already some distance away, looked to be standing motionless in the water with sails slatting; as Lewis approached, he heard Adam say, "Look, he was wung-out, see? And he tried to come about and— Oh-h, brother! What does that turnip farmer think he's doing?"

"Turnip farmer is right," Lewis said. "He ought to take his vessel back into his turnip patch."

Adam glanced around. "Yeh," he said.

Amanda went on watching the vessel.

"Look at it from a seaman's point of view," Lewis said. "If you know anything about it, you know he passed us on the wrong side. He's going to have to beat back, and any steamer coming up or down has got to give him the right of way. Those things are a blasted nuisance, anyway. If they're sailed by somebody who doesn't bother to learn the laws of navigation, well, godfrey, they— Look, Ad, that guy ought to be arrested."

Adam said, "Yeh," again. He didn't look around. Instead, he said to Amanda, "Her after cabin's too high to be one of Neddie's and that coach-house type entrance to it—he never built anything like that."

"What's that, Ad?" Amanda asked.

"Well, like a little entry on the outside, with a door. But she's hogged. She's old, all right. Wonder why they didn't fix that when they—"

"Look," Lewis said. He tried, very carefully, to keep his voice down. "Look, Ad, it's all very well to be in love with sailing ships. But if you're headed for the Merchant Marine, why not start getting interested in diesels? That old tub is so rotten you could poke your finger through her anywhere. She's got to be. What's she doing here on the bay, anyhow? She probably draws fifteen or sixteen feet."

"Yeh," Adam said. "I know how much she draws. Flying light, eleven."

"Okay, smart ass. You know a lot. Maybe you better bother with learning some manners. Dammit, you look at me when I talk to you, or I'll shake some of that out of you."

"All right," Adam said. He still didn't look around.

Lewis reached for him and found himself entangled with a handful of Amanda, who had somehow got in between.

She said, "Don't, Daddy, you'll hurt me," in a helpless voice, and pushed at his hand. The movement was gentle with no force behind it, but Lewis, taken aback, let go. She began fastidiously tucking in the tail of her shirt, which had pulled out.

The skipper of the *Macomber,* the turnip farmer, wasn't going to chance beating back up the channel. He had auxiliary power and he was using it. A puff of exhaust smoke appeared at the vessel's stern; she came back chugging along under bare poles.

"Aw, shoot!" Adam said. "What's the matter with him? Any cluck could beat up that channel."

Lewis turned away. I can't do anything about this now, he thought. Getting mad hadn't helped his head any; walking around had made it worse. He'd better go back to his cabin, take some more aspirin, a good slug of it this time. Then the only thing on God's green earth that would cool that headache was hair-of-the-dog. He had to be in some kind of shape to face his owners, who were already raving mad.

At noon when the ship docked, Charley Anderson and three others carried Lewis ashore to an ambulance which rushed him to a Baltimore hospital. In the afternoon, Pete

Parrott, the second officer, who had gone on the ambulance, brought back word. Lewis had not only alcohol poisoning but aspirin poisoning as well—God only knew how much of the stuff he'd taken. He also had something else, which the doctors weren't sure of yet. They were still trying to find out. They thought he'd pull through, but nobody could say how long he'd be laid up.

"He's still out," Pete said. "Got a whopping high temperature. Been curtains for him if we hadn't got him to the hospital on time."

"So what about his kids?" Charley—now Captain—Anderson demanded, as if they were anybody's responsibility, certainly not his.

"Don't ask me," Pete said. "The skipper must have relatives somewhere."

"No," Charley said. "The thing is, he hasn't. I heard him say once. Hell, somebody's got to do something. They can't stay on the ship."

"Not up to me," Pete said. 'Looks like you're stuck with it. You got the problems now." He went off, swearing quietly to himself. The skipper had got a raw deal and Pete knew it. That jughead in Buenos Aires hadn't had any busted jaw—he'd been paid to lay down, but who could prove it? You could say, but not without losing your job, and Pete had a family.

Captain Anderson was a ravaged man. Not that he wasn't a competent officer, he told himself. He was. But there was a lot of ship's business ashore, and Lewis hadn't left any instructions. Charley wasn't used to having too much to do at once. He was about at the end of his tether. After a while, he went along to talk to Lewis' kids. He had some trouble beginning. As a man with high moral standards, he didn't feel it was decent to mention to kids, cold turkey, that their father was a lush.

"Your dad took too much aspirin," he said. "He's sick, in the hospital. Might be there a week. Now, I'm a busy man, got ten-dozen things I've got to be doing. I want you to tell me right off who there is can take charge of you till he gets back on his feet."

They stared at him with cool, skeptical, still eyes. It hadn't occurred to either of them that they wouldn't be going home to the house on Planetree Hill.

"Come on, there must be somebody," Charley said. "Help me out, will you?"

Adam and Amanda looked at each other.

"I can always get the police to take you up to the Children's Home," Charley said. "One of your dad's friends? Some neighbor?"

"There's Miss Smith," Amanda said. She didn't look at Adam, but was aware of his sudden startled stare. Miss Smith was Old Schnickelpenutz, of ill fame at school and her sworn enemy because Miss Smith, with justice, had blamed her for thinking up the nickname. Lucile had once taken Amanda to call on her, hoping to end the battle, and Amanda had found out that Miss Smith lived in a one-room apartment with a daybed. She couldn't possibly have any place for visitors.

"Good enough. What's her name?"

"Why, Miss Smith," Amanda said.

"Look, for the love of— I mean her whole name. So I can find her in the phone book. There must be five hundred Smiths. What is it? Mary? Sue?"

"Barbara," Amanda said.

This also was true. No one could have accused Amanda of lying. She had seen plenty of notes written in a dudgeon to Lucile and signed "Theresa Barbara Smith."

"I'll get hold of her. You kids pack up and get ready to leave. I'll send one of the boys up there with you."

"How'll Dad know where to find us?" Adam said.

"We'll leave word for him." Much relieved, Charley went off.

"Someone to take charge of us." Adam was outraged. "As if we were a shipment of meat. That old skunk has got Dad's job." He went wandering around the cabin, poking aimlessly at this and that. "What was all that jaw about Schnickelpenutz? What good did that do?"

"If he's ashore going through five hundred Smiths to find a Barbara, he won't be here to see us leave. I'm not going to any children's home. When he finds out no Schnickelpenutz, that's what he'll do."

"You know, he will," Adam said. He stopped in his tracks. "We can sneak out and go home. To our own house."

"How about that!" That was what had been in her own mind, but if Adam thought of it and said, he wouldn't think about all the difficulties first. Looking at him, she thought, he's lovely. Now he'll take over and figure how to do it.

"Let's see," Adam said. "We've got to think. Dad's got the keys to the house somewhere in his things. We'll get them first. How much money've you got?"

"Three dollars and sixty-one cents."

"I got seven-something. 'Tisn't enough. We've got to eat till Dad gets back. Maybe he left some dough in his cabin. He must've left his wallet there. If he didn't, we'll have to sell something out of the house." He swallowed hard. "My ship models, they're worth a lot. My cassette recorder—"

"No. I won't let you. There're other things."

"We can't sell Dad's and . . . Ma's things."

"They'd want us to, if they knew."

"It still wouldn't be right."

"Look. Remember that awful old umbrella stand that M-Ma always laughed at because the antique dealer offered her a hundred dollars for it?" She choked a little and turned the sound into a cough.

"Let's think about it when we have to," Adam said. "We've got enough for bus fare and we know which bus. Number nineteen. Goes past this dock every hour till midnight."

"Okay," Amanda said.

[*17*]

"That's all set, then," Adam said. He didn't look at her, but he could tell. She wouldn't let on, but she was crying. Number 19 had done it. The big lumbering bus to the docks that he and Amanda and their mother had always taken to meet Lewis' ship, because Lucile hadn't liked to drive the car in the heavy waterfront traffic. Adam could see Lewis now—thundering down the gangplank, yelling, "Hi!" loud enough to scare the sea gulls. Everybody there and glad to see each other. He felt under his eyelids the gritty, stinging sensation that meant he was going to cry, too, if he didn't get out of there and stop thinking. "I'll go see where Dad's keys are."

He went past her, still not looking. She didn't cry like other kids, howling out a lot of noise. She just sat still, off by herself, with big, round tears rolling down, not making a sound. It would take her a while to get mopped up. Better to leave her alone, she'd come along as soon as she could.

To Adam's astonishment, he found Joe Bellows in Lewis' stateroom, going through his things or, possibly, packing them. Uniforms and other clothes from the lockers were tossed helter-skelter on the bed beside open suitcases. He had dumped the contents of the desk drawers onto the top of the desk, and what he was doing at the moment was looking through Lewis' wallet, slipping bills partway out, counting. He jumped when he saw Adam, tapped the bills back in, and folded the wallet shut.

"Hey, what's the idea?" Adam demanded.

Joe grinned, winked at him, and tossed him the wallet. "Just checking," he said. "Your old man's got a real wad in there. Guy could go on quite a toot." He turned back to his rummaging, whistling cheerfully a tune which Adam recognized as "Haul Away, Joe."

"You get out of here," Adam yelled. "You've got no right to—"

"Orders," Joe said. "Orders to pack the old lush's duds, so I'm doin' it. Gwan, haul ass. Don't bother me."

Adam's face stung red. The only weapon was the doorstop, a hardwood wedge. He snatched it up and hurled it at Joe as hard as he could. Rage more or less spoiled his aim and the thing was fairly hefty, but it did hit Joe a sideways crack on the anklebone before it glanced off. Joe doubled up with a squall of pain, began hopping around the stateroom on one foot, holding on to his ankle. "Ow, Jeezus! You murderin' little— Oo! F-fft! Wait'll I git my hands on you!" He started, limping, but quite fast for an injured man, and Adam ran.

Joe didn't follow him far. What he was interested in was the wall safe, the combination to which he had found in Lewis' wallet. No sense losing this good chance. In a minute, the world and Charley Anderson would come plowing in here. Joe went to work on the combination and worked fast.

Well, well, he told himself with satisfaction. A couple nice fat wads, one for each sneaker.

He was tying the lace on the second sneaker when Amanda said, pleasantly, from the doorway, "What are you doing, Joe?"

Hell! He hadn't closed the safe door, it was half-open. He said, "Tying up my sneaks, what's it look like?"

"No," she said. "I mean, these are Dad's things. What are you— Oh. You're packing them for him."

She'd noticed the suitcases. "That's right. Skipper told me to. Don't need any help. So beat it."

She didn't. She came in as far as the desk and stood there, staring at him. At the breast pocket of his dungarees jacket. "When did Dad give you his pen?" she asked in a puzzled voice. "But that's his nice one, the one my mother gave him for his birthday."

Joe's ears flamed. He clapped his hand over the pocket. "Don't get funny," he said. "A pen's a pen. Lots of 'em just alike. Gwan. I told you to beat it, I don't need any help."

"You'll get help," Jilson said from the doorway. "From

[*19*]

the toe of my boot. Come on, let's have that pen. What else? Turn out them pockets!"

Adam had gone for the only help he trusted, and Jilson had come on the run.

"Ah, shove it!" Joe said. "I ain't took nothing. This's my pen."

"Had the Cap'n's wallet," Jilson said laconically.

"That kid's a liar. I never even see a wallet. I was—" Joe stopped, his eyes goggling. The revolver in Jilson's hand might be old-fashioned, but its long barrel made it look as big as a cannon.

"Amanda," Jilson said, "I'd just as soon shoot this cuss as not, so you'll want to make tracks before I do it."

"All right," Amanda said. She had been standing by the desk fumbling over a few objects and papers in what had seemed an aimless way. Now she thrust one hand deep into her dungarees pocket and went off without another word.

"Ad," Jilson said, "see'f you can roust out Mr. Parrott. Don't bother old Anderson, you'll start up his stomach rumbles."

"Now, look," Joe said. "You ain't got nothing on me. I ain't—"

Jilson wobbled the revolver at him. "Shell out," he said.

Various possessions of Lewis' came to light out of Joe's pockets. Cuff links and tiepins, an ivory-handled pocket-knife, the expensive Swedish chronograph which Pete Parrott had stowed away in the safe the day Lewis had gone to the hospital. This last item, together with a big bunch of keys, appeared just as Pete himself walked in the door and took a brisk look around.

"Been into the safe," he said. "Had yourself quite a time, haven't you?"

Joe said nothing.

"Those keys would've been nice and handy, wouldn't they?" Pete said. "Duplicates to every damn lock on the ship. Well, we'll know where to stow you, you fancy-fingered louse!"

"Louse, yourself!" Joe said with venom. "You ain't got proof and you know it. All I took was a few of the old lush's odds and ends, you can't send me to jail for that. I never knew what them keys was."

"Let's see what else you've looted. Strip. Take off. Shoes and all," Pete said succinctly.

If I could just get in by them, Adam thought desperately. Dad's key ring's got to be in that pile of stuff on the desk. He could spot it in an instant, he knew—like all Lewis' possessions, it was expensive, a gold chain held together by a small gold knob that would snap apart. Lewis kept his car keys on it, his garage key, and, always, back- and front-door keys to the house. He craned his neck but couldn't see a thing past Jilson and Mr. Parrott, who were watching Joe sullenly take off his clothes and slam them down on the deck.

"What to hell goes on here?" Charley Anderson came thumping up behind him, and yes—in spite of his worry, Adam had to choke back a giggle—preceded by thunderous stomach rumbles. "What'd you tell me that Smith woman's name was?" Charley demanded, seeing Adam in front of him.

Charley had been ashore in a telephone booth calling Smiths. He had got halfway down the list in the book before indigestion brought on by frustration and fury had caused him to stop. Some of the answers he'd got had convinced him that half the Smiths in the city were crazy.

Adam didn't have to answer because Charley, tall enough to see past Pete and Jilson, saw Joe Bellows, stark naked, shaking wads of money out of his sneakers onto the table.

Watching through the space made by Charley as he went roaring in, Adam saw the rest of the scene, heard that the money was ship's funds from the safe, possibly some of it Lewis'. Charley said he would have to check. He was in a fine fume as he took over.

"So you're the one, are you?" he said to Joe. "Now

we'll know whose dunnage to search for ship's stores been pilfered. Okay, Pete, take him down and lock him up and call the cops. Look out he don't break away from you."

"He won't. Not the way he is." Pete, Joe's clothes over his arm, grinned widely. "Git along, little dogie. Don't stub your corns. You must have some, all that lettuce in your sneaks."

Charley stared them out of sight. He seemed to have been holding his breath, for he suddenly let it out in a great gust. "Jeezus!" he said. "What next?" And caught sight, again, of Adam. "Look, you—" he began.

"You got little to do," Jilson said. "Send that sneak thief in here to pack up the Cap'n's stuff." He hadn't raised his voice, but it cut in over Charley's and stopped him short.

"What's it got to do with you? Any of your business who I give my orders to?" he demanded, glaring at Jilson.

"I kind of thought you'd set up the kitchen here, seeing you run off with part of my crew," Jilson said.

"Well, get back down to your pantry and mind your own business," Charley said. "I'm going to want some supper before long."

"Want'll be your master unless you let Joe Blow loose to cook it," Jilson said. "I and the Cap'n's kid are staying here to pack up his things, make sure he gets what stuff b'longs to him. So eat on that. You won't get none of my cooking out of me tonight."

"You've forgot who's the skipper here now, I guess," Charley said. "That was an order I give you."

"No, I ain't forgot. But I damn well know who ought to be, you potbellied old job snatcher." Jilson thrust Adam behind him and shut the door in Charley's face. There was a silence, and then they heard Charley thumping away.

"Gee, I thought he'd fire you," Adam said. He stood looking at Jilson with admiration. "That was telling him."

"Fire me? Not him, he likes my cooking," Jilson said. "Besides, he ain't going to have to. I wouldn't stay on a ship with him if he had a golden crown of roses, wet with pure dew."

Adam grinned. He did love to hear Jilson talk. "That was poetry," he said.

"Well, I've writ a good deal of that, in my time. Want to hear some?" Jilson was already busy folding Lewis' uniforms neatly into his suitcases. He began:

> " 'Oh, gimme back my hard old bolster,
> Gimme back my dirty sheet,
> Gimme old Tom Rocco's diner,
> Gimme back West Wexler Street.'

"I say that sometimes when I'm far from home, git homesick for Mis' McKlosky's boardinghouse," he said. "What's the matter with you? You're nervous as a hen with a stuck aig."

"Nothing," Adam said. He guessed he must have looked nervous, flipping over the piled-up stuff on the desk, and he slowed down. "You really leaving the ship, Jilson? Where you going?"

"To Mis' McKlosky's on West Wexler Street, where else? Always stay there when I'm in Balto. It's a real nice clean place. I only made up that poem to plague Mis' McKlosky. Where're you and Sis going? You know?"

For a split second, Adam considered telling him. If you could trust anyone, you surely could trust Jilly. But what would any older person do if he found out they were going home, to be in the house alone? Flip. Make a noise. What else? Nobody thought kids had any sense. He said, too carefully, "Oh, some friends of Dad's uptown. Name of Smith."

"You don't seem to be dancing jigs about it."

"Well, it won't be for long. Just till Dad gets out of the hospital, is all. By the way, Jilly, I'll probably see him before you do. If we find his key ring anywhere, I better

[23]

take it to him. He'll need to use his car." On purpose, he didn't mention the house keys. Better not, he thought. A dead giveaway.

"That's right," Jilson said. "They'll be here somewhere, I guess."

There'd been some talk belowdecks about the way Charley Anderson was flopping around like a pig in a bag, trying to find a place to dispose of the Cap'n's kids. The general idea was that somebody ought to do something about it. Jilson couldn't quite bring himself to think he was the one.

I like them kids, he thought. We been real nice and friendly together. I s'pose I could take them with me, till Cap'n gets well.

Still, all his life he'd got along by not sticking his neck out. In the Navy, for four years; a man didn't volunteer for anything in the Navy, he'd be a fool to. During his youth, in sailing vessels, it had always been one hand for the sailor and one for the ship. First came first, and by the god, don't ever forget it.

Sailing vessels. And the Cap'n's kid, there. Crazy over them, he was. Knew a lot about them, too. Even knew some hist'ry of that old hoss trough sailed by us in the channel the other day. The *Lizzie Macomber,* he hollers, like his heart jumped right out of him and flew after her on wings, poor little duffer . . .

Jeezus, I got troubles of my own. Got to find a new berth when I leave here. Going to take my time. Find a good one. One I can enjoy myself in, have some fun for a change. This one ain't been no bed of ferns, watching a damn good man drink himself out of his life. I'll go to see him. I'd look a pretty figure, wouldn't I, if he asks me where his kids are and I not know. Oh, blast and dammit! It ain't got to be me.

He packed in a whirl of industry, setting one locked bag after another on the deck beside the stateroom door. Neither he nor Adam found Lewis' key ring.

"Okay," Adam said. "I guess that's it. Thanks, Jilly, I'll tell Dad you helped me pack his things." Something in his voice, the discouraged droop of his shoulders as he made for the door, made Jilson call him back.

"Look, Ad," he said. "You're going to see your dad, why don't you take him his money? The label on the wall-safe drawer says two hundred dollars, here, belongs to him. He may need it."

He caught the sudden flash in Adam's eyes. "Gee, yes, Jilly, likely he will."

"You got a wallet?"

"I've got his."

Jilson took the wallet, counted the money from the pile on the desk, handed it back to Adam. "Shove it deep in your pocket," he said. "Don't lose it, for godsake."

"My windbreaker's got a zippered pocket," Adam said. "I'll keep it in that." He took off on the run.

That made me feel some better, Jilson thought. But I ought t' feel ashamed of myself, all the same. It wasn't exactly shame, it just wasn't good, the way he felt right now.

One thing, he was going to be in a hell of a pickle if old Charley got nosing around and found that two hundred dollars was gone. H'm, he'd better cover that track, deep.

Jilson scooped up some letters and private papers, which he'd sorted on the desk, put them in three manila envelopes. The envelopes he locked into Lewis' attaché case and thrust the key into his pocket. There was still left Lewis' checkbook. He'd take that along, first chance he got, hand it over to Adam. And that was just about it. Nothing left, except a mess of scrap paper on the floor.

Charley came bustling in with an armful of his own dunnage, a seaman behind him carrying more of it. "You finished?" he said. "Hell, you could have cleaned up the floor some."

"I ain't a scrubwoman," Jilson said. "There's the Cap'n's

stuff. His private papers and valuables is in his case."

"Okay, get it out of here," Charley said. "Truck it over to the company offices, and get a move on before they close for the day."

"I ain't a porter, either," Jilson said.

"Goddammit, I want to get moved in here!"

"Does kind of look as though you did," Jilson said. "Now, goddammit, yourself. Being a legal, lifetime resident of the State of Maine, as well as a darn good cook, I ain't about to be nibbled on, yapped at, or red-eyed tomcodded by anybody. You can call a couple of hands to muckle onto them grips, and I'll drop the keys to them off at the hospital, when I go to see the Cap'n tomorrow."

"Well, I don't know— Okay, don't get huffy," Charley said to Jilson's receding back. God, he thought, he couldn't lose Jilson.

As Jilson walked along the deck headed for his quarters, he came on Amanda tucked into a corner in the lee. She was all dressed up in a white windbreaker, a blue dress, white socks, and sandals.

Pretty's a picture, he thought. Looks happy's a lark, as if she didn't have a trouble in the world.

Amanda was happy. She was going home. When she had been fumbling around on the desk in Lewis' stateroom, just before Jilson had asked her to leave, she had found Lewis' key ring, with all his keys. It was now tucked safely in Adam's windbreaker pocket, along with the wallet. She had not been able to get back to the stateroom to tell Adam she'd found it, because old Charley Anderson, after he'd done all that telephoning ashore, had come right into her cabin, red-eyed.

"Look here, now, I've been phoning for more time than I've got, and I can't find no Barbara Smith. What kind of a—" He'd stopped, staring. Holy mud, what ailed her?

Amanda had heard him coming. Thump, thump, along the deck, it couldn't be anyone else. She stood in the middle of the cabin with her eyes closed, her lips moving.

Clasped to her bosom was a large, leather-framed photograph. She held the pose briefly, then started, surprised, opening her eyes. A child come back from far, far away, a child in a dream.

"Oh!" she said. "Sh-h. This is my daddy's picture. He's awful sick. I'm praying for him to get well."

This moving spectacle had affected Charley. He was not a man without sentiment, when it came to some things.

Golly, the poor little kid, he'd thought. Praying for her sick daddy. And her mother dead, too. Grieving. It was kind of holy. It had been all he could do to keep from taking off his cap. He'd stood, shifting from foot to foot waiting for her to get through, but she'd kept right on. Well, Miss Smith could wait. They had bunks, they could stay aboard tonight, and he was too rushed up to go do any more phoning till morning. He had gone quietly away.

So now Amanda was happy. She knew Adam was, too, because they were all set. She waved a hand at Jilson as he came abreast, and said, "Hi!" and he said, "You look darned nice."

Amanda smoothed her skirt. "This is my best dress. And my best sandals and jacket. Everything else is packed up. We're going ashore, you know."

There it was. Still, if she looked that pleased with things, likely they weren't too miserable, he thought, relieved.

Something said to him, Don't ask questions, don't get mixed up in it, but he said, "Where you going? You know?"

Her eyes flickered a little. "Mr. Anderson's going to phone."

"Who to? Anybody you like?"

Don't trust anybody, Adam had said. You know what will happen if you tell a single one. But this was Jilly, hers and Adam's friend. She couldn't tell, but she wouldn't lie to him, either. "I hate her more than anybody in the world. But Dad won't be sick long, then we'll be back with him." She smiled, bright, cheerful. "You know what I'll miss most, Jilly?"

"No. I guess I don't."

"Well, first, you, we've had such good times. And next, those things." She pointed.

Unloading was beginning, and the big dock cranes were clattering along their tracks, getting positioned for cargo hatches.

"I like to watch and see if sometimes they don't make a mistake and go the wrong way," Amanda said. "Come ka-crash into each other and have a fight. They look as if they could have a very good fight. What's the matter? Didn't you want to know that I'll miss you most?"

Jilson was mad; he was furious to be told that she liked him, that she'd miss him most. Dammit, she'd just about broke him up. Back in his quarters, he packed his things. He got everything ready to go. He went to bed, but he couldn't sleep. Rolling around in his bunk, he knew he wasn't going to be able to sleep.

Going to stay with somebody she hated. And happy as a clam. Didn't make sense.

Maybe if he walked around the deck he could walk it off. As he dressed, he caught a glimpse of himself in his shaving mirror, still up on the wall. Forgot to pack it, he thought, and took it down.

Jeezus! Bald as a bedbug. Mean as a snapping turtle, long droopy moustache, nose like the handle on a vinegar jug. Head looks like a aig some kid has drew a punkin-devil on. Who in God's name has ever missed me in my whole life?

He went out on deck, paced the passageways fore and aft. It was about eleven o'clock, bright moonlight, noise like a crazy house, the dock cranes going it, unloading cargo, never stopping. He'd about got himself into a dream, and still that goddam fezzle.

Someone was moving, for'ard, coming down the deck toward him. Ship's watchman, maybe. Must be. Not many people left aboard tonight. Me, the kids, Charley sleeping in the Cap'n's stateroom, couldn't wait to enjoy his first night in there. About everybody had flocked ashore to enjoy the town. Whoever it was, Jilson didn't feel like chewing any rag with him. Or anybody. He stepped back into a cross-passage to let the fellow go by.

Two people. They were pretty shadowy. Moon wasn't high enough to shine inside this side of the deck—one or two stripes of moonlight was all. Up by the gangway, where these characters seemed to be heading, was an over-head light. When they came under that, he could tell who it was. If he was interested, which he wasn't. Not very.

They crossed one of the stripes of moonlight that didn't come up any higher than one fellow's middle but showed clearly that he was carrying a suitcase in each hand. Some of them dreeps who'd been into the ship's stores, maybe, toting stuff off to sell? If that's who 'twas, they had their gall, taking it off the gangplank in full sight of any of the stevedores who might be hanging around down there.

Well, it was the shipkeeper's lookout, not his.

Then the horrid thought occurred to him that those might be his own suitcases—they were packed, ready to go, and he'd come away without locking anything up. He was opening his mouth to let out a yell when the two came out into the full light of the overhead lamp by the gang-way. He closed it again without making a sound.

My God, them kids! Putting foot, all on their own, off the ship and heading where? The boy with all that money on him and the little girl in that pretty dress and white sandals. On this waterfront, a hundred things could hap-pen to them at this time of night.

I can go tonight as well as tomorrow, can't sleep any-way. I can follow along, see where they end up to, needn't let them see me. Then, if the Cap'n asks, I'll know where they'll be. I better make tracks or they'll be out of sight.

In his quarters, he took a quick look around to see if he'd left anything. There was the shaving mirror, still on his bunk. Too bad to leave a good mirror behind. Still, couldn't take the time to unstrap a grip. He tried to thrust it into his pocket, but it wouldn't go, only tore the pocket, slipped out of his hand, and dropped to the floor. Jilson picked it up. It wasn't broken. "You break, damn you!" he told it. "Seven years' bad luck ain't a huckleberry to what I'm going through."

Under the streetlamp at the bus stop, Adam and Amanda waited for Number 19. It seemed to be a long time coming. Adam fidgeted, wanting to look again at Lewis' watch, which he had strapped to his wrist. It was Lewis' nice one, which told the day and the month as well as the time, things anybody in a hospital would surely like to know. Besides, Adam felt responsible for it. Now he wished he hadn't looked at it here under the light, because a queer-looking man going by had stopped and had tried to see the time, too. He'd said, "Hey, little buddy, what's it say?" and had reached for Adam's hand, as if he'd wanted to pull the watch up where he could see.

Adam had said, "Five to eleven," and had jerked back quickly.

The man had gone on by, but he hadn't gone away. He was along the street, in a doorway. Sometimes he would move a little and Adam could see him. There were people around, a few still, and a cab stand across the street, with a driver sitting in his taxi. So Adam wasn't really scared. He only wished the bus would come or that the fellow in the doorway would go away.

"Where could the bus be, Ad?" Amanda asked. "We haven't missed it, have we?"

"I don't think so. We were here in plenty of time. Maybe the bus is late. Want to take a cab? There is one, right there."

"No, we mustn't. We mustn't spend a cent of Dad's money we don't have to."

"S-ssh!" Adam said, horrified.

"Why shush?"

"You want to get us mugged?" He hadn't wanted to scare her, but she just had to stop jabbering about money. Amanda, ashore at last, was flying high, and he hadn't scared her at all. "I don't see any muggers," she said. "Everybody looks like perfectly nice people to me." She hadn't lowered her voice.

Well, I wish they did to me, Adam thought.

It was too late now to get the cab. A tall, skinny man in a hat and overcoat had come up on the far side of the street and was stowing his suitcases into the back seat. The cabdriver had started his engine. Adam could just make out the outline of the skinny man's hat, where he was leaning forward as if he were telling the driver where to go.

Something moved beside Adam and he swung around. The creepy fellow had come back. He was standing there, close by, reaching a hand for Adam's shoulder.

The taxicab's horn beeped twice; a back window rolled down. Out of it poked a long arm, the hand clutching something round and bright that caught light from the streetlamp and focused it on the man's face for an instant before it was withdrawn. Adam caught a glimpse of pale-pink toothless gums as the creepy man's mouth opened wide in astonishment. His reaching hand still poised in the air, he wavered back a step or two. He said, "*What* was that?" and kept on backing.

From inside the black opening of the cab's rear window, a deep, gobbling voice answered him. "That was a Pismo camera, bud. We have just took your picture."

The bright thing had looked like an ordinary round mirror to Adam, but the voice sounded crazy; he felt a cold crinkle at the back of his neck. The creep apparently felt the same way, only worse. He took off, leaning backward, fists doubled and arms bent at the elbows like a distance runner, and vanished around the nearest corner. The clippety-clop of his shoe soles on the asphalt died away.

Someone inside the cab was roaring laughing. It was

the driver, Adam saw, as the cab passed under the street light, going away.

And thank the Lord, there was bus Number 19, rounding the corner and pulling in to the curb.

The house on Planetree Hill was six long blocks from the bus stop. The hill wasn't high, but its slope was continuous. Suitcases got heavier and heavier; halfway up, Amanda dropped her two and sat down on one of them, panting. "I can't, Ad . . . I've got to rest."

"Okay," Adam said. He was glad, himself, to rest. His arms felt as if they were pulling out at the shoulders. He sat down, too, and looked glumly around him. The moon rode high in the sky. Down the hill, the lines of dew-wet rooftops looked gray, as if covered with frost. The pale light made everything seem strange—almost, he thought, like some place we never saw before. As if all the houses were full of people we didn't know.

Well, of course they hadn't lived here long enough to know the neighbors very well. The houses on Planetree Hill were nearly all new, and so were the people.

Adam said, as much to comfort himself as Amanda, "Almost there."

"I wish it was our old good house in Wilmington and that Ma . . . that Ma was there," she said.

Gosh, she must be really tired, to say it right out. Adam tried twice before he could manage "Me, too." Then he knew he'd have to start moving or he'd put back his head and howl like a wolf. "You rested yet?" he asked.

"I guess so." But she didn't get up, only sat looking at her big suitcase. "I wish we had a wagon."

"Would you be okay, not scared or anything, if I went on up and got the garden cart out of the garage?"

She brightened. "What's to be scared of?"

"You wait here. I'll be right back." He took off up the hill, running as fast as he could. He thought at first that he was too tired to run, then, as he went, he realized how great it was not to have anything to carry. She'd be all right, she wouldn't be scared, but he'd probably better hurry.

The house looked the same as when they'd left it. Lonesome. Only more so, now, because it was night and then had been in the afternoon. The windowpanes looked blank and almost white, reflecting moonlight; the shadow of the big maple tree was black across the lawn. He thought suddenly that this was the first time he'd ever seen the house at night without some kind of a light in it; even if he'd got home from a class or a late movie, Ma'd always left a light on in the hall for him. There wouldn't be any thermos of hot cocoa and a sandwich or a piece of cake, either. But there'll be a bed, he told himself with a gulp, and oh, brother, will I crawl into it!

He fetched up, breathless, against the garage door and stood leaning, while he felt in his pocket for Lewis' keys. The moonlight glinted on the bright round of the lock; he could see the keyhole plainly, but the key marked *Garage* wouldn't go in.

He held it up, turning the label to the light. That was the one. He tried it again, tried each of the other two, just in case. None of them fitted.

It must be me, my hand shakes or something, he thought, and tried again; peering closer this time, he saw that this was a new lock. The old one had been a Yale lock, the outside metal dulled by weather. This was so bright it reflected the moon and was a different shape and kind.

Dad must have had it changed when he closed the house. That made sense. He'd always growled about the garage door. Shake it, Lewis would say, and the whole shebang would fall down, all ready for any car thief who came along. Spit on the lock and it would drop off. Well, it wouldn't now. Solid as a rock. So this was just an old key.

Poor Amanda. No wagon. Wonder if I broke a corner of glass out of the window, I could maybe reach in and unlock the door from the inside?

Shading his eyes with his hands on either side of his

face, he stood on tiptoe, peered through one of the slitted garage windows.

There was a car in there. He could make out only a dark outline and see some glints of light on the metal. That would be the Mercedes. Dad had said he'd left it in storage, but sometimes Dad had second thoughts and forgot to tell anyone. Better not even think of busting a window, make it so anyone could get in.

Ma had had a shopping cart she always kept in the back entry. Amanda's suitcases might just jam into that.

The key marked *Back* wouldn't work either. Adam had to try it by feel because the moonlight was on the other side of the house. The key would go into the lock, but it wouldn't turn. He tried, fiddling with it, and finally forced it until it bent and wouldn't come out of the keyhole. While Dad had been at it, he must have had this lock changed, too. What about the front door? Sweating with worry, Adam ran headlong around the house and up on the porch. There it was the same thing.

He collapsed, rather than sat down on the top step. All that planning to get back here, knocking ourselves out. And now we can't even get in.

From somewhere down the hill, a car changed gears and started to come up, grinding a little before it went into high. Whoever it was would see Amanda sitting there on the suitcases. He'd better get on back before, maybe, somebody scared her. It was late—ten after twelve by Lewis' watch. No knowing who might be in that car. He started to get to his feet and, suddenly, was furious.

Pushed around and not told anything and treated like somebody's old junk, he told himself. Amanda and I are not just something to get rid of, we're people. This is our house and we need to get in and I am going to get in.

He stood up, went around the house to the back, and kicked a pane out of a basement window. The shattered glass fell down inside with a muffled tinkle. Adam, reaching through, pushed back the window catch, and wriggled through the narrow opening feet first. Like the glass, he landed on something soft that felt like a big roll of carpet. He couldn't remember one being there, but whatever it was, it had broken his fall. He'd expected to land slam on the concrete floor. He picked himself up from all fours and stared around.

Moonlight lay in two narrow rectangles under the front basement window. There were the familiar furnace and the stairs. As he went up, he clicked the light switch on and opened the door to the kitchen.

From somewhere in the house, a dog—a big one by the sound of it—started barking. There was a flurry and a thump, as if someone had jumped out of bed. Lights came on in the hall. Adam tore out of the kitchen and through the living room, sensing as if in a nightmare that everything was the same but different—the rooms right, the furniture strange and in unfamiliar places. He made the hall and the front door, glancing around long enough to see the nightgowned, hysterically screaming woman at the top of the stairs and, pushing past her, the dog as big as a pony. A man shouted, "Get him, Betsey, stop him, old girl!"

Adam, wrenching wildly at the doorknob, found the lock, twisted it at last, plunged through the doorway into the open yard. He had tried to slam the door but not hard enough; there hadn't been time. It bounced back on a stiff latch, swung wide, and the dog came through. He heard its big paws thumping down the steps, which his own feet hadn't touched—he'd made it in a single leap.

The tree, he thought, the big maple, if I can get to it.

He could go up it like a squirrel; he'd done it a lot of times. But the dog was at his heels. He had to dodge around the tree and cut away at a different angle, thinking, in desperation, I can't outrun it, the tree was the only place.

He didn't even see the taxicab until he heard Amanda's scream.

"Ad! Here! This way, quick!"

It was parked at the end of the driveway. He could see the round white patch of Amanda's face in the rolled-down window and the open rear door with a tall, dark figure standing beside it. Then something went off behind him with a bang like a shotgun; he thought with horror, They're shooting at me. His feet picked up and flew. He dove through the black square of the cab door, aware that he had landed all anyhow on a pile of suitcases. People bleeding and dying didn't feel anything and neither did Adam. He lay, his breath sobbing in his throat, waiting for what was to come.

Outside the cab, pursuit had ceased. Betsey, the dog, was a big old Newfoundland, a good watchdog only because of her tremendous voice which could put the fear of destruction by mangling into the heart of any night prowler. But even in her youth, when she had had her teeth and had not been so stout and clumsy, she had never been known to hurt anybody. She was used to children and quite timid. Chasing Adam had been more of a romp to her than anything else. When he had cut around the tree, she had plowed ahead for ten feet or so before she could change course; when the thing that went bang landed beside her, she had retired without dignity to a safe place she knew of, under the front porch.

Her owner, who had bought the house through Lewis Wyman's agent and, as a safety precaution in these times of thieves and muggers, had had all the locks changed, was also timid. He had come out on the porch in his bathrobe and, like Adam, had not noticed the taxicab, being concentrated on the chase around the tree. Suddenly, someone had screamed. A gun had gone off. He, too, thought someone had taken a shot at him. His house, he thought, was being attacked by a gang; for a moment, he'd been so scared he couldn't move.

Then someone had yelled at him. "You git in the house, you pussle-gutted old laundry stove!" Something hit the steps in front of him, and the gun went off again, spattering gravel all over the porch. He ducked into the house, quivering, slammed the door, and locked it. For half an hour his wife thought he was going to have a stroke. So instead of the police, she called the doctor.

The taxicab whirled away down Planetree Hill, the driver taking many turns into side streets on the way back into town. He kept checking his rearview mirror to make sure he wasn't being chased by a squad car, but at the same time he seemed to be enjoying himself because he kept chuckling and once or twice burst out laughing.

"Where to now?" he asked. "Say we don't end up in court before I get rid of you?"

"You know where West Wexler Street is?" Jilson asked.

"Uh-huh. Down by the waterfront. You going back there? I could take you to a nice hotel uptown. Or are you low on dough?"

"Number twenty-one West Wexler Street," Jilson said shortly.

"Okay. It's kind of a scrummy neighborhood, you know, and you've got a lady here to look after."

"Number twenty-one's a rooming house. It's run by a lady. If you wasn't accommodating as well as nosy, I wouldn't bother to tell you that we got money, only we don't spend it foolish."

"Okay, okay." The driver began to laugh again. "Buh-rother! A looking glass and cherry bombs! You sure go loaded for emergencies. Me, I thought for a minute you'd shot the guy."

"Well," Jilson said, "I do keep a little something handy, just in case, but seldom if ever do I shoot anybody. Tried it once and didn't like it."

PART TWO

Caroline

THERE COULD BE no doubt about it, Susie Warren was the last person known, that day, to have seen Caroline Fling. Caroline's trail stopped short on Susie's front doorstep at 6:30 P.M. Susie remembered the time because of the newscast.

"Just turned it on," she told Pomroy Fifield, the town constable. "If she's the one you mean, and I guess she is. Yuba Fling's girl. Here selling flowers less than an hour ago. Step in, won't you, Pomroy?"

"I can't stop," Pomroy said. "I've got to find that little character. She wasn't home when her mother got back from work, and Yuba's nervous. Which way she go, you notice?"

"Why, around the corner, there. The northwest corner of the house."

"Didn't see her anywheres after that—cross the pasture or anything?"

"All I noticed was she was dressed up. Dressed to kill in her Sunday clothes. Came to my front door and knocked. First I saw, the heads of a big bouquet of delphiniums nodding outside my front-room window. It took a jump out of me, as if my border had come walking. This little girl, twelve years old or so, said, 'You want to buy some flowers?' "

Susie Warren was famous all over the county for her delphiniums. She took a good deal of pride in the fact that nobody she knew, at least so far, had been able to raise such tall ones, with blooms as big as a butter-pat dish. Such iridescence, such exotic bees weren't seen anywhere except in seed-catalog illustrations. She had always had spirited competition, but each year in July, regularly, she won the blue ribbon at the flower show. Her border now was in its second blooming, almost as good as the first one, unheard of for September. The moment she saw these lovely ones, their stems towering over the child's head, naturally she wanted them, for one thing to compare them with her own.

She said, "Where did these come from, honey?" and paused. The youngster was giving her what certainly seemed to be an odd look. The eyes below the white facing of the blue bonnet, which was the style this year for teen-agers, were calm, clear, and ice-blue; their expression gave nothing whatever away.

Then the child said, "My gramma's brought these over from Bradford. To sell. You want them? Ten cents apiece. My gramma needs the money."

"My goodness, she must. Does she know what blooms like that would cost her at the florist's? Who might your gramma be, honey?"

Susie had thought that the grower must be some Bradford farmer's wife who had hit a lucky fertilizer combination. She was racking her brain to think of someone over there who was a delphinium grower and poor, but the child said, without batting an eye, "Mrs. Pollard."

"You can't mean Mrs. Lydia Pollard?" Susie knew Mrs. Lydia Pollard well. Better, she told herself, than she wanted to. In the days when she (Susie) had been the town dressmaker, she had done a good deal of sewing for the fussy Mrs. Pollard, who had never been pleased with any of it, who was rolling in hardware-store money left her by her husband, and who, to Susie's definite knowledge, wouldn't know which end of a delphinium seed to plant.

The child said, with a kind of weary patience, "I'm helping her peddle. She needs the money. She lost all she's got."

There's certainly something more than meets the eye here, Susie thought. This is a cool little cookie, lying her head off, I'm afraid.

"I have got to go," the child said. "You want some or don't you, before these wilt down?" A small, clear drop of sweat rolled out from under the blue cap and down her cheek.

So the little cookie, it seemed, wasn't exactly cool. There was an air of tenseness about her, in the still way she was standing as if she were braced. Something that could be desperation, Susie thought, watching her.

"Mercy, yes, of course I want them," she said. She reached around the corner of the hall and produced an ancient umbrella stand. Not many people nowadays had one of these, most had either broken them or carted them to the dump. This had belonged to Susie's Great-aunt Miranda, now dead and gone. Susie had kept it, not out of sentiment but because it was tall enough for delphiniums. Great-aunt Miranda, who had brought Susie up, was largely responsible for her quick interest in and sympathy for an upset or desperate child. Great-aunt Miranda had had neither interest nor sympathy.

"Why don't you come in, sit down for a minute, honey?" Susie said. "Take that bonnet off, it's hot for a warm evening. You can have supper with me or, if you're in a hurry, some cookies and cold milk."

"Could you pay me? I've got to go."

"Of course. How much? Have you counted?"

"Sixteen. Times ten. A dollar-sixty."

Susie got her purse from the drawer in the front-room desk and counted out the money. "Are you sure you don't want more for them?" she asked. "These are awfully nice ones."

The child took the money in one hand—it might almost be said she snatched it. With the other, she thrust the flowers at Susie and vanished on a run around the corner of the house.

Poor little thing, Susie thought. I wonder what on earth . . .

"I figured," she told Pomroy Fifield now, "that if she was Lydia Pollard's grandchild, she must belong to Yuba Fling. Maybe she's run away. She seemed kind of upset about something." She chuckled a little, thinking of the big yarn about Lydia Pollard's growing delphiniums. "Have you heard anything about Lydia's losing her money, Pomroy?"

"Ain't," Pomroy said. "If she has, she's kept back one Cadillac."

He sounded absent-minded and he was, at least his attention was elsewhere. He was staring through the open window into the kitchen, at the counter where, not long ago, Susie had cut up the meat for the cat's supper. It was beef liver, not too long from the freezer, beginning to bleed as it defrosted. Some of the blood had dripped off the cutting board and had spread into a pool on the counter.

"What's *that?*" Pomroy said, looking from it to her and back again.

"Seeing you've got your eye glued to it for no reason I can see," Susie said, "that's the cat's liver. Makes a bloody mess, doesn't it?"

Pomroy backed away from her, lifting his feet high to feel for the steps.

"What in the world ails you, Pomroy?" Curious, she followed him as far as the top step, looking down. "You look as if you'd swallowed a beetle . . ." Her voice died away as she stared at her border of delphiniums, which, when she'd worked there this afternoon, had stretched entirely around three sides of her backyard picket fence. Now it stretched two sides. The third one was bare of bloom, showing only trampled plants, haggled off flower stalks.

"That little scamp sold me my own flowers!" she said. She turned, strode back into the house.

Pomroy had started off up the walk to his car, but now he came back up the steps and peered curiously through the kitchen window. She was standing in front of an umbrella stand full of flowers, her hands on her hips. Talking to herself, he thought, and leaned closer trying to hear.

"Yes! She certainly did. That's my Summer Skies, my Galahad, my King Arthur. Why! What a little hellion!"

Pomroy couldn't catch it all. She was good and mad, that was for sure. He heard something about "caught up with her in time," and "snatched her to ribbons and braided the ribbons," and "had it coming."

Pomroy was a devout watcher of TV, from after supper to eleven o'clock every night and all day Sunday. Himself an officer of the law, he identified with Marshal Dillon and the sparkling heroes of the F.B.I., and he'd learned much from them that helped him with his own job. Certain types were the ones to look out for—the ugly-looking man was always the criminal; homely old women and old maids living alone were likely to be off their tracks, if not actually crazy. You couldn't call Susie Warren either homely or old, but she sure-God lived alone down here in the woods, on the farm Miranda Cooley left her, half a mile from town.

The trouble was, Pomroy never had very much in the way of crime to deal with. Somebody might swipe a package of Wheaties off a grocery shelf, or a kid like this little Fling character run away after school and worry her mother, but nothing for a real smart detective to get his teeth into. If there ever was anything hot, like a rape or some such, the county sheriff or the deputy here in town,

Fred Montgomery, would come nosing in, get all the credit.

Pomroy had spent a good many hours picturing how he would act if he ran into a real hum-swizzler of a murder or a bank robbery. He saw himself a man clothed with the dignity of authority, keen-minded and cool; what he was would show all over him. When he had backed down the steps, he hadn't really thought that Susie Warren had cut up her cat or that the meat on the counter was anything in the world but the cat's supper. But the blood on the counter had reminded him of clues—any clues. He had a color TV that showed up blood like nobody's business; so he had acted as he considered a smart detective would.

Standing there with his head thrust up to his shoulders in Susie Warren's open kitchen window, he wouldn't have thought, when she turned around and saw him, that he looked like a Peeping Tom.

It was already dusk outside and he was back-to what light there was. She had seen Pomroy start off up the walk —she thought he'd gone. So here was some man with his head stuck in the window, snooping. Without a word she snatched up a cushion from the davenport and let it go full strength. The cushion, stuffed with spruce needles, was hefty; it smacked Pomroy hard in the middle of his face and, as he told the state troopers afterward, "like to tore my head off." He legged it for his car and headed back toward town.

Oh, Lord, that was only Pomroy, Susie thought. Now, I wouldn't have done that if I hadn't lost my temper already.

She had come out on the back doorstep with another cushion, twin to the first one, ready to sandbag the prowler if he didn't make tracks. And there was Pomroy, scrambling into his car.

What on earth had he thought he was doing? Well, probably nothing. All his life he'd been a silly kind of man. She put both cushions neatly back on the davenport and sat down.

Never one to cry over spilled milk, after a while she found her temper. This was a beautiful bouquet to have in the house to enjoy. She'd been tempted, herself, to pick some delphiniums for just that but hadn't because they looked so beautiful growing. She still had two sides of her border left, though that big King Arthur, there, over six feet tall, had been her pride and joy even in its second blooming.

That was quite a career girl, that little cookie. Lied, as calm as a puddle in a plant pot. Smart, too, the way she finagled me. One on me, really. Big sucker, I was. The little devil.

Still, you had to give her credit. She could have had more money for the bouquet than she asked, so she wasn't just out to swindle somebody without a reason to. No, she needed a dollar and sixty cents, had to have it. An emergency of some kind. Me, I wouldn't lift a finger to punish her unless I knew what the matter was.

Maybe there was some trouble up at Yuba Fling's. Could be Lydia Pollard was sticking her nose into Yuba's business again. She'd raised particular Cain ever since George Pollard, her son and Yuba's first husband, had died and Yuba had married again. No wonder that child had been desperate, if Lydia was wound up in it somehow. She was a blistering Tartar of a woman.

Heavens, it was long past suppertime, getting dark already, and here she was half-starved. She'd been too tired to eat when she'd come in from working in the garden, and then there'd been that little Fling and Pomroy, one interruption after another. Susie thought, with anticipation, of those nice pork chops in the refrigerator.

Lord, it was wonderful after all those years with Great-aunt Miranda, and the pull-and-haul of the dressmaking shop in town, to have nobody and nothing to be responsible for but one old tomcat. Everybody thought she was out of her mind, and said so, to be, at her age, which was thirty-two, so in love with her own company. Why, with her looks and her money, they said, she could marry anybody she wanted to, she must have a hole in her ever-loving head. Well, they hadn't had thirty years with Great-aunt Miranda and fourteen in the dress shop. They didn't know that being by yourself and doing what you wanted to on your own time was so great it was almost holy.

You could cook chops in an old black, cast-iron spider without having somebody harping on how much better stainless steel or enamelware was, for instance; stand back and admire the pink meat edged with creamy fat, take your time waiting for them to begin to put out aroma. Nothing like a well-seasoned skillet to start that smell going. When it did, it would be heaven.

And there was Tommy, yowling on the doorstep. "I thought that would raise you," she said, letting him in. "Your smeller beats the world. Put meat on, you know it half a meadow away. Here! Don't you jump up!"

She had spoken too late. He gathered together and in one leap he was up there, landing both his front feet in the middle of that oozed-out liver blood. "You get down this minute, look at the mess! Splattered all over the counter top and on my apron, too!" With her elbow, she nudged him off onto the floor while she scraped the meat into his bowl. "There, I know you're starved, had a bad day hunting. No birds or chipmunks, and I'm glad of it." She set the bowl down. "All right, don't eat my hand off. Tt-t, look at that! Bloody cat tracks all over the clean floor!"

She pulled a paper towel out of the container, wiped off the counter top, and was about to mop up Tommy's tracks with it when she heard the fire whistle blow. From the back porch, looking up toward town, she couldn't see any smoke or flame, couldn't hear the fire truck starting, the way she always could on a quiet evening. Probably a grass fire; they usually put one out with little brass back tanks. Or somebody's oil burner flooded, and chemicals. Susie liked a good fire, but she had a rule—if you couldn't see any smoke, don't go, you'd be disappointed.

The chops were ready to turn, nice and brown. While

[45]

the other side cooked, she washed and polished the sink and counter top until they shone. She made toast, crisp and thin, got lettuce out of the icebox for a salad, dished up the chops, and sat down to eat.

Susie liked to eat and she always bought the best; she could afford to now. She could afford to have a knock-down-drag-out with the butcher if the meat wasn't right. Eating, she thought she'd come a long way from a skinny orphan with a home only by the grace of Great-aunt Miranda Cooley, who had believed that enjoying yourself was a venal sin and who had never served more than one chop apiece, thin, tough, and, like as not, mutton.

True, in simple justice, Susie had to admit she had a lot to thank the old lady for, but not until Aunt Miranda had had her stroke and died of it at the age of ninety-seven. She had left Susie thirty acres of land, the tall farmhouse, and something no one had ever suspected she'd had —a good deal of money. She had kept it in a locked trunk under her bed—her keepsakes and deeds, she'd always said. Susie had cleaned house around it for years and had often wondered why it didn't rot down through the floorboards, because Aunt Miranda would never let it be opened or moved. When Susie finally did open it, after the old lady's death, she'd found the deeds and keepsakes, the last will and testament, and bag after bag of pillow ticking stuffed with bills and coins, some of them old enough to be collectors' items.

Well, Susie had said to herself, cast your bread on the waters and it'll come back with butter and jelly on it. She'd been paying Aunt Miranda board and room for years, and in the trunk she found several fat envelopes marked "Susie" containing every penny of it.

She herself wasn't one who didn't believe in investment. She cast about and looked into and went to trouble to find something simple that people used every day and went on using, no matter what kind of hard times came along. She finally settled on paper bags, which had been no mistake.

The stocks of the paper-bag company she'd chosen went up and went on going. After a while, she'd had enough to retire on—to get so far away from the dressmaking business that the time would come, she'd told herself, when, about a needle, she wouldn't know which end to thread; when she'd have leisure enough to make a real garden and to read books. She had always loved to read; but Aunt Miranda had got twitchy about board and room and had apprenticed her to the town dressmaker, to work nights after school and holidays, when Susie was going on thirteen. Five years later, the dressmaker had died of a felon gone foul on her finger. Susie had taken over the business. After that, there hadn't been time for anything except to take care of Aunt Miranda and rest up for the workday to come.

The tall farmhouse was a fine old-timer, out of repair and with no conveniences at all when Susie had inherited it. The old Cooley farm had been prosperous for generations, almost self-sufficient, with stock pastured in its lush hay meadows, poultry and pig houses, woodlots, and wide fields planted to food crops. It had once occupied nearly all of a peninsula which stretched in a southerly direction down from the town, but, in her time, Aunt Miranda had whittled away at it, selling acreage and shoreline for summer cottages. The house stood on an elevation about a hundred yards back from the eastern shore, overlooking, to the west, a wide, deep bay which ended in islands and mainland and, on the east, the open ocean which poured tides through a mile-wide channel between the peninsula and Whistle Island. Whistle Island, also, had once been owned by the Cooleys. Aunt Miranda had sold that, years ago, to a summer man, an ex-European count named von Wigheln-Bisschner, who had built a big house there around 1920.

What was left for Susie to inherit was a thirty-acre slice which cut across the peninsula from one side to the other. The house and land were blessed relief from slavery and bedpans. She had modern conveniences now such as Aunt Miranda had never dreamed of, and, if she had, the thought of the expense would have dropped her dead in her tracks. Even if the washer-and-dryer, the hot-water heater, the deepfreeze and refrigerator, the electric cookstove and the drilled well might have prolonged her life, she would have dropped just the same. Though she would have resurrected, Susie sometimes thought, just so she could drop dead again, at the sight of four walls of a room in her house lined with books.

The lush meadows of the Cooley farm, overgrown now with trees and alders, were full of privacy for small creatures and birds and for anyone who loved to watch them. On the west shore was a small sand cove where Susie could keep an outboard skiff. But her real pleasure was her flower garden—something which all her life she had wanted to make and never had, except for a few scraggly zinnias in the baked earth around Aunt Miranda's back step. Zinnias were poor things, stiff as corset steels, and hot colors—orange and magenta and red. What Susie'd wanted was something tall and cool and mysterious, as if it carried a secret of its own, and standoffish, as if it would never tell the secret to anything, except maybe to a hummingbird. Delphiniums. She'd found them. And she'd found, too, that living by herself wasn't loneliness. After years of being pulled and hauled around, people schooling all over her life, living alone was security and it was heaven.

That was one reason, Susie told herself, why, seeing some kind of a Peeping Tom staring in her window, she'd let herself go like that at poor old Pomroy. After all, there wasn't any harm in him.

Pomroy had to drive one-handed; with the other hand he held his handkerchief to his nose, which was bleeding a flood. Dammit, everybody knew he had a tender nose. He didn't know but he ought to go to the doctor, but as he was passing the firehouse, the whistle blew. Quite a crowd of people there in front of it, but the trucks hadn't gone out, why was that? Then he saw, parked a little to one side of the ramp, a state-police car—big blue light on top, not flashing, but state cops, all right.

Pomroy pulled up. "What's all this?" he asked Joe Rodgers, a neighbor of his who was standing there.

"Hi, Pomroy. One of Yuba Fling's kids's gone missing and she called the troopers. What's the matter? You got a cold? Holymoly, what happened to you? You look as if you'd been stashed in the bushes somewhere eating a cow."

"I," Pomroy said coldly, "have been out on the job, looking." Blast and damn, state cops took over, had they? This was his job. If anybody called troopers, it ought to been him. Well, he had something he could report if he was a mind to, say anybody run of an idea he'd been loafing all this time. "Ask one of them troopers to step over here, will you, Joe?" he said in a stately voice.

In a moment, the tall trooper came through the crowd and stood outside Pomroy's car window. "What is it?" he asked.

"Constable Fifield. You better git in here with me a minute and we'll drive along a ways. I've got something kind of private to talk over."

"We're pretty busy—"

"Maybe you won't be if you listen to me. I think I got something on this."

"Okay." The trooper walked around the car and got in. "Make it snappy, Constable, will you?"

"We'll just drive around the triangle, here. Now, look, this has to do with one of my neighbors, so I'd ruther not have anyone hear me talking, just in case there ain't nothing in it. This old maid, lives in the woods down the Cooley Road, I think she's gone raving crazy. You can see where she hit me, and she's got a mess of meat and blood in her kitchen. When I asked her what it was, she said she'd cut up a cat. I thought, seeing there's a little girl missing—"

"Godfrey mighty!" the trooper said. "Turn the car

around, bud, and step on it. Why in the living hell didn't you do something about it at the time?"

The police car vanished down the Cooley Road, blue light flashing. Pomroy watched it go. Maybe he hadn't ought to told that in just that way. Prob'ly nothing in it but what she said, the cat's supper. But then, blood around and a little girl gone—things like that ought to be looked into, regardless. Leave no stone unturned. If it did turn out to be something—well, a case—Pomroy Fifield would be right up there, chief witness. Right up there on the stand, giving evidence with the best of them. He saw himself, suddenly, the whole courtroom hanging on to every word he said with their mouths open.

"Yes, sir," he said under his breath, "I was the one found it. First one there. I said, 'What's that?' and she said—"

Groups of men began to separate from the crowd around the firehouse and to head off in different directions, mostly toward the woods back of the town. Now who was that organizing search parties, telling them where to go? Fred Montgomery, the deputy, was in there, phoning from the booth. Prob'ly him, the nosy, interfering son.

Pomroy waited until Fred came out of the booth. "Was it you sending them cordons out?" he demanded.

"Uh-huh," Fred said. "Where've *you* been?"

"Ought to waited till I got back, instead a sticking your nose in where it warn't needed," Pomroy said. "You might find you've sent a lot of fellas on a wild-goose chase."

Fred took a step toward him. Under the powerful lamp over the firehouse entrance, Fred's face showed strained and sheet-white with worry. Yuba Fling was his aunt, his mother's sister; the little girl, Caroline, was his cousin and he was very fond of her. And here was Pomroy, covered with blood. "What've you found?" he said, his voice a croak.

"I ain't sure yet. I sent them troopers down the Cooley

Road, though." Pomroy had trouble holding back a snicker at the sight of Fred's face. "To see your girl friend, down there. No knowing what *they'll* find." Pomroy turned, marched to his car, and drove off, paying no attention to Fred's frantic shout.

Paid him off, by cracky. Learn him, mind his own business.

So far as Pomroy knew, Susie Warren hadn't been Fred's girl friend since some years back, when Old Lady Cooley, who was alive then, had chased him off the doorstep with a kettle of boiling water.

Thinking of that, Pomroy suddenly almost drove into a telephone pole. Miranda Cooley'd been crazy's a coot, the last of her days. Insanity ran in families, didn't it? To be sure! Who but a lunatic would sling a heavy cushion like that at a man, half-kill him, when he wasn't doing nothing but his job, looking in a window? Darned if he wouldn't like to go back down there, see how she was making out with the troopers, be in on it if they arrested her. But the excitement of thinking all that had started off his nose again, dripping like a fountain, and he be dag if he was going to bleed to death in the line of duty. He headed uptown for the doctor's office.

Fred Montgomery stood where he was. Girl friend? he thought. Now who could the blasted old busybody have meant? Susie Warren lived down the Cooley Road, but she was as far now from being his girl friend as she'd been when they'd had to bust up ten years ago. Pomroy's memory must be darn near as long as his nose, if that was what he'd raked up. Or maybe what he'd had in mind was the time last summer when Fred had taken Susie over to Whistle Island in his lobster boat. He was caretaker of the big summer cottage over there and had a day's work to do, and Susie had gone along to walk in the woods and bird-watch. That was all there'd been to that, but no knowing what kind of sinful actions old Pomroy had blown it up into. He could make gossip out of a gull over a hen yard.

[*51*]

The firehouse phone rang, and Fred went in to answer it. It was the sheriff in Bradford saying he'd found the fellow with the bloodhound and was sending him over. Right away.

Thank the Lord, Fred thought. Maybe now we'll get some real action. He began to get the horrors again, thinking of all the things that could have happened to Caroline. She always went right after school to his mother's house to pick up her little brother, Jakie. Ma was minding him while Yuba went to work. Today Caroline hadn't shown up at all.

Susie Warren was getting ready for bed when she heard someone come up the back steps—someone with heavy feet and certainly a heavy knock. She put down her toothbrush with an impatient moan, slipped on her bathrobe, and went to the door. Oh, Lord, she thought, hasn't there been enough for one day? "Whoever you are, you'll have to make it snappy," she sang out. "I'm getting ready to go to bed—for goodness' sake!"

It was a young state trooper, a nice-looking boy, all rigged out in his blue-gray pants with the stripe, coat with slick leather belt, black pistol handle sticking out of holster, and that hat they wore. On the step below him, another one, older, with a face like a chisel, stood there, just looking.

The young one said, "Sorry to bother you, ma'am, but the little Fling girl hasn't been found. Constable Fifield says you told him she was here around six-thirty. Is that right?"

"That's right. She was. I told Pomroy Fifield all that, once."

"Just checking. Fifield said you were pretty sore at the little girl for picking your flowers."

"Oh, I was. I'd probably have said plenty to her if I'd found it out while she was here. But after I cooled off, I was glad I didn't. She didn't look like a very happy little girl to me."

The older man said, "That so? How long was she here?"

"Why . . . five . . . ten minutes, I'd say."

"Mind if we come in, take a look around?"

Susie looked at him, bewildered. "Why, I don't know what you expect to find. But of course, if you want to."

They came pushing in through the entry. The overhead light was on, but the older trooper pulled out a flashlight and began flashing the beam around, on the sink, the kitchen counter, the floor. He said, "You've cleaned up some since Fifield was here."

"Washed my dishes and scrubbed off the counter. What—"

"Take a look at the cat tracks, Paul. Isn't that . . . ?"

Oh, Lord, she'd completely forgot Tommy's bloody tracks on the linoleum, but if they were here to check up on her housekeeping, they had little to do.

The young man, Paul, had got down on a knee. "Hold the light. Looks like it. Yes, I think it is. Blood on that paper towel in the wastebasket, too."

"And on that apron, hanging behind the door. How did you get blood on your apron?"

"That's where I cut up the cat's liver. He jumped—" She stopped, seeing them glance at each other. "What on earth are you talking about?"

The older man said, "Tell me, ma'am," and his voice was nice and gentle and velvety, "how did your cat get blood on his paws? Did you hurt him?"

Susie stared at him, aghast. "Hurt *Tommy?* Tommy's asleep in the chair by the TV. See for yourself."

He did. He went into the front room, and an outraged yowl told her that he'd touched Tommy, who came streaking through the kitchen and shot out through his bolt-hole beside the back door. The trooper came back mopping the back of his hand with his handkerchief. "Nothing wrong with that cat," he said.

"Tommy doesn't care for strangers," Susie said. She was getting good and mad, and she hoped the scratch was a deep one.

"He's still got traces of blood on his paws," the trooper said.

"Yours?" Susie said. "Can I get you some iodine?"

"Let's not get funny." He wasn't purring now. "Why did you tell Fifield you'd killed your cat and sliced up his liver?"

"I didn't—"

"What happened to the bloody mess he said he saw in your kitchen? And that blood on your apron—where did that come from?"

Light dawned on Susie.

"He said you made some crazy talk about tearing the little Fling girl to ribbons and that you hit him in the face when you found out he was listening and heard it. Suppose you tell us—"

"Suppose you listen. Obviously, I didn't cut up my cat. I sliced up some frozen beef liver for his supper, which he ate. It wasn't quite defrosted and Tommy hadn't come in, so I left it on the counter to warm and it bled all over the counter top. When Tommy did come in, he was hungry. He jumped up, landed in the blood puddle, splattered it all over my apron. That piece of liver's gone, you can't find it unless *you* cut him up, but the other half's in the refrigerator, still defrosting."

"Take a look, Paul."

Paul produced the liver, poked at it gingerly with his finger. "That's right," he said. "Still pretty well frozen."

Susie said crisply, "I may have had time to have cut that out of a child, if that's what that irresponsible old liar has made you believe, but I surely to heaven haven't had time to freeze it."

"All right, lady, let's not fly off the handle." The older trooper had turned a little red, she was pleased to see.

"Who's flying?" she said. "I know I said some good strong words about my delphiniums being picked, and I said them out loud. I expect that's what Pomroy heard. I thought he'd gone, he certainly had started to go. I looked around, saw this head stuck in through the kitchen window. Scared me. I live alone here, you know, and the light was off in the kitchen, so I couldn't see who it *was*. So I let go a sofa cushion. I wish now it had been a hammer, the old fool. I suppose his nose bled. Matt Dillon's nose never bleeds."

The young man, Paul, suddenly grinned. "He didn't mention that," he said. "Sure had a nosebleed, though. I guess that's actually what it was," he went on, turning to the other man. "He was pretty mad at this lady here, I thought."

The other grinned back at him. "Okay. I'm sorry, ma'am. You won't mind if we look around the premises outside?"

"You're welcome to," Susie said. "For bodies or tripes or any other kind of insides you may think you'll find. If Pomroy Fifield shows up here again, they'll very likely be his."

"Better not do that. Or we'll have to come back for sure. Sorry we bothered you. We're just doing our job." As they left, he looked back and tipped his hat.

It didn't make her feel any better; for a minute, she thought she might be sick and her legs were shaking. What if I hadn't been able to explain? What if there'd been some one thing I couldn't account for?

She reached for a paper towel from the roller, dampened it at the sink, and mopped Tommy's tracks from the floor. As she dropped it into the wastebasket, she saw that the other towel, the one she'd cleaned off the counter with, was gone. They hadn't given up, after all. Still, if they'd taken it away to test it, all they'd find on it would be beef blood.

But thinking that wasn't much comfort.

Here I was, in my own home, minding my business, and safe. Or thought I was. Born in this town, lived here all my life, a decent person everyone knows. People know who I am, what I am, how I live. Quiet, not bothering

[55]

anybody, not a thought of harming anyone ever in my mind. How could any of my neighbors, even that old idiot, Pomroy, think I could hurt a child . . . in that awful way, with a knife?

She felt her stomach turn over in revulsion as she walked into the living room to sit down. So far as she knew, she didn't have an enemy in the world. Of course, there was Lot Parker, the secondhand bookseller over in Bradford, who'd unloaded all those sets of books on her when she'd gone to him for advice, not knowing what to buy. But to balance him, there'd been Chris Adams, the carpenter who'd remodeled the room for her and put up book-shelves. Chris, like herself, hadn't had much schooling, but he had always been a great reader. He'd looked around at *Decline and Fall of the Roman Empire, The Revised Statutes of the State of Maine,* and quite a number of other boxed sets she'd bought from Lot, and he'd told her how, when he'd been a younger man, he'd gone for a vacation to New York State and had stayed at a big, old-fashioned hotel up in the Catskill Mountains. "Wasn't a damn thing in the hotel lounge to read except a whole set of books by a man named Dummas. Well, you got Shakespeare, Susie, and the rest'll look nice on your shelves. Lot ain't going to take any of the trash back, that's for sure. He's had most of it clutterin' around his store for years. But if you was to take them Alger books and the Grace Fieldings and the Tom Swift sets to a Boston bookseller, he'd pay you a good price for them. They're collectors' items now."

Susie had done that and had got quite a bit of her money back; she'd never mentioned it to Lot Parker, not even to say the biter bit, but somebody had. Anyway, he knew, and he was cool, sometimes quite rude, whenever he saw her. But . . . an enemy? And Jason Pollard, Lydia's husband, who'd tried to buy the Cooley shore property from her after Aunt Miranda died—he'd been furious at her because she'd refused to sell. "A thousand dollars?" she'd said to him. "Oh, it's worth much more than that for summer cottages, even if I wanted to sell it. No, thanks. If anyone makes any money out of that land, it's going to be me." And Jason had rared back on the front seat of his Cadillac and had hollered at her, "That's more'n you need! And you ain't got no right to own so much prop'ty!" But Jason was dead now.

I have got to stop this, Susie told herself firmly. Sorting out people for enemies, for goodness' sake! Nobody's done anything to me but that old fool, Pomroy Fifield, and he lies about everybody.

The state troopers were no fools, though. They'd taken the towel.

She got up and turned on the television, but there was nothing to watch except brave policemen investigating crime and some young people making a bomb to blow something up with. She turned it off.

The thing to do is to call Tommy in and go to bed. Things'll look different in the morning.

In the kitchen she switched on the overhead light and decided to leave it on and to leave the outside lights on, too.

So that that youngster, if she's got lost in these woods, can see lights to come to. A quiet house, with lights on. And I won't lock the door. Though I suppose the poor mite'll think I'm mad at her and won't dare to come in.

Tommy came when she called—thank goodness. He didn't always come, especially on moonlight nights.

"You're a lamb," she told him. "Even if I had ought to slice up your liver for getting me into such a bind."

He didn't seem to be worried about anything she'd do, just jumped to the place on the foot of the bed where he slept and settled down.

In her room on the ground floor next to the living room, she opened both windows.

So if she comes to the front of the house, I'll be able to hear her and call out to come in.

She wouldn't be asleep, she knew that. In bed, the same thoughts went around and around in her head. In spite of the fresh air from the windows, she felt stifled. Moonlight streamed in, making the room light. On the foot of the bed, Tommy had his nightly bath, his back braced against her feet . . . thump-thump, wiggle-jiggle, wash-wash.

"For heaven's sake, Tommy!" she said at last, and shoved him with her foot. As if that would do any good, he'd go right on, he always did, until he was satisfied he was clean. But this time he didn't. He shot up, stiff and straight, his ridge a hackly line, his tail big as a club, and growled deep in his throat.

For a moment she thought, shocked, that he had growled at her. Then a shadow passed across one window, paused, crossed the other. She heard a scrabbling sound. Someone out there! That youngster, maybe? Found her way out of the woods? Oh, please let it be!

She flew out of bed, reaching for her robe.

Four men stood on the lawn by the front step. Four men and a dog—a big, dark-and-white patched, loose-jointed hound, with floppy, long ears. A bloodhound.

So they hadn't found her, poor mite.

One of the men was kneeling, offering some kind of bundled-up cloth for the dog to smell. The child's clothes? Susie watched silently from the open window.

The men stood in the moonlight, vague faces shadowed by hat brims, tall, black figures, motionless as a memorial group on a park pedestal, carved in stone. Not even the dog moved, his tail stretched straight out behind, stiff as a single bone. There was only one sign that these were living creatures. The kneeling man was saying in a soft, husky whisper, "Find." And again, "Find."

Then, suddenly, the tableau broke. The dog leaped, strained to the end of his leash, upsetting the kneeling man, who scrambled to his feet still holding on. The two vanished around the corner of the house, the dog running, his nose to the ground, the man leaping in long, half-stumbling strides. The other men followed, running, too.

Scrabbling sounds came from the direction of the shore road, then silence. The lawn was as empty as if nobody had been there at all, except for the bundled-up cloth the kneeling man had dropped when the dog had started to run.

My neighbors, Susie thought. And not one of them did I know. Or seemed to know me.

The cloth bundle lay tumbled in the moonlight, obviously some kind of child's garment. Whatever it was, it belonged to Caroline Fling, something perhaps she valued, and the night dew would wet it. Susie went out in her slippers to bring it in.

Moonlight was over everything, on the white clapboards of the house, on the beds of daisies and ageratum by the front door. Spruces in the pasture below the house were black; beyond the spruces, the bay was a whitish glimmer, silent to the horizon. The light was cold as if with intent; it had washed color out of everything.

To be out on a moonlight night and not think it's pretty, Susie thought. And the house, the windows looked like closed eyes. She shivered, picked up the garment, carried it into the house. It was a child's coat, dark blue, quite small, trimmed with some kind of fur.

Shoddy material, she thought, holding it to the light under her dressmaker's eye. Poor Yuba can't afford better, I know. But if I were Lydia Pollard, I'd see my grandchild had something to wear besides rabbit fur.

Rabbit fur? *Rabbit?* Does that make sense? For heaven's sake. You'd think they'd have known better.

It had made great sense to the bloodhound. She was a female, not very old, full of the joy of her life and ready to cooperate with anything. She'd taken a hearty sniff of the coat, found it very pleasant indeed. Rabbits? she'd thought. Rabbits they want, for a change? Hoop-la! And

[59]

off she'd gone at a great rate. At the entrance to the shore road, she'd come on a fine rabbit scent and followed it happily for five miles until it petered out at the edge of a deep heath, where leaping rabbits could go but dogs, and certainly men, could not.

Four hundred men from three towns cordoned the woods that night. Almost elbow to elbow, they swept the wild country from the bay shore on the west of Susie Warren's house to the ocean on the east. They did not go into the heath where the bloodhound had stopped; the bogholes in there were six or more feet deep. They scared up forty deer, a large number of annoyed raccoons, foxes, and a big barn owl. One man was hit in the hat by a flying squirrel, scaring him witless. Another got an ankleful of porcupine quills, a third got skunked. They did not find Caroline Fling.

At ten after four in the morning, the fire whistle blew. Susie, still awake, sat up in bed with a jerk.

If they're blowing it now, they're calling the search parties in. That means they've found her. Or, she thought, with a cold clutch at her heart, they know where she is.

Dusky, early morning light was at the windows; to the west, sky and water were the same silvery color, clear and still. No one could have told where water left off and sky began. Over the quiet countryside, the siren wailed, rising, falling, beginning again; wild, inhuman voice, saying, as it so often did, disaster. Or what?

She had better get up, get warm somehow. All night she had felt icy cold, with a kind of dead, inner chill. She was standing by the stove, waiting for the coffee to perk, when she heard a car stop outside. It was the state-police car at the end of the drive, but the man coming down the walk was Fred Montgomery. White-faced, she met him at the door.

"Caroline's all right," he said, without preliminary. "She walked into Aunt Yuba's kitchen ten minutes ago."

"Oh, Fred, thank God!"

"I was with the troopers," he said. "They got it on their car radio. She's home and she's all right." He scowled, looked down at the floor. Apparently he had something more to say but wasn't sure how to say it.

Susie recognized the symptoms. She had known Fred for a long time, and once, years back, she had known him very well. "She's all right? Good, Fred. I've been so scared for her."

"I saw you last night looking out the window," he said finally. "When we had that blasted hound here."

"You did? Mercy, were you with them? I couldn't see faces, and you all looked like a mess of stone statues out there."

"Fellow owned the dog told us not to move or speak. Said it'd take her mind off her smeller. They was all holding their breath for fear you'd make a noise. Talk or something. Not that it would have made much difference. That was a nice bitch but kind of a darnfool, tracking."

"Will you be seeing Caroline? The . . . uh . . . tracker left her coat here. Wait, I'll get it. Pour yourself some coffee, Fred. It's ready now."

He came into the kitchen, waited while she got the coat. "They'll have fifty gallons of coffee ready up at the firehouse," he said. "Thanks just the same, Susie." He took the coat she handed to him, stared at it briefly, folded it over his arm. "Oh, brother!" he said, and grinned. "Well, we had a nice ramble. I *told* the boys she must be on a rabbit. . . . See ya, Susie. I've got one more thing to do and that's follow the toe of my boot till it rousts up Pomroy Fifield."

"You'd do better to go home and get some sleep. You look like the last rag out of the bag," Susie said.

She stood on the back step looking after him as the police car pulled away. He had always been able to tilt back into place a world gone upside-down. Many times, in the days when she'd been half out of her mind with Aunt Miranda, he'd done just that; the way he'd let her

[*61*]

know, a few minutes ago, that he'd understood last night how she was feeling and had made sure she realized why nobody had spoken to her.

If I could have married him, back then, it would have been wonderful, she thought. But Aunt Miranda was on my back like the Old Man of the Sea, and nobody but a relative or a slave should ever be saddled with a thing like that. Now, of course, Fred had his own mother to take care of, though Susie doubted if Flo Montgomery was a patch on Aunt Miranda.

Aunt Miranda, Susie thought with a wry smile. Who, before she had her stroke, used to keep a kettle of hot water on the stove to chase away boy friends, poor, crazy old thing.

Somewhere behind the trees the sun was coming up. The cold-slab look had gone out of the sky. It was beginning to get pink now. Color was coming back, tawny brown to the long grass in the pasture, dark green to the trees. In the border, the delphiniums were showing which were Summer Skies, which Galahad, which a good, but not perfect, King Arthur.

Serenity could be lost in the flash of a moment's time; security, carefully built up over years, could flow away like water or like air. Looking at the flowers, at the dew-dampened clapboards of the tall farmhouse, Susie wondered.

"I went for a walk in the woods and got lost," Caroline Fling told her mother.

"But where? What woods? People looked all over."

Caroline, in bed, her head buried in her pillow, said she didn't know.

"So you left Jakie all alone in the house, put on your good outfit, and went for a walk in the woods."

"I thought Aunt Flo would keep Jakie till I got back. I didn't mean to be gone long."

"Didn't you pick Jakie up at Aunt Flo's after school?"

"No. I thought—" Caroline, worn out, or so she seemed, started to drowse off.

So it had been Flo who'd brought Jakie home and dumped him, all alone here. Yuba'd certainly have a word to say to her about that. Flo was being mean-minded, showing she wasn't going to keep Jakie one minute longer than Yuba paid her for. It wouldn't have hurt her to take him for nothing, seeing she knew how hard Yuba was working to save every penny.

"Caroline! Don't you dare to go to sleep till you've told me where you've been!"

"Mmm, no, Mama."

Yuba had been half out of her mind with worry all night; she had been so glad to see Caroline that she'd almost fainted dead away. Now that it was all over, the child safe, not harmed at all, Yuba was beginning to think of trouble caused, sins committed for a mess of foolishness. Walk in the woods, for heaven's sake!

It had been an awful night. Yuba had got home from work at her usual time, five-thirty; she had a job at one of the big motels down on the Point, cleaning and making up units after tourists had left, sorting laundry and doing odds and ends of other work that took all day. Nearly always, by Labor Day, the tourist trade slacked off, but this year it hadn't; the motel was still full every day. Yuba was tired to death and her feet hurt. She had found Jakie, her three-year-old, bawling his head off in the house, and Caroline, who was supposed to look after him and start supper, nowhere to be seen.

"I don't get it," Yuba said. "Why your best clothes for a walk in the woods?"

Caroline said, "Mmm-hm?" and went sound asleep.

It was certainly a puzzler. Caroline's good clothes were as neat and untorn as when she'd put them on; her new sandals weren't scratched or even wet. And last night there'd been a heavy fall of dew. Yuba glanced out the window to check. Lydia Pollard's black Cadillac was

[63]

parked in the drive, its top soaking wet, its windshield and sideglass running drops of water. Standing there looking at it, Yuba made a face.

Lydia Pollard, Yuba's first husband's old mother; she had been a part of last night's horrors. She'd caught the broadcast about Caroline on the citizens' band and had come flying over, nose-first, to "set" with Yuba and "comfort" her.

And what comfort! At the sight of her, Jakie had started bellering and had kept it up until he'd gone to sleep standing and dropped on the living-room rug, out like a light. If Yuba'd put him to bed when she should have, the old lady'd said, they wouldn't have had to put up with that bellering. Believe you her, she wouldn't have stood that for a minute.

Yuba hadn't tried to tell her that it wasn't any use to put him to bed with Caroline gone. Caroline always did it and stayed with him till he went to sleep. If she didn't, he'd beller till she did.

Then Lydia had started in on what might have happened to Caroline. A hit-and-run could've hid her body in the bushes. If you took time to read the papers, you'd know about all these nasty old men that "got after" girls. Maybe Cad fell off the fish wharf. She was always hanging around down there, Lydia knew for a fact, with all them men. Took Jakie down there, too. It was no place for children, in case Yuba didn't know it.

Yuba had guessed what she was working up to, she'd heard it all before. "Dear George's children" weren't getting proper care, and hadn't been, since Yuba'd married Henry Fling. More to stop her than anything else, Yuba said, "No, Mother, not the wharf. Caroline can swim like a fish. George taught her, remember?" She'd said "Caroline" on purpose, knowing how Caroline hated to be called "Cad."

It had been a mistake to mention George. The old lady

had had the whole thing all over again. As George's mother and the grandmother of his children, she guessed she'd better say she didn't think much of Yuba's going out to work. "All summer you left Cad to take care of that baby. Children need an older person around, someone to lay down the law, see they learn how to behave. That Cad, she's got wild as a hawk. You let her get a little older, she'll be running a *rig* and nobody'll be able to stop her."

Yuba shut her lips tight over what she was bursting to say, and would have said, if it didn't mean so much right now not to make Lydia mad; that Caroline was missing and might never grow old enough to run a rig or anything else. "You know I've got to work, Mother," she said wearily.

"You wouldn't have to if that scalawag ever sent you any money."

"Henry sends me what he can."

"I'll bet! The worst mistake you ever made in your life was to marry Henry Fling. And then to change George's children's names to Fling! Whatever got into you? What kind of a name is that? Them children is *Pollards* and always will be."

Even if Caroline grows up to run a rig? Yuba'd thought grimly. At least, this same old clang about the kids was keeping her mind off how her feet hurt; she hadn't had her shoes off since morning, been on her feet all day. What if the police found Caroline hurt or . . . or worse, and Yuba had to go out, or to the hospital? She didn't dare take her shoes off, because she knew she'd never in the God's world get them on again tonight, she'd have to go in her stocking feet.

"And when they come to live with me," the old lady went on, "they'll be Pollards again and don't you forget it. Hank Fling can call his sprout what he wants to, but not George's children, Miss Lady!"

I'm glad she's at least remembered I'm pregnant. If she

had any sense, she'd shut up and go home. Let me rest. All this trouble and scare, I could mark the baby or even miscarry.

Henry's "sprout" was six months along, really making himself felt. From the way he created around inside her, Yuba was already sure he'd be a boy. Henry was in the Army, stationed in Germany. As soon as they could save money enough for the ticket, Yuba was going to fly over and be with him. She hoped it would be soon. They had awfully good doctors in Germany; if she had to have the baby here it would cost all get-out, take every penny she had saved up for the ticket. Besides, traveling with a little, new baby would be next to impossible—who could say what might harm it? And, oh, God, if anything should happen to Henry's baby!

He was a difficult kind of man; sometimes she had a feeling she couldn't be too sure of him. He'd never really cared for Caroline and Jakie and, times, he showed it. In the summer, he'd written her that she'd have to leave the two kids with their grandmother. Things were rough for G.I.'s over there; what he made wouldn't be enough to take care of a whole family like that. He was sorry, but that was the way the cookie crumbled.

Lydia'd said she'd take Caroline and Jakie, seeing it was her bounden duty, but Yuba'd have to keep hands off from now on out. If they'd behave themselves, not act like such wild little hellions, Lydia'd adopt them, at least, she *might,* and change their name back to where it belonged. In that case, they *might,* just possibly, be the heirs to all her money, but they'd have to mend some of their ways. One thing, she'd cure Jakie of that bellering, and don't Yuba forget it. She was always threatening to back out of the bargain, so that Yuba didn't dare to make her mad. She only hoped the children wouldn't. Jakie had acted terrible tonight, and Caroline, when she'd found out about the plan, had put up an awful row.

"Why can't we go with you?" she'd demanded.

"I've told you. There isn't enough money. Henry can't take care of us all."

"Why can't we go to live with Freddy and Aunt Flo, then? They're just as much related to us as Gramma is."

"I asked Aunt Flo. She won't take you unless I pay your board. And I can't pay board, Caroline. There just—"

"I know. There isn't enough money. I'll bet you didn't ask Freddy."

"What was the use, when Aunty Flo said no?"

"Well, I won't go live with Gramma. Jakie won't either. He hates her. She's awful to him, and—I hate her, too, the old gimlet eye!"

"That'll do. She's the only one that's got the money, and I can't do different. So you stop that talk and be nice to Gramma. After all, she can do a lot more for you and Jakie than I can."

For a while afterward, Yuba had heard Caroline upstairs in her room, throwing things around. She'd hollered up the stairs and told her to stop that, as if it did any good. Caroline at twelve and a half had as stubborn a mind of her own as George had had. Yuba wondered what on earth kind of fur would fly when Caroline and Lydia met head-on, as they surely were going to, when the kids went over to Bradford to live.

And with me gone. And gone for good.

She hadn't dared tell Caroline that after Henry got out of the Army they were going to his people's place in Florida, never coming back here at all. She felt pulled and hauled this way and that; but what could she do? She couldn't risk losing Henry; she loved him.

She would have felt worse if she'd known that Caroline already knew about Florida. Henry's letters were kept carefully tied with a ribbon in Yuba's dresser drawer. All summer, with growing desperation, Caroline had read what might be going to happen to her and Jakie.

Sitting in her living room, now, with Caroline missing and God knew where, while the spiteful clack went on and on, Yuba felt torn in two; but she said, "Well, Mother, I expect you'll just have to do what you think is right."

"Don't you run of an idea that I won't! At least, they'll have a good home. Better than you and that Johnny-come-lately could provide. I've got the wherewithal."

"Yes. You have. I guess I've got to lie down. I'm so tired I can't breathe."

"If you're coming all over queer, you might be going to miscarry," the old lady said briskly.

"No. I'm just worn out." Yuba waited, hoping Lydia'd take the hint and go home. But no. Not a movement to. "If you'd like to spend the night, Mother, you can sleep in my bed. I can bunk here on the davenport. I'd better, anyway, in case . . . just in case I'm needed."

"I'll have to have clean sheets. Have you got any?"

"In the linen closet. In the hall."

I will be damned if I will. One more sheet, one more bed to make, and I die stone-cold dead. Let the old turd make up her own bed.

Under Lydia's resentful stare, Yuba put sofa cushions under her head, pulled the afghan off the back of the davenport, lay down, and closed her eyes.

Lydia said, "Nnffsst!" At least, it sounded like that. A mean sniff, anyway, indicating what more could she expect. She got up and left the room.

After a while, Yuba could hear her thumping around in the bedroom, changing the sheets on the bed.

Oh, God. Don't let her wake up Jakie.

Silence in the house. Glorious, peaceful silence. And before she thought, Yuba had kicked off her shoes.

That did it. Stocking feet. Wherever . . .

But the next she knew, the kitchen door squeaked and Caroline had come tiptoeing across the living-room floor.

Caroline had not been lost in the woods or anywhere else. She had been carrying out a plan. When she had found out for sure that Ma would be going off, forever, and leave Jakie and her behind with Gramma Pollard, Caroline had started working out her plan. She would not, and never would in this world, go to live with Gramma Pollard. It would just be one battleground, all day and every day. How could you bear a battleground, when already you had to stand being left behind, being not wanted by Ma and Henry, so they wouldn't wait a little longer till they had money enough to take you with them?

For two months, she had thought about almost nothing but her plan. She had worked at it whenever she could. If it meant stealing, she would steal; if she had to lie, she'd lie. She was not going to have Jakie get sick to his stomach every day and beller till he vomited, the way he always did when they'd had to go visit Gramma. Ma and Henry could do what they wanted to; the policemen could put her in jail; but if the plan worked out, no one would ever know where she and Jakie were. No one, anyway, until next spring when the Wiggling Biscuits came back, and the Wiggling Biscuits would help, she knew they would. So. If only she could be careful enough, if only she didn't get caught.

She was careful. She always did the shopping for Mama. When Mama needed groceries, she'd leave a list on the table, with the money, before she went to work. Caroline would come away from the store with a separate bagful, bought and paid for with her own money, if she'd been able to raise any money that week. If she hadn't, she'd have in her pockets some of the small things stolen from the shelves—jars of baby food, candy bars, small-sized cans of corned beef—anything that would fit into her pocket and not be noticed. Since she'd always have Jakie with her and he was cute, whoever was at the checkout counter would look at him and not at her.

Then she'd load the groceries into Jakie's express wagon, along with him, and haul everything home. At home, she'd always taken care of Mama's groceries first, putting the list on the table, each item checked, the way Mama liked her to do, along with the exact change from Mama's money. That way, you didn't forget anything.

She'd put Jakie to bed for his nap, stay with him until he was good and sound asleep. He was always a mighty sleeper once he got started; she could be sure of at least an hour before he would wake up. If he did, he'd be all right. He might beller because no one was there, but he couldn't climb out of his crib with the screen over it.

Then she'd pack her own groceries into the garbage pail and slip out the back door across the yard into the woods. Anyone seeing her would think she was just going to empty the garbage can. She always put the groceries into a clean garbage-pail liner first, so they'd stay clean.

The path through the woods to the shore took about ten minutes. Down there was a closed-up summer cottage. The people who owned it, the Fosters, hadn't come this summer. Last fall they'd left their keys with Mama, because one of the jobs Mama had in the spring was to open summer cottages and scrub and get them ready for when the people came. Since the Fosters had intended to come, but had changed their minds later and gone to Europe instead, they had also left quite a lot of canned goods on their kitchen-cupboard shelves. Caroline would put her own groceries on these same shelves, only in the back. It was as safe a storage place as she could think of. If she hid her supplies around home, Mama'd be sure to find them, or Jakie would—he was into about everything. Anybody coming in here would think all these things belonged to the summer people. Nobody would come in anyway, except Freddy Montgomery. He had several cottages he was caretaker of, and the Fosters' was one of them. But he wouldn't bother unless he saw something wrong about the place, and Caroline was careful not to leave any signs. Freddy was hard to fool, she certainly knew that, so she took special pains down here at the Fosters' cottage.

Freddy was a policeman, too, a deputy sheriff; but he was also Caroline's cousin, a relative, who just might not put her in jail if he found out what she'd been doing. Earlier on, in the summer, she'd counted on that. Now she didn't know. She wasn't at all sure of him; she didn't know whether she could trust him. All her life, as far back as she could remember, she'd loved Freddy, and he, of course, was Jakie's dear love of all the world. "Froggy," Jakie called him, which was as near as Jakie could come to his name. She'd always supposed Freddy had loved back; but ever since June she'd been waiting for him to say something about them having to go live with Gramma Pollard. He knew how mean *she* was, and he knew how they both hated her. Never once had he said a word about it, even when his mother, Aunt Flo, had told Mama that she and Freddy couldn't afford to board children for nothing. Of course, you might understand why Aunt Flo had felt that way—she was old, a lot older than Mama, and Jakie's bellering just about drove her crazy, she said. The thing was, Jakie only bellered when he wasn't happy; and if he could have gone to live with Froggy at his house, he'd have been the happiest child in the whole, whole world.

Well, Freddy was probably ashamed, because with people you loved you helped them if they were in trouble. He was thirty-two years old, old enough to be a father and have some say. And he hadn't said. So now she was going to have to fool him along with the rest. The thought of it made her insides feel cold and heavy, as if she had swallowed a rock; but if he was going to be like all the others, then he had it coming.

The Fosters owned a big skiff with an outboard motor which, in the winter, lived in their boathouse. Last fall, when they'd decided to go to Europe instead of coming here to their cottage, they'd told Freddy to use the boat this summer if he wanted to—it would keep the motor tuned and the skiff from drying up as it would do if it was laid up in the boathouse for so long. Having it on this side of the Point had been very convenient for Freddy. He was caretaker, too, of the big cottage out on Whistle

Island. He could walk down the path past Yuba's house to the shore and be off on the island in half an hour, whereas if he used his lobster boat, kept in the harbor, he'd have had to come out around the Point and take three times as long.

Quite often, this summer, he'd taken Caroline and Jakie out to the island with him. He'd had to go every morning when the people were there; sometimes, he'd been too busy to take children. But most days, he'd stop by the house and grin and say, "Did you ask Ma today?" Caroline would grin back and not say yes or no, because in all the times they'd gone with Freddy, they'd never asked Mama. She'd never known they'd gone.

"You stay out of boats while I'm away working," was her word. "I catch you!"

Froggy always brought them back before she got home from work, well in time for Caroline to start supper. Both she and Froggy understood that, about this, the less said the better.

Froggy would scoop up Jakie and away they'd go down the path to the boat, Jakie yelling with joy and hugging Froggy with both arms around the neck. Sometimes they would go fishing, if Froggy didn't have a specially busy day, or they would just go riding around among the islands while he taught Caroline how to run the outboard motor. If they went to Whistle Island, what a day they'd have out there!

The summer cottage was a big one; an old-timer, Froggy said, with shingles so old and mossed up they looked almost like tree bark. It had a big, round turret with a peaked roof and a rooster weather vane riding toward the wind, whichever way the wind was. The rooms in the turret, one on top of the other, were round. From the top room, which Froggy called the "cupolow," you could go out on a little balcony with an iron railing all the way around and see almost all over the world—way out past the other islands to the wide ocean where there wasn't any land at all. One day, the countess pointed out to Caroline that the blue horizon out there wasn't smooth at all, it was hubbly. Since then, whenever Caroline had seen the horizon—and there were lots of places near home where she could—she'd always looked, and it always was. Hubbly.

The summer people who lived in the house were a real count and countess. Their name was Wigheln-Bisschner. Or it had been until the day Jakie had tried to say it and it came out "Wiggling Biscuits." The count and the countess had both laughed. The count said "Wiggling Biscuits" was much prettier and easier to say, so from then on that is what their name would be.

They had both been born in Austria, but they lived now in San Francisco and came to their cottage every summer. They were quite old. The countess was little, not much taller than Caroline, but the count was big and tall with wide shoulders and long hands. They loved children.

"They love you kids," Froggy had said. And then he'd said, sort of under his breath, "It's a damn shame for you and them old folks, too, that they can't take you back to San Francisco with them when they go."

That was the nearest Froggy had ever come to saying anything. And that was all he said. He'd gone right on to tell about the Wiggling Biscuits' one daughter, Lise Wagner, who had married in Europe and then had traveled on her honeymoon all over the world. She'd brought back from Africa as a present to her father three big, awful-looking masks, like Halloween masks only a great deal more dreadful, and the count liked them; but the countess said they were war masks and gave her terrible shivers. So he had hung them, along with some long, shiny black spears that had come with them, on the wall in one of the third-floor rooms, out of sight. One day, when the count had been looking for something for Caroline and Jakie to play with, he had brought the masks downstairs, and after Jakie had got over being scared of them, they all three had had a fine time playing punkin-devil and bogeymen.

Lise Wagner and her husband, Franz, were a couple of old blisters, Froggy said. They'd visited the island summer before last, hadn't liked any part of it, and had said so. They were awful. Summer-resort types. Had to be where there was high society and bright lights and all hell breakin' loose, drinkin'. Bossed him and the cook and maids around till all four of them would've up and left cold, only they liked the old people too much to do that; besides, that Lise and her fat hubby left first. That Lise, she had a big wildcat—an ocelot, she called it—led it around on a leash, scared the cook and the maids and him, too, Froggy, out of their lives. It was an ossle-lot more of a cat than Froggy liked to see around among people. Until one day it got loose and came up to him and he found out all it wanted in the world was to have its head scratched. Name of Walter, Froggy said.

Oh, they'd had picnics on the rocks with lovely things to eat, and the island was lovely to walk around on. The count was so old he was quite lame. He couldn't walk over rough ground very much; so they had had smooth paths made across the island and around shore. On the eastern side was a long sand beach, where you could swim if you didn't mind cold water. At low tide, you could pick mussels and dig clams or hunt for treasures in driftwood piles; or you could walk over to North Meadow where there were deer, and the deer were tame; they would let you come quite close to them. The count had had Froggy put up signs that said WILD GAME AND BIRD SANCTUARY. NO HUNTING.

It was a lovely island, quiet, peaceful, and nice. It seemed to Caroline that nothing, ever, could come at you or hurt you there.

The count was a writer of music. He had music paper, marked in little lines, he was always putting down notes on. He taught even Jakie to play some simple tunes with one hand. He would give him a piece of music paper and say to write notes for a song; then he would play Jakie's squiggles as if they were real notes, and sing words, silly or funny. *"Wunderschön, Jakie!"* he would say. "You will be musician yet."

It was wonderful, Caroline thought, to be with people who really loved you and said so. It would be more wonderful to go with them to San Francisco when they left, to be with them all the time. Once or twice Caroline almost asked, but she never could seem to get up enough courage. And then they had to go away early this year because the count was sick. On the island, he had been quite sick before they went.

He had left ten dollars, five for Caroline and five for Jakie, as a going-away present and had written a little note saying to wait for him, because he'd be back next May, and to buy something nice to remember him by all winter. Freddy brought the money one evening when Mama was home. He had been out on the island all day, closing up the house after the count and countess had gone. Mama said, "Why, wasn't that nice of them, Fred! This'll come in awful handy for winter duds. You children'll have to write them and say thank you." And click! into Mama's pocketbook and that was the last of the ten dollars.

Freddy took Jakie and Caroline to the island with him, once or twice more, while he was closing the house. He had a lot of work to do, putting the heavy shutters on all the ground-floor windows, putting away tools, running the generator that supplied the house with electricity. The count liked to have the heat kept on in the house all winter because of the dampness so near the water. Usually, Freddy had to go over every few weeks and check it. The last day he took Jakie and Caroline, he had a terrible time finding the key to the back door.

"Where on earth?" said Freddy.

Caroline didn't say anything, because she knew where on earth. She had the key. Having it was part of her plan. When Mama went away, out on Whistle Island was where Caroline was going to take Jakie and live in the house without anyone knowing, until the Wiggling Biscuits came back.

On the afternoon of the day Caroline got "lost," she had been carrying out the next-to-last part of her plan, which was to ferry her supplies over to Whistle Island in the Fosters' boat. She had thought of everything as carefully as she could; but there was one thing which surely must be taken care of, and that was to pay Frank Wittlesey for gasoline for the outboard motor. That was the only thing that might leave a trail that could be followed.

A few days before, she'd taken Jakie in his express wagon down to the lobster wharf, where Frank sold gas for outboards, with the oil already put in. She hadn't had the money to pay for it, but she had been sure she could raise it within the next few days. She'd told Frank the gas was for Freddy and to charge it to him. A dollar and sixty cents' worth.

The way she'd been raising money for her plan had been by soliciting—first she'd tried Girl Scout cookies, but she hadn't had any receipt book or anything and some people had acted funny about it. Then one day when she and Jakie had been made to visit Gramma Pollard, she'd found in Gramma's kitchen wastebasket almost a whole book of receipts for the Heart Fund Drive. She and Jakie had traveled all over. She'd had the receipt book and Jakie in his wagon; she was neat and he was cute, and nobody had raised a question. They'd just shelled out a dollar or two. But after school had begun, she hadn't had much time. Junior High, where she had to go this year, was in Bradford, which meant traveling on the school bus and being on hand the minute the bus left. But by skipping lunch, she'd managed to get to a few houses near the school building. She was sure she could raise a dollar and sixty cents; she'd still got three Heart Fund Drive receipts left. But on this day the lady at the door had said, very mean, "Look here, I've heard about you. There isn't any drive for the Heart Fund this time of year. Just whose little girl are you?"

Caroline had got out of there fast. That was finished. She didn't dare try it again, not ever. She absolutely had to have a dollar and sixty cents. Because pretty soon Frank was going to ask Freddy for the money and say who'd charged the gas to him. Freddy would know in a minute she was using the Fosters' boat.

All the way home on the bus, she'd racked her brain. And, finally, she'd come up with the idea of Miss Susie Warren and her flowers. It made a big difference not having Jakie along to help make the good impression; but she could dress up and look nice, that would help. At home, she put on the best clothes she had.

When she had got the money, she had gone up to the lobster wharf along the shore path, where nobody would be at this time in the evening, and had waited behind one of Frank's buildings until she'd seen him leave the office and go down the wharf to the floats. Then she had zipped in, left the money on his desk with a note she'd had ready. "This is for the gas. Thanks. Fred."

She needn't have worried. Frank was just about to take off for Boston with a truckload of lobsters, to be gone three days. He'd come back to the office, had seen the money and the note, and had thought no more about it.

After that, everything had gone exactly as she'd planned. She took a shortcut up through town, a path that went behind the post office and the houses. It was already getting dark. Mama was home, in the kitchen, Caroline saw as she sneaked past the house, and she could hear Jakie bellering. Poor Jakie. He always bellered when he wanted her there and she wasn't.

In the Fosters' house, she changed her good clothes for sneakers and the jeans and heavy sweater she'd hidden away there some days back, knowing she'd need something warmer than school clothes to make this trip in the boat at night. Loading her groceries aboard the skiff took longer than she'd thought it would; she had a lot of stuff, and except for a few packages standing on the front of the shelves, she took all the Fosters' canned goods, too. The motor started on the first pull; she ran it slowly, barely ticking over, until she was well away from the float.

It was full dark by the time she got out to the island, but it wouldn't be for long. Already in the east, the sky was lightening where the moon would be coming up soon. She slid the skiff carefully alongside the landing float and tied it up, bow and stern, as she'd seen Freddy do. Then if you had something to unload, the boat would be steady, not sagging off with the wind or tide.

It was so nice here. Peaceful and still, just a tiny sound of the tide creeping along the shore. There was the house, dark, with the light sky over it, but not spooky or lonesome. Just a place where you'd had a lovely time, always, and would again when the people came back next spring.

She carried her first armload up the slight slope to the back porch, unlocked the door, and went in. It was warm in here as she'd known it would be with the electric power plant running. Now that Freddy had got the shutters on, she and Jakie would be able to turn the lights on at night and nobody could see them. Freddy was the one they'd have to watch out for. He would be coming again, sometime later on, to tow the landing float around to Cat Cove and ground it out so it would be safe for the winter, and he'd have to tend the light plant and do other jobs around. Well, when he came, she and Jakie would just go upstairs and hide in the top round room of the turret, the "cupolow" room. From there, they could see when he left, and Jakie loved the little place with the balcony. They would have to be careful not to leave traces downstairs, where Freddy could see. Of course, he might catch

them; if he did, she'd have to try to make him understand. But think about that when it happened, if it did.

By the time she had all the supplies carried up from the
float and hidden away on the cupboard shelves, with the
people's things in front, the way she'd hidden things at
the Fosters', she was so tired she had to sit down. Just to
rest a minute, she thought, before she started back.

Here in the living room, on the big soft davenport in
front of the fireplace . . . Jakie and I can have fires here,
at night, when no one can see the smoke.

She lay back, feeling very happy. Things had gone well,
and there was one wonderful thing. The big deepfreeze
in the kitchen. She'd peeked into it to see if it was on,
thinking, When Jakie and I run off from Gramma Pollard's, I might be able to steal some meat out of her
freezer and keep it from spoiling, in this one. This one
was certainly on, and it was almost full. Steak and lamb
chops and roasts . . . carrots—ugh, frozen carrots! But all
other kinds of vegetables she and Jakie liked, asparagus
and broccoli and beans. Of course, where the count had
been sick, they'd had to leave early; they hadn't had a
chance to eat the things in the freezer. Probably Freddy
would clean it out, not leave all this stuff in here all
winter. Still, maybe he'd just eat out of it; he didn't have
any freezer at home. If he found it locked, though, he
might think that Marie, the cook, had cleaned it out and
left it locked. He might pull out the plug on it, but after
he left, she could connect it up again. He couldn't get into
it, anyway, if he couldn't find the key. Caroline had locked
it and put the key in her pocket, along with the key to the
back door.

Oh, it was nice here. Nobody to say do this, do that, yell
and carry on. She and Jakie wouldn't be lonesome. They
never were when they were together.

The next thing Caroline knew, she waked up. For a
moment, she lay warm and comfortable, thinking, Where

is this? Then she realized. She jumped up, all standing. How long had she slept? She couldn't tell if it was morning because of the shutters over the windows. She tore to the back door and looked out. It was just beginning to get light. Over the trees in the back of the house, the clouds were pinkish. She could still make it if she hurried as fast as she could.

She ran down to the float, untied the skiff, started the motor. At the Fosters' float, she had to wait for the outboard to cool off. Never, never, never, Freddy'd said, try to put gas into a hot motor. She'd have to top up the tank or he'd miss the gas. While she was waiting, she changed her clothes, rolled the jeans, sweater, and sneakers into a bundle, hid them in a cupboard. When the time came, she'd need them again. Then she went back to the outboard, filled the gas tank, carried the can back into the Fosters' shed. Freddy wouldn't use that one, he had his own.

Then she had second thoughts about the jeans and sweater. They were winter things, and Mama was already going over winter clothes, getting them ready for Gramma Pollard's. She was waiting for word from Henry. No knowing when it might come; any day now, she hoped. So none of the winter clothes, hers or Jakie's, had better turn up missing. Caroline got out the bundle, tucked it under her arm. Then she decided to change to the sneakers. Dew would be heavy along the path and no sense getting her good sandals wet.

She walked home through the woods in the quiet morning, feeling better than she had for a long time. It had been dreadful to see Mama want so badly to go, when she'd not be coming back and they might never see her again. But now that Caroline had things ready to leave when Mama left, now that the plan was worked out all except the last one thing, she felt almost peaceful.

PART THREE

Lewis

IN THE DAYS before he had lost contact with his life, Lewis Wyman had been a sociable man, friendly and interested, a talker who dearly loved to find out, often from the most casual of acquaintances, who they were, what they did, what made them tick. His pleasant manners, his air of really wanting to know (which he did) usually resulted in amiable conversations, even with crusty individuals who might have told another man to mind his own business.

After all, the crusty fellow might think, Here's a decent guy who looks like somebody, treating me as if I were somebody, too, showing he gives a damn, which most people don't bother to do. And he would go his way feeling better, thinking that, after all, he belonged to the human race. He might then drive his car home without handing out to some other motorist a chunk of the ugliness which lived on the top of his mind; he might be decent to his wife this time or just not kick the dog.

Lewis realized on the day he left the hospital how many months it had been since he had taken any interest in the world, in people, even in his own children. In anything outside himself.

Since Lucile's death, he told himself.

He had been in the hospital for eight weeks. A team of

specialists had taken him apart and put him together again, and, he told himself, they had really done a job. He was feeling almost his own man again. He was still shaky, without much endurance, got tired easily, but he was getting over it fast. Much of the spring had come back to his walk. He had lost weight. The fat roll around his middle was gone. He could tie his shoelaces now without grunting and groaning and cussing the soft flab that had been his belly, and the new limberness was wonderful. He had always, before, been slim and leather-tough—a lot tougher than he looked, and, he thought with a wry grin, if he'd been himself that day in Buenos Aires, when he'd slapped Charley Anderson's shill, it could very well have busted the guy's jaw.

Well, that was over and done with. So forget it. There'd be other jobs.

He went first to see his former employers. He hoped they might take into consideration the facts of his illness as the hospital doctors had explained them to him—that the terrible emotional jolt of Lucile's death had caused mental and physical collapse, of which his sudden excessive drinking had been a symptom, not the disease itself.

"So far as alcohol's concerned, you'd better make up your mind you're done with it," one specialist had told him. "Tests show you've developed an allergy. That liver condition could come back, and we might not be able to pull you through again. So watch it."

The owners listened, but they made it plain that this was the last time they wanted to see him. They also handed him Charley Anderson's report, which Lewis didn't bother to read. He picked up his suitcases at the company offices and left.

Nobody said he was blacklisted, but word had certainly got around. Anywhere else he tried, the brush-off was quick and conclusive. Wilmington was out; so was Philadelphia. A New York firm, with which he'd had a fine record some years back, acknowledged his letter and that was all.

He'd have to go elsewhere, but where was elsewhere? San Francisco? Bundle the kids into the car and strike out for greener fields? Who was to say the fields were greener? He'd have to show his credentials, and the first thing they'd do would be to pick up the phone.

In the meantime, his savings were being whittled down at a rate that frightened him. He'd got the money from the sale of the house and a small amount of insurance. His hospital bills had taken a whopping bite. Specialists he'd never seen or heard of had taken a crack at him while he'd been unconscious or out of his head. He couldn't kick about that—he felt better now than he had in months.

Lewis was good at his job. He knew it. His feeling about this was not vanity, but simple acceptance of the fact. It would be, he was sure, only a question of time before he found something. He could always sell his car in a pinch; at present he needed it for job hunting. He had even written to the shipping company in Halifax, Canada, which had started him out as a young man. They'd hated to lose him, way back when. Maybe they'd still remember him.

Today, driving back from Wilmington, Lewis felt discouraged and tired out. The job he'd heard about hadn't been much more than a rumor and had turned out to be exactly that. He'd counted on it more than had been justified because it had been about the last possibility on his list. Ordinarily, feeling like this, he would have stopped at the nearest bar and taken the edge off the gloom with a few slugs. He almost had.

At the first bar, he pulled up at the curb and stopped. The most natural thing in the world—get out, slam the car door, walk in . . . He sat there for a full ten minutes, sweating.

The kids and Jilson were down at Point Milton, on the bay. This was Adam's big day, the day of a sail on the *Lizzie Macomber*. Jilson had fixed it up with the vessel's skipper and had gone along though he was busy job hunting himself. They had gone down to Point Milton by bus and would be back in the late afternoon.

What if I go in here, get started, and can't stop? Lewis thought, gritting his teeth.

In the hospital, he'd laughed dutifully at the story of Jilly's cherry bombs because the kids seemed to think it was funny. At the same time, he'd felt as if his blood were slowly curdling. What if Jilly hadn't been on hand? God, Adam *must* have known the house was sold. But Lewis couldn't remember telling him.

He couldn't help knowing that it was going to take time to get back topsides with Adam. The boy was unusually quiet now, not exactly standoffish, but certainly not outgoing. He seemed to want to be with Jilson all the time. On days when Jilly went job hunting, Lewis sensed Adam's restlessness. Where was Jilly? Why was he gone so long? And when Jilly finally came back, he would be met at the door with Ad's feverish question, "Did you find something, Jilly?" And there'd be no mistaking the look of pure relief and joy that passed between him and Amanda when Jilly said, "No."

Lewis suspected Jilly wasn't hunting very hard. He'd spent a lot of his time with the kids, taking them places, going with them to movies, thinking up entertainment. They hadn't gone back to school and Lewis hadn't insisted on that, knowing that he'd probably be moving on to another city as soon as he got well. It had been a long haul for Jilly; Lewis didn't know how he was ever going to pay him back.

Except with a job with me when I get a ship, Lewis told himself. I had better be there when they get home. And be there sober.

Doggedly, he weaseled the car back into traffic and drove on.

At Mrs. McKlosky's boardinghouse, he stopped and parked the car. A shower would help get rid of the sweat, and an afternoon's rest would get rid of the shakes. As he went through the hall, Mrs. McKlosky called to him.

"Letter for you, Captain Wyman. On the table, there."

Lewis glanced at the postmark. Canadian stamp. Halifax.

"Lew, old onion," the letter began.

There was only one man living who'd ever called him "old onion"—Rhody MacAllister, who had started out with him at the Halifax shipping company and who had stuck with the firm. The letter offered a job. Skipper of the new cargo ship, the *Mary MacAllister,* just off the ways and waiting for him. And where had he been all of Rhody's life, and what had kept him away so long?

In the late afternoon, Adam came crashing against the door to Lewis' room in such a hurry that he had forgotten to turn the doorknob. When he did turn it, his first stride caught the door and sent it back against the wall with a thunderous slam.

Lewis, half-asleep, leaped in the bed. "For the love of God, take it easy!" he bawled, blinking. "What the—oh, it's you, Ad." He hadn't been able to keep the irritation out of his voice, but Adam was full again of his first love and noticed nothing.

"Gee, Dad, she *is!* She's Neddie Macomber's old *Lizzie,* rebuilt. Some nut changed the design, that's why I didn't know her that day in the bub-bay. Captain Brown was darned sore about it. He was telling me while I was steering. He luh-let me steer."

"Good," Lewis said. "Bet you could do it better than he can."

"Oh, wow, no! He knows everything about sailing. He can—"

"The turnip farmer?" Lewis asked, managing a grin.

"Aw, he wasn't even aboard the *Macomber* that day she passed us in the channel. That was his nephew Harold, he couldn't sail a rubber duck in a tub. Captain Brown was sick then, he was in the hospital."

"Fine. You had a good time," Lewis said. "Well, you know, so have I, today. Wait till you hear—" He had been about to hand over Rhody's letter but stopped, wondering whether Adam had even heard him.

"Dad? He even told me how she got here—"

"How who got here?"

"Oh, the *Lizzie Macomber,* you don't listen. Roy Macomber, old Neddie's son, brought her. Golly, she wasn't lost at sea at all, the way the Lunenberg records say. Captain Brown told me. He *knew* Roy Macomber. He's got a tape recording of Roy Macomber's voice, telling how he brought the *Lizzie* here."

"Oh, hey, come on!" Lewis said. "Brown's pulling your leg. Roy Macomber, if he was Neddie's son, was your great-great grandfather. He was drowned, years ago. Nobody could possibly have taped him."

"I could have myself if I'd got here three years ago," Adam said. His eyes had lit up like lamps; he was fairly dancing up and down. "Roy Macomber lived to be a hundred and two years old. He died three years ago, down at Point Milton where he lived and where the *Macomber* hails from now. Before he died, a newspaper reporter interviewed him and took the interview on tape. Captain Brown bought the tape from the newspaper. He let me retape it on my cassette. I've got it right here. Dad? You've got to listen to it, okay?"

"Okay," Lewis said. Resigned, he spread his unfolded letter on his chest and clasped his hands over it. For later, he thought. When Adam can take it in.

Adam fished his cassette recorder out of his jacket pocket. "She's all set up, ready to roll," he said. "You've got to have the beginning that's in the newspaper clipping. When this starts, listen for a glug-glug sound. That's the old boy drinking his rum. He got away with a whole pint before he quit talking."

The glug-glug was unmistakable. It went on for a while. Then Roy Macomber uttered a prolonged "Ah-hhh!" A voice unbelievably old and shaky, but with considerable resonance, said, "It was one helmonious old nor'west blow," and was silent.

A different voice, the newspaper reporter's probably, said, "What was, Cap'n Macomber?"

"The one that sunk them two pizen-meated bastuds. Them ones I have just drunk to the codfish that et 'em and prayed that he warn't too sick a fish when he gut through."

The reporter said, "What about you stealing the vessel?"

"Steal her, hell! She b'longed to me. I earnt her, fair and squar'. Sailed her for that old skunk for years, no more wages than the slops he'd feed a pig. If he ever fed the pig, that is."

"Who was that, now?"

"Pa, who'd you think, the two-heeled old devil. He never knowed she was stole. We was all lost at sea. Long and LaChance was, I know for a fact, and me and the vessel—well, hell's fire, you c'n git lost without being sunk, or you c'n git plain lost. They was a cook once, aboard a mack'rel schooner, says to the skipper, 'Is anything lost if you know where 'tis?' and the skipper says, 'No, you damn fool,' and the cook says, 'Well, I jest dropped your silver teapot overboard.' "

Roy Macomber paused. "I don't b'lieve that old mack'rel scratcher ever had a silver teapot, d'you?"

Silence was punctuated by a glug sound. The reporter nudged it a little. "How about you running the vessel aground, sir?"

"Me? I never run aground in my life. You say that again, I'll bust this rum bottle over your head. LaChance, he done it. Foggy morning, real thick, not much wind. It was his trick at the wheel, and God only knows how, but he plunked her on Anderson's Ledge, off of Star Island. I was b'low, sleeping. I heard her come onto it with a kind of a grind and I come on deck a-roaring. There was him and Long, the' was just the three of us aboard, starting to make off with the yawl boat.

"I says, 'Jeezus Henry George Almighty, what'd you two jassacks think you're doing? This ledge uncovers at half tide. We never went on hard and the tide's coming.'

Sun was kind of breaking through the fog, wind looked to be coming off nor'west, and with lumber, we'd float off. B'god, they never either of'm turned a head my way. So I tackled'm.

"We fit round the deck, I d'no how long, maybe a hour. I'd lay out first one, then t'other. Trouble was, they was both tough devils, kep' coming. But one time I never ducked fast enough, and LaChance laid me out with a belaying pin. When I come to, they was gone, yawl boat and all. Vessel was beginning to bump on the ledge, wind nor'west, sure 'nough, good brisk breeze. I put her aback and off she come.

"Then, that done, I took a look off west'ard, and I see the yawl boat making in for Portsmouth fast as she could hum, and I gut good and mad for the first time. Thinks I, I ain't going to set here dumbfoundered and see them two skedaddlers swipe that yawl boat. So I beat to the nor'ard some, and then I come about and busted 'er wide open. Warn't my fault the wind come on to blow quick, at the wrong time. The old *Lizzie* went over that yawl boat ker-whango! And now, thinks I, I've done it. I looked back and I see the yawl boat ain't ever going t'be the same agin, so I put 'er outa the middle of them shoals before it come on to blow any harder . . . . You le'me alone, mister. Take away your hand or I'll bust it off!"

"Sorry, Cap'n. I thought you'd slipped forward a little."

"I ain't. So I gut to thinking how I'd explain to Pa that I'd lost the yawl boat. And, says I to myself, that ain't possible. So I wung-out and sailed the whole gale down to Virginia. Sold the lumber, made a good thing out of it."

"Sailed her single-handed? Brother!" the reporter said.

"Has been done, many's the time. Man I knew, he sailed hand-pullers single-handed. The *Lizzie* warn't no trouble, she was a wench-hister. I settled down here, done real well with her for a long time. Always done better when the' was a war. They was crazy wild for bottoms during a war, and the *Lizzie* had one, even if it didn't keep out the seawater. German shub-submarine done her in fin'ly. Riz up off the capes one morning, first shell stove a hole in her you coulda run through with an ox. Second one kilt the mate. Blowed him into sixteen pieces. I counted, when I picked him up. Kind of a shock to a man. So I sailed the old girl up Berman's backwater, fur's she'd go, dismantled her and said good-bye. Jasper Brown, the cussed fool's bought the hulk. What's he want the *Lizzie* for? She wouldn't float in a puddle of molasses."

The cartridge finished and Adam slipped it out of the machine. He glanced sideways at his father and was delighted. Lewis was roaring laughing, mopping his eyes with his handkerchief. "Why, the bloody-minded old pirate!" he gasped. "What a yarn! That's great, Ad!"

"I didn't know . . . I seem to be always bending your ear with this kind of stuff. I know you aren't very interested in it."

"A yarn like that I am. Well, that's your big news. How's about if you hear mine now?" He handed over his letter.

Adam read, slowly at first, as if he were having difficulty putting his mind on the news. Halfway through, his gaze suddenly jumped back to the letter's heading. He said, "Canada! Oh, wow, Dad!" He tore out of the room yelling. "Amanda! Jilly! Dad's got his job and it's in *Ca-Canada!*" His voice came out in a croaking roar which ended in a squeak, the way it sometimes still did in moments of stress.

Late that night, Lewis was awakened by a series of thumps and bangs from Jilson's room, which adjoined his. Jilly was, evidently, packing. Suitcases were being snapped shut and set down with loud scrapes and noises in the hall. Irritated, Lewis pounded on the partition.

"Was you knocking at me?" Jilson said, poking his head around the door.

"You know I was. What the hell, this time of night?"

Jilson came in. "I run of an idea you might be awake," he said.

"And I run of an idea you knew I would be, along with everybody else in the house. What's your rush, we can't leave for a day or so, till I get things squared around here."

"I ain't going with you," Jilson said.

"Oh, dammit, Jilly! Why take off now? You know you can have a job with me on my new ship. A good one, too."

"Well, now, Cap'n. I got a good job. Going to be kind of a vacation for me. Cook on the *Lizzie Macomber*."

"Oh, my God!" Lewis reached over, snapped on his bedside lamp, and stared at Jilly. "Have you gone crazy? You, cooking for a bunch of dudes?"

"I ain't saying it'll be a bed of roses, unless I can talk old Brown out of using his great-grandmother's cast-iron scouse pots," Jilson said. "But likely I can do that. Now, Cap'n, you listen to me, I ain't going to mince nothing. You're going to drive you and them two kids and all your stuff to Halifax in that automobile, and with them turn-pikes the way they are and you in the shape you're in, I wouldn't be caught dead. That's one thing. Number two, we won't be sailing dudes here no longer. We're going out into deep water."

"Well, I hope you know what you're getting into."

"We won't be out there long. We're taking the vessel to St. Andrews, New Brunswick, is all."

"And sail dudes out of there? They better take the is-lands out of the St. Croix River, the way he handles her. Jumping Jesus, Jilly!"

"You're worse'n Adam, you don't listen to nothing you don't want to hear. That old man's the best sailing master I ever saw. He was took sick last spring, laid in the hos-pital nigh three months. Whilst he was there, he fell in love with his nurse, sounds like a nice woman, too. She lives in St. Andrews now, and he wants to go up there to git married. Also, whilst he was sick, his nephew Harold took over the cruises. He raised such hell with the vessel, had her aground three times, scairt so many panties off the dudes that it's hard to find anyone to go out now. So Brown's closing up here, going north. Thing is, he ain't a deep-water man, he's leery of it. He needs a pilot. I been talking to him about you."

Lewis glared at him, and for a moment his voice stuck in his throat.

"Talk away," he said at last. "Somewhere else, and for godsake let me sleep."

At the door, Jilson said, "I d'no when I'll see ya again, Cap'n," and closed it quietly behind him.

At three o'clock, Lewis was waked up again. It took him a moment to realize that someone was lying on the bed beside him, pressed against his back. Whoever it was was crying dismally and apparently had been for some time because the damp spot had soaked through the back of Lewis' pajamas.

"Adam?" Lewis said. He turned over quickly and touched the boy's tear-clobbered face. "Adam. What is it, son?"

"Dad? You could pilot a sailing v-vessel to St. Andrews with one hand, couldn't you? J-Jilly would stay with us if you—"

Why, that finagling old devil! Lewis thought.

He put an arm around Adam's shaking shoulders. "Yes," he said. "I expect I could."

"All you'd have to do is s-set courses and stuff. Most of the time you could rest. A nun-nice, kuh-quiet sea voyage, you'd feel better when you got there."

And I know where you got that argument, too, Lewis thought. He said, "Ad, I can't promise tonight. I'll have to look the vessel over, make sure she's fit for deep water. You go back to bed and go to sleep, and I'll drive down first thing in the morning."

I, he told himself, staring into the darkness, have had

that dilapidated old laundry tub shoved down my throat till I could puke up her anchor.

Brown's wharf was deserted when Lewis arrived there early the next morning. Unable to sleep, he had sneaked away from the boardinghouse at daylight. Adam, exhausted, was sleeping dead to the world, and, as Lewis passed Jilson's door, he saw, with grim amusement, that the packed suitcases were still sitting in the hall.

Good, he thought. I'll be damned if I'll stand one ounce of pressure while I look that old hulk over, and there'll be no restful sea voyage for any of us if I find one thing out of line.

There she was, in all her nineteenth-century obsolescence. Stubby masts, but new. Tumble home bulgy as a fat lady's can. Hogged. She'd have trouble beating against the wind; in an offshore sea of any kind, she'd spank the water out of the ocean.

Her bow lay close to the wharf. He stepped aboard, walked the length of the scrubbed and spotless deck, from the bowsprit with its sparkling gold-leaf scroll, to the dark varnished door of the after cabin. The wheel, polished until its mahogany surface sent back glints to the sun, was secured with a becket of immaculate white nylon. Everything shipshape, in order, put in place by a seaman who knew his business. Halyards coiled flat in concentric circles. Hoisting-engine housing dark-varnished to match the after-cabin door. The *Macomber* wasn't a "hand-puller," obviously; she was still a "wench-hister." Lewis grinned to himself, thinking of old Roy, who in his time had been a sailor—who had brought this contraption down the coast from a near-wreck off the Isles of Shoals to Virginia. A man, alone, single-handed, roaring along before "one helmonious old nor'west blow." To his astonishment, Lewis felt the back of his neck crinkle with excitement. The old *Lizzie* was putting out blandishments, some kind of witchery of her own.

[*92*]

"Lady," he said aloud to her, "I can't figure out whether you're a doll or an old whore dressed up for a party."

An indignant voice nearby answered him. "Well! That's an extremely insulting thing to say!"

Aghast, Lewis stared around. He had been at the moment passing the narrow windows on the port side of the after cabin. He now noticed that one of them was half-open. Behind it, glaring at him out of wrathful, cornflower-blue eyes, was a lady with an extraordinary head of yellow hair. She might have been thirty-five, and she was pretty in a ripe and plenteous way.

"I have heard enough fresh talk from one of the officers of this ship," she went on, "and if you're another one, I'm going to cancel the whole clambake. I'm perfectly respectable and a mother!"

Lewis yanked off his cap. "Good Lord!" he said. "I didn't see you and I wasn't talking to you, but I'm sorry and I apologize."

She put her head out the window and stared up and down the deck. "Who else is here?" she said skeptically.

Lewis grinned. "The *Lizzie Macomber*," he said. "She's putting out seductions to make me take her pilot's job, and I was about to tell her I haven't made up my mind yet."

"Oh, thank heaven! If you're the pilot, please forget my bad manners. Actually, I've heard much worse from the boys at rehearsals. The fact is, I've waited around so long for this show to get on the road that I'm mean-tempered as an old hen turkey. Also, I've had to take considerable chat from— Who *is* that young lout who comes around every hour saying he's the skipper and that I've got his stateroom? I arranged my trip with Captain Brown, who says *he* is."

"I'm not sure," Lewis said. "But I think you may have run foul of the Captain's nephew Harold."

"Whoever he is, somebody ought to teach him his manners. Are you really going to take the pilot's job? Please,

please do, so we can get going. I've got engagements all over the provinces next month, and I've got to be in Halifax by the first. I'm Belle Bronson, of the Halifax Folk Singers Band, incidentally."

"Lewis Wyman," Lewis said. "How did you happen to join up with this—uh, clambake?"

"I was broke," she said simply. "We were on a concert tour of the eastern states and a drunk fellow crashed into our van, head-on collision. One of our boys was killed, and it took just about all we had to send his—to send him home. We'll get insurance on the van and the smashed instruments sometime, but it hasn't come through yet. The boys took off hitchhiking—they'll collect the insurance and meet Andy and me—Andy, that's my son, he's ten—in St. Andrews with the new van. But of course they couldn't hitchhike carrying instruments—we salvaged quite a few out of the wreck, among them two bass fiddles. Imagine, hitchhiking with two bass fiddles! So I heard about Captain Brown and his vessel, and I found that he'd take me and Andy and the instruments for just about what we had left, a little under. He's a very nice man, Captain Brown. He lets us eat and sleep aboard, otherwise I guess there'd be some truth in the title you bestowed on me."

She flushed a little and burst out laughing. "I'm outspoken," she said. "And I always talk too much, but it's such a relief! All I've talked to for a week, outside of that unpleasant contraption, Harold, is the ship's cook, Mr. Jilson. I taught him how to make lasagna. He's an awfully good cook, though."

Brother! Lewis thought. He chuckled to himself and looked at her with new respect. Jilly, a lifelong scorner of women's cooking, had not only let one into his cook room, he'd let her teach him something. Also, the lying old scalawag had had this job for a week or longer, all the time letting on he was job hunting.

"There's the Captain coming now," she said. "Do go

and nail down the pilot's job. If you take it, wave to me, I'll be watching. If you don't, just slink away."

"I'll certainly think hard about it," Lewis said.

She had a fine, rich contralto voice—a singer's voice, Lewis thought, and she was very pleasant to look at. Something about her—her yellow hair, perhaps—reminded him of a squash blossom, which, in spite of comedy connotations, had always seemed to him an honest and forthright flower. As she turned away, he saw with interested delight that painted in realistic color on the back of her white jacket, was a landscape—farmhouse and red barn, two cows and a batch of hens, green trees, a lake, and mountain background against a blue sky.

The big man behind the desk in Brown's office looked sick; or if not sick, tired to death. His face was bleached-out tan, accentuated by heavy dark circles under his eyes. The impression of bigness he gave at first was partly because of his suit, made of a thick, woolly material cut for a stouter, huskier frame. He might have filled it out once; now the cloth drooped on him. His voice, however, was brisk, a comfortable baritone boom.

"Cap'n Wyman, glad to see you! Jilson's told me about you, and if you'll pilot me to St. Andrews, I'll—" His voice died away. He stared at Lewis, his eyes bulging a little with astonishment. "I'll be double goddarned!" He reached a long arm behind him and came up with a flat, rectangular object which had been standing against the wall behind his desk. "I brought this down to show to your boy," he went on, and held the thing up into the light for Lewis to see.

It was a battered, faded portrait of a man of forty in a black coat and a white stock, painted in the stiff, wooden style of some itinerant artist of, possibly, the 1880's. Over it, for some reason, had been stretched a protective screen of hardware cloth, which made details a little difficult to see; but Lewis made out a hawk-nosed, lean face, clean-shaven and square-chinned, with something almost electric about it, as if the man, whoever he was, had carried a continual charge of energy, turned on and ready for use.

"Don't know him, eh?" Brown said. "Old Roy Macomber gave him to me. Came out of the forecastle of the *Lizzie Macomber.* That's Neddie Macomber himself, and when you walked in here, I thought I was seeing a ghost."

Staring, still a little bewildered, Lewis at last made out what the old man was talking about. The face of the portrait, with a few variations, was identical with the one that he saw every morning in his own shaving mirror. "I'll be damned!" he said. "Didn't realize."

"That screening bothers," Brown said. "Roy salvaged that picture when he dismantled the vessel. He told me that Neddie hung it aboard her to keep an eye on him and the crew. Said the sight of it gave him the crawling creeps. Used to come in here and chat with me and drink rum, and every time he finished up a bottle, he'd heave it at Neddie's picture. I had to hang it up high with a screen over it, but he said hell, he could spit that high, and"— Brown chuckled—"sometimes he could. So after a while, I took it home, to my house. Your boy's going to be pretty tickled when he sees that."

"Yes," Lewis said feebly. "He will be."

"That's a smart youngster," Brown said. "He's going to make a first-rate hand aboard the *Macomber,* if you and I can get together on the pilot's job. How about it?"

"I'm thinking about it."

"Jilson says you know I've been sick. If I wasn't still a little shaky, I'd take on deep water and think nothing of it. I've got new charts, instruments, whatever you'd need, and the old vessel's fixed up comfortable. For crew, we've got two husky young chaps who know the ropes. Coon— that's my adopted boy, my wife and I got him from a Polish refugee place when he was a shaver—him, I trained myself and he's a crackerjack aboard any craft. Fairleigh's a local fellow, used to sailing skipjacks. And my nephew Harold'll be along."

"Your nephew won't be part of the crew?" Lewis asked. He was beginning to get quite interested in Harold.

"Well, now." Brown hesitated, fumbled with his fingers at a pen on his desk. "Harold's put out, just now, sulky about me getting married again. Says what would a pretty woman want with a sick old man except his money. Harold's a little outspoken when he's sore. Don't mean half of what he says. . . . That sounds like my furniture from the house coming down."

From the street end of the wharf, heavy gears started to grind and Brown jumped up. "Thank God, there it is at last!" He went to the window, peered out, and came back grinning. He had moved with certainty on his feet, his muscles limber and showing a strength not evident when he had been sitting down. Lewis was relieved to see this; he had been wondering just how sick Brown had been.

"That's the one thing outside of the pilot that's been holding us up," Brown said, sitting down again. "My household goods are decrepit, belonged to my grandmother, all old-fashioned stuff I'm sentimental about. Hardly encouraging, though, for a bride starting out. So I made her pick out a living-room set, two chairs and a divan. A 'bride's present,' you might say. I've got a fur piece, too, she'll like, and a case of fancy canned goods, like ham and cookies."

He suddenly brought his fist down on the desk with a bang that made Lewis jump. "Christ!" he said. "I don't feel so goddamned old. Sick, yes, I was. But sickness isn't like old age, something you can't get over." He turned his fist, stared ruefully at the side of his hand. "Now, what'd I do that for? That's going to give me trouble. A bad bruise, darn it. Well, Cap'n? Made up your mind?"

Harold, Lewis thought. What kind of a selfish knothead is he? No one could help liking Jasper Brown, a decent, well-intentioned man, good-natured and humorous, whose marriage intentions were, or should be, his own business.

I've got Jilson's word that he knows how to sail his vessel, and there's Adam, who'll be heartbroken if I back out now.

He grinned and held out his hand. "Okay," he said. "When do we sail?"

Outside, Lewis walked along the wharf, wondering what Brown's illness could have been. Some nervous disorder, perhaps, or a fever that might leave a man's nerves raw? Lewis could well remember his own bout of typhus, years ago, picked up in Hong Kong, when for weeks afterward he'd been on the ragged edge, ready for no reason to climb walls. He'd better get on back and relieve Adam's mind; also, he'd have to make arrangements today to sell his car. He glanced along the vessel's deck and was disappointed to see that Mrs. Bronson was nowhere in sight. She was quite a gal. He'd certainly like to see that landscape on her jacket in full sunlight.

"But there *you* are, you old witch," he told the *Macomber*. "You got your own way with me, didn't you? Took me for my great-grandfather, did you? Or for that crashing old scoundrel, Roy? Brother! That was sure a gene of noble proportions!"

Well, there she was. She was loading, and suddenly Lewis was fascinated. Coal and iron ore he had transported across the seaways of the world, shipments of hides and fruit and tinned meats—never a cargo like this one.

This was the furnishings of an old-fashioned house, a nineteenth-century mansion. There were high bureaus and low commodes—one, at least, complete with chamber pot which fell out of it and was replaced with a shattering crash by the strapping young fellow who was bossing the job. Lewis saw with delight white-painted bedsteads with brass knobs, a whatnot, a varnished oak sideboard, carried from the van, manhandled aboard the vessel, and lowered down a hatch—all kissing cousins to pieces inherited by his mother from his grandmother's house in Lunenberg. The sideboard was a boxlike affair, two bottom cupboard doors decorated with bulgy, glued-on curlicues, tall shelf over a mirror, little shelves on the sides, the whole structure braced by double-curved supports ending in knobby lion feet. After these, came two tremendous chairs and a divan, all modern, upholstered in a purplish fuzzy stuff, related to plush.

The "bride's present," Lewis thought. Wow! She likes color.

Two husky youngsters were loading the furniture on the vessel. Brown's adopted son, Coon, was there—it was easy to tell which one he was. There was the sharp-chinned, upside-down-triangle face, with a merry and innocent eye which managed at the same time to look wise and knowing. A raccoon encountered in the woods might glance around in just that way before it ambled off, minding its own business. Coon was tall and slim; he moved with a casual limberness which Lewis admired, and he wasn't taking any of the hectoring which the strapping fellow was handing out.

"Oh, shove it, Cap'n Bligh," he said in a bored voice. "You want this loaded faster, come and lend a hand yourself."

"You want your nose rubbed in the fresh and lovely?" the big fellow said.

"Appreciate it if you'd try." Coon gathered up a couple of chairs and loped up the gangway.

The van, empty, pulled out. Its place was taken by a taxicab packed with cased musical instruments—bass fiddles, violins, saxes, clarinets, guitars, and mandolins, judging by the sizes and shapes of the cases. Several showed the effects of Mrs. Bronson's van wreck. A yellow-haired small boy darted out from behind the cab, carrying a guitar case. "Harold! Where'll I put this stuff for now?"

There was no mistaking whose youngster he was. The mop of curly yellow hair was unmistakable.

"Throw it." The big fellow held out his hands.

"Come on, Harold. I can't keep the cabdriver forever. Where'll all these cases be out of your way?"

"Throw 'em down. I'll play catch," Harold said.

"These instruments aren't old tin git-boxes like yours," Andy Bronson said pleasantly. He turned to the cabdriver. "We'll stack the stuff here on the wharf. I can carry it down later."

Harold, Lewis thought. The turnip farmer. He stood watching with interest.

Harold was wide across the shoulders but stoutish before and behind, so that his skintight jeans bulged in awkward places. He had on a white-topped officer's cap of the type bought at Naval stores, so new that its gilt trim shot glints to the sun. His T-shirt was pink. His boots were high-heeled, mahogany-red, embossed. Something seemed to be troubling him about one boot; he lifted it to his knee, regarded a darkish blob on its sole. From his concerned look, it appeared that the matter was serious.

From behind Lewis, young Andy said, "Tar or chewing gum stepped in? Tch, oh, my!" He shot past Harold, landed light as a mosquito on the vessel's deck, and vanished into the after cabin.

Harold paid no attention. He pulled out a jackknife, scraped carefully, scuffed his boot on the planking, teetered up and down to test stickiness. That taken care of, he hitched at his belt and let go a blast at the two loaders, who were having trouble getting the overstuffed divan down the *Macomber*'s hatch.

"Well, help us out, numb nuts," Coon said. "It's too heavy for two of us to handle."

Harold let out a bawl. "Hey! You! Old Greasy Spoon, there! Get on out here! On deck!"

A head appeared above the edge of the forward hatch. It remained motionless, as if someone had cut it off and left it there.

Seeing it, Lewis grinned and lifted a hand. His greeting was not acknowledged.

The head reared slightly higher, showing that its owner had come up a rung on a ladder. "Was you hollering at me?" Jilson said.

"Damn right I was. Get over there and help the boys horse that whorehouse settee down the hatch."

Jilson's skinny arms and shoulders, his elongated midriff and thin shanks rose out of the hatch. He stepped over the vessel's rail and strolled along the wharf. Stopping, he let go a fat squirt of tobacco juice, which landed alongside the fancy boots and splattered.

"What the hell!" Harold stared. He couldn't believe it. He took a step forward. 'Look here, you—" His shoulders almost hid Jilson from sight, and Lewis had to lean sideways so that he could see.

"Well, well! See what we got!" Harold said, drawing it out. "Old Greasepot's turned out a ripsnorter, whaddya know!" He doubled a fist. "You want this in the guts or on the beezer? Or will ya crawl down and lap them spots off my boots with your tongue?"

Oh, Lord, he'll massacre poor old Jilson, Lewis thought. I'll have to stop this somehow. He opened his mouth to yell as Jilson spoke.

"Look, you goddam nuisance-puke. You broke the old man's pisspot. Warn't no need of it. You called a nice thing a name that was rotten and also ain't so. You been frigging around me like a fly over a cow-flap for a week. Now, you haul in your horns or we'll settle it."

He had started a kind of double shuffle, a slow, weaving dance, growing faster and faster, until the pat of his feet on the wharf planking sounded like rain.

Lewis realized that he had seen something like this before. In Jamaica, knife fights could start this way; in Hong Kong, he had seen two Malay seamen do almost the same thing. The action moved fast; already Jilson's flying feet had carried him in a half circle, so that Harold, turning, his fists still double, had to face the sun. The knife, flicked out from some hidden pocket, was a seven-inch blade that flashed bright in Jilson's hand.

Harold turned white. He stopped and backed up. "You've pulled a knife on me," he said, dumbfounded.

"I have, sonny," Jilson said. He leaped into the air,

cracked his heels together, and landed close enough so that the point of the knife lightly scratched Harold's chin.

Harold touched his chin and saw blood. He backed away fast and let out a scream. "Uncle Jasper! Uncle Jasper! Help! He's going to kill me!"

Not noticing where he was getting to, he backed off over the edge of the wharf and landed down below with a scattering splash and a sucking sound of invaded mud.

"Mercy," Jilson said. He turned and came over to Lewis. The knife had vanished, Lewis didn't see where.

"You want your lunch, Cap'n?" Jilson asked. "I been buying for the trip, and I got a trade in a big Danish ham. Wouldn't take a minute to scramble up some eggs."

"I could eat," Lewis said. "Is he all right?"

"He ain't if he can't swim." Jilson peered over the edge of the wharf. "He kin," he said.

PART FOUR

Caroline

LYDIA POLLARD was astonished. She had gone over Yuba Fling's house from cellar to attic, and she couldn't find one single piece of the children's clothes. Yuba'd said she'd leave them packed in suitcases marked *Winter* and *Summer,* but Lydia finally had to admit it, there wasn't a suitcase left in the house.

Caroline wasn't any help; she just said, with that blank-eyed, idiot look of hers, that Mama must've made a mistake and taken them with her.

Yuba had got word from Henry Fling at last and had gone in a great hurry and flurry, stricken at leaving the children and scared out of her life for fear she would have the new baby before she could get to Henry. So far, no one had heard whether she had or not. In Lydia's opinion, it would serve her right if she had.

"Don't gi'me that!" she said now to Caroline. "You've done something with them clothes. What you're after, Miss Cad, is for me to stump up all new things for you and that baby. Well, I may have money, but I'm not made of it."

That, however, was exactly what she meant to do. She planned to bundle up every stitch of those shabby, worn-out garments and either burn them or send the lot to the Salvation Army. And do it right in front of those two children, with the new clothes for them laid out on the bed, so they could see how much better off they were with her than they'd been with their mother. The new clothes she'd chosen, all except winter underwear, were at home in Bradford, right now. Lydia had had a pleasant time shopping for them. She'd really let herself go, bought plain things, but substantial. She certainly wasn't going in for the fluff and foolishness the children she saw on the streets were wearing—girls and boys in skintight pants, and all with long hair so you couldn't tell one from the other; or if the girls wore skirts at all, they were stark naked up to their bottoms.

No, sir! Her two children were going to have decent, long-handled woolen underwear for winter and clothes and long stockings to cover. She hadn't found a place where she could buy any, but she had in mind where she could have some made. She'd told Caroline so.

She left the kids in Yuba's house to wait and drove straight down to see Susie Warren.

"Long johns for kids, nowadays?" Susie said. "Where on earth would you get the material?"

"You don't need to bother your head about that," Lydia said. "If I bring the cloth, you certainly could make the garments."

Susie Warren might have inherited money, but to Lydia she was still the town dressmaker. Come up in the world but still no silk purse.

"You know, Lydia," Susie said pleasantly, "if I had all the material in the world, I still wouldn't do it."

"You *wouldn't?*" Refusing an honest job of work and calling first names now, was she?

"No, I'm sorry. I wouldn't. You must know that kids in school would make those Fling children's lives miserable."

"It's certainly none of your business," Lydia said.

"It is, too." Susie was outraged at the idea, and she had held back as long as she could. "It's anybody's business. It's Yuba's business of all, and if I'd known what she was going to do, I'd have offered her the money to take those poor mites with her. Long johns, for heaven's sake! You'd be a laughingstock all over town."

"Well!" Lydia rose to her feet. The cherries on her hat trembled as she made for the door. "You have got the Lord Almighty's gall to call *me* a laughingstock after all the talk that's going round about you. State cops coming down here the night Cad was lost and what they found here!"

Susie burst out laughing. "Oh, come!" she said. "I killed my cat and fed him his liver and he ate it."

"Crazy's a loon, that's what they say," Lydia said. "Headed the same way Miranda Cooley went. Them things run in a family, and don't you forget it!" She slammed the door hard and strode up the walk to her car. I guess I got her told, she thought.

It wasn't so that people were saying Susie Warren was crazy; only with what Pomroy Fifield spread around, certain ones had had it over and wondered what if. Telling her off had been a satisfaction, but it would've been much better if only Lydia could've believed the story was so. She felt mortally offended, all the same.

She drove back to Yuba's house and honked the horn for the kids to come out. She was not going in there and hoist her aching feet up and down and through the lady's chamber, trying to find those suitcases. If Cad had hidden them, Lydia would have it out of her, don't worry.

Nobody seemed to be in any hurry to come. She honked again, this time a long, irritated blast. Still, nobody came. Lydia got out of the car and went into the house. It was quiet as a grave in there, everything as she had left it, only no children.

Hid, had they? Well, they'd find out if they tried to bamboozle her.

Creaking slightly in the corsets, grunting with effort, she climbed the stairs. Nobody in the rooms, nobody in the attic, nobody in the closets or under the beds. At last, frustrated, she came back to the front porch. Yuba Fling's furniture was still in the house, but Lydia wasn't going to use it.

I would not, she told herself, sit down, tired as I am, on even her davenport. Not after the way she's brought up those children to dislike me. When I find them, they'll know it. When I get through with them and I ever honk my horn, they'll come. She climbed into her car to wait.

While she waited, she had a second thought. That bedding in there, sheets and blankets . . . well, after all, George Pollard bought it. It belongs to me as much as anybody.

Caroline and Jakie were in the Fosters' summer cottage down on the shore, having their supper of bread and butter and cold lamb chops snitched out of Gramma's fridge at the house in Bradford before they'd left there this afternoon. The bread was sort of smashed and the chops had some lint and stuff on them from Caroline's pockets—she hadn't had a chance to wrap anything in waxed paper. Gramma was always at her heels now; she'd come very near to catching Caroline at the fridge. But Jakie liked the supper enormously, and he was happy because Caroline had told him they were running away from Gramma and never, never would have to go back there again. He was putting away the last of his chop when he suddenly listened and said, "Froggy comin', le's go see him."

He started to scramble down from his chair. Caroline grabbed him just in time and managed to stifle his indignation with her hand over his mouth. "He mustn't see us! Not even Froggy, Jakie. You want to go back to Gramma's?"

Thank goodness, it worked. She felt his tense little body relax in her lap. He was tired to death anyway from the awful day with Gramma—from all the awful days. Caroline would come home from school to find him bellering just as hard as he'd been when she'd left, and lucky not to find him locked in a closet. He was thin and white now, and his curls, which had been so pretty, were all straightened out and straggly.

Today, after she'd told him that this might be the day they'd run off together, he'd been his old cheerful self for a while. He'd helped Caroline hide the suitcases in the bushes along the path to the shore while Gramma'd been in the toilet—she always had to go the minute she got out of the car, no matter how far she'd driven. The suitcases had been in the downstairs hall closet where Mama'd left them. It had been an awful day just the same, until Caroline had put Jakie in his express wagon, braced a suitcase on either side of him, and started down the path to the Fosters' house.

Now she sat holding him, ready to clap her hand over his mouth again in case he started to holler. You never could depend on him not to; sometimes it was because he felt good. He'd heard Froggy's engine before she had; Jakie had terrific sharp ears. If he started yelling to Froggy, there'd be no stopping him.

It was all right, though. He leaned hard against her and said, "Oh-hh, Froggy," in a long, mournful sigh. Then he went to sleep as if someone had dropped a brick on his head.

Well back from the window, Caroline watched Froggy's boat slide up to the float. He cut the engine, jumped out, dropped a looped rope over a cleat. With a mighty heave he hauled the Fosters' skiff up on the float and started taking the canvas cover off.

With a sinking heart, she watched. What if he leaves the boat there? I couldn't ever push it into the water again. That great big skiff. Yes, I can. I'll push it off if I have to bleed. I'll find another boat. I won't go back.

Some water had leaked into the skiff. Froggy tipped it onto its side, let the water run out, tipped it back again. He tightened the clamps on the outboard motor, felt of the lashings that held the plastic cover over it. He went, whistling, up the walkway to the boathouse, unlocked it, opened the door, and went in.

Was he going to haul the skiff up for the winter? Now? He never put it away this early.

No, there he came, still whistling. He had a pair of oars and a gasoline can; he set them down on the float. With another mighty heave, he shoved the boat back into the water, tied it up, bow and stern, tested the knots. He put the oars and the can into the skiff, fastened the canvas cover; he thumped it with his fist to make sure it was tight on. Then he untied his lobster boat, jumped in, and roared away.

Caroline let her breath go. She'd been holding it, watching every one of Froggy's movements. She heard the sound of his engine grow faint, fainter. Then she could no longer hear it. That meant he was around the point of the mainland, out of sight. What he'd been doing was only what he did every so often—check the skiff, make sure she was all right; but the oars and gas can probably meant that he was going out to the island in the morning. She'd seen him do that, days when she and Jakie had gone with him.

"Take oars and extra gas," he'd always said. "Then, if the outboard conks out, you won't have to swim home."

Poor Froggy. He'd walk down in the morning and he wouldn't be able to go, because the boat would be gone. It would be out at the island, hidden, pushed as far up the tidal brook on the far side of Cat Cove as she could push it, out of sight in the alders. Froggy'd think he'd lost the Fosters' boat. He'd be in trouble.

Caroline felt the tears sting under her eyelids. It was awful to be pushed around and made so scared and worried that you had to lie and steal and get your friends into trouble; it was mean, what you had to do. If only Froggy'd said yes, when Mama asked him if we could go live with him. But he hadn't. He knew what Gramma was like, and he just let us go without a word. I just wish he had to live with her himself. He'd find out.

She hardened her heart against him and crushed back the tears.

I can't help it. I have got to take the boat because Jakie and I have got to go.

She took the suitcases down first.

Susie Warren, walking with her bird glasses along the shore path from her house, stopped short in the edge of the trees. It was already dusk but not so dark that she couldn't see the small, sturdy figure with the child's express wagon, bumping the suitcases down the cleated walkway to the Fosters' float.

What on earth . . . ? she thought, and then, That's Caroline Fling.

Quietly, she watched Caroline take the canvas cover off the skiff, pack in the suitcases, one on each side of the bow, arrange the canvas to make a sort of bed between them, load the express wagon in back of the middle thwart. Going somewhere, certainly. But where, at this time of day?

Caroline went back up the walkway and into the Fosters' house. After a moment, she appeared again, carrying a smaller child who was obviously asleep.

Her little brother, Susie thought. They're running away. In a boat, though? And full dark in half an hour or so? Any responsible person should stop them, and I must.

But she did not. She stood where she was, undecided, while what she knew, what she'd heard about the Fling children and Lydia Pollard went through her mind.

I would have run away from Aunt Miranda at that age if I'd had the courage. This one, this Caroline, she has it. Send these defenseless waifs back to Lydia? I?

Susie, watching, smiled a little. Caroline wasn't defenseless. She knew what she was doing. She had put the baby into the canvas bed, tucked him in, snug and secure. Now she was filling the gas tank on the outboard, expert, careful, testing for fullness with a finger. Lines were cast off, coiled. The motor started with a roar, quickly throttled down, until it was barely ticking over. The skiff moved almost silently away from the float, out from under the land, headed into the strip of pale water.

Through her bird glasses, Susie watched it grow smaller, saw it slide along the dimming outline of the Wigheln-Bisschner float on Whistle Island. She made out Caroline getting out, vanishing, with the baby, into the trees behind the pier. Then it was too dark to see.

She slipped the glasses into their case, got up from her seat behind the ledges, and started home.

I've done wrong, she told herself. But who am I to interfere with an act of desperation and courage? They are all right, so far. There's nothing over there to hurt them. There'll be a way to get into that big summer cottage, and that one, that Caroline, will find it; or she knows about it already. Tomorrow I'll get one of the lobster fishermen to drop me off at Whistle Island, on a bird walk. Or maybe Fred Montgomery'll be going over. I might even let him know where his two young cousins are, let him cope with the problem.

Susie walked slowly homeward through the darkening woods. As she came out of the trees in front of her house, she heard the fire whistle blow.

Maybe I'd better give Tommy cat food for his supper tonight, she thought grimly.

Because that wail in the sky, rising, falling, crying disaster and lost children, meant that the search for Caroline Fling was starting all over again.

From the Wiggling Biscuits' pier to their house was not far, but it seemed so by the time Caroline got Jakie into the living room and tucked up on the davenport. He always felt heavy when he was sleeping so hard; she had to sit down for a moment to catch her breath before she started back for the suitcases. He might not wake up till morning, but if he happened to, here alone, he'd be scared. She'd better hurry. She ran all the way back to the pier.

The suitcases were heavy to haul uphill, both at once. She took one halfway, went back for the other. As she set out with the second one for the house, she heard something, a queer scratching and mewing sound, like a cat, only much louder, and not quite like a cat, either. Whatever it was, it was scary in the dark. Then she heard it coming, its feet going pad-pad on the beaten earth of the path. As she tore up the back-porch steps, something large and furry went past her so close that it brushed her leg. Terrified, she swung the suitcase at it, felt a soft bump as if she had hit it somewhere, caught a glimpse of a long shadowy body as it leaped over the porch railing and vanished in the shrubbery below. Then she was inside, with the door closed. Her heart pounded, feeling as if it had jumped up so high in her throat that she'd never get her breath again.

What was it . . . somebody's big dog? A dog didn't ever make cat sounds. It was here. A big animal that chased people. Whatever would she and Jakie do? Would they ever dare to go outside?

She dropped down on the davenport at Jakie's feet, too scared to think of anything except to get Jakie back into the boat and somehow go somewhere else.

After a while, as she got her breath back and began to calm down a little, she began to think. It couldn't get in. They were safe here in the house. Tomorrow, when she was rested, she'd think of something.

Then she thought, scared all over again, Tomorrow won't do. I have to go back out tonight.

She'd left the boat tied by the bow to the float, where, in daylight, anybody on the opposite shore could see it. The lobster fishermen went by the island before daylight. Froggy, if he came, would come early. Anybody who saw that skiff at the float would know in a minute where to look for her and Jakie. All the long weeks of planning, all the stealing, all the mean and rotten things she'd had to do to get here, would be for nothing; and we'd go back to Gramma's, and Jakie would die, I know it would kill him.

I have got to think what to do. I have got to.

For a while she sat, cold and shivering, trying hard.

At last she got up, went to the door, and listened. Not a sound. Perhaps it had gone away. She opened the door a little, peered out. Nothing.

All right. I have just got to run faster than it does, if it comes. Maybe it's hungry. I could throw it something to slow it down.

She went to the deepfreeze, unlocked it, got out a loaf of bread. Hard as a rock. It would take the Thing, whatever it was, longer to eat.

Her legs didn't want to hold her up to get across the porch and down the steps. But once down and on the path, she flew. It almost seemed she had flown with her eyes shut, because there she was on the float and there was the boat. She jerked hard at the knot in the painter, which seemed as if it would never come untied, thinking, If I take the skiff over to Cat Cove, I'll have to come back through the woods. The knot came apart in her hand; she dropped it, letting it dangle off the bow, and gave the skiff a hard shove out into the tide.

She didn't wait to see which way it went; it would just have to go where it would. She tore up the gangway from the float. The moon was coming up over the trees now; halfway to the house, she could see the full length of the path, nothing on it but a few black shadows of trees. And then she was up the steps, the door closed and locked, her back against it, where she had slid down to the floor, gasping and sobbing for breath.

After a while, she realized that between her armpit and her chest was a hard, lumpy thing, ice-cold. Freezing. She sat up. It was the loaf of bread; she'd forgot all about it.

She got up from the floor, put the bread on the kitchen table. Her head felt fuzzy and she ached all over; but Jakie would wake up first in the morning. If he didn't find something to eat, he'd beller the house down. She opened a can of milk, poured it into a pitcher, left the food where he'd be sure to see it.

Then she kicked off her sneakers and crept in alongside Jakie, snuggling into the warmth of him and his bed.

If they found the Fosters' skiff drifting, they'd think she and Jakie were drowned . . . they wouldn't look any more. But if it's lost . . . oh, Froggy, I meant to hide it and keep it for you, and I'm sor . . .

She didn't hear the Thing, whatever it was, when it came back to the porch door and scratched and cried pitifully to get in.

Jakie woke up at the first light of dawn, rested and raring to go. He tickled Caroline and poked her, but she was dead asleep. She only muttered at him and flipped over, back-to.

Cross, Jakie thought.

He had learned a great deal in his short life about cross people. They had better not be bothered. Of course Caroline wouldn't spank him the way Gramma did; Caroline had never slapped him. Still, the one thing Gramma had taught him was not to bother grown-ups.

He slipped down off the davenport and began wandering about the room. This was the nice place; he remembered it well, but where were the Wiggling Biscuits? He pushed back the lid of the harpsichord, touched a quiet note, sang softly, under his breath, "Ha-hoo-ha." If the nice people weren't here, all the nice things were, it was almost as good. Then he discovered he was hungry and headed for the kitchen.

He was munching bread and oleo and taking swigs out of the milk pitcher when he heard the scratching and mewing at the door.

Kitty, he thought. Kitty wants in.

The door was locked, but the key was there. Jakie knew about keys. The one on the door of the black closet where Gramma'd always locked him in had to be turned before the door would open. He reached, and turned, and opened the door wide.

The kitty that came in was the biggest one he'd ever seen, but it was nice; there was nothing in this place that wasn't nice. There never had been. The kitty, a pretty goldy color, with black stripes and spots, rubbed against him, and he put out a hand and smoothed it all along its back.

It made at once for the table where the food was. That was all right, too. Kitties were always hungry. This one was awful hungry. Jakie's slice of bread vanished as if it had never been there. A second one did, too.

"You be good," Jakie said. "Don't be pig."

Milk. Kitties liked milk. Well, it couldn't drink out of the pitcher, its nose was too big to go in there.

He dropped two slices of bread on the floor to hold the kitty so it wouldn't eat up everything, went over to a cupboard, and rummaged around until he found a big tin pie plate. In a drawer, for himself, he located a spoon. Then he crumbled the rest of the loaf into the pan, poured all the milk over it, put the pan on the floor.

Caroline forced herself awake at last.

Coming on for daylight. She must get up, in case Froggy came. Jakie, she saw, was already gone; she could hear him talking to himself in the kitchen. Fuzzy-headed with sleep, she staggered out of bed and saw, through the open kitchen door, Jakie eating out of one side of a pan on the floor, the big animal gobbling out of the other.

Jakie looked at her and chuckled. "Good," he said. "Kitty wikes it, too. Want some?"

Somehow, somehow, she had to get closer and grab Jakie. Her legs, all by themselves, wanted to run. She went, on tiptoe, across the kitchen carpet. The cat didn't pay any attention; it went on eating as if it had never eaten before. Then she spotted the leather collar around its neck, the tags with letters and numbers.

"WALTER," she read. And the married name of the count's daughter, Lise Wagner.

After Froggy had told her about the pet ocelot on the island, summer before last, she'd looked up *ocelot* in the encyclopedia at school. Now, suddenly, she remembered its picture. This was Walter. He was tame. He wasn't anything to be afraid of. She put out her hand, carefully, and sure enough, he let her scratch his head.

How had he come here? Was somebody else here? Alarmed, Caroline looked around, through downstairs rooms, out of the back door. There was nobody. Anyway, nobody she could see.

Walter, the ocelot, when he had been fed and cared for, had been a magnificent specimen of his kind. Full-grown, almost as big as a bloodhound, he had spent most of his life on a leash as an adjunct to Lise Wagner's costumes, led by the neck to social functions, strictly trained to domesticity and decorum. Now, he was lean and starved, his lovely buff-and-black striped coat scraggly with burdocks, ripped by briers. For some weeks he had been scavenging his food on the island, barely able to keep alive on what his maimed mouth and claws could catch and hold. To make a harmless pet of him, his big canines had been pulled, the rest of his teeth filed dull, his claws clipped. He had caught an occasional mouse or small bird, eaten a dead fish or two washed up on the beach.

Walter had no hunting experience. Only a dimly sensed instinct showed him how. His mother had been shot trying to protect her lair in the mountain forest; her kittens, scarcely old enough to have opened their eyes, had been nailed into crates and shipped to a city pet shop.

Franz Wagner, Lise's husband, had never liked or disliked Walter. He had always enjoyed the sight of his wife, splendidly dressed for evenings, accompanied by what, to the uninformed, would seem to be a savage beast. He also had had great fun on the occasions when he and his friends had used Walter for a hunt—they would take him out into woods, turn him loose, scare him into running, and after a while set dogs on his trail. Walter would run until he was exhausted, then tree. Franz and his friends would then shoot—not to kill Walter, but to frighten him down out of the tree. Walter could leap prodigiously; he could get into the lower branches of a tree and go up from limb to limb; but once up there, he could not trust his clipped claws to help him safely down and, sometimes, would fall. He had learned to be mortally afraid of firearms of any kind. It was because of this fear, combined with an act of cruelty, that Walter had come to be on the island.

The Wagners, at the end of the season, were headed south for the winter in Palm Beach, their cabin cruiser passing Whistle Island, fairly close inshore. Franz was well aware of his father-in-law's wild-game sanctuary and that the unfrightened deer there were tame; he considered this foolishness a symptom of an old man's senility. To Franz, as a sportsman, all forest animals were wild, no matter how tame; they were where they were by the grace of God, to be shot at. He kept telling the man at the wheel of the cruiser to swing in closer. Deer were more than likely to be down on the shore at dusk, and he wanted to be near enough to knock one over.

The seaman at the wheel knew the eastern shore of Whistle Island—a maze of drowned and half-drowned ledges not to be fooled with, particularly in the tricky light an hour after sundown. He edged the cruiser in slowly, sweating under his cap. Wagner was half-soused, or he wouldn't ask anyone to try this, at this time of day and tide. If only the madam would come on deck, she'd straighten him out. Damn foolishness, to shoot from here anyway; no place to land.

Who did come on deck was Walter, who arrived in the cockpit just as Franz let go at something on the shore—a deer, a drift log, a rock; whatever it was, he hadn't hit it. Walter gave a terrified leap at the sound of the gun; he went streaking across the stern seat, upsetting Franz's bottle and his half-full cocktail glass, and ended up at the rail, scrabbling desperately to keep his balance. Franz heard the crash of breaking glass; he swung around without a word, jumped up on the stern seat, and booted Walter overboard.

"All right, get us out of here. Let's get going."

"I could pick him up," the seaman said. "The missus likes him."

"What the hell, I'm sick of the damned brute. If she wants another one, she can find plenty more at the same pet shop."

The cruiser's reversing twin propellers barely missed Walter. When he surfaced, half-drowned and tumbled about by the swirling water of her wake, she was already too far away for him to catch. For a while, he swam hopefully along the wake; then he gave up and turned toward the island, which he could see looming in the darkness.

He had been slowly starving to death ever since. If winter had come to the island before Jakie, Walter would have been dead.

PART FIVE

Andy

ON THE DAY of the *Macomber*'s departure, Lewis and his children arrived on board at daylight, as Brown had suggested. Lewis was a little surprised to find no one on deck or stirring except Jilson, who had already fired up his galley. He offered breakfast, and Adam and Amanda, who these days appeared to be bottomless, decided they had room for more after bacon and eggs and toast at Mrs. McKlosky's.

"Take your stuff below first," Lewis told them. "You know where your staterooms are."

The kids would be bunking below in two of the dude cabins. Lewis regretted this. He would have felt better if they could have been with him in the port after cabin, to which Brown had assigned him. The cabin was spacious and airy, with windows and four bunks. There was room to curtain off a section for Amanda. Lewis had suggested this.

Brown had seemed embarrassed. "Well," he said, "I guess I've told Hal he can bunk in with you. He's a little hurt with my arrangements. Had things all his own way all summer's how it is. I wanted him in with me, but he don't want to. So I guess if you don't mind, Lew, he'll have to be in with you."

Lewis had been puzzled anyway, because the port after

cabin, he'd thought, had been Mrs. Bronson's. She had evidently been moved. But it was Brown's business.

Brown had, with pride, shown Lewis and the kids over the vessel when he had assigned cabins. The staterooms were his brag-piece, he had said. They were immaculate and comfortable, if a little ill-ventilated compared to Lewis' quarters; he wondered how Adam would manage if he got seasick again. Not all of the cabins were accessible, because the overflow of Brown's furniture had been stowed in the for'ard passageway. Lewis caught a glimpse of the "bride's present" braced behind a spidery structure of two-by-fours and wondered how much plush might be rubbed off if the vessel ran into heavy seas.

Brown had also shown off his own quarters, which were in the starboard side of the afterhouse, opposite Lewis'. He explained how the old deckhouse had been ripped out and replaced—the new one built high so that the two staterooms would be pleasant in the daytime and a man could stand up without banging his head on the beams.

He's a little bit of a nut over this, Lewis thought. No sense to spoil Brown's good time, but see one steel waterproof locker, one built-in bunkside dresser with mirror and drawers, see them all. Lewis told himself he'd be a lot more interested in finding out what had become of Mrs. Bronson. He wondered if she and Andy had got tired of waiting and had found another way to travel.

"Now, when you come down in the morning, you move right in," Brown had said. "If I oversleep, Coon'll be around."

Coon wasn't around. No one was. The door to Lewis' stateroom was locked. Brown hadn't locked it yesterday, though, and Lewis hadn't thought of asking for a key.

The kids came roaring back on deck headed for the galley.

"Take it easy, you'll wake up the gulls," Lewis said. "To say nothing of whoever else's asleep."

They cooled off a little and went along. Behind them,

hands in the pockets of his dark blue shorts, Andy Bronson came, stepping in a much quieter and more dignified way. His white T-shirt was immaculate; a pale-blue sailor cap sat far back on his mop of yellow curls.

"You're up early," he said politely. "Good morning."

"Yes. So are you," Lewis said. "Good morning."

"Did Man-Mountain throw you out, too?" Andy said.

"Man-Mountain? Throw me out?"

Andy indicated Lewis' suitcases, stacked near the door of the port after cabin. "Oh. I'm arriving, not leaving," Lewis said. "You and your mother weren't chased out because of me, were you?"

"We didn't mind, really. We just didn't like being chucked out on our ear. I was good and mad. Now we've got rooms down below."

"I should be, too," Lewis said. "Captain Brown didn't do that, did he?"

"Nn-nn. It was the oceangoing cowboy. He said he was the mate and this was his place, so get out. So we did, and he locked the door. My mother has a key, but she won't use it. I'll get it for you, if you want. If you don't, I'll go have breakfast."

"That's all right," Lewis said. "I'll wait."

"Up to you." Andy strolled off toward the galley. "After I have my breakfast, I am going to speak to Captain Brown. I don't like to be pushed around." His outraged back vanished down the galley companionway.

Somebody should certainly speak to Brown, Lewis thought. His nephew Harold doesn't seem quite all there. He settled down against the rail, waiting for Brown to show.

The sun wasn't up, but it soon would be. Streaks of pink and yellow were showing in the east and three foolish-looking pink clouds were plastered on the sky above the horizon, as if stuck on with glue. There wasn't a ripple of wind; Point Milton harbor was like an inland lake, with sunrise, the three clouds and some dark buildings on shore duplicated in the water. Looking overside,

Lewis could see the long shadow of the *Macomber,* deep-down, pitch-black in the greenish-gold depths. He stared at it while the light turned to pink the white undersides of some insignificant small fish, swimming alongside the dark reflection.

Mrs. Bronson came quietly along the deck and ranged herself beside him at the rail. She looked sleepy but neat.

"Good morning," she said. "Our children came up like dawn over Mandalay."

"I'm sorry," Lewis said. He smiled at her. "I try."

"Mm, I do, too. Doesn't work. They've got too much going, all at once. Andy couldn't wait to get up. He is going to tell off Captain Brown."

"I'm sorry about this," Lewis said. "I don't care where I bunk, really. Harold seems to have been pretty offensive about where he does, so your son says."

"Andy is very high on his horse. Since his father died, three years ago, Andy's felt he is the man of the family. He protects me. I only hope he complains to Brown without swearing at him. He's picked up some words from the boys at rehearsals which I ignore when I can, hoping the habit will be outgrown. Would you like to go into your cabin? Here's a key."

"Thanks," Lewis said. "We'll all have a session with Brown as soon as he shows up. Maybe it'll turn out to be a case of us or Harold's being left behind when the vessel sails. Nobody ought to put up with this kind of nonsense."

"Shoot, if it weren't for Andy, I wouldn't even notice it. I'm more comfortable belowdecks, really. There's privacy, a nice big bolt on the inside of the door, and I can practice scales without crinkling anybody's teeth. I got up early, so as to see Brown before Andy does. I'm not going to stop Andy—I like being protected. And I might say, you yourself give a lady confidence, Captain Wyman."

"Do I?" Lewis said. He unlocked the door to the port cabin and swung it open.

"My goodness!" she said, peering over his shoulder.

"Harold must think New Brunswick is much nearer the North Pole than it is."

The stateroom was jammed and littered with Harold's personal possessions. Both clothes lockers were crammed so full their doors swung open, with snappy suits, giddy sports jackets and slacks, and an amazing supply of cold-weather gear. An overflow, consisting of fur- and sheep-skin-lined coats, heavy pants, plaid woolen shirts, oilskins, a snowmobile suit, and half a dozen sets of quilted underwear, was piled up on one bunk. On the other lower was a heap of sports equipment and boots—tennis racket, golf clubs, snowshoes, skis; snowmobile boots, larrigans, moccasins, sneakers, dress shoes.

"What a tremendous pile of stuff! He really does need space, doesn't he?" Mrs. Bronson said. "How awful, Captain Wyman! If you stay here, where would you sleep?"

Lewis lifted a guitar case and three transistor radios off the head of the second bunk and put them on the cabin deck. He lifted one of his own bags to the space he'd made, to stake out ownership. Let him move that, he told himself, and see what I'll do.

"Oh, I'm a nosy woman!" she said. "But the drawer was open, I couldn't help seeing. Look, Captain Wyman. We also have no drugstores in New Brunswick."

Bottles of aspirin, vitamins of all kinds, laxative pills in quantity, drugstore patent medicines crowded the drawer.

"I mustn't *do* this," she said. "It's none of my business. Maybe the poor fellow is sick. What on earth could ail him?"

"God only knows," Lewis said. "But something sure does."

Jasper Brown's talk with his nephew resounded all over the ship. At first, no words could be heard—only an irate, baritone roar inside Brown's cabin. But when Harold came out, the lecture's conclusion was heard by all.

"—and you can cut out playing tricks on people, or by

the god you'll either stay here and fend for yourself or you'll tow in the tender all the way to Canada. You can take your goddam choice!"

Harold apologized to Mrs. Bronson. He apologized to Lewis for locking up the stateroom, forgetting to unlock it.

"I thought I was going to, you know, bunk in here by myself, Cap'n Wyman. On cruises, this summer, I was acting, you know, captain while Uncle Jasper was sick. He still is, he forgets things and he gets, you know, mad easy. He forgot to tell me he'd put you in here. I guess I've got my, you know, stuff all over the works."

"All I need is a bunk," Lewis said. "Any luggage I don't need, I'll stow belowdecks. You might do that with some of yours and stow the rest of it a little more shipshape."

"Isn't much storage space, not for two, is there?"

"Call one of the hands to help you pack your loose equipment belowdecks," Lewis said shortly.

"I'm not in much of a spot to give orders to the, you know, hands. I'm one of them myself, now. It's a peculiar feeling, someone else put in over me to give the orders."

"Look here," Lewis said. "Let's get things straight. I'm the vessel's pilot. I plot the headings, set courses. I give no orders except those in connection with my job."

"Oh, I know all that," Harold said. "I don't think you understand about Uncle Jasper's condition. He's a sick old man, half the time he don't know what he's doing. I have to be on hand to, you know, take over, in case I need to. I take, you know, care of him. Why, I've brought a young drugstore along, say he might need something we didn't have aboard ship. Thank you for the offer of help, all the same, but I'll pack my own stuff out of here."

He left with an armful and, after a while, came back.

"If you don't mind," he said, "I won't move the rest of it. It would be too much to carry alone down to my stateroom belowdecks."

"You've decided not to bunk in here?" Lewis said.

"Yes, I have."

Lewis had had about enough. The talk about Brown's incompetence had been, of course, absurd; you might equate it with what he had mentioned already—that Harold was sulky about his uncle's getting married again.

"Take your sporting goods along, will you?" Lewis said. "I don't want to wake up in heavy weather and find skis or any other loose junk in the bunk with me."

"Yes, *sir*. Okay, *sir*! I hope you understand why I'm moving out."

Lewis glanced at the smooth-cheeked, boyish face, with its look of faultless health and youth. One thing about Harold, he had a beautiful, pink complexion. This isn't a man, this is a baby. A spoilt brat, Lewis thought. Aloud, he said, "Not after hearing about all your reasons for staying nearby. I understood from your uncle that he asked you to bunk in with him and you refused. So why are you moving belowdecks?"

"A strained situation can develop aboard ship. I don't want to cause one, in case my, you know, orders ever conflict with yours."

"If they do," Lewis snapped, "I'll straighten you out."

"Yes, *sir*!"

Carrying his skis and whistling, Harold went out and closed the door behind him.

Strained situation, eh? Harold was the boy who could build one. Lewis was not unacquainted with his kind—at least, with variations of the species. Ships and waterfronts seemed to attract them. They were the boys who bought war medals from the pawnshops, fake officers' caps from the Naval stores. They were the soreheads, the purveyors of malicious ship's gossip, the troublemakers who liked nothing better than trouble, and the hell with them.

Well, since Harold was gone, Lewis could bring Adam and Amanda up here. Rig a curtain for Amanda—Brown surely could produce a square of canvas.

As for Jasper Brown, there was nothing about his performance as skipper to indicate he was incompetent. On the breeze which came up with the tide at noon, he eased the *Lizzie Macomber* out of her berth into the ship channel, headed her down the bay.

Adam, watching, breathed, "Oh-h, beautiful! Look how he's doing it, Dad! Like silk."

Jilson said, "Old girl knows who's boss. See her show off for him."

And, so it almost seemed, she was showing off. The old *Macomber,* with the wind thumping in her rigging, the sun on her new sails, was picking up for Jasper Brown from where she had left off with Roy Macomber, her wake rippling away again to the places she had been— the long wake, stretching green-and-silver, back past the time of mud and rot and sea worms, to Virginia and the Capes, to Boston and New York and Philadelphia and Portland, Maine, to where it had started in Nova Scotia in 1891.

You aren't so darned rickety, Lewis told her. For a beat-up old female, you're putting on a pretty good show.

But Amanda said it aloud. She grabbed Adam around the waist and waltzed across the deck with him. "Oh, she's a bird, a sweet old bird! Hi, bird! How does it feel to have wings again?"

The first days couldn't have been better. The *Macomber* slipped tranquilly along, like silk between the Capes, past Norfolk into open ocean—at home there once again. Things aboard settled down better than Lewis had thought they might. The strained situation did not build. No one could fault the pleasant manners of young Harold Brown. He worked, cheerfully carrying out orders, with the other two hands, Coon and Fairleigh, and did his share. He was polite to Belle Bronson and civil to Lewis, though he had never been back to the stateroom for the rest of his clothes, which still bulged both locker doors. Lewis, relieved, couldn't have cared less. His own possessions lived in his traveling bag; the children, though they slept in his stateroom nights now, kept their things belowdecks, for convenience sake and more space, which everybody needed.

Belle Bronson spent mornings in her stateroom; she had, she said, a lot of program work to do—"And practicing, which is monotonous except to the person doing it." Afternoons she came on deck to a deck chair in the sun, and there, sooner or later, everyone who wasn't busy was pretty sure to be found. "Belle," Amanda said, "is where it's at," and certainly wherever Belle was was laughter, fun, something going on. Lewis, after the long winter of his heart, found himself turning toward that gaiety and warmth almost as much as he was turning toward the sun, which, in those first days, blazed mellow on the *Macomber*'s deck.

Amanda, from the first, had struck up a tremendous friendship with Andy Bronson; the two would disappear for hours and come back at mealtimes, flushed with effort over some project which was evidently a secret between them and about which they were noncommittal. Whatever it was, its net result had been to make Andy very bossy toward Amanda. Adam was scornful about this.

"He's a mama's peewee," he told Amanda. "What'd you want to bother with him for?"

"I like him," Amanda said. "He's different."

"Different-schmifferent," Adam said, and pounded aft to his own true love, which was the *Macomber*'s wheel. Brown was teaching him to steer, letting his brain be picked of information about sailing vessels and their navigation. Adam could scarcely be tolled away even for meals. It would have been hard to say who was having the better time, Brown or Adam.

Jasper Brown already seemed like a different man. He was tanned from the sun, beginning to put on weight and fill out his clothes. Except for the circles under his eyes, which were lighter now, no one would take him for a sick man. He ate for two, and his baritone roar of laughter could be heard along the deck at almost any time of day. He and Belle Bronson kidded each other a good deal.

"I'd marry you tomorrow if you weren't so spoken for," she told him. "You write me in Halifax if you don't find her still waiting."

Brown liked folk songs, the sadder the better, and she could produce almost anything he asked for. She had a tremendous repertoire; he had only been able to stick her once or twice on requests.

"Do you and Andy both play guitar?" Lewis asked her.

"He does. Quite well, too. I can play anything with strings, but what I can make the most noise on is a piano accordion."

She had one with her, which she brought on deck to show, an instrument all gilt and glitter, which, at the climax of some of her numbers, she said, would flash colored lights off and on.

"I go easy on the lights except for exit numbers," she said. "It's awful, the worst kind of burlesque, but it surely wows the audience, especially when I wear my dress to match it, which will do the same thing."

"Your dress? Flashes lights off and on?" Lewis said, delighted.

"My exits are red, green, blue, and yellow. Behind, on my rear elevation, is a picture of the Old Folks at Home Farm. Lights come on in the windows, even the cow's eyes flash. Horrible. But they love it, it always brings the house down. I have to replace the electrical connections when I get home. They burned out in the van fire."

"You had it on that first day I saw you," Lewis said. "I liked it."

"Well, I had to wear it while I did some laundry. That van fire just about wiped me out." She shrugged. "Well, I can splash some, when I get home, so far as clothes go. I wish Captain Brown liked dance music better; and I could change from sad ballads to classical, if anyone was interested."

Lewis liked dance music himself. Apparently, Andy did, too. Walking aft one evening, to check the vessel's heading, Lewis heard Andy say to his mother, "Oh, come on, Belle. Let's slam the old duffer with 'Tijuana Taxicab.'"

"Now, honey," Belle said, "don't let me hear you call Captain Brown an old duffer again. After all, we're his guests here in a way, and if he wants 'The Jealous Lover of Old Green Valley' or the one about the poison viperous snake that bit the man in the heel, we ought to oblige him."

"Oh, balls!" Andy said. "It makes me sick to my stomach, the idea of that dame sucking his heel."

There was a silence. Then Belle said, "I can't help but think it was unsanitary. He probably hadn't had time to wash his heel since it was bit in the hayfield. You, dear, have time right now to go below and wash your mouth out with soap."

Andy let out a howl. "I can't sing with my mouth tasting soap!"

"You had better try," Belle said. "Some things you can say, but others are unpleasant and nasty. Do you go, or do I come with you?"

"Oh, I go," Andy said. "I know you when you get like this."

With dignity, Andy left, headed for the for'ard companionway, and Lewis walked on aft, chuckling to himself.

Most kids would have put up a squall, he thought. Not Andy. Faced with the inevitable, he had gone to cope with it, unhumiliated, not in the least taken down. He would go below, wash out his mouth with soap, come back, and that would be an end to the matter. A day or so ago, Lewis had wondered aloud to Belle how Andy could get away with bossing Amanda around the way he did. "She's two years older, you'd think it would be the other way around," he'd said.

Belle had laughed. "Oh, Andy's of a ripe old age," she'd said. "Nothing fazes Andy. Sometimes I think he's older than I am."

* * *

Coon, the youngster with the perky, triangular face, was at the wheel. He watched Lewis check the course without saying anything.

"Right where she ought to be," Lewis said. "I'll be back at ten. We'll have a change of heading about then."

"I know," Coon said. "Offshore. Wide and deep."

Lewis recognized the reference. "Not quite so wide and deep as the place in the song the skipper likes," he said. "And not too far offshore, yet. We'll probably use the Cape Cod Canal."

"I've never sailed outside the bay," Coon said. "Brr-rr!" He shivered.

Puzzled, Lewis glanced at him. Usually, you wouldn't think anything ever bothered Coon, but evidently something did now. Lewis had been about to say that the more sea room the *Macomber* had, the farther offshore he could keep her, the happier he'd be. Instead, he said, "Nice night. Good sailing weather and we had a clear sunset. Probably we'll get the same weather tomorrow."

"Yeah, sunset. But over east there . . ."

Lewis knew at once what he meant. He himself at sea had seen beginning night too many times not to know how darkness grew in the east. The western sky might still be light, pleasant, with streaks of sunset left, but the eastern horizon was always a portent. The east was where darkness was coming from and saying so.

"You must have seen that a thousand times, sailing the bay," he said. "That gloom's only a trick of light. Doesn't last. The moon'll be up over there pretty soon."

"I'll sure-god be glad to see it. Anything I know as well as I know the moon."

"All right, see you at ten," Lewis said. Still puzzled, he went for'ard. Coon was a seaman who knew his job—at least he gave every sign of it. He must know there weren't any signs of bad weather coming. A nice youngster, quiet, hard to get acquainted with because he never seemed to have much to say. This was the longest conversation Lewis had had with him. Something in the boy's voice, a kind of dread, made Lewis wonder. Well, everyone had the creeps once in a while. A hot mugful of coffee sent down to Coon would be of more use to him than moonrise.

Jilson would have coffee left. He was, Lewis knew, working the big coffeepot overtime, mostly for him. Lacking anything stronger, Lewis had been drinking a lot of coffee. It had helped. He had had to refuse a before-dinner cocktail from Brown on the first night out and had had to explain why. It had started up his devil again, had made him wonder how much longer the damned possession was going to last.

On deck, amidships, guitar music was beginning, a subdued plunking that went well with the sound of the *Macomber*'s bow wave. As Lewis passed, Andy hit a couple of bass notes and began to sing. His voice, a clear soprano, was innocent and pure—not harmed any, Lewis thought, amused, by the taste of soap.

Lewis liked Jilson's galley, where Brown's good sense had kept out the fancy frills that decked the passengers' quarters. Its plain pine cupboards and counters, scrubbed deal table and black cookstove made it, to Lewis, the most pleasant place on the ship. Jilson had trouble keeping people out of it and out from underfoot. Functional and simple, it was roomy as galleys go, with built-in bunks for the cook and his helper, though Fairleigh, the crew member who pinch-hit as cook's helper, slept elsewhere, because Jilson's thunderous snores kept him awake. Fairleigh had already cleaned up and put away after supper. The place was neat and polished; the coffeepot was on the stove, giving off a noble smell of coffee.

Jilson was stretched out on his bunk reading a paperback. He muttered something but did not look up as Lewis came in.

"What was that?" Lewis asked. He made for the coffeepot, found cream and sugar, filled a mug with a fine, steaming brew. Then he stuck his head out of the companionway and whistled, and presently Adam came loping along the deck.

"Mind running this down to Coon, Ad?" Lewis asked.

"Deckhands sending you after their coffee now," Jilson said.

"Coon sounded as if he could use some. Seems to have the creeps."

"Hell, them young jaybirds can always use coffee. They'd put up a tent in here all day long, if I didn't stomp on the first sneaker that comes down the steps."

"You sound mean and ugly," Lewis said, grinning at him.

"Feet hurt. My corns is talking in tongues. What's he got the creeps about?"

Lewis brought his own mug over to the table, sat down, leaning comfortably on his elbows. "Said he didn't like the way the dark looked in the east."

"He kidding?"

"No, I don't think so. You know how the east looks, just at dusk."

"Hell, yes. Had a bad dream about that myself once. Dreamt the dark come out of a drum like a churn, with a big hand turning the handle, so's to spread the night slow all over the world."

"Why a bad dream? That's pretty, like poetry."

"Pretty, hell. Old skin-on-bones flipper, yaller fingernails, fat black wart on it that jumped up and down every time the churn handle come up and over. I come to, screeching."

"Well you might have," Lewis said.

Adam came down the companionway steps, his sneakers flopping limberly on the linoleum. "Coon says thanks. The coffee's just what the doctor ordered."

"Overet," Jilson said morosely.

"What's the matter?" Adam asked. "You sore about something?"

"My slipped disk is killing me," Jilson said.

"Want some coffee?"

"You won't put enough sugar in it."

"Three spoons. What you like," Adam said. He handed over a mug, went back to fix another for himself.

Outside on the deck, Andy slid effortlessly into the chorus of another song and Jilson moaned.

"Pu, them sad ballats!" he said. "Busted hearts and stobbed wimmen! Now he's gitting to where the mermaids are at the bottom of the sea, a-shedding their sad tears for me. Feller wrote that never see a mermaid. Nor you, nor I."

"Oh, it's an all-right song," Adam said. "What's the matter with it?"

"Gives me a bellyache, is all. I could sing you a song I writ myself, ain't creepy and ain't sad. I've writ a whole collection of ballats about the Coast Guard Light List."

"Come awn!" Adam said. "I bet you never wrote a song in your life. I bet you a quarter you can't sing!"

"I wouldn't take your money, it'd be sinful."

"Okay, there's a quarter. Sing one."

Jilson stared up at the ceiling of his bunk and all at once began to sing in a voice so nasal that it sounded as though it actually came out of his nose.

> "Here I be, a shipwreck sailor,
> Long time gone from home,
> Setting on a rock in the middle of commotion,
> A-cussing and a-swearing at the damned old ocean,
> Up to my ass in foam.
> > Feet wet, pants wet, sick and tired of trying,
> > And Old Man Ledge lighted-whistle-buoy crying,
> 'Home, for godsake, go home.' "

"I take it all back," Adam said.

"You better. In my time, I been known as the sweet singer of Belfast, Maine. You going to give me that quarter?"

Without a word, Adam handed it over.

"Canadian!" Jilson said. "I ain't going to take it." He tossed it back to Adam, who, not expecting it, made a grab and missed. It fell behind a cupboard door which was open a crack and fetched up against something inside with a clink. Adam got down on all fours to root it out.

"Hey," he said, coming up with it. "What're all those old iron kettles doing in there?"

"Taking up good room," Jilson said. "Them is Jasper Brown's grandmother's cast-iron scouse pots, come out of his house along with all them other beat-up goods. He thinks they're great to cook a chowder in. Taste of iron rust makes the dudes think they're roughing it. You couldn't scrub 'em clean with the left-footed Carborundum boot sole of Judas Isacarot. What to hell's going on on deck?"

From outside had come a series of thumps, followed by a crackling sound of light wood breaking and a sudden, clear, high-pitched scream. Something metallic dropped with a clang and a discordant jangle.

Lewis leaped for the companionway. He came out on deck in time to see Andy Bronson slam down the remains of his shattered guitar.

The scream had been his mother's. She had evidently been sitting with her accordion in her lap and had dropped it when she had jumped up. She was saying in an appalled voice, "Andy, are you sick? What's the matter?"

Andy stood staring down at the splintered mess of strings and wood. He put both hands over his eyes. He said, "Belle?" in a questioning tone. "I see . . . oh, funny . . . lights . . . Belle?" And suddenly screamed.

Belle leaned, swiftly picked him up in her arms. "I'm here, honey. It's all right—"

From the deck chair where he was sprawled, Harold said, "Maybe it's that soap you made him wash his mouth out with, Mis' Bronson. Tch, tch! Never ought to do that to a high-strung kid."

Amanda said suddenly, "You shut your fat mouth!"

and Lewis put a hand on her shoulder, shaking it slightly. He said, "Belle, can I help? Can I take him?"

But Andy buried his face against his mother and burst into sobs. The sobs were spasmodic, hysterical; Belle held him close. "Thanks, Lew, but if you could gather up our things—the instrument cases are there by the deckhouse." She went off along the deck toward the companionway.

"Gawd," Harold said. He unfolded himself, lazily, from his chair. "Little punk went off like a firecracker, didn't he?" He sounded amused, complacent, as if he might be enjoying himself.

The moon had come up, not yet high enough to give much light. Belle's accordion lay, spread open, where she had dropped it. Some sparkles of moonlight on its glittering metal were blotted out by Coon's slim shadow as he came swiftly across the deck. He was as silent as his shadow; the sound he made was the solid smack of his fist on Harold's face. The sound Harold made was the *thunk!* of his head against the deck planking. He rolled over and lay still.

"Coon!" Jasper Brown came striding along the deck. "What goes on here? What in hell d'you mean, leaving the wheel?"

"I lashed it," Coon said. Neatly he sidestepped Brown. "You better pick up titty-baby, he's dropped his marble."

"Fairleigh, get the wheel," Brown said. "Coon, I want to see you in my cabin right away."

But Coon was already gone, his tall figure melting into the shadows by the afterhouse.

Jasper took an uncertain step forward; a piece of the broken guitar cracked under his foot, and Amanda said sharply, "Don't step on it! Maybe it can be fixed."

"What is it?" Jasper leaned and peered. "Busted git-box. Hal, you do this?"

Harold, already stirring and sitting up, held his jaw and moaned.

"Well, you come along aft with me," Jasper said. "We'll put something on that." He stood, watching Harold

[*134*]

scrabble to his feet. "Was that thing insured?" he demanded of nobody.

There was a silence. Then Amanda answered him. "Nobody can insure the tone of an instrument. This was special. Andy loved it." She choked a little, whether with tears or fury, Lewis couldn't tell. He said quietly, "Amanda," and put out a hand, but she had already moved, picking up the pieces of the guitar, putting them carefully in the case. "Not what any dope could call a 'git-box,' " she burst out.

"Aw, hell, Uncle Jasper," Harold said. "Kid got sore at his ma, had a temper tantrum is all. Nothing to do with me."

"Dammit, I told you and Coon," Jasper said, "if you were coming along with me, you'd have to—" The door of his stateroom closed, and Lewis was left alone with his children.

They were quietly picking up Belle's possessions, not saying anything. Adam put the accordion into its case, snapped the case shut. "Want us to take this stuff down, Dad?" he asked.

Lewis held up his watch to the moonlight. "Yes," he said. "Tell Belle I'll be down as soon as I check the heading."

"Temper tantrum, nothing!" Amanda said fiercely. "Andy wouldn't have one. Unless—"

"Unless what?" Lewis asked. He himself was deeply puzzled; she was right. You wouldn't expect Andy, ever, to fly off the handle.

"Unless something awful," Amanda said. "That big slab of . . . of slob acted as if he was glad of it, whatever it was. I'm glad Coon hit him. I wish he'd knocked his head right off."

"He hasn't got any head," Adam said. "It's just a mess of clanks. Could Andy maybe have got food poisoning, Dad? That was funny, about his eyes. What if he needs a doctor?"

"Could be," Lewis said. "Don't worry, we're not too far

offshore. We can head in any time we need to, get to a doctor before morning. Tell Belle that, will you?"

He had tried to think of something that would comfort them; they were shocked and upset, and he didn't blame them. So was he. After they had gone, he stood where he was, leaning against the rail, thinking. Not food poisoning, probably; not with Jilly handling the food. But soap poisoning? So much chemical stuff chucked around nowadays, you hardly knew what was in the food you ate, let alone something like soap, which you weren't supposed to. He made up his mind to ask Belle what Andy had washed his mouth out with, and if he'd swallowed any of it. He'd better find out how the youngster was before he changed the *Macomber*'s heading, just in case.

At his knock, Belle said from behind her closed door, "Lewis?" and, when he answered, let him in. "He's better," she said. "I think he's going to sleep. He's had about as wild an attack of hysterics as I ever saw, but I gave him a good dose that made him throw up, and he's got rid of whatever it was that upset him so. I can't imagine . . . well, he's always liked Coke and it's never bothered him before. But that's what it looked like, a bottle of Coke or some soft drink."

"Well, that was quick," Lewis said. "Thank God." He mentioned the soap and she laughed, the deep, rich chuckle that he liked and had begun to listen for.

"The thing is," she said, "Andy doesn't. We had this out quite a while ago. He would go when I told him to, but he wouldn't wash out his mouth. When I accused him of it, he said it did no good, anyway, and destroyed his dignity. So I said, Don't destroy mine then, by using those words. He said he'd much rather apologize, it made more sense. So there it stands. I tell him to go, a kind of warning, and he goes. And that's all."

"Not the soap, then," Lewis said. "I'll get Jilly to check into the soft-drink situation. Would it help if I slept in the stateroom next to yours tonight, just in case?"

"No need. But it's nice of you and thanks. I'll be all

right. And with that smack on the nose, I doubt if Harold does much prowling tonight. Whatever got into Coon, do you suppose? Harold?"

Lewis stared at her. "Good Lord, Belle! Is that cretin bothering you?"

"Not too much. There've been some meaningful glances and a few remarks I'm careful not to hear. He does have a curious habit of blowing through the keyhole at all hours of the day and night. It annoyed the children, Andy and Amanda. Andy was teaching her guitar in here— Oh, dear, I've told. Amanda was keeping that as a surprise for you. Don't let on about my big mouth, will you?"

Lewis was suddenly furious. "I'll go and speak to Jasper right away. We aren't too far offshore yet. Brown had better put a halter on his Harold, or we'll fetch a coast port in the morning anyway and clear us all out of here."

She reached both hands for the lapels of his jacket and stood holding on against the rise and fall of the deck. "Don't do anything drastic," she said. "Andy and I are broke till we get to St. Andrews, and we've also got all those band instruments aboard here. I haven't wanted to make any trouble—we won't be here much longer, anyway. Besides, I've had much worse to contend with around hotels and concert halls, and I'm prepared. I've got an unpleasant little aerosol can which squirts a very stingy spray, not to hurt or maim, but to make think twice. For myself, I don't think I need it here, but I wouldn't hesitate to discommode anybody I caught fooling around with Andy."

A quick sideways roll of the vessel slanted her against him. For a moment, her hair was silky and fragrant under his chin, and Lewis held her close, realizing that he himself didn't want the voyage to end at some coast harbor, where he'd have to say good-bye and very likely never see her again.

"Goodness!" Belle said. "This kind of transportation's unpredictable, isn't it?"

Brown sat behind his cabin table, studying a chart. He glanced up with his usual friendly smile. "Hi, Lew. Have a seat. Coon told me you were changing course, and I was charting it myself."

"I'm not sure yet whether we will change the heading, unless it's inshore," Lewis said crisply. "Look here, Jasper, your nephew's making a hell of a nuisance of himself. What's the matter with him? Is there anything wrong with him?"

Brown's astonishment grew on his face, and it was part anger, as Lewis could see.

"Hal? What are you talking about? What'd you mean, is there anything wrong with him?"

"He's ruining the trip. He's been plaguing the kids and annoying Belle, prowling around nights. And look at Coon. He was certainly up in a heap. God knows what Hal did to him."

"Oh, he and Coon have punched each other all their lives. I've put the stopper on that, good and solid. You've got Hal all wrong, Lew. He's a high-spirited young feller, likes to kid, play jokes. Sometimes he don't have good judgment, goes a little bit too far, and he's high-strung, too. But great balls of fire, Lew, I brought that boy up from a pup, know him inside and out. There ain't a mite of real harm in him."

"Maybe not," Lewis said. "Let's say, if you want to, that his kidding goes too far. Maybe you feel your boy's a practical joker with a heart of gold, but blowing through keyholes in the middle of the night is plain childish pestering, and I want it stopped."

"You sure your judgment ain't a little warped, Lew? Hal says you're kind of carrying a load for Belle yourself, and I can't say I blame you. I think what's happened is Hal's been having a little fun with her about it."

"Think what you like," Lewis said between his teeth. "You aren't helping any, Jasper. This is what I've got to say. If you can guarantee that all this damned foolishness will stop, we'll go on to St. Andrews. If you can't, we'll head inshore tonight and call the whole trip off. It's up to you."

"Why, shoot, Lew, I'll give him holy hell. I guess I ought to. All right? Now, about this heading, Lew. What would you say to this?" He moved his hands on the chart so that Lewis could see his penciled line.

Lewis reached for the pencil, stood for a moment holding it in his hand. "You know, this *could* be darned nice, Jasper."

Jasper grinned. "Hell, Lew, we can't let anything spoil this trip. Hal's nothing but a big kid."

Right, Lewis thought. A big kid with God only knows what mental age.

He made up his mind quickly. From the beginning, he had trusted Jasper's judgment and good sense; and Jasper, now, believed what he had said. Lewis couldn't bring himself to agree with him; but the truth about Hal might lie somewhere in between.

"I think we'll use the Cape Cod Canal," he said. "Offshore, we might run into November weather this time of year."

He would not head so far offshore as he had intended, to gain sea room, but would set a course parallel with the coast, swinging easterly to give a wide berth to the sand traps of the New Jersey shoals.

"Like this," he said, and ruled in the light line that would be the *Macomber*'s wake to Cape Cod, on up past the Isles of Shoals and the Maine coast, between the islands into the St. Croix River.

PART SIX

Froggy

FRED MONTGOMERY did not go to the island on the day after Caroline and Jakie had disappeared. He stayed up all night with the search parties. At daylight, so worn out that he could barely walk, he went home to rest. In midmorning, a fisherman spotted the Fosters' skiff drifting some miles offshore and towed it into the harbor. In it were found a pair of oars, a gasoline can, the plastic cover of the outboard motor, and a small, woolen mitten.

Nobody questioned what must have happened. The mitten told the story. The children had stolen the skiff and somehow or other they'd got overboard. Knowing them both as he did, Fred reasoned that Jakie had fallen in and Caroline had tried to rescue him; Fred's heart broke and stayed broken.

People recalled the first disappearance of Caroline, so far a mystery to all, because she'd never said where she'd been. Well! She'd been in that skiff, that was where! A few mentioned what a little hellion she'd been; some recalled being taken for a bogus Heart Fund contribution, but now that she was certainly drowned, the consensus was, "Poor little thing!"

Lydia Pollard said there was no doubt in her mind— those kids had been trying to run away. It was a judgment on them. God saw to it that wrongdoers got punished, in this world. She got very little sympathy from anyone. Weeks ago, word had gone around all over town about the miserable way she was treating Yuba's children. Now, she took to her bed, with two doctors, and was said to be suffering from a nervous breakdown. Certain ones of her neighbors, more calloused than others, were of the opinion that it served her right.

The search through woods, abandoned cars, and buildings was called off. For a week or so, fishermen patrolled surrounding waters, keeping eyes open for floating bodies. The Coast Guard searched the tidal shores of islands, finding nothing.

On the day they searched Whistle Island, Caroline was ready for them. She heard the engine of the picket boat, saw it tie up to the float and watched the coastguardsmen getting out. She took Jakie up to the turret room for his nap. She had already fixed a cot for him and a bed for Walter, who was delighted to have a bed of his own.

They all stayed quietly in the turret room playing with the horrid, funny-looking African masks from the third-floor room, where they usually lived on the wall. Jakie loved them—they reminded him of Halloween. He found that one of them would fit on Walter's head, and Walter didn't seem to mind having it there, but he looked so dreadful and funny, like some awful nightmare animal, that Jakie began to scream laughing and Caroline had to take the mask off quickly in case some of those men might hear. Then, after a while, both Jakie and Walter took their naps.

While they slept, Caroline watched, standing well back from the turret-room window. A few lobster boats went by, heading home; she could see the closed-up summer cottages along the eastern shore of the mainland, the people all gone back to the cities now. Above the trees on the Point, she could see the roof and attic windows of Miss Susie's tall house where it stood on its hill.

Someday, when I'm big enough to fight off Gramma

Pollard and can take Jakie back to Mama's house, she told herself, I'll go to see Miss Susie. I'll give her back her dollar and sixty cents and say I'm sorry I spoilt her flower bed. I expect she's still awful mad at me.

The men were gone a long time. Finally, she heard them coming back along the shore. She held her breath. Of course they must be looking for her and Jakie—would they come in and search the house? But they went on, down to the float. The picket boat cast off and roared away.

After that, for a time, nobody came.

Things were different, living on the island, harder than Caroline had thought they'd be. Watching, every minute, was the worst. She hadn't realized before how Jakie would be everywhere over the place like a butterfly, with Walter at his heels. She had to keep an eye on them all day long to make sure they didn't go down on the beach or the float, where they could be seen. Jakie loved the beach and the float. Froggy'd always let him fish for flounders off the float at high tide; Jakie couldn't see why he couldn't do it now. He didn't care if lobster boats went by there at almost any hour of the day. He was a little terror and very smart about waiting till he saw she wasn't looking, and then he'd be off and away.

She tried tying him to a piazza post on the end of a long clothesline, with plenty of room to play. Jakie sat down and bellered till anyone over on the mainland could have heard him. Then she tried tying up Walter, because Jakie stayed around where Walter was. Jakie picked out the knot and before she knew it, they were headed for the float, she after them as fast as she could run.

She found places in the deep woods toward the middle of the island where they could go and play and not be seen. For a while, she got Jakie interested in building a brush camp, the way she'd learned how in the Camp Fire Girls.

"A lovely playhouse," she told him, "and every bit of it is yours, only you and Walter have got to stay here and help me build it." Then she wished she hadn't said that, because the idea of being told he had to do something didn't sit well with Jakie. It did with Walter, though. Walter loved any sheltered place. She and Jakie hauled load after load of nice dry leaves into the brush camp, spreading them deep and soft on the floor, for Walter— and sometimes, Jakie—a place to take naps.

Along toward the last, when she had the playhouse almost done, she looked up one day from where she was putting spruce boughs on the roof and saw that Jakie and Walter were gone.

She had hauled Jakie over from the house in his express wagon and had left the wagon in the bushes alongside the path. Mr. Wiggling Biscuits' paths were just the right width for Jakie's wagon. The ones through the woods were great to take walks on; she had to be careful, of course, about using the one along the shore. Not many people came to the island because of the NO TRESPASSING, NO HUNTING signs, and the big ones that said WILD GAME AND BIRD SANCTUARY. Froggy always had to go around and check the signs every fall when the hunting season began in November, and of course it was November now. Once, when he'd taken her with him, they'd found a lot of the signs torn down or gone altogether. Froggy'd been good and mad.

"There's always some jerks," he'd said, "who'd tromp on anything or anybody if they thought there was a deer to shoot." He'd shown them the deer in North Meadow, nibbling twigs and not moving even when she and Froggy came close. "Nobody bothers them all summer," he'd said. "They don't get scared of people. Those jerks might just as well shoot somebody's cow."

Now, tearing as fast as she could run back to the path where she'd left the wagon, Caroline wasn't thinking about that. She was trying to guess where those two darn scamps would go, once they'd got away from her. Down to the water, of course. The path, here, went all the way to the shore on the east side of the island. There was a sand beach down there, which Jakie knew about and would remember. He never forgot any place where he'd had a good time. They'd gone there often with Froggy and the Wiggling Biscuits. Now, they used one end of it as the only place they could go and not be seen from the water.

Where the sand beach stopped and became ledges, a high point covered with trees curled out and around in a hook, making a hidden cove. The cove was sheltered, on a sunny day now, warm as summer. Its floor was clean white sand. In the ledges were caves to hide in and wiggle through, with stones and shells to play with and big piles of driftwood to hunt through and find interesting things left by the tide.

At low tide, they could dig clams and pick mussels. Caroline always took along a clam hoe and a bucket to fill. Clams and mussels tasted good after all that bread and butter and meat; they helped to feed Walter, too. His appetite was something awful; it would have made a big hole in the groceries if Caroline hadn't remembered clams and mussels and found out that Walter loved them. All she had to do was boil and cool them and put them down. He would pick his own out of the half-open shells.

That beach was surely where they'd be headed for; but Jakie wouldn't know enough to keep down if a boat came by. Caroline raced along the path, hauling the jangling wagon behind her. And there they were. She caught up with them just before they got to the four-foot bank of sand and driftwood, topped with a hedge of frost-bitten beach peas at the edge of the beach.

"Jakie! Come here! You know you've got to be—" She stopped, gasped, and ducked down. This end of the beach was open to the ocean; she was always careful coming along here because lobster fishermen hauled traps outside the ledges on almost any good day, and there was one there now. Only this one was anchored off the beach and four men with guns were getting out of a dinghy on the shore.

Caroline crawled the rest of the way, grabbed Jakie by the back of his shirt. He opened his mouth to beller, but she clapped her hand over it, good and hard. "Jakie, if you cry, I'll put a clam worm in your mouth!" she whispered fiercely in his ear.

It was the worst thing she could think of. Clam worms came out of the flats and were creeping and slimy. She'd tried everything. She'd told him once that big animals in the woods would get him if he ran away, but he'd already seen the big animal that came out of the woods and he loved it. This was awful, though. Tears came into his eyes, but he clamped his mouth shut, even when she took her hand away.

She put him in the wagon flat on his back. "Stay down, Jakie," she warned, and crept along the path pulling him behind her until they were out of sight behind the trees. She looked around for Walter; he was bounding along ahead. As she looked, he made a great leap into the underbrush and went out of sight. Then she got up and ran.

When she got back to the house, Walter wasn't there. She shoved the wagon out of sight under the front steps, took one wild look around before she rushed Jakie into the kitchen and locked the door. No Walter anywhere. Oh, why hadn't he come home with them?

Walter, peering through the beach peas, had seen the same sight Caroline had. He had reason to remember men with guns. Terror-stricken, he raced for cover in the underbrush, driving through it to the playhouse, where he lay down on the leafy floor, panting and shivering. But he could hear the men's voices as they walked along the path. They could find him here; they could get in. He raced off into the deep woods, the thickest he could find. There he climbed into a tall tree, rasping his way up through the prickly boughs nearly to the top. Now that his claws had grown out, he could climb faster and more easily. He sat there waiting for the sound of the dogs which would surely come.

Caroline, behind the locked door of the turret room, finally managed to get Jakie to sleep. She had a time with him. He didn't beller. He kept his mouth tight closed, but tears ran down his cheeks. He kept looking at her and pointing to Walter's bed. She didn't dare to comfort him too much; once he got over the clam worm, he would surely let go with all his lung power; but at last she said, "I can't leave you to go down and let Walter in until you go to sleep," and that did it. He lay down, quiet as a mouse. He'd sleep for an hour or so, she knew. He always did.

She was so tired herself that she didn't know how in the world she could do anything but lie down and rest. She felt jumpy all over, her skin felt wiggly. She was really scared for Walter. She couldn't help remembering the time, back in the town, when Pomroy Fifield had seen the big cat in the woods. He'd been out, one winter, cutting cedar posts. He'd said it was either a lynx or a panther. First, he'd said he'd only got a glimpse of it; then it had dropped out of a tree right 'longside of him; the third time he'd told the story, it had dropped right on his back. Most people didn't believe a word he said. Then another man saw some tracks in the snow, and Bessie Updike, who was fourteen, came home one night from the movies with her dress ripped. She'd told her mother that a big cat had jumped out of the bushes at her. Her mother got out of her later that her boy friend had torn the dress, but the story went all over town how Bessie Updike had had her clothes ripped right off her back by a panther.

Pomroy Fifield had come to the school and made a speech to the schoolchildren. Nobody must go out after dark, he said. That Thing was a dangerous animal. Everybody was scared to death until a mess of men went out into the woods and tracked it down and shot it. It had turned out to be a sick old bobcat that had already been shot once and bitten all over by dogs. It only weighed about twenty pounds, and everybody knew it was a bobcat; but there were still people around now who'd tell about the time the panther came down out of the mountains.

Caroline knew what would happen to Walter if those men with guns, out in the woods now, got a sight of him—the same thing all over again. And if they didn't shoot him today, they'd carry back word about a big cat, a panther, over on Whistle Island, so that until someone did shoot him, the woods would be full of men with guns, all ha-ho together because they had something to kill.

She got her arm out from under Jakie's head without waking him and tiptoed down the stairs to the second story, where the windows weren't shuttered and she could see out. She went from room to room, looking. Both yards, front and back, were empty. From the front room she could see a little way along the path, but that was empty, too. Walter might be down at the door waiting to be let in, though. She didn't know how she would ever dare to open it. Those men, by now, might be over here, right around the house.

Still, if he were there, he'd be scratching and crying. She could listen. If she heard him, she could open the door *snip!* and *snip!* shut it again. They'd shoot him anyway, even if they saw him on the back porch. She went downstairs, stood with her ear right up to the keyhole of the back door. She couldn't hear Walter, but from quite far away in the woods, she heard four shots, quick, one after the other.

She started to cry, and then as the tears began to come hot down her cheeks, she was furious.

I won't have it! I won't stand for it. I won't let them shoot Walter. If they have, I'll sink their boat, I'll *kill* them!

She took the short length of clothesline with the loop in one end of it which she used for a leash for Walter. In her pocket, she put four slices of the meat she was saving for supper. She let herself out of the back door, quietly closing it, putting the key deep in her dungarees pocket. Then she ran for the woods as fast as she could go.

As she ran, she heard two more shots off toward the north end of the island. That was where North Meadow was, where Froggy had shown them the deer last summer. He'd said then that the north end of the island was where the deer usually hung out. If those men were over there, she was lucky and so was Walter, because he'd run in the other direction, toward the playhouse. Maybe she'd find him in there, hiding in the place where he was used to being safe.

She ran fast, looking ahead along the path, ready to duck if she saw anybody. Walter wasn't in the playhouse. She didn't know where next to look.

She had to drop down for a moment to catch her breath. Or to get it back from where it had gone; she didn't have any left.

I have got to think. I can't just run around in the woods, I'd never find him. I have to think where he would go.

But the first thought that came to her was an awful one. Walter was tame; he was used to people.

He came right to Jakie and me the night we got here. What if he followed those men, friendly, the way he is?

The thought was so awful that she couldn't stand it. She put back her head and hollered, using up what breath she had in one good loud yell. "WALTER! COME HERE!"

He didn't come, and she couldn't hear a sound.

I s'pose they've heard me. And Jakie and I'll have to go back. But I would rather, than have anything happen to Walter.

The tears began again, and this time she couldn't stop them.

I'll have to holler again if he doesn't come. Maybe we could run fast enough, before they get here.

Walter's tree wasn't too far away, and he had heard her.

It had taken him a while to come down. He came loping through the underbrush and landed plop in Caroline's lap.

She pushed the loop of the leash through under his collar, tucked the free end through, and took off for the path. Walter, who felt safer now and better, smelled the meat in her pocket and had room in his head for thoughts of supper. Besides, he liked a good run. They made it to the back porch of the house and tore up the steps.

As Caroline fumbled in her pocket for the door key, she heard Jakie laugh, the kind of laugh that always sounded as if he were happier at this one, certain, single moment than he had ever been before in his life.

Froggy, in sadness, hauled the Fosters' skiff into the boathouse, padlocked the door, and left it. He'd never use that boat again, he told himself, he didn't think he could bear to. If he hadn't been so damn lazy, and had hauled it up for the winter when he should have, instead of keeping it tied off the float because it was handy to use . . . if he hadn't showed Caroline how to run the outboard . . . if Aunt Yuba'd asked him to take the kids instead of Lydia Pollard. . . . Froggy brooded, blaming himself.

Why hadn't someone mentioned to him that Lydia was abusing the kids? He hadn't known. For a while, everybody'd said weren't they lucky, going to Lydia. She had all that money.

Hurt and bewildered as well as grief-stricken, Froggy kept asking himself, Why didn't Caroline come to me if things were so tough she had to run away? She must've known I'd have helped. Ma should have known about it; she kept in touch with all the talk going around town. She never said a word to me. Why?

He put off going over to the island to do the last of his chores in closing up the place for the winter. He'd got the shutters on earlier, but he still had to tow the float and gangway over to Cat Cove. The job had to be done on a high-run tide. He let a high-run tide go right by.

Sometime soon he'd have to start up the power plant, generate enough juice to keep the house warmed up and the pipes from freezing when the cold weather came. Everything was still running out there. The deepfreeze—well, he couldn't disconnect that with all that stuff in it, and no key. Damn that Marie, what had she done with the key?

He knew he ought to go, but the place would remind him of Caroline and Jakie. God, he'd loved those kids. And now they were dead, and mostly on account of him.

His mother, Flo, was worried about him. She told the neighbors she was. She, herself, of course, had been flattened right out flat when she'd heard that awful news— she'd thought she'd drop down dead, then and there, but Time healed all.

She worried more about the possibility of Fred's losing his good job. That old count was nice to work for, but he was fussy. Suppose someone who wanted Fred's job— and she guessed she knew of several who wouldn't look sideways at the rocking-chair money—well, suppose some one of them men took it into his head to write the old geezer and say, I see your float and gangway out at the island ain't been hauled up yet and I wonder if Fred Montgomery's still working for you. If he ain't, would you let me have the job?

Once them summer people found out they couldn't trust you, look out. There went your job with the breeze.

Flo didn't consider herself a nagger. She wouldn't keep after Fred about anything, only drop hints—of course it wasn't the same. She'd only say, "I see there's a high-run tide this week," or, "My, look at it rain! I hope this wind ain't took any shingles off of the Whistle Island house, don't you?"

One day she thought of something that might just possibly get Fred moving. She said, "Oh, I almost forgot, Fred. Susie Warren called. She wants to go out to the island with you when you go."

Susie Warren hadn't called, but, times back, she had, when she'd wanted to go to Whistle Island, bird watching. Before Miranda Cooley died, when Susie hadn't had a nickel to rub together, Flo certainly wouldn't have thought much of *that;* she and old Miranda had worked hard to bust Fred and Susie up and had had a good success. But circumstances altered cases; now Susie had that big house and all that money. Thinking about things, Flo had decided she might just kill two birds with one stone.

Fred had come in to his dinner and had sat down, looking at it without lifting a fork. Her good fish-and-potatoes and squash and apple pie. It was enough to drive a woman crazy. And it seemed as if he hadn't heard one word she'd said.

He said, "Lydia's got over her nervous breakdown."

"Land sake, she has? She was in bed carrying on and bawling, last I heard."

"She was in Bolton's half an hour ago, buying new curtains for her bathroom. Raised the roof because they didn't have anything good enough."

"Who was the clerk?" Flo asked, interested.

"Old Miss Sadie Bolton. She dunned me for a payment on a new living-room set. You know anything about that?"

"Sadie say anything back to Lydia?"

"Told her to go suck her toe."

Flo's jaw dropped. "Told Lydia that? My Lord in heaven!" Flo savored this, for a moment, along with a mouthful of squash. "Well, Lydia's stock's fell low in this town, I must say. Of course, everybody knows now how she treated them two yow'uns of Yuba's. She only wanted them, anyhow, to show everyone how she'd got her own way. Never cared a hoot about them, any more than—"

"Than you did or I did," Fred said. "Than Yuba did. Or one of us would've done something."

"Freddy, don't talk so. You know we couldn't afford to take Yuba's children. I told her when she asked me that we just didn't have the money unless she paid board, which, of course, she couldn't do, and—"

Fred shoved back his chair. He had turned a funny shade in the face, it almost seemed to Flo, green. "You mean," he said, and choked a little, "you mean Aunt Yuba asked you and you said no? And never even mentioned it to me?"

"Freddy, dear, what else could I have done? You know—"

"Goddammit, I know we could have shoved over somehow! So you"—his voice rose to a shout—"so you ordered a new living-room set from Bolton's!"

"Fred! Don't you dare to yell at me like that! I've saved for that living-room set for—"

"Saved, hell! You didn't even give Bolton's the down payment!"

The only way, when he got huffered up like this, was to swamp him with talk. "It wasn't my business, it was Yuba's entirely, all she talked about was how much better off they'd be with Lydia, and be left her money when Lydia passes on. Lydia promised to take out adoption papers with Yuba's consent, you know that, don't you? There's been talk, let me tell you, about Yuba because she never come home when she heard about the kids, only wrote. I know why. She never intended to come back here, she told me so."

"She told you that?" Fred's voice was quiet, but his face was still green.

"Why, why would she? The kids was well taken care of and Henry Fling didn't want them."

Fred pushed back his chair and got up. He made for the door, grabbing his hat as he went. "They're well taken care of, all right," he said.

"Fred, you come back here and eat your dinner. Where you going?"

He didn't stop or say.

Fred made for the town pier and rowed off to his boat. That was one place he could be alone, away from that yak. He'd head off somewhere for a while, he didn't know where. He had a goddamned good mind to go for good.

My God, Aunt Yuba and Ma! And telling him that now.

He opened the throttle of his big engine wide and roared down the harbor.

Flo, peering out of the window that overlooked the harbor, saw him go. 'N there! All you had to do was nudge! a little, once in a while. She hustled to the telephone and called up Susie Warren.

"Susie? Freddy's headed for the island this afternoon. He wondered if you'd like to go too. You be out in your skiff, because he's in some tearing old hurry to catch the high tide, and he likely won't stop unless you flag him down." And, good mother that she was, she added, "Oh, and I'm ashamed of myself for not reminding him, but he's gone off and left his lunchbox right here on the table. If you could take something—"

"Fine," Susie said. "I've got a ham. Thanks, Flo."

Well, Flo thought, if he takes her along, he'll have to come back tonight.

She set about putting away the untouched food while she had a private daydream. What if Susie's still after Freddy? Of course, she's kind of a nut, but, my Lord, all that money, he could do worse. The dream ended with Susie being put away in an insane asylum and Flo living with Freddy, just as she was now. We could paint the house, get all new carpets. And have a new car. And pay cash for that living-room set . . .

Fred, barreling down the harbor, hardly noticed Susie Warren's skiff. He was nearly past when he saw the skiff was anchored and she was in it, waving frantically at him.

Hell! Outboard's probably conked out and no oars. Women! They ought to stay out of boats if they didn't know enough to take along the equipment they might need. I'll bet ten dollars she hasn't even got a jug of water.

He slowed down, came around in a circle, and stopped alongside. He was astonished when she handed up a heavy lunch basket and scrabbled in over the gunnel of his boat.

"Hi," she said. "This is darn nice of you, Fred. Don't let me hold you up. Your mother said you were in a hurry to catch the tide."

Ma. She'd called Susie up. Blast and damn! But what could he do now without sounding like a gump? He said, "That's okay, Susie," and shoved his throttle ahead, this time not quite so far as it would go.

He might as well go out to the island, get the work done. It had to be done sometime, and the tide would serve just about right a little later on. Susie wouldn't be any bother to him—when she'd gone before, she'd always taken off into the woods with her bird glasses, and she never kept a man waiting when it was time to go home. He glanced back at her and saw she'd taken up roost on an empty trawl tub and was building sandwiches out of stuff she'd got out of her basket—good hefty slices off a big, pink ham and a whole loaf of bread.

She caught his glance and grinned, holding up a jar of mustard inquiringly—did he want some on his sandwich? Nobody could hear any talk, on account of the engine, and he nodded. Darned if that ham didn't look good!

She came up behind him with a loaded paper plate— two big ham sandwiches, cold boiled eggs wrapped in foil, a big hunk of chocolate cake. "More if you want it," she said in his ear, and put the lunch on the pilot shelter shelf in front of him. "That's instant coffee in the thermos. I hope you like it, it's all I had time to make."

One thing, he thought with relief, as she made her way aft without saying any more, she don't talk your ear off, she never had.

He ate all the lunch, drank the coffee, felt better. Even going out to the island didn't seem so awful now. He guessed it was because someone was along. Out there alone, that was what he hadn't been able to face. He'd hear those kids' voices everywhere he went. He'd hear Jakie laugh.

Them flapperjaws around town can blister their tongues about Susie all they want to, he thought. He could hear his mother now. "Oh, she walks around. Plants seeds. Watches birds. You know how she is."

Yes, I do know how she is. How she is, is like a good apple. With her along, it would be like having good sense and decency and a friend walking beside you. That's what it would be like.

Susie would have enjoyed talking with Fred. But when you went out with a fisherman in his boat, he stood back-to, steering; you sat on the trawl tub or the bait barrel and didn't talk; that was the custom. She was glad she'd got a grin out of him. He looked so peaked and unhappy, as if he'd been sick. She knew why, and she could guess why he was so grim as the island came closer and the turreted roof of the big house began to show through the trees. Watching him, she began to doubt the wisdom of keeping what she knew to herself.

So far, she had kept her counsel. She had let the search go on without opening her mouth to tell anyone. And if anyone found that out, she dreaded to think what people would say about her then. She had not gone out to the island, because she'd found a way to make sure the children were there still, and safe. From the narrow attic window of her house, she could see out over the peninsula trees and almost into the front yard of the Wigheln-Bisschner cottage. With powerful binoculars, she had been able to make out the small moving figures that must be Caroline and Jakie, and a third speck which looked like a big dog. She'd worried over whether they were getting enough to eat and where food for a dog that size could come from. She didn't worry over their being able to keep warm. The whole town had talked for years about the old count's extravagance, heating that big house all winter. So long as she could check every day, see them running around over there all right, Susie would keep still. If Caroline had an emergency, such as a hurt, or sickness, she could easily flag down a lobster boat as it went by the pier.

When real winter came and the thing got really impossible, she'd have to tell Fred, and she'd planned to. He would have to help her get the children away somewhere, out of Lydia's clutches. It might not be too hard a job—everybody, including their mother, thought they were dead. It would be kidnapping, of course, and where she'd take them she didn't know. But she was not going to have a hand in returning them to Lydia.

Now, seeing Fred's face, she suddenly felt awful, guilty all over. He was obviously eating his heart out, and had been.

I wish I dared tell him. But there must have been some reason why Caroline didn't, and I can't. Not until I know more. Fred's terribly law-abiding, maybe she knew he'd make her go back. Perhaps I could find Caroline today, talk to her and find out.

Fred tied up the boat, helped her out on the float, but he made no move to go anywhere. He only stood staring bleakly up the path that led to the house. "I've got to go up there, start up the power plant, generate some juice," he said at last. "I can leave the engine running while I tow the float around. Then I'll come back and cut it off, and that's when I'll be ready to go."

"Can I help?"

He shook his head.

"Well, I've brought my camera and my bird glasses—they're in the basket with the lunch, if you'll hand it to me," she said. And that's a bald-faced lie, she told herself cheerfully. What made the basket so heavy was food—the remains of the ham and chocolate cake, loaves of bread, cans of soup and evaporated milk, tucked in and hidden under a big linen dinner napkin. There was, also, in the bottom, a small-sized pair of woolen mittens.

"You ain't going to lug that far," Fred said as he hefted the basket onto the float.

"No, I don't plan to. My camera's the heavy thing. I'm going to take some pictures of . . . of the house. Of course, there's the ham. And I've probably brought more

[*156*]

film than I need to . . ." I'm burbling, she thought. She stopped and smiled at him.

Fred didn't smile back. He said, "I guess I'd better go start up the generator," and still didn't move.

He doesn't want to go up there alone. I have got to tell him, she thought. I can't let misery like this go on any longer . . . but wait. Those kids are somewhere around. Hidden, I expect. They must have heard the boat come in. Maybe he'll see them. Living here, they've got to leave some signs around.

"Can't I come along? I'd love to see the power plant," she said, and started up the path ahead of him.

No sign of anyone around the house. Not a track, not a trace of the litter, sticks, stones, seashells, that children playing usually left around. The place was just a closed-up summer cottage, its lower windows shuttered, its upstairs windows reflecting trees and sky.

The dog, Susie thought desperately. Maybe they won't be able to keep the dog quiet.

Yes! There in a damp spot on the path, in mud that was partly dried and cracked, was the print of a small sneaker. Susie saw it, stepped over it, waited hopefully. But Fred came on behind her, and, glancing back, she saw that he was staring straight ahead. His eyes looked blank and unfocused; he had put his big rubber boot squarely on the footprint. Not a trace of it was left.

"We better go round by the front," Fred said. "Grass ain't been cut out back. Here, let me go ahead. I'll show—"

From somewhere above their heads, for all anyone could tell out of the sky, Jakie laughed.

Fred said, "Oh, my God!" He turned white as paper, his knees bent under him and he folded quietly to the lawn, fainted dead away.

PART SEVEN

Harold

THE MACOMBER *SAILED* northeasterly, into changing weather. Off Montauk, she ran into a blow which lasted a day and a half, with head winds and chilly, driving rain. It was not a bad blow for November, but the seas were steep; sailing against the wind she was an uncomfortable ship, hard on the wheel and logy. Brown, after a full day of beating back and forth and making little headway, was disgusted.

"This isn't getting us anywhere," he told Lewis. "I'm going to haul down sails and start the auxiliary."

He seemed nervous and jumpy and, Lewis thought, with reason. Brown had been at the wheel for most of the day, refusing to let even Coon relieve him. He had a right to be tired. He was bad-tempered, too, which wasn't like him.

"Goddammit, what are you, scared or seasick?" he snapped at Coon, when, earlier, Coon had suggested longer reaches offshore.

"Haven't any cause to be scared," Coon said reasonably. "And I haven't been seasick since I was ten."

"Poor old Adam's laid out again," Lewis said. "And I haven't seen Harold on deck for quite a spell."

"You leave Hal out of it," Jasper said. "I know you

don't like him, but you don't have to downgrade him all the time."

Lewis let it go by. "Well, Jasper," he said, "you know sailing ships, but I've had considerable experience with November blows, and this one isn't bad enough for a man to wear himself out over. Why not hand over to Coon and you get some rest?"

He got no answer to that, but shortly after Brown got the sails down and the engine started, he put Coon on the wheel and disappeared into his cabin.

For six hours the *Macomber* thumped along under bare poles. She made a little headway against the wind, but she obviously needed the balance and equilibrium lost when her sails came down. She spanked out a thunderous white wave on either side of her bow, occasionally shoving her nose deep into a big one which came over green on the deck. But at suppertime, when Lewis walked aft with a can of hot soup for Adam, in case Adam felt like eating, he caught a brief glimpse of the moon before it plunged out of sight into the clouds.

Clearing weather, thank God, he thought. We'd better have some before this old tub flies apart. "Excuse me," he said aloud to the *Lizzie Macomber*. "But you are acting like one, you know."

He got no answer, nor did he expect any. Adam would have known what it was. "You should have seen me, before plain damn fools made a logy old tub out of me."

Amanda took her supper down to eat with Andy in his stateroom. He was feeling himself again except for a kind of vertigo which bothered him at times; tonight, the *Macomber*'s antics had been too much for him, and he had not come up to eat. He was in his and Belle's cabin with the door bolted; it was a moment before he answered her knock.

"How're you feeling?" she asked. "Hungry? This looks good."

"I hope you don't think I'm seasick," Andy said. He bolted the door behind her and went back to his bunk, where he had been propped up on pillows, reading.

"Of course not," Amanda said. "You're getting over food poisoning."

"The hell I am," Andy said. "What have you got there, anything besides the slops Belle's been choking me with?"

"Steak," Amanda said. "Jilly sent it, with his regards."

"Filet mignon," Andy said. "Thank God!" He picked up knife and fork. "Begin, please, Amanda, so I can. I'm starving to death. Who says I had food poisoning?"

"Didn't you?" Amanda said. "I thought Belle said—"

"I'm glad she thinks so. She ought to know better." Andy took a bite, chewed, and swallowed. "Yum!" he said. "That's something like. I think she does know better. She just doesn't think I do."

"But, Andy, what, then?" Amanda asked. "You were awfully . . . well, sick."

Andy went on eating, in silence. At last he said, "Angleworms." He blinked and shook his head a little. "I still have 'em, sometimes."

Amanda choked. For a moment, she had a horrid picture.

"Not real ones," Andy said. "Look, Amanda. A fellow doesn't go absolutely off his nut from food poisoning. And rave and smash and yell and then not remember it. I remember yelling but not a thing about busting my guitar." He stopped, then went on mournfully, "I don't see how I could have, not that one. The first really good one I ever had."

"There'll be another," Amanda said. "Of course there will, Andy."

"Don't be an old false comforter," Andy said. "I liked that one."

"All right," Amanda said meekly. "Will you want to give me any more lessons now?"

"And don't be a child," Andy said. "Of course I will.

We'll use one of the band guitars. Joe Richards' wasn't hurt when we piled up the band, and it's a very good instrument. We'll begin again, just as soon as sounds stop hurting my head."

"Does your head still hurt?"

"I've just told you it does." Andy finished his supper and set the tray carefully on the deck, where it rattled. He tossed a pillow over it. "See? Angleworms. Hurt my head. It won't last, fortunately. Now, look, Amanda. If you won't tell, I'll tell you what it is. I don't want Belle to know I know. She's worried enough already."

"Of course I won't tell."

"Promise? Okay, then. I freaked out."

Amanda stared at him, horrified. Anybody at school had known what that meant. "Andy! How could you . . . !"

"I couldn't. Not by myself. Did you ever see me be a fool? It was in a bottle of Coke Hal had. He gave it to me. Now, Amanda. Don't ever touch one single thing he gives you, and don't let Adam. I think Lover Boy takes it himself. He's just like Rodney Miller, the fellow that was killed in the van wreck. He acts just the same. Rod used to tell me what he saw, he said it was pretty. Wouldn't I like to see long colored angleworms? he said. I said no, I wouldn't. Be like Rod? No, sir! Besides, I have to take care of Belle."

"Andy, how awful, I could scream . . . !"

"No, don't. You'll bust my head wide open."

"I won't. But whatever would anyone do such a dirty mean trick for?"

"I made remarks. About his guitar playing. He *is* awful. Just thumps. I told him to get a ukulele, it wouldn't sound so loud. I guess he wanted to see me ground down small. Well, I was," Andy said. "I was ground down pretty small. I think I'll go to sleep, now, Amanda. You surely won't tell?"

"No," Amanda said. "I'd like to kill him, but I won't tell."

"Don't worry," Andy said. "I'll tend to it."

Amanda gathered up the two trays as quietly as she could.

"Don't drop one, for godsake," Andy said, wincing.

"No. They'll be easier to carry now than they were coming down," Amanda said. "We aren't bouncing around the way we were this afternoon. I think it must be clearing off."

Andy didn't answer. She saw he had buried his head in a pillow, but as she left, he said drowsily, "Tell Jilly that was the best steak I ever had."

As she passed Harold's stateroom, he opened the door and put his head out. "Ah," he said. "The little mother. Kid feeling better, is he?"

"Oh, yes," Amanda said. "Are you?" She went on without waiting for an answer, feeling her blood curdle at the sight of him.

Harold watched her out of sight. If there was anything that really got his goat, it was a fresh kid. It might please them all to know he hadn't been seasick in his stateroom, just lying in his bunk making plans. Wouldn't hurt to remind the Bronson dame's kid that he, Harold, didn't care for smart cracks, either.

He tiptoed along the passageway to Belle's stateroom and tried the door. As usual, it was bolted on the inside. Harold got down on his knees and blew loudly through the keyhole. He could hear a slight movement from the inside. Heard it, did he? Harold took a deep breath and blew again. A gust of some kind of foul-smelling spray shot back through the keyhole into his mouth, covering his throat and the front of his shirt. It began instantly to sting, and tasted horrible—my God, what was it? Insecticide? If it was, it was deadly poison, get rid of it fast.

Harold plunged into his cabin, headed for the bathroom and some soap and water. He barely made it before he threw up. No matter how much he scrubbed and gargled, he couldn't get rid of the smell. And that taste!

Why, that murdering little devil! he thought. Or maybe Bronson herself had done it. What if it had got into his eyes?

No, must have been the kid. Here came Bronson along the passageway with Wyman, he could hear their voices.

In growing rage, Harold soaped and rinsed one more time. He thought, after a while, that he'd got rid of most of it, but his anger hadn't cooled off any. Play tricks on him, would they?

Well, he had his plans about perfected. He'd thought he wouldn't start anything quite so soon, but why not? Might as well get it over, and he could see out his porthole that the weather was clearing.

Coon, coming away from the wheel, worked his shoulders inside his jacket, trying to get the ache out of his muscles. The old *Lizzie* had sure given him a workout this time. With clearing, the wind had come around southwesterly, with a squall that had practically spun her out of the water; a couple of times, she'd felt as if she actually had bounced clear of it. She was all right now—fair wind, back on her proper heading. The seas were still high, but nothing Fairleigh couldn't handle. Coon was tired; he thought yearningly of his bunk, but first he wanted to go check on his father. He'd thought the old man would have come on deck the moment the auxiliary stopped—he always kept an ear peeled for changes; but he hadn't shown up. Of course, he'd got himself worn out, which he wasn't supposed to do, and that bad temper hadn't been a good sign either. Concerned, and not thinking of anything else, Coon walked around the corner of the afterhouse. Someone running and solid as a rock slammed full tilt into him.

"What the hell!" Coon gasped. His wind was knocked out, and in the shadow of the house he could see only shadow. The fellow didn't move or say anything. He put both hands against Coon's chest and gave him a powerful, running shove.

It might have been ten feet to the vessel's rail. Coon, heels skidding, off balance, felt himself rushed backward toward it. His whole body recoiled, arching up and away from the rail, as he realized what was happening. He reacted automatically—he had no time to think. He let himself go limp and drop flat to the deck. The fellow—no need to guess who it was—went plunging across him. A punkin-hollow sound indicated that he had bumped his head.

"Not this time, either, damn you," Coon said. He got to his feet, stood braced against the wall of the cabin. "I hope that cracked your goddamned skull. Hang on, or you'll go overboard yourself. I hope you do."

Limping, because he had taken an almost crippling fall, Coon went along the deck to the door of Jasper's cabin. He stopped there, his hand on the latch.

The moon had at last broken through the clouds and shone now with a cold glitter on the long, empty stretch of humped-up rollers to the horizon, on the foam-patched curled wave flaring back from the *Macomber*'s hull. Coon turned cold as he looked. He had no wish to die in the icy waters of the Atlantic Ocean. Though, he thought, it might not be much lonesomer than the spot I'm in now.

He had come close. Closer than he had last summer, when Hal had picked up the foot of the ladder he'd been on and had walked away with it. Another one of Hal's playful tricks, and you couldn't convince Jasper Brown it was anything else, or that the guy was off his rocker. And it didn't take dope, either, to put him there.

If you did anything drastic, it would just about kill the old man.

But that's twice, Coon told himself. And I've had it.

He left the door to Jasper's stateroom, walked for'ard to his own quarters. In the bottom of his valise, neatly boxed for concealment and to keep oil off his clothing, was his revolver. He had got it last summer, more for protection than for anything else—the sight of a gun in his hand, he knew, would scare Hal into a fit. The bugger was a coward, the kind who hit when you couldn't hit back. He slid the gun into his pocket, rummaged out a small flashlight. From now on, he wouldn't be without either one.

He went back to Jasper's cabin, paused with his hand on the door, hearing voices inside. Hal? Getting a good story in first? No, Cap'n Wyman. Maybe he ought to tell Cap'n Wyman a few things. He almost had, a few nights ago, when he'd let Wyman think the dark in the east was what he was scared of.

No. Better not. It wasn't far to St. Andrews now, three or four days, maybe, less if the weather held. Wyman might go straight to Jasper, demand, the way he already had once, to be set ashore here and now. And Coon had sworn he'd see Jasper got to St. Andrews and his girl. He opened the door and went in.

Lewis had been going to bed when the squall struck. The deck had tilted under his feet; he heard a crash and clatter as the booms slammed over and a thunder of flapping canvas.

Blast and damn a sailing ship! Up sails, down sails, change of wind, change course, change back again. He struggled into his jacket and went on deck.

The wind, having boxed the compass, was back southwesterly, fair for the needed course. Coon and Fairleigh had had things under control. The hoisting engine was already started, and the big foresail broke out and creaked aloft as Lewis watched. He went aft, set the new heading, and then, feeling useless, started back for his stateroom, longing for the comfortable hum of diesels under his feet, the solid thud-and-return of pistons.

As he'd passed the starboard cabin windows, he'd seen that Brown was up. The old boy couldn't be as worn out as he'd seemed. The gimbaled lamp over his table was lit, and he was sitting back-to within its rectangle of light. Lewis hesitated a moment and then knocked and went in.

"Hello," Lewis said. "Get some rest, did you?"

Brown said thickly, "To hell with you, Wyman. Clear out."

Astonished, Lewis stared at him. Good Lord, he thought. Is he drunk?

There was no smell of liquor in the cabin. He could not see Brown's face, which was bent over a heavy, paper-bound book on his table. Stepping closer, Lewis saw that the book was a mail-order-house catalog. As he watched, the old man lifted a hand to his lips, wetted a finger, and turned a page. He was looking at women's dresses.

"Jasper," Lewis said sharply. "What's the matter?"

Brown started slightly and raised his head.

Lewis stopped in his tracks, shocked and appalled at the change in the man since afternoon. His face, cream-white under its tan, appeared to have fallen in. He sat, lax in his chair, sagging as if he could no longer command his muscles to hold him up.

"Jasper, what's happened?"

Brown mumbled something. He fumbled with the drawer of his desk, trying to pull it open. What he had said, as near as Lewis could make it out, was, "Three, four hundred miles."

"What is it you want? Let me help you, there," Lewis said.

But Jasper had the drawer open. What he'd wanted was a candy bar, which, after a couple of tries, he thrust into his mouth and started to chew, wrapping and all.

From the door Coon shot by Lewis in a rush. "Don't swallow that foil, it'll poison you!" he said, and wrenched the bar out of Jasper's mouth. "Here, have it now." He handed it back, minus the foil. "Easy does it. You'll be okay in a minute, and then I'll help you turn in."

Jasper sat blinking, looking from Coon to Lewis. After a silence, he said, "Thanks," in a clear and normal voice. "For a minute, there, I didn't see how I could manage it alone. Got too tired, I guess."

"I'll say you did." Coon had the top drawer open, looking sharply in. "You didn't take your shot this morning," he said.

"Now, Coon, boy, stop fussing. Of course I did."

"Here it is, full hypo, just the way I fixed it for you," Coon said. "How come?"

Jasper grinned at him. Some color had come back into his face, and his grin was as usual, even affectionate as he looked at Coon.

"Didn't seem to take hold this morning," he said. "I filled 'er up again, just in case I needed more."

"Oh, for— Pop, you know you can't fritz it up like— Darned stubborn old nut! What do you want to let yourself get so pooped for? I can handle the old gal all right, you ought to know. We had an old bouncer of a squall while you were asleep. Fair and I did okay."

"We did?" Jasper listened. "That's right, auxiliary's stopped. Got fair wind again, have we?"

"Southwest again."

"Ought to have called me," Jasper said. "I told you to."

Coon flushed. "I'm not bragging any," he said shortly. "Okay, Pop. If you want me to help you get to bed, I will."

"No need of it. You get to bed yourself."

"All right." Coon took off his jacket, sat down on the bunk opposite Jasper's, began untying his sneakers.

"What's the idea?" Jasper said.

"I'm sleeping here." Coon finished undressing quickly, snapped back the blankets, and crawled under them, where he lay with only the top of his black curly head showing.

"Well, sleep there if you want to," Jasper said. "But you get worried too damned easy, Coon, boy. You have something on your mind, too, Lew?"

"No," Lewis said. "Just stopped by to say good night. See you in the morning, Jasper."

Thoughtfully, he went into his own stateroom and to bed, where he lay wide awake for a while. He had never heard Coon talk so much at any one time. Well, yes—the night he'd said he was scared of the dark, he'd said more than a word. He'd been worried then about something more than that, Lewis was sure. Hal, of course. Something Hal had done to him. One of Hal's blasted tricks? It seemed more likely now that Coon was jealous. Young, wanted praise for a job well done, and Jasper hadn't given him the time of day. Hal, of course, was the white-headed boy, damn him.

Still, Coon was worried about Jasper's health—something the old man had to take shots for and might be expected to neglect doing it. Worried and, it was obvious to anyone with half an eye, desperately so.

Harold lay in his bunk, knees up, hands behind his head. If anyone thought that a little crack on the nub was going to bother him, they had another think coming. The bump had come up big, and he was probably going to have a black eye. But it only throbbed a little now. Didn't hurt at all. He could get up and go out whenever he felt like it. He grinned to himself, and the drug running wild in his blood turned two spots of moonlight, slanting through the porthole to the wall of the stateroom, into pure gold coins —coins that spun and flashed and threw off sparks like a catherine wheel. Pretty.

Damn that Coon. Well, I can wait. Thought I had him when I dumped him off the ladder last summer. Not even a blood relation and coming in for a good chunk of Uncle Jasper's dough. And that St. Andrews bitch, too, thinks she's going to get away with a potful of it. If she marries him. Which she ain't going to.

I'm going to need every cent of that dough if I go into this Newfoundland thing.

How about that Newfoundland thing? Hey, how about that?

He was bored out of his life, ready and waiting for a spell of good, red-blooded action. Had a little fun with the Bronson kid, but what was that? A few fireworks, was all.

Better luck next time, maybe. Wyman's kids. Serve Wyman right for turning me out of my stateroom.

Old Uncle Jasper. Have to be sure to get to him early, explain this black eye. He always had to know about your lumps. Damned old fool, give you hell, then stop and wait, hoping you could explain everything. You could always explain everything. Then he'd cry on your shoulder. Be a good boy, now, Hal. Oh, sure. And while I'm in his cabin, I can sneak his insulin back where it belongs, or he'll conk out. Wouldn't want that, not right now. Just let him have another spell or two, look more natural. Besides, Coon's got some ideas; he's watching the old boy like a damn mother.

Who'll I say gi'me this eye? Coon won't open his trap, he'll just creep around, sneaky, till he gets a chance to get back at me. Oh. Sure. I know. It'll be a ball.

This Newfoundland thing. It was going to take real doing. In that book, which was supposed to be the truth and not a story, the guy'd written that there was a town in Newfoundland where the people had been wreckers for generations—stuck bogus lights out on the shore and when ships came piling up on the rocks, they'd loot them, take everything. It went back to the time when ship captains traveled with chests of gold coins aboard. Or pirates did, anyway. Jewels, too.

This guy'd said in his book that there wasn't a family in the town that didn't have a chest or a stockingful of gold pieces and stuff stashed away in their house. Old gold coins. He had bought a coin book, looked up values, just in case. Worth a lot now, not only for the gold, but for what they'd bring from antique dealers. A fortune. People there sounded like a low-grade bunch. Ignorant, shirttail fishermen. What if some guy got hold of a good, fast cabin cruiser and some strong, tough kids with guns? Highball in there some dark night, take over the town. Stand the shirttails up against a wall. They'd rather tell where their chestfuls were than take a bullet in the back. Get the works and buzz out of there the same night. Nobody'd ever know who'd done it.

He lay thinking, the dream taking shape, gilt-edged and pieced out with TV and movie plots, in which, if the bad guys changed places with the good guys and came out on top, what difference would it make? Just another set of guys, that was all. Be a nice change. You might make a fortune if you wrote a TV show like that. Men younger than nineteen had made it, in their time, and not all good guys, either.

Hal's planning took no account of ice-bound coves and harbors, frozen over now until spring. If it had, he would have found no problem. For, tonight, he was king of the castle, the reckless horseman, riding them all down; the blood-stained pirate flying a skull-and-crossbones to terrorize the Seven Seas. Ice? Breathe on it and melt it, what the hell?

Toward morning, still feeling great, he got up and made his way in stocking feet to Lewis Wyman's cabin.

Lewis woke early in the morning. Something had waked him, he wasn't sure what. Some sound from outside the cabin, or perhaps a change in the *Macomber*'s swing and sway? Rearing up, he glanced out of the cabin window and saw the sun beginning to tip the horizon in the southeast. Pleasant weather again. Good sailing. He lay down again. Might as well sleep awhile longer. It was still early.

What had waked him, he saw, was two bottles of orange pop, rolling around on the bedside dresser by Amanda's bunk and clinking together. Well, he'd gone to sleep to worse noises than that in the past few days. As he was making himself comfortable again, he saw the canvas curtain that screened Amanda's bunk stir. She looked out, stared sleepily for a moment, then slid from under the canvas and stood up.

Bathroom, probably, Lewis thought. He grinned a little.

You sure couldn't call these mother-of-pearl deals aboard the *Macomber* "the head."

No, she was zeroed in on the pop bottles. She picked them up and looked them over, then, carrying them, made for the door of the cabin.

Unlocked, Lewis thought suddenly. Didn't I lock that last night? I'm sure I did.

She was back almost at once, without the bottles, climbing into her bunk when Adam put his head over the rail of the upper, where he slept.

"What'd you do with them?" he asked in a half-whisper. "I was looking forward to one when I got up."

Amanda stared at him, frozen motionless. After a silence, she said, "Oh. I'm sorry, Ad. Did you bring those in last night?"

"No. I thought you did. All thoughtful for morning."

"Maybe Dad did," Amanda said. She got into the bunk, pulled the curtain, and was silent.

"Hunh! Sleepwalking, I guess," Adam said, showing disapproval. He got no answer, and presently, from his regular breathing, Lewis judged he had gone back to sleep.

Now what was that all about? Lewis wondered. Something between them—they had all kinds of privacies he didn't inquire into. But it was no use his trying to go to sleep again. Amanda, in her pajamas, and with that soft, thoughtful voice, so like Lucile, had resurrected his old pain, dimmed now somewhat, but there and ready. He might as well get up, take a turn or two around the deck, try to walk it off while he waited for breakfast.

He swung his legs over the side of the bunk and put one foot into his valise, open and ransacked, the contents tipped out and tumbled on the floor. This was the only piece of luggage he had kept in his stateroom, the rest he had stowed belowdecks. It had contained nothing but daily necessaries and some odds and ends, none of which seemed to be missing. Checking, he saw that nothing had been taken, not even his old brandy flask, which lay at the bottom of the heap. The flask, silver-plated once, but worn by long use so that swatches of brass-colored metal showed through, was still full. It had lived for years behind a buttoned flap in his valise, and he had not forgotten it was there. He might be kidding himself, he'd thought more than once, when he'd told himself it was for emergencies.

However, he hadn't taken it out. The prowler had done that and then hadn't touched it. Hadn't taken anything.

Only one person aboard who'd do this. Hal, of course, had kept his key. Lewis was sure, now, he'd locked the door last night. He repacked his belongings and locked the valise. What had Hal wanted to find?

The kids had gone back to sleep. No sound at all behind Amanda's curtain, and Adam lay sprawled, still breathing through his nose. Lewis shivered. He had brought them here to his own cabin for safety; there was no safety anywhere on this vessel. Staterooms belowdecks had bolts on the inside of the doors. He could unscrew one of those, bring it up here, and he'd do that before the day was out. Meantime, he'd go to see Jasper, and this time, by God, he'd make the old man see the light.

As he left the cabin, he came face to face with Hal, who had been in to see his uncle and was just closing the door behind him. Hal had a purplish lump on his forehead which had spread downward into a magnificent, greenish black eye.

"Cap'n Wyman," he said. "Say, I'm sorry about, you know, last night. I guess I lived it up some. God knows, I was feeling no pain when I ran into you. I hope I didn't hurt you. If you hadn't gone down, we'd both been in the drink."

"What are you talking about?" Lewis said.

"Uncle Jasper's just getting dressed. Oh, and another thing. I got into your cabin by mistake last night. Used to be, you know, mine, and I was groggy with this head. I kicked something over in there, a suitcase, I guess. Hope I didn't do you any damage. If I did, I'll be glad to pay for anything I, you know, broke." He fumbled in his pocket, handed over a key. "I meant to give this to you before. Forgot it." He grinned and the grin was sheepish, sincere. "I hope you'll tell Uncle Jasper I've had my whacks, what with this lump on my head and this eye." He stepped past Lewis and went on for'ard, whistling.

Lewis stared after him. After a moment, he knocked on Jasper's door and went in. There was no sign of Coon. Jasper sat on the edge of his bunk; he was still in his nightshirt, and his big, bony feet, knobbed with bunions, were bare. He sat rubbing them together, sole on instep, as if they were cold. He gave Lewis a thoughtful look and glanced down, as if embarrassed, but his greeting was cordial.

"Morning, Lew. How are you? Feeling better?"

"I haven't been sick that I know of," Lewis said.

For all he could see, Brown was all right. He looked it, certainly.

"Now, Lew," he said, "there's times when a feller needs a friend."

"That's right," Lewis said. "What can I do for you, Jasper? Are you all right this morning?"

"Me? Sure, I'm okay. Finest kind. Who to worry about, I guess, is you. Now, Lew. Why don't you just hand that flask over to me? If you don't have it around, it won't be a temptation to you."

"Jasper," Lewis said quietly, "what do you remember about last night?"

"What should I remember? I came off the wheel, dead tired, et my supper, went to bed. For godsake, Lew, don't change the subject on me, I'm trying to help you. I've got to depend on you, and I've got to be sure you're in good enough shape so I can."

"All right, Jasper. Who told you I was drunk?"

"My God, Lew, Hal's face is proof enough. That boy, I never see such a looking sight in my life. It's a wonder you didn't kill him. He says he don't know what you hit him

[*173*]

with, but it must have been something besides your fist. Now, Lew. I can't have you mauling the boys around, that ain't right. I know you've had your troubles with liquor before, son. I don't hold it against you if you've slipped. But no sense making it harder for yourself than you have to, is there?"

He sounded like an elderly schoolteacher, sanctimonious and full of compassion, advising an erring pupil. His round brown eyes, liquid with sympathy, fixed on Lewis, he paused and waited for the schoolboy's answer.

Lewis, controlling himself, let him have one. "Shut up, Jasper. The next port within reasonable distance is Boston. We're headed in there. I'm getting myself and my children off this vessel as soon as I can."

"My God, you can't mean that! You can't leave me in the lurch now, Lew, my wedding's next week. I've got to get to St. Andrews. What's got into you? Are you still drunk?"

"I haven't been drinking," Lewis said crisply. "I'm not even going to bother denying the bunch of lies you've been told. Hal broke into my stateroom last night, prowled around, went through my suitcase."

"But, Lewis, you hit him! The boy's got a temper—"

"I didn't hit him. There was no fight, not with me. I want him locked up until we're tied up in Boston. If you won't see that he stays that way, Jilson and I will."

"Lock up Hal? Are you crazy? I don't know what you can be talking about."

Lewis got up to go. "I'm sorry you don't believe me," he said. "Since you won't, I've got to break my contract with you. I've got my kids to look after, and there's already been enough going on to make me wonder just how dangerous your boy is. He's certainly a flashy liar."

"What happened last night? Why wasn't I called?"

"You had a sick spell last night. You don't seem to remember it."

"I did?"

"When I walked into your cabin last night, I thought *you* were drunk."

"By the god, I wasn't! I don't drink, not much. I can't. I'm diabetic."

Light dawned on Lewis. "Are you an insulin taker?"

"God, yes. Before I got the dose regulated I used to have spells, made me act drunk as a skunk. I thought I'd told you."

"No. You didn't tell me."

"Anything with sugar in it'd bring me out of it. You see me eat any candy?"

"Yes. I did."

"That was it. Doctor told me not to get too tired. I guess I did, so I had one of them spells. I ain't had one for a long time, but I ain't been feeling too well lately, either. I keep boxes of candy bars around, though, just in case."

"Jasper, I've known you to be a reasonable man," Lewis said. "I think you believe I am. Let's get together on this. I do have a flask. It's full. You can taste it to see if it's watered. I tell myself I carry it for emergencies, and so far, I haven't had it out of my bag. It's been buried there for months. How could anyone know I had it?"

Brown's shoulders suddenly sagged under his voluminous nightshirt; he looked miserable and old. He began rubbing his feet together again. It made a rasping sound. He said, "Yes. I guess so, Lew."

"My door was locked," Lewis said.

"Hal's got duplicate keys to all the staterooms. I'll get them away from him. Then he couldn't . . . I can't lock him up."

"Even if you believe these tricks of his are nothing but jokes, he still can't be allowed to . . . to go around . . ."

"You needn't try to make it sound better than it is, Lew. He was always a heller as a youngster, but not mean. He was an awful cute little baby. My brother Luke's boy. Luke and his wife both died young, and we raised their youngster. I've done everything for him, Lew. Everything.

Bought him any toy he asked for, a car when he was old enough. . . . I was pretty lonesome when my wife died. I guess . . . I think the world of him. I ain't able to believe he'd do anything downright bad. If I promise to keep an eye on him, you wouldn't—just to St. Andrews? I guess it's like my life depends on getting that far. I'm in one hell of a bind, Lew. Please, for godsake, help me." He huddled himself together, his forearms leaned hard on his knees, his shamed eyes on his feet.

Torn, Lewis looked at him. Something about Jasper's big, callused feet—the swollen purplish knobs of bunions, which must be sore, must hurt him—hit Lewis where he lived, shook his determination. Like the man, those feet had come a long way—homely, dependable, decent, doing the job demanded of them; strong, until stress and wear had asked too much, more than tendon and bone could bear. It was as if those honorable feet themselves had called for help and Lewis couldn't stand it.

"All right, Jasper," he said. "We'll all help. Keep an eye on Hal, yes, get him off our backs. The thing for you to do is get the rest you need and don't worry." He managed a grin. "You know you told me you wouldn't want to get to St. Andrews all tuckered out."

Shaken, he left the cabin and walked along for'ard to the galley.

The damned, selfish, smooth, young bastard! he raged to himself. He'll be watched, all right.

[*176*]

PART EIGHT

Fred

WHEN FRED MONTGOMERY began to come to, his first thought was that he was either dead or crazy. He was lying on his back on the ground. Somebody had poured cold water on his head, and it had run down inside his shirt. It was uncomfortable, so he couldn't be dead, but he certainly could be crazy. He remembered Jakie laughing, and now he could hear Jakie bellering. Once Jakie opened his mouth and let out, you didn't forget the sound. Shivering and still groggy, Fred didn't open his eyes for fear of what he might have to face up to.

Then someone wiped the water off his face. A hand came down on it, comfortingly, and rested there. Something like a big rough tongue went *smirp* across one cheek, leaving a warm wet trail. Fred opened his eyes and stared into the liquid eyes of Walter, who sat beside him.

He moaned, "Oh, my God!" and shut his eyes again, quick. The whole weight of Jakie landed on his chest—no ghost but solid Jakie, hugging, scattering wet kisses, hollering, "Froggy, wake up! Wake up right now!"

Susie, whose hand was on his forehead, said, "It's all right, Fred. It's the kids. They're real. Don't sit up yet if you still feel dizzy."

But Fred sat up. His senses came back with a whirl. There were the kids, Jakie and Caroline, and they were real. Something warm and glowing grew inside his chest and seemed to explode, as if the sun had risen there and blown up, scattering little pieces of itself all over him. He said, "Oh, glory!" and choked, and couldn't think what to say except, "Where'd you get Walter?"

"He was here," Caroline said. She stood, a little apart, looking at him. "It's all right for you to hate me, Freddy. I stole the skiff and outboard and I lost them."

"You could steal my everlasting underpinning so long's you two are all right," Fred said. "They found the skiff okay. It was you and Jakie lost."

"I had to steal them," Caroline said in a hard voice. "It was all the way I could get away. Now we'll have to go back. Now that you've found us, and *she* knows." She stared inimically at Susie. "I wouldn't have come out, except I heard Jakie laugh and knew he'd gone out on the balcony. I had to run and grab him for fear he'd fall. *She* saw me and hollered to bring cold water. I thought you were hurt, so I got the water. That was why Jakie bellered so, he thought you were hurt. Now she'll go and tell where we ran away to."

"I will not," Susie said. "I'd never in the world tell anyone where you are."

"Yes, you will," the hard voice went on. "All you, you always tell each other."

Susie remembered that look. On the day of the delphiniums, she had seen it—ice-blue, cold, still. Oh, my soul! she thought. She's—what? Twelve? Thirteen? and she hasn't found a person or anything in her world she can trust. Except Jakie . . . who's too young. "Caroline," she said, "on the night you ran away, I saw you."

"You did not!"

"I was walking along the shore path. You made a bed for Jakie in the skiff. I watched you go and I saw where you went. I didn't tell anyone, not even Fred, who's been feeling awful ever since they found the boat and thought you were drowned. Why should I tell anyone now?"

[*178*]

"Did you, Freddy?" Caroline said. "Did you feel awful?"

Fred had scrambled up, with difficulty because of Jakie hanging onto his leg. "Dammit, I just about died," he said. "What'd you think? Why couldn't you have told me how it was? You ought to know I'd have done something."

Caroline said nothing. She stared at him.

"I didn't know," Fred said. "I'd have had you with me like a shot if I'd known anything about it." He whirled on Susie. "My God, Susie, how come you didn't speak up? You must've known how I felt."

"I wanted to," Susie said. "Only if Caroline hadn't, I couldn't. Don't you see? It was for her to say." She could tell from the way he looked that this was going to be hard to forgive.

"Them over here alone, with nobody to look after them," Fred said. "What if one of them got sick or hurt? Could have died for all anyone would have known."

Caroline said disdainfully, "I would have hung a sheet out of an upstairs window. You'd have taken us back to Gramma Pollard, you know you would have."

"Well, it would've been the law. She adopted you."

"She did not. She said we acted so, she didn't believe we belonged to any Pollard. She said our father was probably some old rammer down around the shore that Mama went with. She said she wasn't going to fix it so we'd get any of the Pollard money," Caroline said.

"Oh, that sad, horrible old woman," Susie said. "How could she say such a thing to a child! You might be sorry for her, lonely and eaten up with meanness, but it's a crime to let her have anything to do with children or anybody else not strong enough to stand up to her. I guess I know. I went through the same thing with my old aunt. A whole childhood without being loved, and children have got to be loved." She stopped, hoping Fred would say something. He didn't. All right, let him be mad. He'd know what she thought, at least.

"I think Caroline did right," she said. "Law or no law.

She took over, did what she had to, with a whole townful of people standing around saying how awful Lydia Pollard was to those kids. Not a soul lifted a finger to stop it. Do you wonder Caroline doesn't trust anyone now?"

"I cut down your flowers," Caroline said. The still, cold gaze had narrowed. It said, now, as the tone of her voice did, So what are you up to?

"I figured out long ago that you had a reason for that. Anyway, it was a nice bouquet to have in the house. I've worried some about your having enough to eat over here." Susie wasn't going to mention the binoculars and the attic window. Caroline wouldn't like one bit the idea of having been spied on. Susie might tell Fred later, if it would make him feel any better about her sense of responsibility. She went on, "I brought along a ham and a chocolate cake. If anyone's hungry, we might go eat some of it."

At the mention of ham and cake, Jakie was lured away from his love, which still was Froggy's leg. He said, "Eat? Come, Walter. Eat." He and Walter made a beeline for the back door, where they stood waiting hopefully.

"No," Caroline said. "We've got to get ready to go back. Freddy's going to take us back there." Head high, she turned and started for the house.

Fred suddenly came to life. He had been torn apart and put together again; his nerves were still raw. He was freezing from cold water down his neck. He let go with a bawl that outbellered Jakie at his best.

"Caroline! I ain't either going to take you back there! You won't see Lydia Pollard ever in your life again, you can forget about that right now! And you can cut out looking at me as if I was a mad dog, I don't relish it. I never knew until this morning that Ma wouldn't take you kids when your mother asked her, nobody mentioned it to me. If I'd known, I'd have raised particular Cain, and you know it. I'm freezing to death, this wet shirt, and you don't give a darn about me, either, if I die of pneumonia. You get going and find me something to put on whilst this dries.

[*180*]

And you come down off that high horse and quit acting like a little fool or I'll tan your britches!"

The indignant, baritone bellow appeared to comfort everybody. At least, it comforted Susie. Male and bossy, she thought. What everybody needs.

Caroline took off for the house and went up the steps like a scared rabbit. Walter reared up on the kitchen door and as usual peeked through the keyhole to where the food would be. Jakie pointed his finger at Froggy and said, "Zz-zzt!" whether congratulation or admiration for another male, it was hard to say.

Fred himself sniffled and let go with a tremendous sneeze.

"God Almighty!" he said plaintively. "I'm cold."

Now they could have a fire in daytime in the big fireplace, because people would see Fred's boat at the float and know he was there. They had hot soup first, mainly to warm up Fred, though he said he didn't need it, he was blistering already. He sat in front of the blazing fire, wrapped in a purple and white afghan with zigzag orange stripes, which belonged to the Countess Wiggling Biscuits.

"Golly," he said. "The old lady's afrighan. Never expected to find it on me."

Caroline had been fussing over him, stiffly, but fussing. She had hung up his shirt to dry behind the kitchen stove. She had brought the afghan and, after he had draped it, shawllike, over his shoulders, she'd insisted that the ends be tucked under his belt to keep it from slipping. The thing was bulky; Fred had to let out his belt to the last hole. It made him look twice his size.

"You look like a fat Turk, all those wild colors," Susie said, laughing at him. "I hope nobody sees you."

Fred grinned and Jakie laughed, but Caroline didn't crack a smile. She said, "You drink your soup, Freddy. You'll catch a cold."

Fred drank the soup, set the cup down. He reached a

long arm and gathered her in against his knees. "Come on, poker stick, bend," he said, and then she was in his lap, with his cheek pressed against her hair.

Susie, cutting sandwiches at the kitchen table, glanced around once and then was content to listen to the peaceful silence in the living room.

Maybe this'll come out all right, she thought. Now we have to figure out how to get them away.

From somewhere, fairly close behind the house, a gunshot rang out, then another and another, and a confused babble of men's voices yelling. Walter leaped from under the table where he had been enjoying his handout. His claws scrabbled desperately on the linoleum; then he fled through the living room and vanished like a shadow up the front stairs. Jakie said, "Oh, bang, oh, dear!" and began to pucker. He ran to Caroline, buried his face against her.

Fred put both of them aside and came to his feet. "Everybody stay put, don't go out!" he commanded. He tore out through the kitchen door, banging it behind him. The sound of his boots thumped on the back steps and died away down the path.

Caroline, comforting Jakie, looked over at Susie. "Deer hunters," she said. "We saw them in the woods. Have you got a sandwich ready? If I can stuff one in Jakie, he won't beller."

"Let's all have one," Susie said. She brought in the plate of sandwiches.

Caroline gave one to Jakie, took another for herself, munching composedly. "Freddy will fix them," she said proudly. "They'll be sorry they ever came here."

Fred raced through the woods in his afghan, which, in his rage, he had forgot he had on. He hadn't any objection to shooting deer himself, when it was legal and in season; but nothing made him so boiling mad as the knotheads who poached a protected area, where the animals were used to people and wouldn't run. To shoot anything in a wild-game sanctuary was like shooting fish in a barrel, and hunters who came here knew it. What they wanted was easy hunting—haul home a deer to brag about, even if it might as well have been somebody's cow. The faster he ran, the madder he got.

He spotted the hunters, four of them and strangers to him, in the middle of a clearing. They had evidently seen a deer and fired off in all directions, hitting nothing but one man in the hat. At least, there was no dead or wounded deer in sight. They were all standing in sober silence, staring down at the hole in the hat, when Fred burst, yelling, out of the bushes.

He was yelling as a precaution, in case they'd heard the bushes crashing and took what some lunks called "sound shots" at him. He wasn't prepared for what did happen.

The man who was holding the hat dropped it. He pointed a shaking finger, made a gargle sound in his throat, and ran headlong into the underbrush. The others whirled around, stared. Then they all took off after him. One fellow started to climb a tree, thought better of it; he dropped his gun and followed the others, leaving Fred alone and astonished in the center of the clearing.

"Be darned!" he said aloud. He had expected a row and had been ready for that.

He walked across the clearing, picking up the hat on his way. Pretty fancy hat. Fellow's name and address inside on the sweatband. Out-of-state hunter. Well, the woods on the mainland were full of them just now. One of the other men, judging by the load of sporty equipment he had on, certainly was, too. Who in his right mind would want to pack all that weight through the woods—rifle, hunting knife, sure, okay. But full cartridge belt, big revolver in holster-on-hip—what was the guy out gunning for? Game wardens?

The remaining two men looked like locals. Nobody he knew—they could be from Bradford. Probably had company from the city; brought them over here to make sure they'd get a deer to take home.

Fred picked up the dropped gun and jerked the shells

out of the magazine. He noted with disgust the rifle's caliber, the soft-nosed bullets which would tear an exit hole as big as a dinner plate in any kind of flesh. He got blazing mad all over again.

Their boat would be over at the sand beach. If he could catch up with them before they got off to it, he'd have some words to say about hunting here, hunting anywhere with a cannon like this. Carrying the gun and the hat, he trotted through the woods to the cross-island path.

The hunters had made time, seeing they'd battled the underbrush back to the beach. High tide had peaked; the ebb had grounded out their skiff on the sand. They were frantically trying to shove it off. As Fred looked over the four-foot bank at the top of the beach, one of them glanced up, saw him, and let out a yell.

"Hey, look! There he is! My God, it *is* a wild man!"

Fred yelled back. "You hold on! I've got something to say to you, damn you!"

The boat, embedded in soft wet sand, slid into the water; the men waded after it over their boot tops and scrambled in. One grabbed an oar and shoved off; another started the outboard motor.

Fred, about to jump over the bank, stopped short and ducked down. The fellow with the revolver had it out and was taking aim. The bullet zinged over Fred's head and smacked into a tree. Astonished, a little dazed, Fred stayed where he was while the outboard revved up, the skiff went roaring out to the lobster boat anchored off the beach. Then he peered out through the screen of dried-up beach peas at the top of the bank.

That was a Bradford lobster boat; he'd seen it before. He didn't know who owned it, but he could find out, know it next time he saw it, for sure. Whoever that joker was, he'd hear about it, going around taking potshots at people.

Wild man, what the hell! Who'd they think was a wild man?

Fred looked down. For the first time, he realized what

he'd been galloping around the woods in. Godfrey mighty, the old lady's afrighan! It had pulled out of the back of his belt so that the ends of it were flapping out behind him, but shoot, any fool could see that it was nothing but a purple and white and orange-striped afrighan. Still, he did need a haircut—hadn't had the heart to bother much about his looks since he'd thought he'd lost the kids. And his hair was all streeled out in peaks, the way it always got after it had been wet.

He sat back on his heels and roared laughing. Wild man, sure enough. Wild man of Borneo! Scared the living bejee-zus out of them fellas, no wonder. After a while, he got up and trotted back along the path, still chuckling.

As he neared the house, he calmed down and began to look at the affair more soberly. Those fellows might not want to let on they'd been over here poaching deer, but he'd bet a good deal that not one of them would be able to keep his mouth shut about seeing a wild man on the island. They might say they'd just landed to eat lunch or been beachcombing. And that guy that had dropped the gun, he'd sure want to come back after it.

Fred glanced at the gun which he was carrying. Two or three hundred dollars' worth of rifle; a darned expensive gun; probably fine, if you wanted to blow up an elephant. If it didn't make you sick, thinking what one of those dum-dum bullets would do. Serve him right if I was to sink it, he thought, glancing at the water beginning to show through the trees. Take a couple twirls around my head and let 'er go. It was a temptation, but of course it wasn't the gun's fault.

The sight of the water made him think of something else. He'd lost the high tide. Couldn't tow that float around to Cat Cove now; wouldn't be able to get it far enough up the brook, even if his boat could tow it against the ebb tide. Well, he could do it tomorrow. There'd be another day or so of the springs.

Ordinarily, what he'd do would be to stay here overnight, work until he had everything cleaned up. If he'd been alone, he would have. But there was Susie, he'd have to take her home. That would leave the kids . . . The kids.

If those lunks shot off their mouths about the wild man, there'd be a hunt over here after him, a hoot'n-holler all over the place, with a bunch of men, maybe dogs. Like enough they'd search the house, because that would be the only place on the island anybody could shelter. He'd better take Susie home right now, hustle back as soon as he could.

But what if those poachers got over their scare and came right back to get the lost rifle? They'd been scared all of a heap, but they had guns to help them get over it. They could be over in the woods right now.

I can't leave here at all, not till this wild-man business is settled away. Leave the kids and poor old Walter?

He marched up the back steps into the kitchen. He wasn't surprised when everybody there took a look at him and began to laugh.

"Wild man of Borneo," he said. "Where's my shirt? Wet or dry, I want it."

It was dry enough. He felt better when it was on and he had combed his hair.

"Now, I've got to tell you we're in a bind," he said, and explained as briefly as he could. "There's two things we could do. I could take you, Susie, and the kids across to-night, you could hide them in your house. After dark. I wouldn't know how to manage taking Walter, though. The other thing is, we could all stay here. If there's a hunt tomorrow, I'm a deputy sheriff, I've got as much law as anybody, and if I'm here, they won't search the house. Staying here all night would be rough on you, Susie. It'd make an awful lot of talk."

"Abandon Walter and break Jakie's heart? Never!" she said. "My cat Tommy is the only problem I've got, and he isn't one really. I left out food for him, and he's got a nice warm box in the barn he can get to. If people talk, they'll talk. If it isn't about one thing, it's another. Besides, I like it here. I wouldn't mind staying forever."

It occurred to Fred that that might be an extremely pleasant thing to do. Still, he couldn't help but be concerned.

"You sure?" he asked. "Ma knows you came with me. This'll jiggle pendulums all over town."

"Let 'em jiggle. Even at that, I won't be taking half the chances that Caroline took. We are all going to stay here and make sure that what she did wasn't for nothing. That no hearts get broken and nothing gets lost, Fred."

She smiled at Caroline and was surprised to get a shaky smile in return. Even a shaky smile, she thought, is something. Aloud, she said, "Come on, Caroline, you're the lady of the house. Let's go upstairs and fix me a bed to sleep in."

Jakie toiled up the stairs after them, carrying a slice of ham with which to comfort Walter, who was wedged in the darkest corner he could find, under a bed in a back bedroom. He took quite a lot of coaxing before he would come out.

They all stayed inside the house for the rest of the day, lying low. Fred had started to do a few outdoor chores but suddenly found himself worn out. He slept on the davenport in front of the fire. Jakie and Walter played punkin-devil with the African masks. Susie said it gave her cold chills to see how Walter looked with his mask on. "Like some awful animal out of a horror story," she told Caroline. She and Caroline found a box of dominoes. At dark, Fred went down to the float to check the lines on his boat.

Nobody had come, and wouldn't now, today. Peace and quiet, he thought. Why don't more people try to manage so's they'll have some, instead of racking each other to pieces? His mother was going to flip; hell would break loose. She might be so torn out by the idea of the scandal that she wouldn't tell one or two dear friends about it, but Fred didn't believe so.

Serve her right if Susie and I got back together, after the way she lied to old Miranda Cooley that time and broke us up. She'd told Aunt Yuba and Aunt Yuba had told somebody else and word went around until it got back to Fred, that Ma'd told Miranda Cooley Fred had said he'd be damned if he'd put up with two old women on his hands. Which Fred had never said and never would have thought of saying. You didn't, though, get married to spite your mother. That wasn't the reason. A man got married because he thought so much of somebody he couldn't help it.

He stopped on the path to sniff woodsmoke from the fireplace chimney and to look at the sky. Overhead was clear, with big stars, but in the west, so low down on the horizon that he could just make it out, was a long line of dark cloud.

Mean weather, tomorrow or next day, he thought.

The shuttered house looked lonesome, closed for winter, the people gone away. But he knew what was inside. Supper getting ready and a warm fire and company; all out of reach of the day-after-day nagging voice, the snatching, grabbing hands.

In the morning, a big powerboat slid alongside Fred's boat at the float and tied up there. Out of it climbed Pomroy Fifield carrying a shotgun and following him a party of ten or eleven men, also with guns, plus two dogs. Fred watched them come up the path. He noted with satisfaction that all four of yesterday's poachers were along, three carrying rifles, the fourth empty-handed. The fourth gun leaned against the porch rail beside Fred; on a chair behind him was the afghan, topped by the holed hat.

Pomroy led, bustling along, ready for good fast action. He stopped dead at the sight of Fred's face.

"What's the idea, Pomroy?" Fred said. "You know you can't bring hunters over here."

"Now, Fred. Word's come round that there's a wild man, a crazy man, running the woods over here. I'm doing my duty, according to law. We got to ketch him. You never come home last night, and your mother's out of her mind with worrying. Says the only reason you didn't was you and Susie Warren was prob'ly tore to pieces by the critter."

"Are you nuts?" Fred demanded. "I'm over here closing up the cottage for the winter. Never got through yesterday, so I stayed all night. I know all about that wild man. There ain't one."

"There is, too! These fellas see him. He come at 'em in the woods, hollering and screeching. Say he's an awful sight—no clothes, but a lot of old colored rags. They just made it to their boat."

"Which fellas is that?" Fred said.

"Them, right there. Mr. Graham, he's from Waban, and him, there, Mr. Pease, and Joe and Herb Packard from Bradford. Four witnesses. Now, Fred. Four of thum see him."

"Mr. Graham," Fred said. "Is this your hat?"

Mr. Graham looked uneasy. "I don't reckernize it," he said.

"Funny you don't, it's got your name and address in it. Like to tell me how it got this bullet hole? You wouldn't? Well, is this your gun? Full of soft-nosed bullets? What might you boys have been doing over here yesterday, when you saw this wild man?"

Graham flushed a little. "Why, exploring around. Just visiting. Joe and Herb, here, took us for a sail in their boat. Always wanted to land on a Maine island. So we did."

"What were the guns for? Maybe you were going to hunt each other? Was that how Mr. Graham got the hole in his hat?"

[*189*]

"Fred, these gentlemen is visitors to the state," Pomroy began. "You hadn't oughta—"

"Visitors, hell! These gentlemen are poachers on private property, with NO HUNTING, NO TRESPASSING, and WILD GAME AND BIRD SANCTUARY signs plastered all over the place. And one of them, Mr. Pease, there, him with the pistol, took a shot at me. Now, I'm the caretaker of this island, and I'm also a deputy sheriff of the county. I want your names and addresses, all of them. It's serious business to take potshots at the law."

The pistol carrier burst out, "It was self-defense! I fired at that crazy . . . that wild . . ."

"Even if there'd been one, it would have been murder to shoot him," Fred said coldly. "You fired at me, from a boat twenty feet off the shore. You ever see this before?" He reached around, brought out the afghan, which he unfolded and dropped across the porch rail. "Well, I'm glad to see your faces turn red. It's about time."

"What's that thing got to do with it?" Pomroy demanded. "If I didn't know ya, I'd say you was off your rocker."

"I got my shirt wet," Fred said. "I was choring around inside the house waiting for it to dry. Had that thing over my shoulders when these buddies of yours started the Battle of the Bulge out behind the house." He grinned. "I wasn't about to worm into a wet shirt, so I went in what there was."

He picked up the afghan. "This is a lot wilder than a tame deer to haul down the freeway on your fender. If the old lady's afrighan was what you boys were after, I don't know as the district judge'd fine you more than two dollars."

Pomroy was mad; he was giving up hard on the wild-man hunt. Had it all planned out how he'd cordon through the woods like a fine-tooth comb. All the trouble I went to to set up this posse, and that cussed Fred racking round the swamp in a blanket.

"Dressing up like a wild man ain't legal, it's uttering menaces, like," he said. "I could arrest you for it, and I could arrest you for adult'rous actions over here with Susie Warren. I'm a good mind to do it, too. Your Ma said—"

Fred took his hands out of his pockets. "Well, now, Pomroy," he said. "You travel back and tell everybody that Susie and I are married. If my nose bled as easy as yours does, I'd be a little mite careful what I stuck it into."

Happily, he watched the wild-man hunt embark. Now that, he told himself, was one hell of a way to propose. If she says no, I'll have to tell Ma we had a quick divorce.

He stood watching the boat grow smaller, made aware by the look of things that he had better get going if he wanted to get that float secured over in Cat Cove before the weather caught up with him. There was no wind yet; the water was smooth and still as a windowpane, except where the boat's wake spread out like two rolls of glass. The sky was overcast, a uniform, dead gray. Growing colder by the minute, too, and from over on the east side of the island, he could hear the rollers beginning to boom on the ledges. Something stirring out over the ocean, that was for sure. A northeasterly, probably. He took a deep sniff and then another. There was no mistaking the smell of snow.

He spent the rest of the morning dismantling the float and gangway and, on the peak of the tide, did the towing job, got everything made fast over in the cove, including his boat. No sense to leave her out tied to the pier if an old rouser of a storm was heading in.

As he stepped ashore, he saw Susie and the kids, with Walter, on the path waiting for him. They were jabbering together, ten to a dozen; Caroline, too, seemed to be back on an even keel again. Everybody began talking louder as he came climbing up the steep bank of the brook. He saw that this wasn't any chance to talk to Susie. All this company.

"Big surf rolling in over on the east side," he said tentatively, as soon as he could get a word in. "You kids ought to go over and see it."

"We've just been," Caroline said. "And lunch is ready. We've waited for you, and we're starved."

"It looks quite threatening," Susie said. "No wind at all, just big glassy rollers heaping up green and smashing over. I see you've anchored the boat, Fred. You don't think you'd better take me home today?"

Well, he couldn't. Leave her over there alone, after what he'd told Pomroy Fifield? He cast around for something to say and came up with, "Well, I could. If you really want to go."

"She doesn't," Caroline said. "She's going to stay with us until we find out how we can all get away."

"Unless you want to get rid of me, Fred," Susie said.

"Can't say I do," Fred said. How in hell did you put your mind on two things at once? He went on helplessly, "How much food did you leave down for your cat?"

PART NINE

The Macomber

THE MACOMBER *MADE* knots before a fine, following breeze. With lucky weather and comfortable sea room, she bypassed Boston and Portsmouth, New Hampshire. Then, off the Isles of Shoals, the sky turned overcast and cold; off the coast of Maine, it was winter.

On a gray morning, the wind boxed the compass and died, leaving the old schooner becalmed, wallowing in an onshore swell. Brown ordered the auxiliary started, and the nightmare of pounding along under power began again, worse than ever because of the size and authority of the swell, which came rolling in in glassy gray-green humps from the open Atlantic.

Even in the good weather, Brown still had not been feeling well. He had, evidently, kept his bargain with Lewis; what he had done or said Lewis didn't know, but there had been no further trouble with Hal. Hal was again sincere and pleasant to everyone, doing chores, helping trim sails, cheerfully taking his trick at the wheel. He was terribly worried about his uncle, he confided to Lewis. The old man wasn't doing well at all. If they weren't so close to St. Andrews now, Hal would certainly insist that they put in at the nearest port and make Uncle Jasper see a doctor.

He was outgoing with the kids, who politely ignored

him. Amanda had consulted Andy about the mysterious bottles of orange pop, which she had thrown overboard.

"I've got to tell Adam," she'd said. "I know it must've been Hal who left those there, and if I hadn't waked up before Adam did he'd have drunk them. What if he hands one out to Adam when we're not looking?"

"I'll tell Adam," Andy said. "You let me handle it, Amanda." Andy was getting over his angleworms, at least he said he was, but he still got giddy when the weather was rough and certain sounds still hurt his head. So far, he hadn't made any move to break out Joe Richards' guitar and go on with Amanda's lessons. Amanda could tell by the way he sometimes would come to a dead stop, catch hold of something and shake his head. She was sure he ought to tell his mother what the matter was; but, "I'll slap you on the wrist," Andy said. "And never speak to you again if you do."

"Of course he ought to tell her," Adam said. "Darned little mutt!" He had been silent for a long time after Andy had talked with him after exacting the same promise.

"Well, I'm glad you know," Amanda said. "Maybe together we can figure out what we ought to do."

"What could we do?" Adam said. "Shove that fat-tailed acid-head overboard?"

Right now, he sounded disgusted, but Amanda could tell he felt more than that. He was as horrified and as furious as she was. Maybe not so scared, and he was thinking.

Adam was. That was before the weather had changed; the sun was still warm enough to be out in. For a long time, he stayed by himself, sprawled on top of the after cabin. Tell Dad? Dad would go after that wart and get himself hurt . . . after all, that long spell in the hospital. Brown was the one who ought to know about it, but he thought Hal was the greatest. Coon or Fairleigh? Coon, maybe, knew already, look at the way he'd dumped Hal that night; but if Coon knew, why hadn't he done something about it before? And Fairleigh was just a guy aboard; he was quite chummy with Hal, too. That left one person who'd have any good sense about what to do.

Having made up his mind, Adam felt better; but not much.

The *Macomber*'s blunt bows thrust, reared, and chunked down; she rolled miserably, pitched worse, every lunge accompanied by creaks, groans, thuds of slatting rigging. Thumps and bumps from belowdecks were beginning to be significant—Brown's furniture was breaking loose. Coon and Fairleigh had tried to rebrace it, but the braces had broken and there turned out to be nothing on board to replace them. The "bride's present," along with assorted bureaus, commodes and chairs, began to walk up and down the passageway. Surprisingly, Brown didn't seem to be too concerned about it, except that he asked Lewis to get Belle and Andy on deck.

"Make them as comfortable as you can in my cabin, Lew," he said. "That's too tough for them, all the stuff slamming around down there."

He looked pale and exhausted, and Lewis said, "I'll put them in my cabin, Jasper. There're four bunks and my kids'll be glad of their company. I can sleep in your extra bunk, if you don't object. You'd better turn in awhile, hadn't you?"

Jasper grunted something which Lewis couldn't hear and started aft. He went into his cabin and shut the door. Lewis made a note in his mind to go and check on him as soon as Belle and Andy were settled away. Coon was busy at the wheel and would be until things quieted down. Somebody ought to look in on Jasper, after a while.

Things were worse belowdecks than he'd realized. The "bride's present" was not only walking, it was tumbling, mixed up with other objects he didn't try to identify. The mass was still for'ard of Belle's stateroom, however. He made his way from handhold to handhold to her door.

"Thank God!" Belle said, letting him in. "Oh, I am glad to see you, Lew! I haven't known what on earth to do; I've been afraid all that stuff thundering around out there would block the door. Andy, poor lamb, is so sick again, and I didn't see how I could manage to move him out of here alone."

A staggering sideways roll sent her plunging into him. He had just time to brace himself before he caught and held her. She clutched him with both hands.

"I've been just in desperation," she said. "It's so stuffy in here with everything closed. Makes him feel worse, and I'm scared something besides seasickness is wrong with him." She buried her face in his jacket and held on.

Lewis steadied her with one hand, holding on as well as he could with the other, not surprised at the tumult stirred in him by her closeness, only regretful that this, which he now knew he had been waiting for, couldn't last longer. "We'll get him on deck right away," he said. "My stateroom. The air's fresh up there, he'll feel better."

Andy sagged limply in his bunk. His face was greenish, shading into blue on his closed lids and around his mouth. His hair was wet and plastered into peaks with sweat, but Lewis, lifting him, found he was ice-cold. Seasickness while it lasted was likely to turn anyone green, and of course some got it worse than others, but Lewis, looking at the shivering youngster, wondered if Belle might not be right. Andy had had one stomach upset already; this might be a return of it, aggravated by seasickness.

"Come on, son," Lewis said. "We'll go up on deck, you'll feel better in the fresh air."

"You can't carry him in this merry-go-round," Belle said. "Maybe both of us could, in a blanket."

"I can walk," Andy said. "What's the matter with you, Belle?"

With Lewis' arm steadying him, Andy managed to, but barely. His mother tucked him into Lewis' bunk. She was, anyone could see, desperately worried. "If only he could get warm," she said. "Do you suppose Jilson could make some hot tea?"

"I'll see what he can come up with." Adam had been sitting in the opposite bunk, where he and Amanda had been trying to keep checkers from skidding off a checkerboard. Now he gave the board a shove, sending the checkers flying, got up and made for the cabin door.

"You come back here," Lewis said. "On deck's no place for you, right now."

"I'll get him his tea," Adam said, and was gone.

"Oh, dear," Belle said. "I wish I'd asked him to find out if Jilly has anything I could use for a hot-water bottle, too."

"I'll ask him," Lewis said. He started for the door and on second thought came back and rummaged out his brandy flask. A little brandy in the tea might help. He'd known it, in his time, to settle a seasick stomach quite well.

In Jilson's galley, everything was rattling and banging. Pots and pans and other objects inside closed cupboard doors were clashing together; knives, forks, and spoons clinked in their drawers. A bottom cupboard door had been battered open by three of Brown's grandmother's cast-iron scouse pots, which now careened in bacchic irresponsibility around the galley deck. A heavy lunge of the *Macomber* sent Lewis staggering in among them, and they converged as if with intent on his ankles, getting in some solid thumps as they rolled past.

He said loudly, "Ouch!" and "Damn!" and made it across to Jilson's bunk, where he tucked up his feet.

Jilson was in the bunk, and Adam, who shoved over into a corner to make room for Lewis.

"Jilly's heating water," Adam said. He put his arms around his drawn-up knees and buried his face in them.

"You aren't going seasick on us again, too, are you?" Lewis said.

"No. I'm all right," Adam said, but Lewis wondered. He had caught a glimpse of Adam's face, which looked white and drawn.

Jilson at the other end of the bunk had his eyes closed. He did not acknowledge in any way Lewis' presence.

This is a hell of a time for him to get sore about something, Lewis thought. "Jilly? Can you find something Belle can use for a hot-water bottle?"

Jilson did not open his eyes. "Anybody'd be lucky today to git cold stew wrapped in my kisses," he said. He put a foot down off the bunk, yanked it back as a tumbling iron kettle headed his way.

"Why don't you shove those things back in the cupboard where they belong?" Lewis said, irritated.

"I already did, twelve times. Once more'd be unlucky." Jilson got across to the stove, laid a hand on the side of a big teakettle wedged into the recessed cover. "Ketch on the cupboard door is busted."

He dodged across the deck, yanked out a drawer. "Tea," he said. "Where in the ever-loving green-eyed God is the sugar bowl? Ow!" He whirled around, hooked a toe under the big iron pot which appeared to be nibbling at his heel, lofted it up the companionway steps, from which it rolled back, clanking. "Sugar bowl's gone. No sugar here, except that little tinnikinful I send Andy down on his tray. Now what did that creepin' night owl want with all that sugar? Well, I guess there's enough here to fix up the tea."

"Wait!" Adam said. "Don't use it, Jilly. That could be the way he"—his voice broke, came out in a hoarse squeak —"did it this time."

"What goes on?" Lewis said. "Who did what this time?"

"I woke up early this morning, see him ransacking around," Jilly said. "What woke me, he yanked that ketch off the cupboard door; in a hurry, seems so. He was back-to, there, a minute. Yes, he could've, Ad." He rummaged around in a drawer, came up with a sealed tin, which he opened. "Nobody's been into this," he said, and began adding tea with alternate spoonfuls of sugar to the boiling kettle.

"Look here, Jilly," Lewis began. "Is Hal prowling nights again?"

"Now, Cap'n. Ad's going to take this tea back, soon's it's ready."

He didn't go on, and Lewis, looking at him, saw that his eyes were blank and hard as two stones. He had known Jilson for years and had seen this only a few times that he could remember—the last time on the day Jilson had walked Hal off Brown's wharf. Jilson, now, was coldly and furiously angry. The thing to do was to let him alone; if he wanted Lewis to wait until Adam was gone, Lewis would wait.

He brought out his brandy flask. "Put a little of this into Andy's tea," he said. "Maybe it'll settle his stomach."

Jilson took the flask. He regarded it with no expression, unscrewed the cap, smelled of it. "Lewis," he said. "It ain't moral to give this to a little sick kid." Upending the flask, he began to empty it, in long swallows.

Lewis watched him. "Damn it, Jilly, I wouldn't want to come between a man and his morals, but it just could be the youngster needed some of that."

Jilson said nothing. He decanted the tea into the brandy flask. It took doing; a good deal of the boiling mixture slopped and ran down his fingers, which apparently were made of asbestos. " 'N there!" he said. "Biling hot tea *and* a hot-water bottle. That little fella can hold that onto his belly and sip out of it, from time to time. Gi'me that sock, there, at the head of the bunk, Ad. Got to wrop it up or it'll blister your fingers."

Adam held the sock open while Jilson forced the flask into it, and went off up the companionway steps without saying a word.

"What gives?" Lewis said. "Come on, Jilly. I know something does."

"You think I was a hog drinking up your brandy."

"Oh, shoot, you were welcome to it. Only—"

"Thanks. It warn't unwelcome. You recall the time the young fella almost died aboard the cargo boat?"

"Of course I do."

"Some cluck give him a slug of whiskey on top of a freak-out."

"So?"

"It could've killed cold a kid as little as Andy."

"Andy?" Lewis said, stunned.

"Andy says Hal gave him something in a bottle of Coke. There ain't any real proof of it, Andy don't remember too good what happened. He only told Amanda, didn't want to worry his Ma. They was two bottles of orange pop come to roost in your cabin, nobody knew where they come from. Why? Amanda had the sense to heave 'em overboard, and then she told Adam, just in case he might accept a free present from Hal."

"What ailed them they didn't tell me?" Lewis said. "We could have locked him up before—" Anger choked his voice. "He . . . my God! He . . . feeding drugs to kids? He ought to be shot."

"I'm going to do some ransacking myself," Jilson said. "In his cabin. If I find any proof I can be sure of, I'm going to shoot the bugger in the laig. That'll hold him still, till we can git to a constable."

"Which will be soon," Lewis said. "I've had it up to here. This time, we'll let Jasper sleep. We passed Green Mountain, in on the coast there, around one o'clock. The chart shows a deep-water channel at the foot of the mountain, with a sheltered harbor at its western end and a fair-sized town where there'll be a doctor, with any luck. I'll have to check the chart—"

"Green Island Channel," Jilson said. "It's tricky as all hell."

"You know it?"

"I ought to. I've sailed it times enough."

"That's right, I forgot you come from these parts some-where, don't you?"

"Near enough," Jilson said.

"You know the channel well enough to take the *Macomber* in there?"

"Well, I never took the *Macomber* in there. I could do it if we hit it in daylight. Nobody but a fool'd try it in this creation after dark."

"We'll make it before dark, then. We can keep her on power until we get some wind. What do you figure the weather's going to do?"

"Once it starts it ain't going to fool around none. The way the clouds been curdling up, there to the west'ard, and the way the air smells like somebody's washing right off the line, we'll likely git a no'theaster with snow. How's the tide, you know?"

"Of course I know. The ebb here has got about three hours to run."

"Hell of a big coast tide along here," Jilson said. "That bullgine of Brown's wouldn't do no more'n keep her head to it till it slacks off some. H'm. You can tell from them oily swells that some kind of a ruckus is raising particular hell offshore, right now. Likely we'll get a good breeze be-fore long, too. Then we could set sails and bust 'er wide open into Green Island Harbor."

"Good. I'll change heading right now."

"You need any help, holler," Jilson said. "Right now, I've got some other fish to fry."

Lewis glanced at him. "Hal? Better let him alone till I can come with you, hadn't you?"

"I won't bother him for nothing except my sugar bowl," Jilson said softly. "That one that was on young Andy's tray, I'd touch about as soon's I'd touch a rattlesnake."

Maddening old devil, Lewis thought as he went up the companionway steps. Maddening, yes; but when you needed him he was there.

Not a breath of wind. The weather was changing but not in too much of a hurry. The air was steadily growing colder, colors darkening down. The swells were gunmetal now, their glassy tops reflecting sky.

Harold was astounded, when he opened his stateroom door to a knock, to see Jilson standing there, poking the long barrel of a huge, old-fashioned pistol at him.

"You git back into your bunk," Jilson said. "Stick your leg out if you want a bullet in it."

Hey, what the hell, the old boy wasn't, you know, fooling. Hal did as he was told. "What's the matter with you?" he asked. "Have you gone nuts?"

Jilson didn't answer. Not turning his back on Hal, keeping a cautious eye out when he had to, he began to search the stateroom. His hunt didn't have to last long. In the top drawer of the elegant bedside dresser he found what looked to be a young drugstore—bottle after bottle of pills, medicines, packets of one kind and another. Still watchful, he unscrewed the top of a bottle marked *Aspirin,* shook a pill out into his hand. It was unmarked; otherwise it might have been what the label said it was.

"You got a headache?" Hal asked politely.

"Nope. I take it you have one often. Where's the key to your door?"

"In the lock."

Jilson shoved the drawer shut. He went out, locked the door on the outside, and went along the passageway, carrying the key and the aspirin bottle in his hand.

Left alone, Harold lay for a moment quietly in his bunk. Old fat ass had caught on. How? Probably missed the sugar and took an educated guess. Been around, that old boy. A lot of good it'd done him to lock that door, though. Twice Uncle Jasper'd asked for that bunch of duplicate keys to the staterooms. Tch, tch, too bad. Both times I forgot to hand them over to him.

*   *   *

Fairleigh, at the wheel, said to Lewis, "Thank God! That land in there, we could hit a harbor before dark, couldn't we, Cap'n?"

"We could," Lewis said. "That's the heading. Okay?"

"I'll say okay. Much more of this and I'm upside down. Hal promised to relieve me, and he hasn't showed up. I don't know where Coon is."

"I'll send somebody down," Lewis said. "Can you make out a while longer?"

"Oh, sure. She's easier on the wheel now."

Headed westerly, the *Macomber* was easier. As the ebb tide slacked, she even made headway toward the coast. The rounded hump which was Green Mountain lost its hazy outline, became a mountain. There was still plenty of daylight left, and when the flood tide made, it would help, though by that time, Lewis hoped, the help would be where it was needed, up Green Island Channel. There had even been a few puffs of wind, vague and wandering, and Coon and Fairleigh had got the sails up to catch anying that might blow from the northeast and fair. Adam, with pride, had taken the wheel while Coon and Fairleigh broke out the sails, and Lewis had had a few words with him then.

"Andy's better, Dad. That tea helped a lot. When I came out, he was asleep."

"You ought to have told me about this, Ad."

"Well, Amanda promised Andy. Still, I would've, if you hadn't just come out of the hospital. You'd have tackled Hal, you know you would."

Lewis smiled a little and tapped him lightly on the shoulder. "Yes," he said. "Thanks, Ad. I see. I guess you were in a bind."

Adam grinned back. "Gee, I sure was," he said.

There had been no sign of Brown. It wasn't like him to be unavailable when sounds on deck let him know he was needed, but actually he hadn't been needed and Lewis was glad he was still asleep.

He'll find out soon enough that we've had to turn the show around, Lewis thought, and, with a sinking heart, I'm going to have to tell him why.

Could it be possible that Brown didn't know already? He had talked about being in a bind. Remembering that morning and that talk, and the old man's distress, Lewis wondered. If Brown knows and still, without warning us, turned that cruel and irresponsible boy loose aboard here, then he must be sick. A lot sicker than he thinks. Impossible to believe he'd have done it, knowing Hal would be around among children.

So. I don't believe Brown knows or would credit a word of it if I told him.

Coon does, though. He was expecting something to happen that night, and it wasn't any dark that came out of the east. That sock on the jaw he gave Hal, I'd be willing to bet dollars, wasn't because of anything Hal had done to him. It was for Andy.

Braced against the after cabin, where he could see the land coming closer, Lewis could by turning a little see in at one of Brown's stateroom windows. Jasper was asleep, back-to in his bunk, only the top of his head with its grizzled hair showing.

Let him sleep. Poor old devil, by the time he wakes up, we could, with luck, be anchored in Green Island Harbor.

"Cap'n Wyman?" The voice behind him was tentative, and it was Harold's, but Lewis, swinging around, for a moment was bewildered. All he could think of was Harvey, the man-sized rabbit. All it lacked was ears. Then he realized that the rig Harold had on was a snowmobile suit, cream-white in color, heavily quilted over some kind of acrylic or goose down. His enormous boots were of fur, spotted black and white, to his knees.

"My God!" Lewis said.

"What? Oh, my suit? I was just cold. Best thing in the world for keeping a man warm, and I guess my blood pressure's low from being seasick. Cap'n Wyman, I saw you looking in at Uncle Jasper. Has he moved yet?"

"Not while I was watching him," Lewis said.

"I'm worried. I thought he'd be on deck like a shot when you changed the course. Would you come in there? There's something I want you to see."

"Why not let him sleep? He's had a day of it."

"We won't have to wake him up. Please come."

Lewis stared at him. The smooth, boyish face, the pink cheeks, the look of health and well-being were set off by the white fur of the close-fitting hood, and Lewis' stomach turned over.

"I won't disturb your uncle," he said shortly. "Whatever it is can wait till he wakes up." He thrust his doubled fists into his jacket pockets. Let the law take care of him. The police'll see he has a fine place to go.

"No, it can't wait," Hal said. "I think somebody's fritzed up his insulin dose. I think that's why he's been feeling so pooped these last few days."

"Who'd do a thing like that?" Another joke? More fun and games?

"Well, I don't know, but I could make a guess. Something's sure wrong. Uncle Jasper always acts like that, tired and, you know, sick, doesn't eat, when his dose isn't right."

There might be something in this, the way Jasper had been for the best part of a week—morose, listless, off his feed.

Lewis took another look through the window. Something about the immobility of the man in the bunk made up his mind. "All right," he said.

Inside the cabin, Harold made for the top drawer of Jasper's table. "See, here's his stuff and the needle that goes with it, been used, see? And now look, taste this."

Lewis took the opened bottle, poured a couple of drops into his hand. The colorless liquid had no taste whatever, no medicinal smell. But had insulin any taste? He didn't know.

"We can compare it," Harold said. "This other bottle here hasn't been opened." He produced another bottle, twisted off its cap. He said, "Oh, my God, Cap'n Wyman!

He's been plugging water into himself for who knows how long!"

"Shut up!" Lewis said. "What's Jasper's dosage? How much of this stuff does he take?"

Hal stood where he was, turning the bottle around in his fingers.

"Well, if you don't know, go get Coon. Get a move on, for godsake!"

Horrified, cold to his heart, Lewis turned toward Jasper, turned his back on Hal.

The heavy kick at the base of his spine sent him sprawling. The full weight of Hal landed on his back, flattening him, crushing out his wind. Something slammed hard on the side of his head, and he blacked out.

"That's for you and for any other cluck sticks his nose in my business," Harold said. He picked up Lewis' unconscious body, thrust it into the lower bunk, opposite Jasper's. "For a cent, I'd give you the heave-ho overboard," he muttered. But he couldn't do that. Coon was at the wheel now, and he'd see it. Well, on this side of the cabin it couldn't be seen from the window, and laid flat and covered with a blanket, it wouldn't be noticed from the doorway, unless whoever came in looked twice.

Now he had to work fast. When he'd come around the corner of the house, had seen this guy snooping in the window, he'd been scared stiff. God, he was still shaking! He hadn't been in yet to put the insulin back where it belonged. If Wyman decided to look closer and realized how Uncle Jasper was now, oh, wow! Harold had had to think fast.

He poured the water out of the first bottle, dropped it into the drawer. He was about to restore the second bottle to its proper place when the auxiliary engine, which seemed to him to have gone on forever, suddenly stopped. The *Macomber* yawed, swung into a trough. Harold grabbed a handhold just in time to keep from falling to the deck, and the bottle in his hand dropped and smashed.

Oh, hell, now he'd have to go down to his cabin to get another bottle. He had the rest of Uncle Jasper's supply stashed away down there.

Wait, though. If old Greasy Spoon with the gun, there, had done any checking, he'd know Hal wasn't in his stateroom. Wasn't fooling about shooting me in the leg, not much he wasn't.

He heard Coon, at the wheel, yell something. Fairleigh went by the window, lunging from handhold to handhold. After a little, Hal followed him. Coon, already halfway down the hatch that led to the engine, shouted at him to help Fair on the wheel.

Gone to fix the engine, hanh? Fat chance of fixing it now. It was about time that sugar worked up through the gas line to where it would do some good.

Could be things would work out all right. For a while Hal had been scared to death they wouldn't. He'd stolen the sugar, just in case someone, say, Coon, found Uncle Jasper too soon, and they'd headed inshore to a harbor, where some doctor might bring the old man to.

Cheerfully, Hal lent his muscles to Fairleigh on the wheel.

"I was just in talking to Uncle Jasper," he confided to Fairleigh.

"He awake? Why don't he come on deck?" Fairleigh asked nervously.

"He's still tired. I told him he ought to rest."

"Gee, I hope Coon fixes that engine pretty soon or we get some more wind. This is enough to kill the devil."

"Coon won't fix it," Harold said.

"How'd you know that?" Fairleigh glanced at him curiously.

"I got antenna out." Hal grinned. The way he was feeling, he almost told Fair then and there why Coon wasn't going to fix the engine.

Why, me and my big mouth, he thought, and considered with indulgence his big mouth. "I've got to go

[207]

for'ard," he said. "You can handle this all right, can't you?"

"No, dammit, I can't. You come back here!"

But Hal only waved a carefree hand and vanished around the corner of the house.

Fairleigh liked no part of what he saw happening around him, to the *Macomber,* to the Atlantic Ocean. The sight of those big oily rollers was enough to scare a man to death; it took all his strength to keep the vessel from swinging sideways into the trough. He began to pray for Coon to get the engine fixed or for some wind out of the east.

Jilson in his galley heard the auxiliary stop. The first sideways careen almost took him off his feet, and he thought it was a good thing he'd got those scouse pots stowed. He was busy decanting a gallon or so of canned stew into a kettle; no use to try to cook anything decent in this fandango, or even heat a pot of stew, and he didn't intend to try. Cold stew and bread and butter would be better than nothing. People could dip in. He himself expected to be busy, taking the vessel up Green Island Channel; Fairleigh'd have to have something he could hold on the stove with one hand, which was all the cooking he knew how to do.

The kettle Jilson was using was Brown's grandmother's biggest scouse pot, which was the heaviest one he had, harder to tip over than a light one. It also had a tight cover, with ears and a bale, so that it could be lashed to something. Looking at it, Jilson suddenly saw that it was twins. He did a double take. Sure enough, two kettles.

Couldn't be seasick. Never had been.

Drunk the Cap'n's brandy. No kind of liquor ever had any effect on me. Never in my life.

Can't leave them two—that kittle to roll around full of stew.

He set it down on the deck and lashed it to a table leg.

Old gal was sure bouncing around.

Kind of foolish to stop that bullgine before there was more wind.

Cap'n Wyman had Coon to help him. Coon knew what to do.

If they need me, they'll holler.

Jilson staggered to his bunk, feeling very strange indeed.

Whoever was poking around, rubbing his face and the back of his neck, was hurting. Lewis muttered, "Cut it out, will you?" and saw, as though through a slowly clearing fog, the pale, triangular face of Coon.

"You all right?" Coon said. "I thought you'd never come to."

Lewis' head made a loud thump and seemed to keep on thumping.

"Where'd he hit you?" Coon's hand, rough as gravel, went on massaging the back of Lewis' neck. The hand was unsteady; Lewis could feel its tremor down into his shoulders.

"Who?" he said. He moved to sit up, and his back, it seemed to him, screamed, a sound almost loud enough to be heard. He lay still again, rigid and gasping, but the pain had helped to clear his head.

"Here," Coon said. "Aspirin. Maybe it'll help."

"Pills?" Something about pills. What had it been?

But the two Coon offered, along with a cup of water, had the well-remembered taste of aspirin.

"Kicked me," Lewis said. "I guess I'm all right. Will be in a minute." The thumps weren't inside his head. They were from on deck.

Coon took his hand away. He let himself sag down to the side of the bunk, holding to a stanchion for support. "I'm glad I could do something for you," he said thickly. "I got here too late to help my father." He brought up his other hand, brushed it quickly across his eyes. The knuckles of the hand were bruised and swollen, spattered with flecks of blood.

Lewis began to remember. This was Jasper's cabin. Across it, in the other bunk, Jasper still lay. Someone had pulled up his blanket to cover the thick cockscomb of grizzled hair and had rigged rope lines to keep him from rolling out of the bunk. Lewis felt his mouth go dry. He tried to swallow, managed to stop the nausea rising in his throat, recalling the water in the insulin bottle, his own brutally stopped effort to help Jasper.

"I tried," Coon said. "I worked over him, seemed like hours, tried mouth-to-mouth, everything I knew. I didn't quit till he—till I could feel how cold he was . . . his arms were stiff. . . . I can't seem to think or stop bawling."

"Let it come," Lewis said. "You'll feel better."

"I'll never feel better. Not till I kill that bastard. He had you both locked in here. The door's locked now. I had to bust in a window." Coon held up his bloody hand, glanced at it briefly. "Busted it in with my fist."

The boy was half out of his mind with grief and shock, Lewis could see. He himself was still somewhat fuzzy-headed. It was hard to think straight. How long had he been out?

"I found one bottle empty. One on the floor, broke. That was all. Pa had a lot of it, somewhere. I couldn't find any."

Lewis sat up, gritting his teeth against fiery quivers of pain. The aspirin had helped, but he'd have to give it more time. The *Macomber*'s fantastic motion, the sideways lunge and roll twisted his body; he wouldn't be able to stand. Not yet. Sitting up, he could see beyond the narrow cabin windows a darkening piece of sky, with somewhere behind it a queer, whitish glow. What time was it, and where was the *Macomber* now? Not in Green Island

Channel or any other sheltered place. And where the hell was Jilson?

"Coon," he said sharply. "Come out of it, boy. We've got to get moving, get out of here, find out what's going on."

Coon shook his head slightly. He sat staring at the opposite bunk; two bright runnels slid down his cheeks. He scrubbed them away with the back of his hand.

"It's getting dark," Lewis said. "Stick your head out the window, see how close under the land we are. See if you can tell what the weather's doing. That glow in the clouds—what is it? Sunset through overcast? Snow? Snap it up! We've got to know."

Coon jerked to his feet. He headed, not for the window, but for Jasper's table, crawling on all fours for the last few feet.

"Cut it out!" Lewis said. "It's too late to do anything now."

If Coon answered, Lewis couldn't hear him. He had yanked open the lower drawer of the table and was rummaging around in it. He came back, still crawling, dragging behind him by its lanyard Jasper's big waterproof flash lamp, the one the old man had always carried at night, powerful as a searchlight. Coon had known where to find it. He flung the lanyard over Lewis' head.

"Hang onto it, Cap'n. Stay here. I'll see what I can do and then find a key or come back with an ax." He made for the broken window, wriggled through, and was gone.

I could maybe get out that way, too, if I could get myself over there. Lewis measured the narrow opening with his eyes. But Coon, thin as a lath, had had trouble and Lewis' shoulders were somewhat wider than Coon's.

Where was Jilly? He must know by this time what was happening. It he isn't on deck, it's because he can't be. Frantic with worry, Lewis thought of the kids and Belle in the other cabin, the sick boy . . .

I've got to stop thinking of anything except how to move, how to break out of here. Maybe I can pick that lock with my penknife.

At the top of a towering upward swing, the *Macomber* checked. She hung motionless, not as if her hull had met any obstruction in the water, but as if some force had laid hold of her sails and rigging as she leaned for the plunge into the trough of the next wave. Then she slammed sideways and down and kept on going.

Lewis, flung backward in a tumble of blankets, heard from outside a confused yelling and one gravel-throated roar, cut off in the middle by a wild shriek of wind and the thunder of falling rigging. A hard, heavy object crashed on top of the cabin with a tremendous impact which shook the whole structure.

A mast, Lewis thought. Maybe both of them. Whatever it was lay there thudding and pounding, then, as the vessel heeled, rolled or was washed off, for the sounds ceased and the wavering light from the sky coming through the windows was blotted out as if someone had snapped it off.

Scrabbling around, trying to untangle himself from the smother of bedding, Lewis found he could move.

He guessed he wouldn't need to, there was no sense to try. Because she's going. She's done for. She can't possibly come back.

To die penned up like a rat in a cistern was horrible, but to die in darkness was a thousand times worse. He felt for the switch of Jasper's flash lamp, snapped it on, and found himself staring upward at the opposite bunk almost directly above his head. He could see Jasper's body sagging against the lashings that held it in. A great dollop of water roared through the window Coon had broken, crashed against the cabin wall and into the bunk, soaking Lewis to the skin, filling the bunk like a horse trough. Then it began to pour away.

The *Macomber* wasn't giving up, by God! She was still

trying. She was hurt—that crash had been a mast, all right, he could make out rigging and some flapping canvas mashed against the cabin windows; but the plucky old lady was slatting her fat bottom right-side-up again where it belonged.

He had better do the same with his.

Flat on his stomach, sometimes crawling, Lewis wormed his way toward the door. Water continuously in motion washed over him; he couldn't tell how deep it was, but deep enough to wash him loose from a handhold once, roll him over and over, back to the opposite wall. He timed his movements, clinging to whatever there was while the big slosh went by, making as much way as he could till it rolled back.

Lord, the things that went on in a man's mind. All he could think of was a louse in a washing machine.

Under his body, flattened to the deck planks, he could feel a steady continuous vibration, as if the tough wood within its own grain were tearing apart, letting go. He got to the door, reared up to his knees, clinging to the knob. Here, he could realize more clearly the confused and terrible racket going on on deck. Crashes, bangs, squeal and roar of wind, swash and thud of water . . . Who'd open a door to go out in it? Who'd let it in?

The *Macomber*'s stern mounted as a big roller thrust under it. Lewis braced himself, waiting for the sickening drop that would come. To his numbed astonishment, it did not come. Instead, the vessel steadied. Under his feet he could feel some of the strain go out of her as she swung heading into the wind. There must be some gear left—the rudder, a sail or two—and somebody on deck who knew what he was doing, because she seemed to be bow-on to it and holding, at least for now.

He clung to the latch, focused the light beam on the door lock, started to raise himself an inch at a time. The pistol shot a few inches from his head half-stunned him and the bullet parted his hair. He heard it whang into the opposite wall of the cabin as he ducked and the wash of water carried him sideways. Wood splintered with a second shot and the door swung open.

He saw a snowman; behind him, a blind, impenetrable smother. Gusts of it drove into the cabin, tiny, steel-hard needles that flicked past the flashlight beam and stung his face. A second snowman materialized behind the first, staggered, fell across Lewis' legs. A roll of seawater splashed over them both, leaving a gob of yellowish foam. Someone reached, took the flashlight lanyard from around Lewis' neck, hauled the weight off his legs. He yelled words nobody could hear, indicating with the light beam the closed door of the opposite stateroom. Now, Lewis could see three figures silhouetted against the light. Like crippled men, they moved into the senseless, screaming blankness, in which the powerful searchlight beam was little more than a milky glow. Brown's prized coach-house entrance to the cabins was as if it had never been. Then the door of the port stateroom opened and closed behind them.

One of the snowmen slid down by Lewis, clutching his arm. A wet, ice-cold nose bumped against his cheek. "Dad?" Adam's voice said in his ear. "Dad? Are you okay?"

"Adam," Lewis said. It was all he could manage. He put his arm around the boy, held him close.

Coon was sitting flat, as Lewis was. The light, hanging from its lanyard on Coon's chest, was still milky, crusted with melting snow. He put up a hand which, after a couple of tries, wiped it clear. His feet were braced against the second snowman's feet; the two sat, as if wildly staring at each other, toe to toe. The second snowman, Lewis saw, was Jilson.

Jilson looked to be in hard shape. His breath came in a series of grunts. His eyebrows were fierce with hardened snow, his moustache icicled with it. He put up a hand, knuckled the snow from his face; he had a lump on his jaw, another, purplish-black and swollen, on his forehead. He was, however, alive and still able to yell.

"I see . . . you ain't dead, Cap'n . . . we thought . . . you was."

"Where in hell were you?" Lewis yelled back.

"Doped. Skunk juice planted in your brandy." A crash from out on deck drowned out the yell. Lewis made out, ". . . mistake. Turned me into a flickering flame of fire, b'Jeezus!" The continued hoarse roar turned now on Coon. "Shift . . . goddam flashlight. You're blistering m'eyeballs . . ."

Coon swung the light quickly away. The beam passed across Lewis' bunk, steadied there. Belle had done what she could to cope. She was braced behind a big roll of blankets, stuffed against the sideboard of the bunk, and had padded both ends of the bunk with other bedding. Behind her capable back, Amanda and Andy looked out with wide-open, terrified eyes.

Lewis moved, cautiously, holding on to whatever handholds he could find. He reached, put a hand over Belle's where it gripped the sideboard of the bunk, feeling its strength and tension. She leaned her head toward him so that he could hear.

"Lew, thank God! We thought you'd gone overboard." She relaxed her hand long enough to give his a brief squeeze. "We're all right. Andy's better. Only scared now."

It was quieter in this cabin—no broken window to let in the outside tumult. Yet he could hardly hear her, and he was still too breathless himself to raise much volume. He managed, "God bless you, hang on."

"Dry clothes," Belle said. "Get some on. In the lockers. Get some for the others, too. Harold's. God knows there're plenty."

Scrabbling and clawing, he pulled himself along the side of the bunk to the steel locker at its foot, reached and wrenched open the locker door. A thick, heavy mass of assorted clothing gushed out as if blown ahead of a blast.

The legs of a pair of wool pants hung on a hook, clasped themselves in a friendly way around his neck. Suddenly, he realized how desolately soaked and frozen he was.

The others, too. He began rooting in the locker full of Harold's clothes. Warm stuff. Dry. Ironical, at last to get something decent out of Hal. Where was he? Lewis didn't much care.

Sheepskin-lined vest. Quilted ski jacket with a hood. Heavy pants. Tough, heavy stuff. He realized that Coon had come up alongside him with the light and begun shoving things, by the armful, to him. And bracing himself, shuddering, as the *Macomber* almost threw him flat again, he thought, At least we're going to drown warm.

At the first touch of the dry material against his skin, he felt better. He shoved along the side of the bunk with an armful of jackets and pants for the kids.

He found Coon already there, hauling down more bedding from the upper bunk—the mattress, which apparently Belle hadn't been able to handle, more pillows, blankets. "Get 'em braced against that . . . when . . . hit . . . the jolt . . . break bones," Lewis made out. "Do . . . same thing . . . other bunk."

"I'll help," Lewis said, and found he couldn't. His back, which he hadn't felt since leaving Jasper's cabin, contracted with pain, doubled him up. Coon clutched his arm to steady him; his hand fumbled until it found Lewis' hand, pressed into it a small rectangular tin. Aspirin.

For a moment, Lewis was furious. Not at Coon—it was damned nice of Coon to remember—but at whatever Providence had hold of him now, plastering on bad luck, refusing to let up. Go ahead, damn you, make it worse! he thought. What difference does it make whether or not I drown with my back eased up?

Coon helped him into the other bunk, eased him down next to Adam. Jilson, after he had changed his clothes, had climbed into the bunk and lay braced against the wall. He must be still groggy, because he made no move to help Coon with the bedding from the upper bunk. He was, however, not unconscious, for he suddenly yelled out, "Turn that light off! Burn the battery down, we won't be able to see the bottom of the kelp bed!"

Close to Lewis' ear, Coon said, "Hang 'er tough, Cap'n. I'm going over there with them, help 'em hold on." He moved away, climbed into the opposite bunk, and snapped off the light.

At once, Lewis regretted it. In the sudden pitch blackness, the howl of the wind, the thuds and crashes from outside sounded louder, the *Macomber*'s plunges seemed more violent. Adam, beside him, jerked a little, began to shiver. Lewis put an arm over him, held him closer.

Chances were, with the vessel driving fast on the coast, that Jilson was right—it would be the bottom of a kelp bed for everyone, but Lewis wished the old fool would shut up about it. He thought of the long coast, stretching thousands of miles, north and south from Labrador to Cape Horn, and nowhere in it a hole of shelter to be found in this darkness.

So here we huddle, not a damned thing we can do. And my fault for letting us get into this.

Nevertheless, he swallowed a couple of aspirin and to his surprise almost at once felt better. Not his back, which was tuning up again, but, he supposed, the idea that the aspirin might help, give it time. If there should be time. The homely gesture of taking medicine was on the side of life. And so was Coon. It was as if Coon had been saying all along, "Hold on, we've got a chance to get out of this, I'm not giving up, don't you."

Lewis' mind began slowly to function.

We're driving stern-first, we've got to be, and steady. How? Someone on deck? No one could hold her head to it in this, only a fool would try, there'd be no sense to it. He reached across Adam and nudged Jilson. "Is anyone on the wheel, Jilly?"

For a moment, he thought Jilson hadn't heard him.

Then Jilson said, "Ain't no wheel. Ain't no nothing. Both masts gone. For'ard house carried away."

From beside him, Adam said clearly, "Jilly and I and Fairleigh rigged a sea anchor." His voice shook a little, but in it was a certain amount of pride.

"Foremast laid half-overboard," Jilson said, leaning across Adam. "Riggin', shrouds, sails, never saw such a mess. We got the windlass cable hitched onto it, chopped 'er loose and over she went. Tailed out good. Took a-holt of us like a cat with a kitten. Don't know how long she'll hold, ain't much of a rig. We headed aft here, one of them seas come over, wound me around the stub of the main-mast. Fairleigh went. I thought Ad had gone, too." He subsided.

"He found me hanging onto his foot," Adam said. "Jilly was surprised." He giggled, a little hysterically. "Jilly was also crazy. He flailed around like King Kong."

"It was that cussed skunk juice," Jilly said. "A while there, I felt like God."

Adam. Lewis' throat tightened. He said huskily, "That was close."

Adam said, "You're not just whistling 'Dixie.' "

Fairleigh gone. It could so easily have been Adam as well. Hal—where was he? Evidently he hadn't been around to help or Jilly would have said so. If he had not gone overboard when Fairleigh went, he must still be around, somewhere belowdecks, huddled in a stateroom, alone, with what he had on his conscience for company. An act of cold-blooded murder which no man who was any part of human would care to take with him, fresh, to his death. There was no doubt in Lewis' mind now. And Jasper Brown, dead in his flooded cabin, could not be more lonely.

Lewis said to the pitch blackness in front of him, "We lose Hal, too?" and Jilson's gravelly roar answered him.

"Hal left us quite some time ago."

After a silence, he went on, "So shut up, will you, Cap'n?

My head feels like a turnip with a crow on it. Pick, pick, pick."

There was in the voice the same stonelike coldness which Lewis remembered from the day on Brown's wharf —the misbegotten day when he had decided to sail with the *Lizzie Macomber*—when Jilly, peering down at the water, had said, "He ain't if he can't swim."

Lewis had a sudden picture, clear before his eyes, of the pale-colored snowmobile suit tossed and tumbled in black water, before the air was forced out of its expensive fabric and it went down.

The *Macomber* struck the coast at the height of the storm tide, in darkness and a smother of snow. Fifty feet from shore, her keel ground over a flat-topped ledge, normally a foot or so out of water at high tide, but tonight drowned deep in surf. Before he heard the breakers' heavy growl, Lewis sensed what was coming from the violent change in the vessel's motion, the sharp, jerky lift and fall. He sat up, yanked Adam to a sitting position, shoved him hard against the padded end of the bunk, realized that Jilson, too, had felt the difference. The sudden sharp check slammed them hard against the mattress and layers of bedding; Lewis thanked God for Coon's foresight. A crack like that against a hard surface, against wood, would certainly have broken bones, might have killed a man. As it was, it knocked the wind out of him. He managed to gasp, "Everyone all right?" and heard Jilson say, "Wouldn't be, if the old gal had fetched up all standing on that."

That she hadn't was evident. He could hear the solid, grinding drag as the *Macomber*'s momentum and the weight of water behind her drove her across the ledge. Then she was free. The next big roller drove her, smashing and splintering, stern-on, into the ledges on the shore.

The sudden upward thrust as the stern rose to the slant of the shore threw Lewis out of the bunk. He was aware of somebody else on the deck with him; flailing arms beat against his jacket, grabbed and held on; someone else had him by the collar. He found the sideboard of the bunk and clung to it while another big roller churned under the vessel's bow, carrying her higher on the ledges. He hung on, waiting for the drag-back that would come when the wave receded. It did not come. She stayed where she was, wedged, apparently, slanted back on what had to be a steep and sloping shore.

The flashlight beam cut through the dark. Coon was on his feet yelling. Lewis could hear the yelling but not what was yelled. He was yelling himself—get out quick, because whatever was wedging the stern wasn't likely to hold it stationary for long.

The flailing hands that had gripped his jacket, he realized now, had been Andy's; Jilson had the boy, a firm grip under his armpits. He saw the moving shapes of Belle and Amanda following the flash lamp's light, and he looked for Adam. Adam was beside him, helping him to his feet.

In the roaring tumult outside, they followed Coon around the corner of the afterhouse. The house made a lee and Coon stopped there, while he aimed the light out over the stern. The powerful beam stopped short a few feet in front of his face, against a wall of parallel-driven snowflakes. More opaque than fog, yet alive in a way fog could never be, the white hissing streamed past the light, reducing it to a small, yellowish cone. The lens was already spongy with snow; Coon wiped it with his hand to clear the snow away. For a second they saw the reflected shadow of his hand, a tremendous black claw as if reaching out of the solid wall of snow.

Coon said loudly, "Jeezus!" and snatched the hand away.

Lewis heard this only because Coon's mouth was almost against his ear. Coon was going on shouting, shoving the light at him, flinging the lanyard over his head. ". . . drop off the stern," Lewis made out. ". . . hold light on me."

Lewis crawled past the splintered stump where the

wheel and binnacle had been. The stern rail was gone, the tender from its davits. Flat on his stomach, in a mass of tangled rigging, he pointed the flash lamp downward. At first, he could see nothing but swirling flakes. Then he found that by lowering the light to the length of its lanyard, he could get it into a lee under the stern. He made out something, a gleam of wet wood, not far down—the *Macomber*'s rudder and sternpost lying there; beyond it, snow-blasted and solid, was a curve of ledge. He couldn't see Coon. Or hadn't Coon gone down there?

A hand tugged at his leg. Coon crawled past him, vanished into a dark shadow over the stern. For a moment, Lewis thought he had jumped; then he saw that Coon was using a rope, made fast somewhere behind them, going down it hand over hand. The rudder skidded as his feet struck it, slid sideways out of sight. Under it was ledge; not rockweed-covered ledge, but a slightly rounded slab of grayish-white granite. Sun-bleached granite, wet now, but granite above high-water mark.

Jilly, creeping in beside him, hauled up the rope. He tucked Andy into the looped end of it and lowered him into Coon's arms. Amanda went next, and then Belle, who said with a gasp as she went over the stern, "It's going to take more than you to handle me." Lewis, beside them, clinging to his lamp, heard Jilson's gallant reply. "Gwan! Git! You ain't no heavier'n a cow . . . many's the cow I've h'isted in my time."

The *Macomber* died hard. She had struck on the peak of the tide, a flood driven high up the shore by the storm. Her sea anchor had fetched up on the flat-topped ledge briefly, but long enough to slow a little her dizzying drive toward the finish. A towering breaker carried her high up the shore; the next one had slammed her stern between two massive shoulders of granite and had wedged it there. The rest of her battered length lay churning up and down, slowly giving to the grind of her keel against the rock.

Breakers drowned her deck, their crests ripped off in great veils streaming into darkness.

When the center of the storm passed, her warped keel gave up the fight and broke in two. The wind had started to go down, but the sea had not; for a time, the ebbing of the tide was imperceptible because of the weight of water, the tremendous surf still thundering in. The broken-off section of her bow swung sideways, crashed against the ledges, was borne up and over them to a sand and pebble beach. What remained of her stern, a chunk of naked hulk about forty feet long, stayed wedged between the granite shoulders.

PART TEN

Fred

FRED MONTGOMERY, waking in the night, heard the sound of the storm and realized that it was something out of the ordinary. The wind roared around the house, rising sometimes to a wild squeal that petered out to a moan as it drove past a chimney or a corner. He was sleeping in an upstairs east bedroom; last night he'd opened a window an inch or two. What had waked him was sharp needles of snow blown all the way across the room into his face.

That sure hit blunt-end-foremost, he told himself.

He got out of bed, padded over to the window. Already snow had built up a layer on the sill and was icy and wet underfoot. His toes flinched away from it and he shivered as he shut the window.

Something hit the porch roof outside with a crunch of breaking wood. That loose gutter he'd been going to fix earlier on. Now it would have to be a new one. Serve me right.

But he didn't care now what work there was to do. Welcome, work! Welcome, anything! Welcome to a November snowstorm, two weeks earlier than snow was supposed to come, that would make outdoors work twice as hard as it ought to be. Who cared a hang what happened now? Jakie and Caroline were alive, sleeping in the bedroom off the living room, along with Jakie's kitty. He'd better make a trip downstairs, make sure the fireplace screen was up good and tight and that nobody had been waked up and scared by the storm.

Halfway down, he thought of something else that warmed him almost as good as a fire. He was in love.

By gum, you know, I am, he told himself.

He plodded soberly down. That was a wind! He'd even felt the house shake a little, that last gust. Hope the roof stayed on. Some of those old shingles would likely go.

The fireplace screen was up where it belonged—fire was nearly out anyway. These darn tight shutters made it dark as a pocket in the downstairs rooms at night. Be nice to take off one or two.

But I guess we won't be here too much longer.

He put on a living-room lamp, let it shine briefly through the door of the kids' room. They were fine— sound asleep, snuggled up one on each side of Walter. Only Walter moved; he turned his head and gazed at Fred, his eyes deep and glowing softly with the light.

Looked just like that spring, back of the rocks in the cave on China Hill. Turned a flashlight on it and there it was, almost as if it were looking back at you—as if it had a secret that nobody who wasn't a deep dark spring in a cave could ever know.

Fred turned off the light. He stood for a moment on the hearth, which was still slightly warm, trying to get some feeling back into his cold bare feet.

So, if we can't stay here very long, where will we go? Away from any place where people know us, that's for sure.

Lydia Pollard would be on his back in a ton of trouble if he ever let on about the kids or took them back to town. He could maybe write the count, they'd help. Maybe they'd take them.

But I don't want anyone to take them. I want them myself. Kids have got to be loved, that was what Susie'd said, and she'd been right. The Wiggling Biscuits would love them all right; but San Francisco's a hell of a long ways away from me.

I wonder if Caroline's right about Lydia's not adopting them legally or if that was just the old bat saying just about the rottenest thing she could think of to say. It was rotten, too—say a thing like that to a kid! Aunt Yuba might be in 5,000 different pieces over Henry Fling, half out of her mind with him and trouble, but she'd always been decent.

Sure like to know what she'd say if I was to write her and tell her that. Like to know, too, what Judge Higgins would say to it if he was to know. If people abuse children, the state'll take them away, even their own kids. I could go see Judge Higgins. I'd have to have some good, straight, eyewitness evidence, something besides the kids', about the way Lydia used them. Still, if I couldn't get anyone to speak up . . .

Fred knew his neighbors. Not one of them but would rather have every tooth in his head pulled out than go to court as a witness.

And if I told the judge those kids were alive, and things went against us, we might have to send them back to Lydia.

I would take them to Timbuktu first.

At the thought, Fred felt colder, and lonesome as the last peeper in a spring swamp—the one that hadn't found another peeper to join up with. There always seemed to be one that got left out, and he kept going on and on about it, long after all the others had quieted down and set up house for the summer. Coming home after dark some nights, even late as August, you could hear him saying, "Where?" and waiting; and then, "Where?" again. It was about the lonesomest sound on earth.

I'm a lonesome man in an old house at night in the middle of a raging storm, he told himself. But it ain't any use standing here and going on and on about it.

He went back up the stairs. An icy draft blew down

them from somewhere in the upper regions, curdled his ankles. As he passed the door of Susie's room, he found where it was coming from. It was blowing through the crack under the door. Even here in the hall, he could feel the snow needles in it.

God, she'd be buried up to her ears by morning.

He opened the door. Sure enough, window wide open. He stalked across the floor, shut the window with a bang.

From the bed, Susie said, "Fred? Is that you, Fred?"

"Yes, it is," he said. "I'm lonesome and froze half to death and—"

"Well, get in here with me," she said. "I've been waiting and waiting, and it's about time, isn't it?"

Waiting and saying, "Where?" Like me, Fred thought. Yes, I guess she must have been.

PART ELEVEN

Coon

TWICE JILSON HAD to rest. Once, he fell flat and Adam, coming behind, plowed into him. Jilson got up and went on, ducking the wet tree branches slatted into his face by the wind, staggering over uneven ground, until he came flat up against an almost impenetrable thicket of young spruce. If he had had any breath left, he would have let out a yell; this was what he'd been looking for. He knew this kind of country. Before he had gone to sea, he had been a hunter and a fisherman from the time he'd been old enough to keep up with his father's easy pace in the woods. This wasn't the first time he had been caught outdoors at night in a snowstorm, and not always with a flashlight as good as this one, either.

The middle of the thicket would be cold, but sheltered. There'd be dead saplings to start a fire with. He got down on his knees and wormed his way through saplings interlaced like a hedge. After a while, when he could no longer feel the wind on his back and the spruce needles under his numb hands were free of snow, he said to Adam, "This's a good place. Better'n the lee side of that bank. You think you can find the others if I give you the light?"

"I can follow our tracks back," Adam said.

"Don't depend too much on tracks," Jilson said. "Just

[227]

go straight's you kin and remember 'tain't far. Hold the light whilst I bust up some of this dry stuff."

"M-matches?" Adam had trouble holding still his chattering chin.

"I ain't ever been known to of been without dry matches to light my pipe," Jilson said. He had some, with his tobacco, in a waterproof tin.

The heap of dry twigs caught, flared up. Adam hunched over it, fed on more twigs, lengths of dry saplings, which Jilson broke over his knee and handed along. The fire grew steadily, a beautiful sight.

"Don't git too close to it," Jilson said. "Burn your feet off, you won't be able to go back after the rest. 'N there! Now I can see to keep this going. You hyper. You sure you can make it back there all right?"

Adam wriggled back through the thicket, wincing as the snow needles stung his face. Among the trees, he could still follow his and Jilly's tracks, but in the naked bedlam near the shore, they were blown over and gone. He stopped for a moment, bewildered. What if he couldn't find the others? They were huddled down here somewhere behind a four-foot bank at the top of the shore. Coon had hollowed out a kind of cave in the snow for them. Andy had had to rest and Belle hadn't wanted to leave him, so the others had stayed, too, while he and Jilly went on ahead to see what shelter they could find. What if they were snowed under, the way the tracks had been?

He flashed the light around and was relieved to see, not far away, a single pinpoint of light and a whitish figure coming toward him. He managed a croak and then a hoarse calf-blat, which he could hardly hear himself over the howl of the wind and the thunder of the breakers. To his surprise, it was answered; Amanda came plowing through the snow to him.

"We saw the light," she said. "Bug in a bottle."

The others were close behind her. Andy was walking; he staggered and his legs spraddled, but he was making it on his own. He lasted partway into the thicket, when his mother had to help him. After a little, they saw the yellow glow of the fire through the undergrowth.

Jilson had been breaking and throwing on the flames everything he could reach. "Git up to it," he said. "Git the kids close to it." He had made quite a hole in the thicket and the fire blazed high. He vanished briefly, and they could hear him crashing around in the brush, and the snap of dry saplings broken off at the base. The towering armful he brought back this time, he dropped on the ground, a reserve pile.

"All the comforts," he said, spreading his hands to the blaze, and stopped suddenly, staring bleakly around. "Where's Coon?" he demanded.

"He was right behind me with the other flashlight," Belle said. She, too, stared around, bewildered, because it was obvious that Coon wasn't there.

"Oh, for godsake!" Jilson reached over, plucked the flash-lamp lanyard from around Adam's neck. "He'd be the last one I'd think I'd have to haul out of a snowbank. Ad, keep the fire going." He stalked off, sounding very put out. For a while they could hear him swearing as he thrust his way out of the thicket.

It seemed to Adam that he couldn't move. He was sitting close to the fire, getting warm, too exhausted to brush the snow off himself. Amanda, seeing it was melting and would wet him through, did it for him. "I'll get some wood," she said. "What did he do—just pull up trees?"

"Broke them off, dry little ones," Lewis said. He tried to get up. "I'm sorry," he muttered. "I can't seem to bend."

"I'll help," Belle said. "If you could take Andy, Lew." She sat with her jacket, a heavy, fur-lined one from Harold's locker, open to reflect heat on Andy, who was backed up against her. As she got up, Andy winced and said loudly, "Ow, Ma! I think I'm ruined."

"What is it, honey? Where does it hurt?"

[229]

"This damn jug in my shorts. It's slid down my front."

"Let's see." Lewis reached a hand, unbuttoned a button. The hard object was his own brandy flask, which had been faithfully tucked against Andy's stomach. The sock it was wrapped in was damp and it was stone-cold, but as Lewis took it out he felt a slosh of contents. "Great guns, Andy, no wonder you had to walk spraddled out. Didn't you drink any of this?"

"Some," Andy said. "It was still hot when I went to sleep."

Lewis reached for a couple of sticks near the fire, laid the flask across them. "That'll heat up in no time," he said. "Look what this fellow of yours came up with, Belle. Tea."

Belle flung down the sticks of wood she carried and paused a moment by the fire. "Why, we can piece that out with snow water, maybe all have a warm drink. Andy, you're a miracle! Imagine even one swallow of hot tea!"

Nobody mentioned Coon; not aloud, but the silence grew heavier as time went on and Jilson did not come back.

Jilson floundered through the thicket until he arrived at his point of entry, at its edge. He saw no sign of Coon, heard no answer to his calls.

Must be around here somewhere. Snow ain't deep enough to bury him. Yet. But where, in this mess? Much more traipsing, I'm going to be flat on my face, myself.

This place here, now, was where they'd come up to the thicket. Big trees, with snow under them. You could see traces of tracks. What had that careless damn knothead done, walked back and gone to sleep in that hole in the snow?

He realized suddenly that he couldn't feel any snow now driving against his face. Flakes weren't blotting out the beam from the flashlight. Wind was going down some, too. Gusts not half as hard as they had been.

He blinked. Down there, off the shore, there'd seemed to be a flash, like some kind of reflected light. Well, Coon had a flashlight. Couldn't be him, though, unless he was wading around out there in the breakers.

Jilson pushed along, trying to keep his eyes on the place where the light had been. He turned off the flash lamp so that he might see better, in case the light came again. As he did, he caught a glimpse of sky. Big clouds, scud, barreling along; behind, a yellowish light. The moon. A small slice of it appeared, quickly hidden, and he caught the flash again.

Poof! Nothing but the moon on the water. Clearing off. That was one hell of a fast-traveling storm.

Now he could make out the line of boiling surf on the ledges, a vague grayness behind it that was the ocean. Tide would have had to ebb some, by now, but that sea hadn't gone down any. It was still making noise enough to deafen a man. The moon bobbed out, shone full for a moment from behind a black, scudding cloud. He saw that a shadow down there that he'd taken to be a ledge was the *Macomber*'s stern. He thought, awe-stricken, she's still there. She can't be.

He turned the flash lamp full on her to check. No mistake. There she was, cocked up like a cat on a barn roof. Well, I will be! It was as good as seeing a ghost.

Down on the *Macomber*'s stern, a light suddenly shone out. Its beam shot across his eyes, showed up briefly the narrow, cleared field between him and the shore, the bank he was looking for crested with snow, like a breaker ready to let go. Jilson let out a yell and started running through the snow.

That couldn't be Coon. Not even a simple damn fool would've climbed back aboard that wreck tonight. It's got to be somebody we left aboard, signaling. Couldn't be Hal, I know where that bugger went. Fairleigh? Thought he went overboard, too, could've been mistaken. And the old man's dead, Coon said. Could he have come to?

Climbing the bank, Jilson had to stoop down and claw through the slippery snow. As he started to rear upright again, something went whizzling over his head, landed with a clang on the rock behind him. A big, heavy, soft bundle hit him full in the chest, bounced off into the snow. He staggered, sat down hard, and began commenting in a loud voice, his words blurred somewhat by rage and by the tumult of the surf.

". . . know no better'n . . . heave stuff at a man . . . knock him arse over teakittle. . . . Who are you, blast you! Who's aboard there?"

"I was," Coon said, beside him. "You hurt any?" He was carrying something—a square wooden box, Jilson saw, playing the light beam on him.

"You crazy? Go back on there?"

"No. That's a bundle of blankets. Can you carry it? I've got all I can lug here."

"What good's wet blankets?"

"These came from the locker in Pa's cabin. They're pretty dry."

Coon stepped around Jilson, began playing his flashlight beam over the snowy rocks. "That was an ax I almost beaned you with," he said. "See it anywhere?"

The idea of an ax brought Jilson to his feet. Firewood. No more damn saplings, tear your hands to pieces on. He added the beam of the big flash lamp to Coon's, and they found the ax, half buried in snow at the foot of the ledge it had landed on. It was one of the emergency axes—the *Macomber* had carried several clamped to the outside walls of both her for'ard and afterhouses, just in case. Jilson and Fairleigh had used two of them to chop away the mess of fallen rigging which had made the sea anchor.

Jilson began to get over his rage. By gum, that youngster! If it wasn't something he'd done! I wouldn't of gone aboard there for a million dollars. He picked up the ax without a word, came back, and shouldered the bulky bundle of blankets. Maybe they *were* dry. They were lashed up inside a set of oilskins, pants and jacket.

Jasper's, I wouldn't wonder. Been in there, too, where

the old man lay dead. Well, I could say a little something decent to him.

He stepped out, caught up with Coon, who had walked off through the snow. "Pretty bad on there, was it?" he said.

"Yes," Coon said. "I got on and off all right."

What he had really gone back for, Coon wasn't going to talk about. He had seen everybody ashore and sheltered as much as possible in the lee of the bank, had waited until he'd seen the light which meant someone was coming down from the woods. Then he had quietly slipped away over the ledge, climbed the rope up over the *Macomber*'s stern. He had had trouble getting into his father's cabin. The door was ripped off, hanging on one hinge; a lot of wreckage and stuff had blocked the doorway. Breakers were still piling over the vessel's bow and up her deck; she was grinding, churning up and down. But she was canted back steeply—as he stood on the stern, the edge of foam from the biggest rollers washed over his feet, but he'd told himself that the ebb tide would surely have made by now.

Coon was still somewhat in a state of shock; otherwise he might not have tried what he was doing, which was to get somehow into the stateroom and carry out his father's body. It seemed, now, the least he could do. Get it ashore, see it buried decently somewhere, not abandoned to be pounded and battered by the sea, left as if nobody cared. Coon did care; he had loved the old man. The weight of grief was heavy in his chest as he ripped the ax off the wall of the afterhouse and chopped his way into the stateroom.

Inside, he stared around him wildly, with a sinking heart. The flashlight showed that the for'ard wall of the cabin was gone; the place was gutted. One stanchion of the bunk where Jasper had lain swung aimlessly to and fro, loose at its bottom end. The only thing left intact was the steel clothes locker, bolted to the wall.

He took the blankets from the top shelf of the locker. They were dry, except where his wet hands touched them.

He stuffed them into the pants of his father's suit of oil-skins, folded back the legs, buttoned the jacket around the bundle.

God, there was other stuff he ought to take—those candy bars of Pa's, boxes of them . . . might save all our lives, and he'd be glad of that, if he could know. Coon stuffed into his pockets and down the front of his shirt as many boxes as would go.

He was turning away when the flashlight caught a corner of the wooden box, shoved behind the clothes at the back of the locker. That, too—the case of fancy groceries Pa had been taking along for a present to his girl.

Coon's knees went weak. He leaned his exhausted body against the cold steel side of the locker, thinking, Oh, God, she'll wait a long time.

If I could let go, just slide out there into the water . . . a couple of those breakers would be all it would take. And quick.

But if this stuff would save some lives, maybe it was the next best thing; it might make up to Pa for the dirty, underhand, scabby way he had had to go.

Carrying his load, which was heavy, he watched his chance and made it to the peaked stern of the *Macomber,* a little higher above the furious water, now that the tide had begun to ebb.

Lewis woke, surprised to find himself waking up. When he had lain down, the pain in his back had been bad—he'd thought he'd never go to sleep again. But he was waking up, so he must have gone to sleep sometime. Cautiously, he stretched out a foot and found he could. Legs stiff, but not so bad as yesterday. Maybe, today, he'd be able to do his share of work. Could be, his share might be figuring out where they were, what part of the coast they'd got stranded on. Hopefully, the mainland; but there were hundreds of islands, some lived on, some not. Jilson had said last night the uninhabited ones were bleak and lonely at this time of year, seldom visited by anyone. "If this turns out to be one of them, we've got it tough."

He had got back with Coon last night deep in gloom, which had been surprising, considering Coon's haul of food and dry blankets. Everybody had had fancy canned meat, Hershey bars, and a drink out of the brandy flask, which, after it had been passed from hand to hand and diluted several times with snow water, could hardly have been called tea, but at least it was hot. Adam and Amanda, hunting through the thicket for dry wood, had come on a rough shelter, built out of brush and floored with leaves. A new fire, kindled on the open, lee side of it, reflected heat back inside, and with blankets spread on the leaves and others piled on top, it was infinitely better than bare, open ground.

"Somebody's been here not too long ago," Adam had said. "This brush is still green. Maybe they're still here."

"Summer people's kids, most likely." Jilson wasn't listening to anything hopeful from anybody.

Perhaps he'll feel better this morning. Lord, I hope so, Lewis thought. Someone was up. The fire was burning high; off in the thicket, he could hear the thumps of an ax, chopping wood. Jilly or Coon? Jilly. By firelight, Lewis could see that everyone else was here, asleep. Packed in like seeds in a pod. Coon, at the far end of the row, was jammed partly through the brush wall; Adam, next to him, appeared to be half on top of him.

Nighttime in the thicket; no light except from the fire. Through the laced brush above his head, Lewis couldn't see the sky. He held his watch to his ear, surprised to find it still ticking. Well, it was a good watch, self-winding, waterproof. He turned it toward the firelight. Five-thirty. Morning.

Jilly came into the light with an armful of wood, dumped it down by the fire. He stood for a moment, humped over, warming himself, turned, and went back into the woods.

The man must be made of piano wire, Lewis thought. And looks like a piece of limp string.

He slid quietly out from under the blankets and stood up.

Mobile again, thank God. His back was still sore, but he could walk. He went over to the fire, picked his boots out of the row left standing there to dry, began to worry them on. They were dried stiff as sticks, but warm.

Jilson, seeing him, came back. "Awful combination, warn't it?" he said.

"Never saw worse." Lewis supposed Jilly meant the wreck and the storm, but not at all.

"Deviled meat, choc'late bars, warm snow water, Jeezus!" Jilly said.

Lewis grinned at him. "Something made you feel human again, I see. Sure did me. Snow water and Hershey bars may not fill a man up, but seems they're just the ticket for a lame back. You have any notions about where we might be, Jilly?"

"Could be anywhere. Somewheres off Green Mountain last night. Wind no'theast, flood tide running hell-a-hootin westerly. By daylight, maybe we can tell. If my head would clear up, I could think better."

"Still feel rotten? How did you get that crack, anyway?"

Jilson moved over to Lewis' side of the fire, sat down near him. "I was in my galley, caroling like a bird," he said in a low voice. "My head felt like the inside of a one-hundred-watt 'lectric light bulb. Couldn't think, and as for moving, all I could do was twitchel some. Hal come down the companionway, knocked me flat with what felt like a chunk of two-by-four. I see he was going to kill me, and all I could do was roll over. Coon was right to his heels and Coon shot him. He lugged him on deck and heaved him over. Come back and told me, told me about poor old Jasper. I don't see how anyone could've done different."

"Neither do I," Lewis said. God! he thought. It takes a coward to put on a real ugly show.

Jilson was silent a moment. "I have killed better men than him in World War Two," he said at last. "That was a long time ago. I ain't used to any such of a sight now."

He got up, stalked out of the firelight into the thicket, where he began using the ax again. Presently he came back with another armful of wood.

"Weather's warming up," he said. "Going to be a nice Indian summer day. If the *Macomber* ain't broke up, she'll be setting there like a bird on a nest, and the tide ought to be out far enough, pretty soon, so's we can get aboard, find something we can use or eat. If I could get a-holt of just one of them scouse pots I benigrated so much, we could get us a mess of shellfish. There's got to be clams and mussels along the shore here somewhere."

The snow, in the morning, was beautiful. On the west side of the island, the wind had blown most of it into the water, but there were snowbanks left on the lee sides of thickets and buildings. The warm sun was melting it fast, making it just the right texture for snowballs and snowmen. After breakfast, Caroline and Jakie made a whole family—a snowman and woman, two children, and Walter, who was very hard to get exactly right. Fred had let him out early, when he himself had got up, and Walter was off by himself in the woods for a while. Fred said it was a shame to keep him tied up all the time, and he'd be all right if they were careful when they let him go. Like this morning, when the sea was so rough on the east side of the island that there wouldn't be lobster boats out. Besides, Fred and Susie were here now to take care of everybody.

Caroline couldn't make a very good snow-Walter until he came back, and the man and the woman didn't look too much like anybody. Jakie lost interest in them quickly, but he really zeroed in on the one she told him was Jakie. He worked hard on it and finally topped it with his woolen cap, so that everybody else would know. He got his mittens soaked—he had only the one pair, which Susie had brought him. Susie said she'd get him another this afternoon in Bradford. She and Fred were going over to town today.

She had to go to her house and get Tommy, her cat, who had been left alone there for two nights. "Poor Tommy," she said. "He'll have eaten up all the food I left, and he'll think he's been left alone forever."

She was appalled when Jakie, hearing this, burst out into a terrific beller. He rushed to Caroline, buried his head in her lap.

Caroline stared at Susie. "He can't stand it to hear about anybody left alone," she said stiffly.

"I know. I'm sorry. I said the wrong thing." Susie went over and put her arms around both of them. "Nobody here will ever be left alone again, Caroline," she said. "And Tommy won't either, Jakie. I'm going to bring him with me when I come back."

Jakie's dark cloud cleared away. He gulped and swallowed his beller and presently looked up at Susie. "Come back?"

"Yes. Right away this afternoon. Fred and I have got to go to Bradford. We'll buy you some mittens and then go to my house and get Tommy. We won't be gone very long."

Jakie wormed out of Caroline's clutch and started for the kitchen. He came back with a bucket, which he plunked down in front of her. "We and Walter go get muskels for Tommy, Caroline."

Fred, who had been out looking for storm damage around the buildings, heard this as he came through the door. "Better stay away from there today, Jakie," he said. "That old surf's roaring, sounds like houses tumbling down over there, and the water'll be way up over the mussel bed."

Jakie said firmly, "Tommy hungry." He picked up the bucket with an air of not having heard a word. Jakie seldom heard anything he didn't want to hear, anyway.

"Well, you can walk over and see," Fred said. "But don't get near the surf, Caroline. You ready, Susie?"

She was buttoning her coat. She said, "What color mittens do you want, Jakie?"

Jakie considered. "Yeller," he said, but he wasn't to be sidetracked for long. "Muskels, Caroline. Now."

"This afternoon," Caroline said. "You'll have to eat lunch first and have your nap. Besides, we have to wait for Walter to come back."

"We'll hustle," Susie said. She smiled at them and at Fred and took his hand as they went out the door.

Jakie had started his well-known pucker, which suddenly dissolved into a smile of his own. The sight of two people besides himself and Caroline—and Walter—loving each other was unusual and wonderful, something like Christmas. He ate his lunch without a word, went by himself to the davenport for his nap. As he lay down, he looked at Caroline, who was tucking him up in Mrs. Wiggling Biscuits' afghan. He said, in a marveling voice, "And Tommy, too!" and went peacefully to sleep.

Fred didn't want to make the long trip out around the Point to the harbor. First, it would have taken too much time, and, second, there'd be a lot of people around the harbor side and he wasn't going to expose Susie to any cheap remarks, in case there might be some. He was a little later than he'd planned to be in starting. His boat in Cat Cove was full of mushy snow which had to shoveled out. Some of the meltage had dripped through the engine box onto the engine. Fred had to operate, dry off the points, blow on this and that before the engine started.

"We'll leave the boat at Fosters' float," he told Susie. "I'll walk up through the woods and down through town and pick up my car. Then I'll drive back and get you, if you don't mind waiting."

"Why?" Susie asked. "I'd be proud to walk through town or anywhere else with you."

"Same to you," Fred said. He flushed a little. "I ain't sneaking around, Susie. But Pomroy Fifield'll have spread his news all over town by now, and I don't care to put up with any wisecracks. Ma's going to give me a hard time, too, and I don't want you to have to listen to it. You do as I say."

"Of course," Susie said meekly. "I'll wait for you on Yuba Fling's back steps."

At Yuba's back steps, he kissed her hard on the mouth and left her there, saying over his shoulder, "That'll keep you warm till I get back."

"Well, it surely ought to," Susie said. A little weak-kneed, she sat down on the steps to wait.

The steps gave under her; they were rickety and rotten; the sun didn't reach them at all. They were still damp, uncomfortable to sit on. She got up and began wandering around Yuba's backyard.

Snow had mostly melted out past the shade of the house, uncovering various kinds of trash—an old, collapsed wooden barrel which had spilled out rusty tin cans, junk, and paper. Food wrappers and pieces of old newspapers had blown around the yard and lay sodden. A clothesline still had pinned to it a length of drab, purplish material which might once have been a couch cover but looked now as if it had soaked for a long time inside a dead ox. From the empty house behind her came a smell of must and decay, heavy, she thought, as the misery and loneliness which had gone on inside. Yuba Fling, pulled and hauled this way and that, without help from anyone, hadn't been able to take the strain any longer and had gone off to the husband whom she loved, after doing everything within her power for the two children she'd had to leave behind.

What a choice for a woman to have to make! Suppose I had it, now, with Fred? It was like a shadow over happiness to wonder.

A car stopped out front, a car door banged. Thank goodness, there was Fred. To stay near this down-spent place any longer was more than anyone could bear—anyone who had once blamed Yuba Fling and now suddenly understood why no one could.

Susie walked around the corner of the house and came face to face with Lydia Pollard.

Lydia stopped in her tracks. "What are *you* doing here?" she demanded.

"Walking," Susie said. "It's a nice day for a walk, isn't it?"

"I thought you might be looking for a place to hide your face," Lydia said.

"No. I wasn't. Were you?" Susie had to step out of the drive into snow to get around Lydia, who seemed suddenly to have swelled to twice her size. Like a hen, Susie thought. Something more dangerous to cope with than a hen. She went on past, catching sight of the blazing eyes, the bitter, spite-eroded face.

Suppose you were a child confronted by that! Jakie, with his passion for living, for loving; Caroline, with her goodness, her gentleness when she was let alone, allowed to live her life in her own way. Susie shivered and went on to the corner, where Fred in his car shortly picked her up.

"That old bat say anything to you?" he demanded.

"Nothing to worry over. How did you make out?"

"Oh, Ma hauled me over the coals. She cooled off some when I told her we were headed over to Bradford to pick up a marriage license. Now she's happy as a clam planning the wedding. Thinks we ought to be."

"Clams get married, do they?"

"They do something. They go on and on somehow. I don't guess they have to get a blood test first."

"I wish we could just get the license and find a minister, today. Oh, Fred, I love you."

"Yes," Fred said. "There does seem to be a good deal in it, don't there?"

"Who needs a wedding?"

"Ma does," Fred said, looking grim.

"Is she put out about your marrying me?"

"She ain't disappointed, that's for sure."

He didn't go on to say that what Ma was interested in was using Susie's money to fix up her house. She'd hovered over him while he shaved, put on his good suit, and packed his suitcase with things he'd need at the island, buzzing gossip to him like a tape recorder.

Pomroy Fifield. Flo had dropped down dead and cold when he'd come peddling that story. "Now, I knew you and Susie wasn't married, Freddy, think how I felt! I'm awful glad you've brought her home today, in time so's I can tell around that you was caught over there in that awful storm. Tomorrow I'll go right down there and welcome her into the fam'ly." Flo paused a moment, reflectively. "She'll have to do something about that old tomcat, I ain't going to put up with a cat in the house. Scratch up all the upholstery, puke on the new carpet."

"You better hold your horses a little, Ma. I ain't married yet. You said so."

Flo nibbled at that for a moment. Better not rush too hard, Fred was funny sometimes. She changed the subject. "I don't suppose you saw a sign of them poor little dead bodies anywhere out there," she said.

"No. No dead bodies."

"I would've thought if they was washing around in the ocean, that storm would've brought them in. I had a letter from Yuba. She still feels awful bad."

"That so?"

"I wrote her back that we'd take them like a shot, if they wasn't dead. I had one good old knock-down-drag-out with Lydia about it, too. She said take them and welcome, they wasn't any kin of hers and never would be."

"I s'pose you'd swear to that in court, wouldn't you?"

"Yes, I would, on the Bible. You never heard such a mess of cultch in your life, Fred. I went up to Yuba's one day to kind of air out the house, see the bedding wasn't getting too damp, and who but that old besom was there in person. She had every sheet, blanket, and pillercase out, folded ready to take, on the table. Says, 'Anything in this house George Pollard bought and it belongs to me.' 'Anything in this house belongs to *my sister,*' s'I, 'and to George Pollard's children if they wasn't dead, thanks to you.' 'They wasn't George's children and never was,' s'she. 'The most you could expect the way they acted, they belonged to old Flipper Wilson or some such.'

"Well, let me tell you, that made me mad! I says, 'You mis'able bitch! Of all the gall I ever heard, saying a thing like that about a poor woman grieving for her dead children,' I says. 'The likes of you,' I says, 'cannot insult my sister Yuba to me. She is a decent woman, whatever sour milk you are dribbling all over town like a dead cow's tit,' I says. 'Added to which,' I says, 'here you are, a thief in the night, making off with her sheets and blankets. You ought to be ashamed,' I says, 'and glad I don't call the constable.' And I turned right around and picked up that whole pile of sheets and blankets and brought every one of them home with me. The idea! She don't need them, and I do. We," Flo finished, "ain't speaking."

Fred buckled the last strap on his suitcase. "Well, Ma, I'll see you when I see you."

"Now, Fred. When? I've got to know, all these plans I've got to make."

But he was gone, clattering out of the front door and down the steps.

Tch! Seems as though he might have been a little mite definite about his wedding, seeing the blunt of it's going to come on me.

She sat down to plan. She could hardly wait.

They shoved out through the thicket into melting snow. Morning was somewhere over the horizon; the sign of it was a clear bar of yellow light in the east. The storm, which had been the first kick of winter, had gone, leaving behind it Indian summer. The air was chilly enough to make a man shiver, but it was well above freezing. The snow was already wet enough to make snowballs, as Adam and Amanda proved when they waded the drift above the shore. The party was complete except for Belle and Andy, who were still asleep, buried in blankets, with a good fire going. It had seemed too bad to wake them, and Andy, at least, would probably have to rest longer.

Jilson said, "Ad, why don't you and Amanda scavenge along the sand beach down there, see what stuff you can pick up? Might be a bucket or anything else I can cook in. Might be some canned stuff out of my cook room washed up, but gorry, I d'no. Looks like a godawful mess down there to me."

With the growing light, they could see now the flat-topped table of granite where last night they had landed. At the far edge of it, the crumpled stern of the *Macomber* was a shadow between the shadows of the ledges. She was still wedged there; the rope still dangled from her stern. Coon went up it like a monkey and Jilson followed him.

Lewis knew better than to try climbing a rope. He realized with relief that no one expected him to. If there were anything usable left aboard, somebody would have to be on the receiving end, carry whatever it might be up to the bank. He stood waiting, looking for any sign that might give him a clue as to what benighted place they were stranded on. He could see now the ocean to the horizon. Far out, the lightly colored water seemed calm, no breath of wind touching it; nearer shore, the rollers lifted, curled, and thundered over a hundred yards of rockweed-covered ledges. Seeing them, knowing now what the storm and the high tide had carried the *Macomber* over, Lewis was shaken. That black devil out there must be the one we dragged across, he thought.

To the east, no land, only open ocean. Northerly, jumbled ledges buried in surf stretched away below a heavily wooded shore. South, beyond the ledges where he stood, was a hook of land which he couldn't see over; leading to it was a pebble-and-sand beach, dotted with boulders of various shapes and sizes and topped with a towering windrow of rockweed driven up by the storm. One long black ledge the shape and size of a railway car loomed up near its far end. He could see the kids now, running toward it.

This was an outpost, last land before deep water. It had to be. Otherwise he would have been able to see islands.

Still, this was only eastern shore. He tried to picture the chart for the area. So far as he could remember, there should be no islands out of sight of land, or each other. As soon as he could get a look at the western side, he might be able to figure. There'd certainly be islands, hopefully the mainland, within sight—if this turned out to be an island, which he suspected it was.

He glanced back at the beach and did a double take. What he had thought was scattered boulders was wreckage from the vessel. The thing like a railway car was fifty feet or so of the *Macomber*'s bow.

Damn it to hell, he thought. The poor old fat lady.

Someone called from above, "Stand away!" and a big bundle of wet canvas landed beside him. "Got to the sail locker," Jilson said, from the peak of the vessel's stern. "Whole new set of sails. Dry 'em out, we got shelter till we get squared around." He waved and backed out of sight.

Lewis began packing salvage up the shore. There was the canvas, more of Harold's heavy clothes, more blankets. Plenty of rope. No food, Lewis saw with a sinking heart, no bucket or cookpot. Everything of that kind must have gone with the galley.

The sun was breaking above the horizon when Coon came down the rope. "It's one awful mess in there," he said. "You can walk right out through the hold to the ledges. Jilly's gone down that way to the beach. He fixed a canvas bag, says the tide's uncovered a mussel bed out there. We'll have to roast them in front of the fire."

Coon's face was dead white; he was shaking. Lewis put

an arm around his shoulders. "You've about had it," he said. "Go on back to the fire, crawl into the blankets. Get some rest. There's no need to run yourself any raggeder."

"J-Jilly said to go down on the beach. Hunt out whatever there is before the tide comes in."

"Never mind what Jilly said. Go along."

Coon hesitated. "I got for'ard as far as Hal's stateroom," he said. "I found this." He held out a soaked cardboard box, which was full of broken glass. "Pa's insulin." He relaxed his hand, let the box drop to the ledge. "An insulin bottle's rigged with a tight cork stopper to keep it pure. You push the needle through the stopper, draw the stuff out. The bottles in Pa's cabin had tin caps."

"Yes," Lewis said. "We know what happened, Coon. You can't blame yourself for it."

"I could've done something quicker, besides plug him for doping Andy." A note of hysteria crept into his voice. "H-Hal tried to kill me last summer, darn near shoved me overboard one night on the vessel. I didn't think he'd go so far as to— God, I ought to have known—"

Lewis said sharply, "No one could have, not for sure. Go up and sleep. You did a noble job last night, something not many would have had the guts to do. Saved our lives. Take it from there, and try to be easier, son."

"Okay," Coon said. "I'm . . . sorry." He walked off up the bank and across the small field toward the trees.

Andy dreamed that a black-spotted cat as big as a dog was licking his face and purring. Then the cat jumped and went away. Andy snapped awake. No cat. Nobody but Coon, putting wood on the fire. Coon came and got under the blankets and was cold at first, shivering. Then he got warmer and went to sleep. Andy's back was comfortable against his mother's front. He went to sleep, too.

Adam stared at the jagged timbers where the *Macomber* had broken, the yawning dark cave that led to her for'ard hold. Behind his eyelids he felt the gritty sting of tears, and he let them come. He had run along the beach, not paying any attention to the messed-up gobs of seaweed-strung wreckage scattered there. He had outrun Amanda, who was lingering, looking for things; or maybe she realized, when she saw it too, that he'd want to be by himself for a while. To say good-bye.

The things in the world that seemed real were all going, neglected, dumped, smashed. What you could have now was cars, motorcycles, outboards, snowmobiles. Stuff like that. And they were fun, but that was all they were. Rip and tear and stink along a highway or a lake—sure, you liked that, while it was going on. But after you got dirty, you had to get clean. After you made noise, there had to be quiet. A house, even a new one, was a place where doors wouldn't shut, tiles fell out of plaster on the bathroom wall, and the time you stayed in it didn't last long.

What you needed was something plain and strong and tough, so that you could care about the work your hands did. Why should you bother, learn about building a car that would last a year or two, a house that fell apart before you could grind out the money to pay for it?

You thought about it and you looked at your hands. You knew by heart the names of the woods Neddie Macomber had used. White oak. Hackmatack. White pine. Swamp cedar. You knew the long list of the *Macombers. Josiah, Edward B., James, Susan, Gertrude, Lizzie.* You read about Neddie's reputation. His schooners—plain and strong and tough.

Lost at sea. Missing. Wrecked on rocky shores and breaker-drowned ledges from Nova Scotia to Cape Horn; left to rot and die in the scum of muddy harbors, where you could still see the hulks, poke around and find trunnels as solid as the day they were driven in.

This was what it was, that he could never make Dad see.

Adam said good-bye, mopping at his tears with a sodden, wrinkled handkerchief. "Good-bye, old girl. You were the last one. You tried and did darn well, the way they all did. So good-bye."

Amanda, coming along more slowly, found a battered, unopened gallon can, half buried in seaweed and sand. She rooted at it and couldn't budge it—the sand was beaten almost as hard as rock. She found a stick, stuck it into the sand upright, worrying it down a few inches beside the can. Adam would get it out when he came back. Muscles, she told herself, is what we need.

A little farther on, a small bright object caught her eye— a stainless-steel fork, sitting there as if it had just been washed and put down with care by somebody's hand. She picked it up and put it in her pocket.

As she came up behind Adam, he was stuffing his handkerchief into his pocket. She saw he'd been crying and she knew why; he wouldn't like it if she noticed. She said to his back, "I found a can of something stuck in the sand back there. And I found this." She produced the fork.

"Good," Adam said stolidly. "What was in the can?"

"It's still buried. I couldn't tell. You'll have to howk it out for us."

"You know, I think we could walk in there," Adam said.

"That hole looks nasty," Amanda said. "All that slimy seaweed, yeck!" Still, he'd feel better if she agreed with him. "Okay. I will if you will."

It was dark inside the *Macomber*'s hulk. They stumbled along, feeling their way, climbing over broken, jagged pieces of plank and timbers with nails in them, going slowly toward what after a while was a gleam of sky.

"I think that's where the for'ard house carried away," Adam said. "Hey, look, here's another can." He had found it by putting his foot on it, slipping sideways. It was wedged under a broken plank, but he managed to dig it out, clawing into a packed mat of seaweed.

"Label's washed off, but it sloshes. What'll you bet it's

[*248*]

tomato juice?" He hated tomato juice. "Must've come from the galley," he went on. "The galley was along here somewhere."

They came out into the morning's half-light, into the roofless place. There was no way to tell that this had been the galley except for the companionway steps which were sagged sideways into the hole, and under them, the top of Jilson's table, split in two and canted backward, with one broken leg thrust helplessly into the air. Another leg lay half buried by seaweed. Still lashed to it was the biggest of Jasper Brown's grandmother's cast-iron scouse pots.

"Well, how about that!" Adam said. He tugged at Jilson's knots, which were swollen tight by seawater; finally, he had to use his jackknife to cut the rope and to slice away the tough, strangling strands of weed.

"Got something for Jilly to cook in, if we had something to cook," Adam said. "If we had some ham, we could have some—"

"Shut up!" Amanda said. "I know that, it's got whiskers. Now you've made me think of ham and eggs and I'm so hungry I could die."

"Okay, I'm sorry."

In the dusky light, she could see his grin. Thank goodness, he felt better. She said, "Let's go out on the beach. Maybe there's something in this can good to eat, and in the one I found, too. We could go back to the fire and hot up whatever it is."

Adam said in a sickened voice, "Yah, hot tomato juice!" He put the can into the scouse pot and started back the way they had come. "Watch it, Amanda. This is lousy going."

Lewis let himself cautiously down over the ledges to the beach. He plodded along past the windrows of weed and kelp, keeping an eye out for anything usable. He spotted the can Amanda had marked and dug the sand away from it. No telling what it was—label gone, sand-scoured, battered, it was fairly heavy—a food can, he hoped. From the look of things, he couldn't expect to find much more. The galley had carried away offshore, and in the storm last night this beach must have been turned upside down two or three times. Most of the wreckage from the vessel's passageway was scattered here—Jasper's furniture, smashed and splintered; chair legs, tabletops, chunks of bureaus and commodes, the top half of the old-fashioned sideboard with the mirror gone, except for a few jagged shards of glass. Lewis recognized, but barely, one of the overstuffed chairs from the "bride's present." Its plush covering was gone, all but a few shreds of discolored material held by the upholstery nails. Wads of stuffing bulged out of it, and as Lewis pressed on the seat with his boot, muddy water squirted out of it in all directions.

If Providence had used the instruments of its justice to pay off Hal, it had certainly finished in the process some assets which could reasonably be thought a part of its concern, valuable, deserving care. Fairleigh. The *Macomber*. A decent and helpless old man.

Feeling grim and discouraged, he walked on. Near the remains of the hulk, the beach looked as if it had been plowed over by a mindless and elemental bulldozer. The black cave of the hold was choked with kelp, boulders, weed, sand, and unidentifiable objects. From somewhere inside it came a weird, jangly bong, like the sound of a cracked metal drum, and a voice singing. Lewis jumped, feeling, momentarily, the back of his neck creep.

Adam had taken a thump on the side of the scouse pot and had begun singing to cheer up Amanda's slippery advance out of the darkness.

> "Here am I a shipwrecked sailor,
> Long time gone from home,
> Setting on a rock in the middle of commotion—"

It had worked, for she began singing with him:

> "A-cussing and a-swearing at the damned old ocean—"

They came staggering and sliding out of the slippery hold, to confront Lewis, who looked horrified—Amanda supposed because he had heard her singing Jilly's cuss words.

"I know," she said primly. "I'm not supposed to sing it, but I thought the occasion called for it. Look what we've found, too."

"So long as you've got out of there without breaking your fool necks," Lewis said, "I'm not listening."

Blue mussels were abundant on the bar below the beach; the storm had rooted quantities of the big red variety from their holdfasts, only needing to be picked up from the sand. They filled the kettle and Jilson's canvas bag and carried a bushel of the things up the beach, where piles of driftwood were melting out of the fast disappearing snow. Jilson rooted out some fairly dry stuff, whittled away the surface moisture, and made shavings for kindling. Nobody wanted to go back into the thicket. The sun had come up warm; where he built the fire in the shelter of the ledges at the top of the beach, it was warm as summer. There was no way to tell what was in the two salvaged gallon cans. Jilson put them aside.

"Don't want nothing to spoil because we can't eat it," he said. "Besides, mussels is as good as a beefsteak dinner."

Adam went racing up across the field to see if the others were awake and ready to come down, and by the time the first kettleful of mussels was done, they were there. They all looked rested. Andy was even lively; he had color in his cheeks, his eyes were bright, his appetite tremendous.

"We look like what we are," Belle said cheerfully. "People out of a shipwreck. Willy off the pickle boat. Andy and I can't comb our hair. You'll have to put up with it until we can locate a comb."

"Andy's hair's on end because he had a bad dream," Adam said, grinning at Andy. "Dreamed it twice. About a big old spotted panther came out of the woods and kissed him. That cat's going to claw you one of these times, Andy."

'Oh, he's a nice cat," Andy said. "I wasn't scared. I liked him."

Battered and bruised, mostly thankful, the survivors ate, rested, and dried out in the sun. Adam and Coon moved long enough to rig a line between two stout alders, where extra blankets, damp jackets, and some of the *Macomber*'s spare canvas began to flap dry in the breeze; the breakers boomed on the ledges, louder as the tide came in; they seemed now almost like a background to peace.

Lewis glanced over at Belle. She had finished eating and lay relaxed in the sun, her back propped against a flat-sided granite ledge. "Here we sit," she said. "Like birds in the wilderness. What's next, Lew?"

Not a word of complaint about her predicament, the loss of all her band instruments, which, considered from the financial side alone, must be tremendous. Only, what's coming next, what's to be done?

He said, "Well, next, Jilly and I walk around the point, there, see if we can figure out where we are." He smiled at her. "The rest of you had better take it easy."

"Take it easy, nothing," Belle said. "I'm slept out. I'm going too."

"So'm I," Coon said. "You don't need to go, Cap'n Wyman. You're lame again, ain't you?"

Lewis hadn't been going to admit it, but the slippery, skidding walk along the ledges and sand had stiffened his back again. The thought of another rough journey filled him with dread.

"You let us go," Coon said. "We can see anything you can and come back faster. Come on, Jilly."

Jilson sat, his legs stretched out to the fire. His boots and the lower part of his pants legs had begun to steam. "I ain't going," he said. "Now I have ate, I ain't capable of nothing. I am going to have to caulk off. A man can handle just so much." His face set in stubborn lines, he stared around with an irritated glare. "I would be glad if you wimmenfolks would clear off out of here, so's I can git these wet duds off."

Belle chuckled. She got up. "Come on, Coon. Come on, kids. Let's go see if we can locate the cities on the mainland."

I ought to be the one doing that, Lewis thought, watching them climb the ledges toward the north end of the land. But, Lord, I couldn't. Not now.

He might as well give in and rest. The ledge behind him sloped at just the right angle to lean his sore back against.

Jilson got up, set the last kettleful of mussels back from the fire. He paused, picked one out of the boiling broth, thoughtfully ate it, without cooling it.

"Lined with asbestos, too," Lewis said drowsily.

Jilson paid no attention. He went up the bank to where the canvas was drying on the line, pulled it down, along with a couple of blankets.

"Is that stuff dry enough to sleep in?" Lewis asked as he came back.

"I slep' in wet blankets before you was born," Jilson said.

Lewis grinned. "I didn't mean that kind," he said.

"What's wet is my goddam boots. Feels as if I had my feet in a pan of raw dough. Wish I did. I'd have biscuits." He folded the canvas down on top of a flat ledge near the fire, dropped the blankets beside it, began dreamily to take off his clothes. "I had better spread them duds out so's they'll dry."

Far from spreading them out, he left each item in a heap as he shed it before he crawled under the blankets and began almost instantly to snore. The series of heaps led from his jacket by the fire to his hat beside his bed—one boot, the other boot, pants, shirt, socks, long johns.

Lewis sighed. He stared at the heaps for quite a while before he scrabbled and got painfully to his feet. Those clothes were going to be devilish to put on again unless they were straightened out and hung where they'd dry. Moving stiffly, staggering occasionally, Lewis finally got everything up the bank and hung on the line in the sun. Something heavy thumped in Jilson's jacket pocket—his long-barreled pistol, with two unopened boxes of cartridges. The boxes were sodden, beginning to fall apart; he shook out the cartridges, spread them out at a safe distance from the fire. The gun was partially loaded—two shots fired. The two which had taken the lock off Jasper's door, very likely, he thought. Phew! He could still feel the wind of the one which had parted his hair. He unloaded the gun, left it on a board near the fire.

If those cartridges aren't drowned out and the gun'll still fire, we might be able to shoot a seabird or two, or rabbits if there are any. He built up the fire, went back to his place against the ledge.

Warm in the sun. Tide coming. Still high surf, but going down . . . roar not so loud now . . . pleasant for a man to sleep by. . . .

By the time Jakie woke up it was nearly midafternoon, but he hadn't forgotten anything. He presented Caroline with the mussel bucket at once. She knew it wasn't any use trying to get mussels now—the tide would be up over the bed; besides, as they left the house, she could still hear surf, which they mustn't get close to. Jakie, though, wouldn't be satisfied until he'd seen for himself, and, anyway, she'd have to see where Walter was. He was still roaming.

The snow was nearly gone in places where the sun had got to it, but here and there on the path and in the woods, it was quite deep. After a while she abandoned the express wagon and let Jakie walk. He plugged along, head down, carrying the bucket, not letting it out of his hands in case Caroline should change her mind.

Where there was still snow, she could see Walter's tracks. He had come quite a way over here—he'd even turned into the path that led to the brush camp in the woods and then had come back, she saw. So he wasn't in there now. She and Jakie were at the edge of the field going down to the shore when she smelled woodsmoke and another smell, too, almost like someone cooking. Of course, it couldn't be.

Goodness, what a racket the surf was making! A lot louder over here than it had been at the house. Great big rollers coming in, one after another. Pretty to watch.

There *was* smoke, she could smell it plainly, and something cooking, down on the shore. Somebody was there. . . .

Jakie was about ten feet ahead of her. She ran after him as fast as she could and caught up with him just as he started to plow through the snowbank at the top of the beach. There, she could see out over. A fire, burnt down to coals; alongside it, a big black kettle, upset, and a pile of mussels that Walter was nosing into; two men asleep, one in blankets, the other leaning back against a ledge.

She said in a husky whisper, "Walter! Stop that! Come here." But Walter didn't move. He had mussels.

Terrified, she scooped up Jakie and ran. Walter would have to come by himself—first, she had to get Jakie away. "Jakie, people! Men down there!" she said fiercely into his ear as she raced up toward the path.

Jakie put both arms around her neck and held on with both hands to the bail of his bucket, which he wasn't going to drop here for any mean and ugly men to find. The bucket went rattley-bang against Caroline's back. It sounded to her as loud as a gun going off.

Out of sight in the trees, she had to put Jakie down to get her breath. He ran by himself for a little while; then she had to carry him again. It was slow going, especially in snowy places. She couldn't go any faster, with Jakie, and he was so out of breath now and scared that he couldn't go by himself.

They were nearly back at the house when Walter went by them, traveling in great jumps, the way he did when he thought someone was after him. He ran up onto the back porch, stood up with his paws on the door, scratching frantically to get in. Then he must have heard something because he took off over the railing and vanished like lightning into the thicket behind the house.

Voices. That was what he'd heard. Caroline could hear them now herself. They were coming along the path that led over to Cat Cove—where Freddy kept his boat now, and, for a hopeful moment, she thought it might be Susie and him coming back. But it wasn't. Walter wouldn't have been scared of them. This was a gabble of voices, more than two people.

She plunged with Jakie up the steps, unlocked the door, poked him inside. Then she dodged back onto the porch to show Walter that the door was open, that she was there. She didn't dare to call him. The voices were quite close now. He wasn't in sight, anywhere. She went in, closed and locked the door.

There were two sandwiches left from lunch on the table; she grabbed them and the opened can of milk, hustled Jakie up the front stairs. As she passed a second-floor window on the way to the turret room, she saw the people— a tall man, quite young, a big woman with a lot of yellow hair, and three kids.

Lewis' head snapped upright with a jerk. The fire had burned down to coals, the sun was on his face instead of his back now. He'd been asleep for quite a time. Something, some noise, had wakened him. Momentarily blinded by the sun in his eyes, he glanced around and stiffened where he sat.

Jilson was still asleep, stretched out in his blankets. His chin, covered with bristly, iron-gray stubble, was stuck straight up into the air. Beside him, licking the stubble, was a yellow-and-black-spotted cat, which looked to Lewis like a young panther.

"I'm dreaming," Lewis said aloud, and jolted wide awake. But if I am, Andy had the same dream.

The thing was certainly real. Close to three feet long,

with a tail as thick as a man's wrist and nearly the length of its body; yellow-colored coat, dotted and striped with glossy coal-black. It was hunkered down there, licking Jilson's whiskers and purring. The purr sounded as if someone were shaking a bagful of rocks.

What can I do? Lewis thought. If I move or yell, scare that thing, it could be chewing on Jilly's throat before I could stop it.

The gun over by the fire was unloaded. How could he get it loaded in time? It had been wet; it might not even shoot. Suppose Belle and the kids came walking into this, not knowing! Lewis stared at the cat.

It seemed friendly enough, purring away like a big tabby. It lifted a paw the size of a teacup and patted Jilson's cheek. Not a claw showing. Playful. The way a cat pats a mouse when she wants it to wiggle.

Jilson wiggled. He grunted, "Dammit, cut that out!" reached a hand and pushed the cat in the face. His fingers groped, pulled back, froze in the air. His eyes flew open. For a second, the two stared eye to eye, before Jilson came roaring to his feet in a flurry of flying blankets. He stared around horribly, jumped into the air, a leap which took him high over the cat's back, made a running scrabble for the gun by the fireside.

The animal flattened its ears, spat, and took off in a beautiful standing jump of its own, which carried it over Jilson's back as he stooped to grab the gun. A second jump carried it out of sight beyond the top of the bank. It had vanished like silk lightning, but not before Lewis had caught sight of the collar and tags around its neck.

"It's all right, Jilly," he called. "Don't shoot it, that's somebody's pet." He choked and stopped. Jilson's emergence, bare, his jump over the cat, and the cat's jump over him were too much for any man. Lewis broke up.

Jilson pulled the trigger three times before he discovered that the cat was gone and the gun doing nothing but click. "Somebody's pet, hell! You let me git some bullets into this gun, I'll drive that thing so far into the ground that—" He came to a stop, put the gun down with measured movements. "You," he said, "would set there and let a sleeping, nekkid man be et by a tiger and never turn over a goddam hand."

"No," Lewis gasped. "No tiger, Jilly. And I was asleep, too."

"And not only set there, but laugh. I ought to pound you over the head with a rock."

Lewis, beyond help, put his head down on his knees and strangled.

"You ain't worth a rock. You ain't worth the time I've took up telling you you ain't. Where's my clothes? Hid them, too, have you? By the jumped-up— Where are they, you sprangle-footed runt?"

Lewis jerked a thumb at the clothesline. In the silence that followed, he recovered somewhat, glanced around, saw Jilson standing at the top of the beach, yanking up his long johns with solid powerful jerks. A sock, apparently deteriorated from seawater, tore in two; the top half he pulled nearly to his knee, left it where it was, and hauled his pants on over the ruin.

Lewis said, "Look, Jilly. That was a tame cat. It had a collar on. Its people can't be too far off. You realize what that must mean. Somebody lives here."

"I don't want nothing to do with them, they must be crazy. Keep a varmint and let him loose to rack around the country clawing people to death." He stooped to the snow-bank and scrubbed his chin and whiskers with snow, making a thorough job of it. "Tiger spit!" he said, giving Lewis a baleful look.

"I don't think he'd have hurt you. He was probably just saying thanks for a fine meal," Lewis said.

Jilson came down from the bank, walking delicately over beach rocks which hurt his feet. He glared at the scouse pot lying on its side and empty. "Et every damn one," he muttered. "So that's funny, too. You shut up, Cap'n, or I'll haul this kittle down over your head."

Someone called from the field and Lewis caught sight of Coon's tall head pushing past a stand of alders. "Here comes Coon," Lewis said. He grinned at Jilson. "Stow it, Jilly. Let's see if he's got any good news for us. Hi," he went on as Coon came down the shore. "Where'd you leave the others?"

"We found a house," Coon said. "They're over there."

"Anybody in it? Hey, Jilly, maybe we're rescued," Lewis said.

"We thought there was somebody in it," Coon said. "Still got smoke coming out of the chimney. But I don't know what kind of people they can be. They knew we were here, and they must've known what's happened to us. Their tracks are all over the top of the bank there."

"What!" Lewis said.

"Yes!" Coon said. He was frustrated, mad, and worn out. His shoulders sagged. "No, we ain't rescued, dammit! They took off in a big powerboat. We missed them by about ten minutes. We hollered, jumped up and down. Didn't see us or didn't want to. Man and a woman aboard, I could make them out. Must've had at least one kid and somebody else. And a big dog. Tracks, of two and the dog." He jerked his thumb at the field. "Up there. Didn't you see anybody?"

"Jilly and I were asleep," Lewis said. "Damn! Saw us and left without a word?"

"Sure did. Big powerboat . . . tearing along." Coon blinked and set his jaw. He was, Lewis saw, very close to tears. "That house . . . big, old place, locked up tight. Shutters on the downstairs windows. I think we could break in."

"We not only kin, we will," Jilson said. He clanked the scouse pot, filling it with the remainder of the mussels from his canvas bag. He walked past them, his head in the air, carrying the pot in one hand, the ax in the other. He paused briefly on the other side of the bank. "Look there!" he said, staring at the tracks. "A woman and a kid. A woman with the heart of Jezebel, and a hellcat's kitten." He went on, muttering. Coon followed and then Lewis, making slower time.

The house was huge, a cedar-shingled affair, four-storied, with turret and gingerbread in the best Victorian tradition. It had been where it was for a long time. High on the eastern wall, a wooden gutter sagged rotted halves down to a wide porch roof. There were no shutters on the upper-story windows.

Jilson hove to in front of Lewis and stared at the house with bloodshot eyes. "Summer cottage!" he said. "I've always wanted to bust into one of *them*. Go off and leave us to starve and freeze, would they? Well, by the god, they're going to have boarders!"

Belle, sitting on the back steps with the kids, grinned at him. "In that case, welcome home, Jilly," she said. "The place is plastered with NO TRESPASSING signs. Maybe we'll end up in a nice warm dry clink."

"There's also a law concerning the rescue of castaways," Lewis said grimly. "If they make trouble, we'll wave it at them." He sat down on the step next to Belle, and she slipped her hand under his arm. "Still gimpy, Lew?"

"Some," he said. "But better since I rested."

The kids had lined up watching Jilson, who had gone at once to a porch corner post and had shinnied up it. He used the ax like an ice ax to help himself over the overhang and to pry up one of the second-story windows. Then he climbed in over the sill and disappeared.

"That was quick," Belle said.

"Jilly's always quick when he's sore," Adam said. "And he's sure sore now."

Amanda said, "What's he doing? Why doesn't he let us in? I'd like to sit down on something that isn't wet." She glanced around, wondering where Andy was, and saw him standing at the corner of the house. As she looked, he caught her eye, put one finger on his lips, and beckoned. Then he went out of sight around the corner.

Thumps came from somewhere inside the house. They caught a whiff of smoke and saw it, gray and heavy, pouring from the chimney.

"Building up the fire," Lewis said.

"Yeah," Coon said wearily. "First things first. We'll be lucky if he doesn't cook his mussels and eat a meal before he lets us in."

This was something of an exaggeration, because the mussels were sitting in the scouse pot on the porch. They all stood waiting, watching the door. Amanda got up, slipped quietly around the corner of the house.

"What?" she asked Andy.

"Ss-h," Andy said. "Look, it's my cat. He's real. He's coming."

He was, in long, easy leaps up the wood path, his yellow-and-black coat glossy in the sun.

"It's an ocelot," Andy said. "It's one of the loveliest animals in the world. I saw one once, in a zoo. Look, he's tame. He's got a collar on." He called softly, "Here, kitty, kitty, kitty."

But Jilson, just then, opened the back door, and Walter, seeing him, plunged back out of sight into a thicket.

Jilson's triumphant entry into the house had restored his temper. He stood with a roof over his head and anyone would have thought he owned it. "Come right on in," he said. "Key was in the door. All you've got to be is a good back-door man. Them skunks left coals in the fireplace. Bring along them mussels, will you, Coon?"

Walter had been lurking, waiting for a possible chance to get into the safety of the house. Over at the beach, he had reasoned that anyone who had the sense to cook mussels for him was a friend; he had tried to repay friendliness with goodwill. But the friend had yelled and jumped and had pointed the thing that sooner or later would explode in his face with a loud bang. He had been too scared even to notice Caroline and Jakie on the path. The back door was closed tight, and he had raced for the shelter of the trees.

Now the back door was closed again, but with no one in sight. Walter raced, went up the porch corner post like a thrown, limber rope, and vanished through the open window.

Caroline, hearing the familiar sound of him on the stairs, opened the turret-room door wide enough to let him in. He plunged at once for Jakie and shut out terror in the shelter of Jakie's lap.

Caroline stood, stiffened, listening at the door. They were in. They were *inside the house.* They must have seen Walter. He couldn't have got in unless they'd let him. She began to shake.

From time to time, she opened the door again and listened. If only Freddy were here. He would scare the daylights out of them, maybe send them to jail. Because they had no *right;* they had broken in. When would he be back? Not for hours yet, because he and Susie had had to go to Bradford.

Then, as she heard the sounds grow, heavy feet clomping around downstairs, she began to get mad. Opening the door a little wider so that she could hear better, she made out an unmistakable sound. Somebody had slammed the refrigerator door. Somebody yelled, "Look, there's a whole big roast of meat in there!"

Our supper. They're going to eat our supper that Susie'd said to put in the oven about four o'clock if she wasn't back in time. These robbers would eat it and then go, and who knew what of the Wiggling Biscuits' nice things they'd make off with!

If I could only think of a way to scare them, the way Freddy scared the deer hunters! But the afghan was downstairs in the living room. And suddenly, she thought of a way.

She started out through the door. Jakie lifted an alarmed head. He said, "Where to?"

Oh, dear. She'd thought he and Walter were both asleep.

"I'll be right back," she said, and saw, horrified, that he was puckering up to beller. She flew to him. "Ss-h, Jakie. Walter's scared. He needs to be loved. I'm just going out a minute. You stay and love him."

"Come back? You come back, right now?"

"Mm-hm. Okay?"

It worked, but she'd have to hustle. She tiptoed down the stairs to the third floor and into the room where the African masks were. They were on the bed in there. She and Jakie always took care of them after they'd been playing punkin-devil or bogeyman. She put one on, fastening it tight around the back of her head, so she could be sure to see all right out of the eyeholes. Then she reached up and pulled down one of the long, black-handled spears off the wall. Freddy'd said okay to play with the masks but never to touch the spears. He'd understand, though, when she told him what she'd taken one for.

She stood at the top of the stairs, trying to make herself go down.

Jakie waited. She'd said she'd come back *now*. When she didn't, he moved Walter gently out of his lap, opened the door, crept out, and peered down the stairwell. He saw Caroline come out of the room on the third floor. She had one of the bogeymen masks on, and she was carrying the spear. The spears, forbidden, had always fascinated Jakie. He began to giggle, at once clapping his hands over his mouth.

"Ss-h, Walter," he whispered. "Come on. Play boobie-man." If Caroline was going downstairs, there was nothing to be afraid of. Walter followed him down and into the third-floor room.

[*263*]

* * *

Jilson remembered that he'd left the window over the porch roof open. The warmth in the kitchen and living room was wonderful—no sense heating up the whole out-doors.

Caroline heard him coming. Clump, clump, up the stairs. Oh, a terrible-looking skinny man with a bald head like an egg and a great long drippy moustache and whiskers. She dodged back into a room and got behind the door. He must have seen her. He was coming right into the room. She was so scared she forgot she had the mask on. But he went right on by toward a window that was open. So that was how they'd got in.

Jilson heard a sound behind him and looked around. It was not Caroline's awful visage which scared him. She was peeking out from behind the door; but in the doorway stood some kind of an outlandish pygmy, or a midget, with a horrible stiff black head, white circles around the mouth and eyes, and beside him, a big animal, with, for chrissake, the same kind of a head, only on an *animal*. A third head peered from around the back of the door, and the pygmy emerging carried a long black spear.

Jilson let out a yell, "EE-yow!" and dived headlong through the open window.

Caroline saw Jakie and Walter and realized. She grabbed Jakie, put for upstairs as fast as she could go. The three of them huddled down together on Jakie's bed in the turret room.

People came rushing upstairs to see what had happened to Jilson. They found he had disappeared. They found nothing else. Then they heard an indignant bellow from below and all trooped back down.

Fred and Susie, coming along the path from Cat Cove, saw a strange man come shooting through a second-floor window and land on all fours on the porch roof. Without a pause, he scrabbled to his feet, raced across the roof, and jumped off. He landed in what remained of the snowbank

[*264*]

beside the porch, where he sat, apparently unharmed, when Fred confronted him.

"What in the living hell," Fred bawled at him, "goes on here?" And stopped short in amazement as what seemed to be a multitude of people came streaming out of the back door of the house.

The Coast Guard came and went. Lewis, as the only officer of the *Macomber* left living, made his report. He gave the exact information which, at firsthand, he knew to be true—the owner dead on board of diabetes; his nephew and one seaman overboard in the storm. Anything more, he told himself, would be hearsay. If Coon or Jilson wished to add anything, they were welcome to. Neither did. It wasn't any of *his* business, Jilson said, and Coon was silent.

The doctor provided by the Coast Guard had strapped up Lewis' back; nothing was wrong with any of the other survivors, he said, except exhaustion. He recommended a day or so's rest, if that could be made possible, before they left the island. Susie and Caroline made up beds all over the house.

Coon left on the second day. He was going, he said, to St. Andrews to see his father's girl. "Not that anything I can say to her will help much," he said. "But there're some things I can tell her about him she might be glad to know. It seems only decent to go." He had lost his look of wise and secret innocence. His eyes were shadowed and sad.

"Where to after St. Andrews?" Lewis asked him.

"Home, I guess. Back to the bay. I'm used to that."

"If you're ever in Halifax, look me up," Lewis said. He mentioned the address of the shipping company which had hired him, and held out his hand. "We all owe you a lot more than thanks, Coon."

"I owe you a little something, too," Coon said.

Lewis' fingers remembered for quite a while the strength of Coon's good-bye handshake.

Newsmen came for photographs and interviews; crowds

of people flocked to the island to see the wreck and, if possible, the survivors. Not all of them were available. Lewis, resting in bed, was not. Coon had gone. Jilson refused, with considerable violence, to be photographed or interviewed. He gave his name—Charles Jilson—to the newsmen, got himself out of sight, and didn't reappear.

Probably has good reasons, Lewis thought. He had never questioned Jilly about his past, but he did know from having seen signed articles aboard ship that Jilly's name wasn't Charles. It was Moses. Lewis wasn't surprised on the morning of the following day to find Jilson gone.

He had left word with Adam, who was very glum about it. "Went off in a sight-seeing boat last night," Adam said. "Says he'll write you later. I tried to coax him to stay, but he said he couldn't. Said he'd been slobbered on by a tiger and scared out of his manhood by a three-year-old child, and the only thing that would bring him back to life would be to go and look at the shapes and condition of his damned old relatives. You think he'll write?"

"He always has," Lewis said.

"Well, I wish we could get out of here," Adam said. "That bunch of goggle-eyed gawpers picking over the beach for souvenirs makes me sick. Picnics, they have, and leave all the bottles and trash."

"For the birds," Lewis said. "It's a wild-life sanctuary."

"Yeck!" Amanda said. "They can't stand it that something's more welcome here than they are. Are we going to ride to Halifax in Belle's van, Dad?"

"Would you and Adam like to?"

"We'd love to. We don't want to lose touch with Belle and Andy."

"It'll be swell, having some friends in Halifax," Adam said.

In time to come, more than friends. Lewis knew that now, and so did Belle. She had mentioned the van to him last night.

"One of the boys should be waiting in St. Andrews with it by now," she'd said. "I've asked the Coast Guard to see if they can get in touch with them, tell them to pick us up in Bradford, it's not far, just a nice easy drive . . ." She plunged ahead, not waiting for his answer. "And, you know, I could solve a problem for you, if you'd like to think about it. I don't take Andy on tour, he's too young, I leave him with my father and mother. They've got a nice house in Halifax, plenty of room, and the kids like each other, if you wanted to board Adam and Amanda with them, when you take your ship out . . . I'm being very forward, but . . ."

Lewis reached for her hand. "Belle. You could solve all my problems for me if you wanted to think about it."

She would not, she said, have to think at all, not being at the moment capable of it.

On the afternoon of the third day, Fred and Susie slipped over to Bradford and were quietly married by a justice of the peace.

"Not much of a honeymoon," Fred said as they came away. "All that mess out at the island to tend to. I couldn't leave now, Susie."

"Well, first things first," Susie said. "I'm delirious now. If I went off with you alone, Lord knows what would happen. Just a couple of ready-made, settled-down old householders, we are. Ready-made family. I like it. Did you mail the letter to the Wiggling Biscuits, telling how their house and their island have had to be turned into a picnic table?"

Fred nodded. "I was going to send them a copy of the Bradford *Times,* the story's spread all over the front page." He grinned, a little sheepishly. "Forgot to. Under the circumstances, I guess." He reached in a back pocket, brought out a tightly folded newspaper, which he spread out so that they could both see. "Haven't even read it," he went on. "Just glanced at the head— Oh, my God!" he said in a choked voice. "How did that happen?"

The Bradford *Times* photographer had taken plenty of pictures—of the castaways, of the wreck, of the Wiggling Biscuits' house. The front page of the paper was clogged with them. But the one which had shaken Fred and stopped his voice in his throat was of young Andy Bronson, proudly leading Walter on a leash down the path to Cat Cove and, walking with him, unmistakably, Jakie and Caroline.

"We'd better get back as soon as we can," Susie said. "Oh, Fred! I did keep them in, I thought. I don't know when they went out."

"No," Fred said. "Wait. I'm done hiding, Susie. Come on."

He made for the parking lot where they had left the car. Susie, sitting beside him as they shot down the highway out of Bradford, thought, idiotically, Arrested for speeding on our wedding day! And then, But law officers don't—and then sat alone with her worry about the children because Fred was off somewhere, separate from her and silent, concentrated on what he planned to do. He hurtled the car at last into the drive at his mother's house.

Flo came to the door, all smiles and welcome. "There you are at last, the two of you," she began. "I was just finishing planning some— Heaven sake, Fred, what ails you?"

She may well ask, Susie thought. She herself had never seen him like this. She caught a glimpse of the rocklike set of his jaw and stayed where she was.

"Ma, where's Aunt Yuba's overseas telephone number?"

"Mercy, Fred, you're never going to call her up, it'll cost the earth!"

Fred picked her up by the elbows, shook her in the air, set her down hard. "You find it! You got it from Lydia when the kids were lost. Git! Dig it up!"

"Oh, yes. Yes . . . in my writing box . . ." She fled and Fred, following, slammed the door behind him.

He was gone a long time.

Andy, who had inveigled Caroline into taking a walk, had had no idea in the world that the photograph had been taken, because the newsman who had taken it had been hiding in the bushes. He had not got as many pictures as he wanted for his story, and his camera had a telefoto lens. He had seen the kids sneaking out through a door that led from a back shed. Sure, sneaking, he'd thought, because the two older ones had been looking around carefully, and one of them, the boy, had gone dancing on ahead, saying, "It's okay, they've all gone. Come on." Then the newsman had been fascinated and flabbergasted at the sight of Walter. He had got, and had congratulated himself on getting, the best picture of the day. That had been on yesterday.

Today came Pomroy Fifield, in a hired boat, paid for by Lydia Pollard. He came, pigeon-breasted in triumph, up the path from the pier, pistol on belt, constable's star pinned to the left side of his braces, hat patterned after the well-known half-Stetsons of the state police. He guessed he had caught up with that cussed Fred at last. Kidnapped them two kids, stashed them away over here on this island, let everybody, including their poor grandmother, think they was dead. Pomroy had a pair of handcuffs in his pocket for Fred Montgomery. He strode up the back steps, knocked briskly on the door.

Andy had, on yesterday, wormed out of Caroline why she and Jakie and Walter had to be so cagey about going out when people were around. He thought this was dreadful; he even told her that it was unconstitutional. "Life, liberty, and the pursuit of happiness are for everybody, Caroline. Anything else is against the law."

"So make a speech." Caroline shrugged. "Kids are anybody?"

Andy regarded her. For two kids as nice as Caroline and Jakie, with whom he had set up as satisfactory a friendship as he had ever had in his life, and for Walter, to have this kind of prison life forced on them, shook him to his independent depths.

"Life, liberty, and the pursuit. And stop right there, period," Caroline said. "So pooh, Andy!"

So something ought to be done about it, he told himself. How could anybody feel like that!

He was in the upstairs front room, where he slept, making his bed, when he saw Pomroy coming up the path. His mother and Lewis had gone for a walk; Adam and Amanda had gone over to the sand beach again, Andy supposed to look at the wreck. He didn't see why anyone would want to—he certainly never wanted to see any part of that horrible old ship again. Caroline, with Jakie and Walter, was in the kitchen—he was glad, now, that she'd locked the back door, even though he'd kidded her for doing it.

He called firmly down the front stairs. "Caroline! Scatter. Here comes the fuzz."

"The what?" Caroline called back.

"A policeman. Skinny, with a gun. Got a hat on, like Western. Face looks like—well, a mashed cupcake. Know him?"

Caroline, herding Jakie and with Walter following, came tearing up the stairs. She had known Pomroy Fifield well, had observed him from afar, and had expertly avoided him a good many times. By the time Pomroy began knocking on the downstairs door, she and Jakie and Walter were in the turret room. She had not been able to grab anything to pacify Jakie, in case she had to, except a paper bag half full of gumdrops, which someone—possibly one of the newsmen—had left on the living-room table yesterday, but as she rushed past Andy, the bottom of the bag knocked against a newel post and gumdrops went flying all over the stairs.

Andy was indignant. That is a hideous, wicked shame! he told himself. Anybody to have to be so scared, and of that poky little grunt downstairs, too!

He gathered up the gumdrops, making sure to find them all, went back into his bedroom, leisurely finished making his bed. Downstairs, the knocking got louder. Then it stopped and the cop began to holler. "Anybody home? Hey, there, ain't anybody home?"

Andy quietly opened the window, climbed out to the porch roof, and crept along it until he could hang his head over the edge. He said politely, "How do you do."

Pomroy jumped. He stared officially, here and there. A voice had come from somewhere.

"Up here," Andy said. "Look up. Illo, illo, boy, come, bird, come."

"What's that? What say?" What kind of . . . ? Godsake, on the piazza roof! Pomroy made out, a few feet above his head, the round-eyed, expressionless face of Andy.

"Shakespeare. *Hamlet*," Andy said. "Can I help you in any way?"

Funny name. And funny-looking kid. Face looked to be all swole up. "You off'n the wreck?" Pomroy asked.

"Yes. I'm Andrew Bronson. Because if I can't help you in any way, I'll have to ask you to stop making such a racket. We have two young children here and a pet ocelot. The children are resting. You can imagine what a terrible ordeal the shipwreck was and how such a fright might shatter young nerves for days. They have to be kept very quiet, now and after we get them home. The ocelot is also very sick. We think he may have swallowed seawater, and I myself am in agony from a terrible toothache. So if you could, for chrissake, pipe down, Mr.— I don't believe I caught your name."

"I'm Constable Pomroy Fifield from—"

"Pleased to meet you, I'm sure." The swelling in Andy's face was caused by two thunderous gumdrops, one in each cheek; they made his story of toothache believable and Pomroy lowered his voice.

"I reckernize you now from your picture in the paper," he said. "You was walking along leading a wildcat on a string and they was two kids with you. Now, I want to know—"

"That was the ocelot," Andy said. "I took him for a walk, hoping to make him feel better. Seawater is very bad for ocelots."

"You had that critter on the wreck with you?"

"We had on the wreck," Andy said, "old Uncle Tom Cobleigh and all." Wow! he thought. Some skunk with a

[*271*]

camera must've been stashed in the bushes. What I did! Oh, thunder! He went on, talking fast but somewhat impeded by the gumdrops. "Those two kids— Well, you know, a great many people came to see the wreck. Those two joined me on my walk. They didn't tell me their names. I suppose they went away with their family when the sightseeing boats left."

Well! That was a puzzler. "You mean Fred Montgomery ain't got them two Fling kids hid over here?" Pomroy said.

"I don't know, I'm sure. You'd have to ask Mr. Montgomery. He's over in Bradford today."

"Well, who's them two here you was talking about? You tell me that, mister."

"Why, how nice!" Andy said. "You know you are the first person *ever* to call me 'mister.' It's very polite of you. Thank you. You must mean the two Jilson children, Joe and Charisma. Poor Charisma, she is just all to pieces. Mr. Charles Jilson. The ocelot is his, too. And now I would appreciate it, Constable Fifield, if you just got the hell out of here, because I have got to go give him his nerve medicine. A man like you of course will understand . . . A sick animal . . ."

Andy withdrew his face slowly, like the Cheshire cat, went back, and crawled in the window, leaving Pomroy standing.

Now that was a nice little boy, real polite, kind of pro-fane in his talk maybe, but that was all the style, kids nowadays. Pomroy walked back down the path to his hired boat, pondering. Don't believe he was lying, either. I'll have to tell Lydia it ain't Fred's got them kids. Or newspaper pictures—you can't tell by them. Or maybe it was just a remarkable resemblance.

Andy watched him going away. I sure goofed, he thought. Well, we'll just have to take those kids on the van with us.

He turned his head sharply and listened. From upstairs, yes. The beginnings of what was probably going to be a sustained beller, and Andy ran, pulling gumdrops from his pocket.

"It's the Good Samaritan of the Gumdrops," he said, outside the turret-room door.

"Adopted, good and solid," Fred said to Susie. "Ours, with Aunt Yuba's full permission. All we've got to do is get the papers and she'll sign. She never has signed any paper for Lydia, and she's got letters from her, saying she doesn't want the kids, she's putting them in a children's home. I got hold of Henry Fling and he got hold of Aunt Yuba and she got hysterics. I was so mad I was pretty plain about it, I guess."

"I imagine you were," Susie said. "You scared me. I was afraid you were gone for good, you were gone so long."

"That," Fred said, "is something you'll have to get used to, if you make me mad." He grinned and kissed her and spun the car so fast in the driveway that gravel crackled out from under the wheels and flew. "Come on," he said. "Now let's go home."

Caroline, at last, won her battle. She survived.

But Adam Wyman, in his notebook, rounded off the roster of Neddie Macomber's schooners. He recorded the date; and the place where the last of the green-and-silver wakes had ended.